"But Dal," Bergen protested. "Somec is like immortality. I'm going on the ten-down-one-up schedule, and that means that when I'm fifty, three hundred years will have passed! Three centuries! And I'll live another five hundred years beyond that. I'll see the Empire rise and fall, I'll see the work of a thousand artists living hundreds of years apart, I'll have broken the ties of time—"

"The ties of time. A good phrase. You are ecstatic about progress. I congratulate you. I wish you well. Sleep and sleep and sleep, may you profit from it. . . . But Bergen. While you fly, like stones skipping across the water, touching down here and there and barely getting wet, while you are busy doing that, I shall swim. I like to swim. It gets me wet. It wears me out. And when I die, which will happen before you turn thirty, I'm sure, I'll have my paintings to leave behind me."

"Vicarious immortality is rather second rate, isn't it?"

"Is there anything second rate about my work?"

"No," Bergen answered.

"Then eat my food, and look at my paintings again, and go back to building huge cities until there's a roof over all the world and the planet shines in space like a star. There's a kind of beauty in that, too, and your work will live after you. Live how you like. But tell me, Bergen, do you have time to swim naked in a lake?"

Bergen laughed. "I haven't done that in years."

"I did it this morning."

Tor books by Orson Scott Card

The Tales of Alvin Maker

ORSON SCOTT CARD

THE
WORTHING
SAGA

TOR

A TOM DOHERTY ASSOCIATES BOOK
NEW YORK

THE WORTHING SAGA

Copyright © 1978, 1979, 1980, 1982, 1989, 1990 by Orson Scott Card

A Tor Book
Published by Tom Doherty Associates, Inc.
49 West 24th Street
New York, N.Y. 10010

Cover art by Wayne Barlowe

ISBN: 0-812-50927-7

First edition: December 1990

Printed in the United States of America

0 9 8 7 6 5 4 3 2 1

Contents

Author's Introduction

This book brings together all the Worthing stories for the first time in one volume. In a way, the Worthing tales are the root of my work in science fiction. The first science fiction story I ever wrote was an early version of "Tinker"; I sent it to *Analog* magazine when I was nineteen years old.

At the time, *Analog* was the only science fiction magazine that listed itself in *Writer's Market*; since I had never read a science fiction magazine in my life, I knew of no others. "Tinker" reached *Analog* just at the time that longtime editor John W. Campbell died. His immediate successor rejected the story, but sent along an encouraging note.

I took this to mean that I was on the right track, and continued working on "Tinker" and several related stories—"Worthing Farm," "Worthing Inn," and a much longer but never finished work about the first contact between the children of Worthing and the outside world. Soon after, while living in Ribeirão Prêto, Brazil (I was serving as a missionary for the LDS church), I used my spare time to plot out and begin writing a novel-length prequel that explained why these people had psychic abilities and how they came to live on the planet Worthing. It was then that I thought of somec, with its torturous but forgotten pain; the planet Capitol; and the rather bizarre starship that Jason piloted. At the time my grounding in both science and science fiction were weak. I had read Isaac Asimov's *Foundation* trilogy—Capitol's derivation from Trantor should be obvious. But I had read little else, and as a result spent much time reinventing the wheel, so to speak. Eventually I left the work unfinished as I turned my hand to playwriting and, after my mission was finished, to starting the Utah Valley Repertory Theatre Company.

In 1975, my theatre company in dire financial straits, I turned back to fiction. Since "Tinker" had received an encouraging note from *Analog*, I pulled out the manuscript and reread it. Apparently I had learned much in the intervening years, because I found it necessary to rewrite it from beginning to end. Again I sent it to *Analog*; again it was rejected with an encouraging note. This time, however, Ben Bova, who had since become editor, let me know why the story wasn't working. "*Analog* doesn't publish fantasy," he said, "but if you have any science fiction, I'd like to see it."

It hadn't occurred to me that "Tinker" was fantasy; *I* knew that there was ample science fictional justification for everything that happened. Furthermore, I had read a collection of Zenna Henderson's stories and knew that tales of people with extraordinary powers were within the realm of science fiction. Yet the impression "Tinker" leaves *is* that of fantasy—medieval technology, lots of trees, and unexplained miracles. I toyed with the idea of going back to the story of Jason Worthing, which would establish "Tinker" and all the other stories as true science fiction, but I was too impatient to work with a novel. Instead, I wrote the novelette "Ender's Game," which became my first fiction sale and the foundation of my career as a fiction writer.

Still, it was not long before I returned to the Worthing stories. Even had I been inclined to neglect them, I could not have forgotten them: My mother kept asking me what I was going to do with my "blue-eyed people." She had typed those early manuscripts for me—I was already a fair typist, but I couldn't match her error-free 120-word-per-minute artistry—and, as the first audience for the stories in the Forest of Waters, she believed, as I did, that there was some real power in them, even if I did not yet know how to tell the stories as well as I should.

By then I worked at *The Ensign*, the official magazine of the Church of Jesus Christ of Latter-day Saints (the Mormons). Two other editors there, Jay Parry and Lane Johnson, were also working on fiction writing. We would spend lunch hours down in the Church Office Building cafeteria, eating salads, drinking nasty cheap soda pop, and developing story ideas. Most of my stories immediately after "Ender's Game" emerged from that creative maelstrom. It was then that I began using the idea of somec in stories like "Lifeloop," "Breaking the Game," and "Killing Children"; but the stories were never *about* the science fiction elements. Always they were about people and how they created and destroyed each other.

When Ben Bova invited me to submit a novel to him for a new series of books he was editing with Baronet and Ace, I immediately thought of my Jason Worthing novel, and started writing it. I showed the first fifty pages or so to Jay Parry, who told me it was too long. Too long? In fifty pages I was most of the way through the story. If I cut any more it'd be nothing but an outline. Then I realized that what Jay was really telling me was that the story *felt* long. I was trying to rush through the story so fast that I merely skimmed over the surface, never pausing long enough to show a scene that would allow the reader to become involved in the story, to care about a character.

I went back, slowed down, started over. Still I had trouble structuring the story as a coherent whole. My only experience was writing short stories, so in desperation I rethought the story as a series of novelettes, each from a different character's point of view. The result was a pretty good story marred by a weak, diffuse structure. Even so, it was deemed publishable, and under the title *Hot Sleep* it began to wend its way toward publication. In fact, I finished the final draft the night before my wedding to Kristine Allen, and on the morning of the wedding I photocopied it and dropped it off in the Church Office Building mailroom before going through the tunnel leading under Main Street to the temple, where my bride was waiting for me. She had some understandable doubts about what it meant to our future that I was a few minutes late for the wedding because I had to get a manuscript into the mail.

In the meantime, Ben Bova suggested that I collect the somec stories he had bought for *Analog*, and some new ones, and publish them in a collection with Baronet. The result was the book *Capitol*. Some of the new stories were good enough that they have found their way into this book. Some, however, were purely mechanical and soulless, and I have, out of mercy to you, dear readers, let them quietly expire. Yet at the time I wrote them, they were the best I could do with the subject matter, and *Capitol* came out in the spring of 1978 as my first published book of fiction—roughly at the same time as the birth of my first child, Geoffrey.

Hot Sleep followed a year later, with a hideously ugly cover from Baronet that embarrassed me doubly because it faithfully illustrated a scene in the book. I learned then—as I have re-learned since—that if there is a scene in a novel which, if depicted on the cover, would destroy the effectiveness of the book, that is the scene that will appear on the cover. Worse yet, the blurb writers had written "Hugo Award Winner" on the cover, even though I had come in second for the Hugo Award in 1978; it was the John W. Campbell Award (for new writer) that I had won at the Phoenix WorldCon (World Science Fiction Convention).

Soon after the book's publication I received a letter from Michael Bishop, a writer I had admired for some time, but had not met. He was apologizing in advance for his review of *Hot Sleep* in *The Magazine of Fantasy & Science Fiction*. The review had not yet appeared, but it was too late to correct it, he said—he had criticized me for allowing "Hugo Award Winner" to appear on my book, only to discover a short time later that his own publisher had done the same thing to him, crediting him with awards he had not received. Thus began a friendship that continues today, though not without occasional tensions caused by our very different ideas of what good storytelling consists of.

His review of *Hot Sleep* was highly critical, but it was also the most helpful book review I've ever seen. He called attention to the structural flaws in the novel in a way that helped me see what I had done wrong. I was then beginning work on my third novel, *Songmaster*, and was set to use a fragmented, diffuse structure just like the one in *Hot Sleep*; with Bishop's review as a spur, I found ways to bind a long story together as a single whole. It was the beginning of my understanding of story structure; my narratives came under my conscious control, and a whole new set of tools was available to me.

In the meantime, though, what could I do about *Hot Sleep*? I now knew how to write it properly and was deeply dissatisfied with it in its current form. Yet it was also selling steadily, which meant that to some readers it was adequate at least. Furthermore, I was now quite unhappy with the weaker stories in *Capitol*—and it too was still selling, bringing readers to associate my name with stories I no longer approved of.

I discussed this with Ace editor Susan Allison at dinner during a convention in Santa Rosa; she agreed to withdraw *Hot Sleep* and *Capitol* from print in favor of a new novel, called *The Worthing Chronicle*, which would tell the same general story, but with much stronger artistry. I did not write the new book until the autumn of 1981, as I was in the midst of my first semester as a graduate student at Notre Dame. By then I was aflame with my newfound passion for medieval literature and my theories of how and why storytelling works, and, armed with the marvelous book *The Lost Country Life* as a resource for details of daily life in a pretechnological society, I made *The Worthing Chronicle* the most structurally complex yet thematically unified of my works of fiction. Far from being my weakest novel, the story of Jason Worthing was now my best.

Years passed; my old books went out of print. This is always painful to an author; like a parent whose children have stopped writing, the author thinks wistfully of his out-of-print books and wishes he could hear from them again. I'm grateful that Tom Doherty and Beth Meacham, my publisher and editor at Tor, have seen fit to let me assemble in one volume *The Worthing Chronicle*, the better stories from *Capitol*, and the original fantasylike stories that started me, not just on this series, but on my entire career as a writer of science fiction.

In the process of writing *The Worthing Chronicle*, I did not have the original Worthing stories at hand—"Worthing Farm," "Worthing Inn," and "Tinker." So where I needed elements from them, I relied on memory, and freely adapted to fit the needs of the novel. Now, going back over the original stories, I find that they are so inconsistent with the novel that to reconcile them would require rewriting them completely. I even made notes on how to revise them, but finally decided to publish them here as they were originally. After all, one of the major themes of *The Worthing Chronicle* is the nature of storytelling; it is more true to the intent of this work if I present these stories in such a way that you can see how the tales have been transformed over time.

Some of the transformation arises from the fact that I became a better writer over the years. Some of the differences come from the fact that I have lived a bit longer now, and understand people a little better. Most of the changes, however, arose from the needs of the novel. The stories became what I needed them to be. I believe that's what all our stories are. Not just our fiction, but our news, our gossip, our histories, our biographies, our memories. They are what we need them to be.

Yet I believe in these tales. I have lived with them in my memory since I was in my teens. It took me a long time to acquire the skill to tell them as I wanted them told, yet I never ceased caring about them over the years. Now I offer them to you in the hope that you will find them powerful and true.

The Worthing Chronicle

*For Laird and Sally
because the right tales
are true to you*

1
The Day of Pain

In many places in the Peopled Worlds, the pain came suddenly in the midst of the day's labor. It was as if an ancient and comfortable presence left them, one that they had never noticed until it was gone, and no one knew what to make of it at first, though all knew at once that something had changed deep at the heart of the world. No one saw the brief flare in the star named Argos; it would be years before astronomers would connect the Day of Pain with the End of Worthing. And by then the change was done, the worlds were broken, and the golden age was over.

In Lared's village, the change came while they slept. That night there were no shepherds in their dreams. Lared's little sister, Sala, awoke screaming in terror that Grandma was dead, Grandma is dead!

Lared sat up in his truckle bed, trying to dispel his own dreams, for in them he had seen his father carry Grandma to the grave—but that had been long ago, hadn't it? Father stumbled from the wooden bedstead where he and Mother slept. Not since

3

Sala had been weaned had anyone cried out in the night. Was she hungry?

"Grandma died tonight, like a fly in the fire she died!"

Like a squirrel in the fox's teeth, thought Lared. Like a lizard in the cat's mouth, trembling.

"Of course she's dead," Father said, "but not tonight." He took her in his vast blacksmith's arms and held her. "Why do you weep now, when Grandma has been dead for such a long time?" But Sala wept on, as if the grief were great and new.

Then Lared looked at Grandma's old bed. "Father," he whispered. Again, "Father." For there lay her corpse, still new, still stiffening, though Lared so clearly remembered her burial long ago.

Father laid Sala back in her truckle bed, where she burrowed down against the woven straw side, in order not to watch. Lared watched, though, as his father touched the straw tick beside his old mother's body. "Not cold yet," he murmured. Then he cried out in fear and agony, "Mother!" Which woke all the sleepers, even the travelers in the room upstairs; they all came into the sleeping room.

"Do you see it!" cried Father. "Dead a year, at least, and here's her body not yet cold in her own bed!"

"Dead a year!" cried the old clerk, who had arrived late in the afternoon yesterday, on a donkey. "Nonsense! She served the soup last night. Don't you remember how she joked with me that if my bed was too cold, your wife would come up and warm it, and if it was too warm, *she* would sleep with me?"

Lared tried to sort out his memories. "I remember that, but I remember that she said that long, long ago, and yet I remember she said it to you, and I never saw you before last night."

"I buried you!" Father cried, and then he knelt at Grandma's bed and wept. "I buried you, and forgot you, and here you are to grieve me!"

Weeping. It was an unaccustomed sound in the village of Flat Harbor, and no one knew what to do about it. Only hungry infants made such cries, and so Mother said, "Elmo, will you eat something? Let me fetch you something to eat."

"No!" shouted Elmo. "Don't you see my mother's dead?"

And he caught his wife by the arm and flung her roughly away. She fell over the stool and struck her head against the table.

This was worse than the corpse lying in the bed, stiff as a dried-out bird. For never in Lared's life had he seen one human being do harm to another. Father too was aghast at his own temper. "Thano, Thanalo, what have I done?" He scarcely knew how to comfort her as she lay weeping softly on the floor. No one had needed comfort in all their lives. To all the others, Father said, "I was so angry. I have never been so angry before, and yet what did she do? I've never felt such a rage, and yet she did me no harm!"

Who could answer him? Something was bitterly wrong with the world, they could see that; they had all felt anger in the past, but till now something had always come between the thought and the act, and calmed them. Now, tonight, that calm was gone. They could feel it in themselves, nothing soothing their fear, nothing telling them wordlessly, All is well.

Sala raised her head above the edge of her bed and said, "The angels are gone, Mama. No one watches us anymore."

Mother got up from the floor and stumbled over to her daughter. "Don't be foolish, child. There are no angels, except in dreams."

There is a lie in my mind, Lared said to himself. The traveler came last night, and Grandma spoke to him just as he said, and yet my memory is twisted, for I remember the traveler speaking yesterday, but Grandma answering long ago. Something has bent my memories, for I remember grieving at her graveside, and yet her grave has not been dug.

Mother looked up at Father in awe. "My elbow still hurts, where it struck the floor," she said. "It still hurts very much."

A hurt that lasted! Who had heard of such a thing! And when she lifted her arm, there was a raw and bleeding scrape on it.

"Have I killed you?" asked Father, wonderingly.

"No," said Mother. "I don't think so."

"Then why does it bleed?"

The old clerk trembled and nodded and his voice quivered as he spoke. "I have read the books of ancient times," he began, and all eyes turned to him. "I have read the books of ancient times, and in them the old ones spoke of wounds that bleed like slaughtered cattle, and great griefs when the living suddenly are dead, and anger that turns to blows among people. But that was long, long ago, when men were still animals, and God was young and inexperienced.''

"What does this mean, then?'' asked Father. He was not a bookish man, and so even more than Lared he thought that men who knew books had answers.

"I don't know,'' said the clerk. "But perhaps it means that God has gone away, or that he no longer cares for us.''

Lared studied the corpse of Grandma, lying on her bed. "Or is he dead?'' Lared asked.

"How can God die?'' the old clerk asked with withering scorn. "He has all the power in the universe.''

"Then doesn't he have the power to die if he wants to?''

"Why should I speak with children of things like this?'' The clerk got up to go upstairs, and the other travelers took that as a signal to return to bed.

But Father did not go to bed: he knelt by his old mother's body until daybreak. And Lared also did not sleep, because he was trying to remember what he had felt inside himself yesterday that he did not feel now, for something was strange in the way his own eyes looked out upon the world, and yet he could not remember how it was before. Only Sala and Mother slept, and they slept together in Mother's and Father's bed.

Before dawn, Lared got up and walked over to his mother, and saw that a scab had formed on her arm, and the bleeding had stopped. Comforted, he dressed himself and went out to milk the ewe, which was near the end of its milk. Every bit of milk was needed for the cheese press and the butter churn— winter was coming, and this morning, as the cold breeze whipped at Lared's hair, this morning he looked to winter with dread. Until today he had always looked at the future like a cow looking at the pasture, never imagining drought or snow. Now it was possible for old women to be found dead in their beds. Now it was possible for Father to be angry and knock Mother to the floor. Now it was possible for Mother to bleed like an animal. And so winter was more than just a season of inactivity. It was the end of hope.

The ewe perked up at something, a sound perhaps that Lared

was too human to hear. He stopped milking and looked up, and saw in the western sky a great light, which hovered in the air like a star that had lost its bearings and needed help to get back home. Then the light sank down below the level of the trees across the river, and it was gone. Lared did not know at first what it might be. Then he remembered the word *starship* from school and wondered. Starships did not come to Flat Harbor, or even to this continent, or even, more than once a decade, to this world. There was nothing here to carry away to somewhere else, nothing lacking here that only other worlds could possibly supply. Why, then, would a starship come here now? Don't be a fool, Lared, he told himself. It was a shooting star, but on this strange morning you made too much of it, because you are afraid.

At dawn, Flat Harbor came awake, and others gradually made the discovery that had come to Lared's family in the night. They came, as they always did in cold weather, to Elmo's house, with its great table and indoor kitchen. They were not surprised to find that Elmo had not yet built up the fire in his forge.

"I scalded myself on the gruel this morning," said Dinno, Mother's closest friend. She held up the smoothed skin of her fingers for admiration. "Hurts like it was still in the fire. Good God," she said.

Mother had her own wounds, but she chose not to tell that tale. "When that old clerk went to leave this morning, his donkey kicked him square in the belly, and now he's upstairs. Too much hurt to travel, he says. Threw up his breakfast."

There were a score of minor, careless injuries, and by noon most people were walking more carefully, carrying out their tasks more slowly. Not a one of them but had some injury. Omber, one of the diggers of Grandma's grave, crushed his foot with a pick, and it bled for a long, long time; now, white and weak and barely alive, he lay drawing scant breath in one of Mother's guest beds. And Father, death on his mind, would not even take the hammer in his hand on the Day of Pain, "For fear I'll strike fire into my eye, or break my hand. God doesn't look out for us anymore."

They laid Grandma into the ground at noon, and all day Lared and Sala were busy helping Mother with the work that Grandma used to do. Her place at table was so empty. Many a sentence began, "Grandma." And Father always looked away as if searching for something hidden deep in the walls. Try as they might, no one could think of a time before this when grief had been anything but a dim and wistful memory; never had the loss of a loved one come so suddenly, with the gap in their lives so plain, with the soil on the grave so black and rich, fresh as the first-turned fold of earth in the spring plowing.

Late in the afternoon, Omber died, the last blood of his body seeping into the rough bandage. He lay beside the wide-eyed clerk, who still vomited everything he swallowed and cried out in pain when he tried to sit. Never in their lives had they seen a man die still in his strength and prime, and just from a careless blow of a pick.

They were still digging the new grave for Omber when Bran's daughter, Clany, fell into the fire and lay screaming for three hours before she died. No one could even speak when they laid her into the third grave of the day. For a village of scant three hundred souls, the death of three on the same day would have been calamitous; the death of a strong man and a young child, that undid them all.

At nightfall there were no new travelers—they always became rarer as the cold weather came. It was the only good thing about the night, however, the fact that there were no new guests to care for. The world had changed, had become a harsh place, all in a single day. As Sala got into her bed, she asked, "Will I die tonight, like Grandma?"

"No," said Father, but Lared heard in his voice that he wasn't sure. "No, Sala, my Sarela, you will not die tonight." But he pulled her truckle bed farther from the fire, and put another blanket over her.

Lared did not need to be told, once he had seen. He also moved his truckle bed from his place near the fire. He had heard the sound of Clany's screams. The whole village had heard them—there was no shutting them out. He had never been terrified of flames before, but he was now. Let the cold come— better that than the pain. Better anything than this new and terrible pain.

Lared fell asleep nursing the bruise on his knee where he had carelessly bashed the woodbox. He awoke three times in the night. Once because Father was weeping softly in his bed; when Elmo saw that Lared was awake, he got up and kissed him and held him and said, "Sleep, Lareled, sleep, all's well, all's well." It was a lie, but Lared slept again.

The second time he awoke because Sala had another nightmare, again about Grandma's death. It was Mother who comforted her, singing a song whose sadness Lared had never understood before.

> Saw my love at river's side
> Across the stream.
> The stream was wide.

> Heard my love say come to him
> Across the stream.
> I could not swim.

> Got myself a little boat
> But the day was cold.
> I had no coat.

> Got a coat and put it on
> But it was night.
> Now wait till dawn.

> Sun came up and night was over
> I saw my love.
> I saw his lover.

Lared did not know what else Mother might have sung. He was lost in the dream that wakened him the third and last time that night.

He sat beside the Endwater in spring flood, with the rafts coming down, the lumbermen poling them a safe distance from each other. Then, suddenly, there was a fire in the sky, and it fell down toward the river. Lared knew that he must stop the fire, must shout for it to stop, but though he opened his mouth he could not speak, and so the fire came on. It fell into the river, and all the rafts were burned at once, and the men on the rafts screamed with Clany's voice, and burned, and fell into the river, and drowned, and all because Lared did not know what to say to stop the fire.

Lared woke trembling, filled with guilt at his failure to save anyone, wondering why it was his fault. He heard a moaning sound upstairs. His parents were asleep. Lared did not wake them, but climbed the stairs himself. The old clerk lay on the bed. There was blood on his face, blood on the sheet.

"I'm dying," he whispered, when he saw Lared by the moonlight through the window.

Lared nodded.

"Can you read, boy?"

Again he nodded. This village was not so backward that the children had no school in the winter, and Lared read as well as any adult in the village, even when he was ten years old. Now he was fourteen, and beginning to get a man's strength on him, and still he loved to read, and studied whatever letters he could find.

"Then take the Book of the Finding of the Stars. It is yours. It is all yours."

"Why me?" whispered Lared. Perhaps the old clerk had seen him eyeing his books last night. Perhaps he had heard him recite the Eyes of Endwater to Sala and her friends after supper. But the clerk was silent, though he was not yet dead. Whatever his reason, he meant Lared to have his book. A book that is my own. And a book about finding stars, on the day after the Day of Pain, the day after he had seen a star fall into the forest across Endwater. "Thank you, sir," he said, and he reached to touch the old clerk's hand.

Lared heard a noise behind him. It was Mother, and her eyes were wide.

"Why would he give his books to you?" she asked.

The clerk moved his lips, but made no sound.

"You're nothing but a boy," said Mother. "You're lazy, and you argue."

I know that I deserve nothing, said Lared silently.

"He must have family—we'll send his books to them, if he dies."

The clerk tortured himself by shaking his head violently. "No," he whispered. "Give the books to the boy!"

"Don't die in my house," said Mother, in anguish. "Not another dead in my house!"

"I'm sorry for the inconvenience," said the old clerk. Then he died.

"Why did you come up here!" Mother whispered fiercely to Lared. "Now see what you've done."

"I only came because he was crying out in his—"

"Coming to get his books, and him on the edge of death."

Lared wanted to argue, to defend himself, but even his own dream had blamed him, hadn't it? Her eyes looked like a ewe's eyes, when the pain of birth was on her, and he dared not stay or quarrel. "I have to milk the ewes," he said, and ran down the stairs and out the door.

The night had turned bitterly cold, and the frost was thick on the grass. The ewes were ready for the milking, but Lared was not. His fingers quickly became too cold, despite the warmth of the animals.

No, it was not the cold that made his hands tremble clumsily. It was the books that waited for him in the old clerk's room. It was the three new graves heaped up in the moonlight, where soon a fourth would rise.

It was, above all, the man and woman who walked across the river, angling their steps to combat the current. The river was ten feet deep from bank to bank, but they walked as if the water were hard-packed dirt, whose only oddity was that it slid away underfoot as they walked. Lared thought of hiding, so they would not see him; but instead, without deciding, he stood from his stool by the ewe, set the milk bucket up high where it could not be kicked over, and walked out across the cemetery to meet them.

They were on the riverbank before he reached them, looking at the new graves. There was sorrow in their eyes. The man was white-haired, but his body was strong, and his face was kind and sure. The woman was much younger, younger than Mother, yet her face looked harsh and angry, even in repose. There was no sign that either of them had been in the water—even their footprints on the riverbank were dry. And when they turned and looked at him, he could see even in the moonlight that their eyes were blue. He had never seen eyes so blue that even without sunlight their color was brightly visible.

"Who are you?" he asked.

The man answered in a language that Lared didn't understand. The woman shook her head, said nothing: yet Lared felt a sudden desire to tell them his name.

"Lared," he said.

"Lared," she answered. His name sounded strangely twisted on her tongue. He felt a sudden urgency not to tell anyone that he had seen them walk on Endwater.

"I'll never tell," he said.

The woman nodded. Then he knew, though he still did not know how he knew, that he should take them home.

But he was afraid of these strangers. "You won't hurt my family, will you?"

Tears came to the man's eyes, and the hard-faced woman did not look him in the face. The thought came into Lared's mind: "We have already hurt you more than we can bear."

And now he understood—or thought he understood—his dream, and the falling star on the Day of Pain, and the Day itself. "Have you come to take away the pain again?"

The man shook his head.

The hope had been brief, but the disappointment was no less deep because of that. "If you can't do that," he said, "then what good are you to us?" Still, he was an innkeeper's son, and so he led them carefully through the cemetery, past the sheepsheds, and into the house, where Mother already had the water boiling for the morning gruel.

2
The Making of Parchment and Ink

Mother greeted them. "Do you want a meal? Have you been traveling all night?" Lared watched for her surprise when they spoke inside her mind, but there was no surprise; there was no answer at all, it seemed, for she repeated her question, and it was into Lared's thoughts the answer came.

"They're not hungry, Mother."

"Let the guests speak for themselves," she said sharply. "Will you eat?"

The man shook his head. Lared felt an urgent desire to get the Book of the Finding of the Stars. He started for the stairs.

"Where are you going, Lared?" Mother asked.

"To get the book. Of the Finding of the Stars."

"Now is not the time for playing. There's work to do."

"They want me to read it to them."

"Do you think I'm a fool? They haven't said a word, I don't even think they speak Worren."

Lared did not answer. Instead, Sala said, "It's true, Mama.

13

They speak to Lared and me without words, but they don't want to talk to you and Papa."

Mother looked from Sala to Lared. "What is this? They only talk to you, and not to—" She turned to the strangers. "I don't need people coming into my house and telling me I'm not worth talking to. We don't need you."

The man put a single shining jewel on the table.

Mother looked at it with contempt. "What can I do with *that*? Will it draw grain out of the soil? Will it make my husband's forge burn hotter? Will it heal the scabs on my arm?" But she reached out and took it. "Is it real?" she asked them; and then, helpless in the face of their silence, she asked Sala, "Is it real?"

"It's perfect," said Sala. "It's worth the price of every farm in Flat Harbor, and every building, and all the earth that's under it and all the air that's over it and all the water that runs through it." And she put her hand to her mouth to stop the torrent of words.

"Get the book they asked for," Mother said to Lared. Then she turned sullenly back to the gruel.

Lared ran upstairs, to the room where the body of the old clerk lay. The eyes were closed, with pebbles on them. The belly under the blanket was slack. Did it move, just a little, with a faint breath?

"Sir?" whispered Lard. But there was no answer. Lared went to the pack the old man had so heavily borne. Five books were within it, and a sheaf of parchment, perhaps twenty sheets, with a small horn of ink and several quills. Lared knew something of making parchment, and one of the first lessons of winter school was to sharpen and split a quill for writing. The ink was a mystery, though. Lared reluctantly set the inkhorn back in the pack; he had been given books, not the tools of making books. He quickly sorted out the titles from the decorations of the tooled leather covers; never did cattle and sheep so docilely lie together as in the sheepskin pages and the cowskin covers of a book. The Finding of the Stars.

He had barely set the other books aside when he heard footsteps on the stairs. It was Father, come with Han Carpenter to take away the corpse. Their boots were lightly crusted with soil—the grave was already dug.

"Come to rob the dead?" asked Han cheerfully.

"He gave the books to me—"

Father shook his head. "Han thinks there's jests to make in death rooms."

"Keep the ghosts at bay," said Han. "If they're laughing, they'll cause you no pain."

Lared looked suspiciously at the old clerk's body. Had he a ghost, perhaps? And did that ghost bear sharp penknives, ready to carve Lared like a quill, perhaps when he slept? Lared shuddered. To believe such things would be the end of sleep.

"Take the books, lad," Father said. "They're yours. But be careful with them. They're worth the price of the iron I'll use in my life."

Lared made a wide circle around the bed, where Father and Han were winding the old man in a faded horseblanket—it would make no sense to send the good cloth into the ground with the dead. Lared left the room and fairly flew down the stairs. His mother's fingers caught him at the bottom, stopping him, nearly pulling him off his feet. "What, do you want another burial today? Be careful, there's no angels now to pick up your feet when you start to fall."

Lared pulled away, answered sharply: "I didn't stumble till you near pulled me down!"

She slapped his face harshly, hurting his neck and leaving his cheek stinging. They looked at each other in surprise.

"I'm sorry," Lared whispered.

Mother said nothing, only turned back to the table to set out the horn spoons for their guests. She did not know they had walked on water, but she did guess the worth of the jewel they gave her, and that was miracle enough to warrant the best treatment.

Lared did not want to go to the strangers now, however, for they had seen him ashamed and in pain. In spite of himself there were tears in his eyes—no one had purposely hurt him in his life, and though the pain was fading, the fear of it was not. "She never," he began to explain in a whisper, but they spoke into his mind again, spoke calmly to him, and he handed the Finding of the Stars to them.

The man held the book, opened it and traced the words with

his finger. Lared saw at once that he could not read, for his finger moved from left to right instead of from the top to the bottom of the page. You can do miracles, but you cannot read, Lared thought triumphantly.

Almost at once an image leapt into his mind, of pages of strange words in even stranger letters, letters that spread across the page loosely, as if the parchment were not hours of labor and the ink not worth its volume in hard-earned tin. Then he saw, as if in memory, the young woman bending over the page. "Sorry," he murmured.

The man pointed at the first word, drew his finger down the first sentence, and asked with his eyes. Read, said the silent voice in Lared's mind.

"After the worlds were slain by Abner Doon, ten thousand years of darkness passed before the fires again burned their threads between the stars."

The man's eyes grew wide. "Abner Doon," he said aloud.

Lared pointed at the two words.

Only two letters to say this man's name? asked the silent voice.

"No—those are words, not letters." Lared got a kindling twig from the firebox and drew in the thin dust on the floor. "Here's *ab*, and here's *un*, and here's *er*, and they fit together like this. This tie tells you that the *un* is quick, and this one that the *ab* is longest, and the binding tells you that the words are names."

The man and woman looked at each other in surprise, and then laughed. At Lared? He thought not.

No, said the voice in his mind. Not at you. At ourselves. We thought to learn your language and your writing, but it's plain your letters are too hard for us.

"No, they're easy," said Lared. "There are only a hundred ninety-eight letters, and thirteen ties, and seven bindings at the ends."

They laughed again, and the man shook his head. Then he got an idea. "Jason," he said, pointing to himself. "Jason." And the voice in Lared's mind said, Write.

So he wrote: *J* and *es*, and *un*, and joined them to make it say *jesun*, and bound it to say, not name, but name of God. It was a dignity only offered to great rulers, but Lared did not hesitate to use it with this man. With Jason.

But apparently the man could understand somehow what the binding meant. He took the stick from Lared's hand and put the binding of God's name on the word of Abner, and put the common name binding on his own name.

An image came into Lared's mind, of a small man dressed in a strange and ugly costume, smiling with mocking amusement. Lared didn't like him. The voice in his mind said, Abner Doon.

"You knew him?" asked Lared. "The Unmaker of the Universe? The Breaker of Man? The Waker from the Sleep of Life?"

The man shook his head. Lared thought he meant that he did not know Abner Doon. How could he, after all, unless he was a devil, too? That thought crossed Lared's mind. Their powers were more than human; how did Lared know that they were good?

In answer came a soothing feeling, a warmth, a calm, and Lared shuddered. How could he doubt them? And yet, even deeper, he still asked himself, How can I not doubt them? They come too near to the Day of Pain.

Jason handed him the book again. Read, said the voice in his mind.

He understood only some of what he read. Making the sounds was easy, since he knew the alphabet. But many of the words were too hard for him. What did he know of starships and worlds and explorers and embassies? He thought that perhaps the two strangers would explain to him what the words meant.

We can't.

"Why not?" he asked.

Because the words mean nothing to us. What we understand is your understanding of them. What you don't know, we can't know.

"Then why don't you learn our language, if you're so wise?"

"Don't be fresh," said Mother from the kitchen, where she was grinding the dried pease for the pot.

Lared was angry. She understood nothing of the conversation, but still could tell when Lared was doing something wrong. Jason reached out and touched him on the knee. Be calm. It's all right. The words weren't put in his head, but he understood them all the same, from the gentle hand, from the calm smile.

Jason will learn your language, said the voice in his mind. But Justice will not.

"Justice?" said Lared, not realizing at first that this was the woman's name.

She touched herself and echoed his word. "Justice," she said. Her voice was uncertain and soft, as if little used. "Justice," she said again. Then laughed, and said an incomprehensible word in a language Lared had never heard before.

That is my name, said the voice in his mind. Justice. Jason's name is mere sound, the same no matter what language you speak. But my name is the idea, and the sound of it changes from language to language.

It made no sense to Lared. "A name's a name. It means you, and so what if it means something else besides?"

They looked at each other.

Tell us, are there words about a place named—

And Justice said a word: "Worthing."

Lared tried out the name on his tongue. "Worthing," he said. Then he wrote down the name in the dirt, so he would be sure to know the sign for it, if he met it in the book.

He did not notice that at the saying of the name Mother's eyebrows rose, and she slipped out of the kitchen without so much as an I'll-be-back.

He found Worthing at the end of the book. "It was believed for thousands of years that two of Doon's Arks had gone astray, or their colonies had failed. Indeed, if Rivethock's Ark resulted in a colony, it remains unfound to this day. The world called Worthing, however, from Worthing's Ark, was found at last, by a Discoverer IV–class ship in the Fifth Wave, whose geologer marked the planet as habitable—and then, to the shock of the crew, as inhabited."

This time, where the words were hard, brief explanations often came into Lared's mind, using ideas that he was familiar with. Doon's Arks were huge starships equipped with everything that 334 passengers would need to start a world. A colony was a village in newly cleared land on a world without human beings. A Discoverer IV of the Fifth Wave was a starship sent by the government to chart the inner reaches of the galaxy some five thousand years ago. A geologer was a machine, or a group of machines, that looked at a world from far away and saw where lay all forests and oil and iron and farmland and ice and ocean and life.

And if we read at this rate we'll get nowhere, said the voice in his mind. The impatience on Justice's face matched the words, and for the first time it occurred to Lared that it might be *only* Justice who spoke to him. For Jason only smiled at whatever she silently said to him, and when he answered her it was in words from their strange language, spoken aloud.

"Who are you?" demanded Father.

He stood at the door that led into the kitchen shed, his strong arms and massive shoulders filling door, silhouetting him against the light from the kitchen fire.

"They're Jason and Justice," said Sala.

"Who are you?" asked Father again. "I'll not be answered by my children's voices."

The words came into Lared's mind, and he spoke them. "You'll not be answered any other way. Don't blame us, Father—they only speak to me because they don't know another way. Jason plans to learn our language as soon as he can."

"Who are you?" asked Father a third time. "You dared to cause my child to say the dark name, the hidden word, and him not yet sixteen."

"What hidden name?" asked Lared.

Father could not force himself to say it. Instead he walked to where Lared had written the sign of it upon the ground, and scraped the mark away with his foot.

Jason laughed, and Justice sighed, and Lared spoke without waiting for them to give him words. "Father, I found the name *Worthing* in the old cleric's book. It's just the name of a world."

Father slapped Lared sharply on the face. "There is a time and place for uttering the name, and that is not here."

Lared could not help but cry out from the pain—he had no strategies for coping with this unhabitual distress. It was too cruel, that with the coming of pain the greatest danger of it should be, not from fire or water or beast, but from Father. So even after the first impact of the pain wore off, Lared could not keep himself from whimpering like a bee-stung dog.

Suddenly Jason slapped the table and jumped to his feet.

Justice tried to hold him back, but he stammered out a few words that they could understand. "Name of my," he said. "Name this mying be."

Father squinted, as if seeing better would help him understand the twisted words. Lared translated for him. "I think he means that *his* name is—is *the* name."

Jason nodded.

"I thought you said your name was Jason."

"Name of my is Jason Worthing."

"My name is Jason Worthing," prompted Lared.

The moment Lared uttered *Worthing*, Father's hand snaked out to slap him again. But Jason was quicker, and caught the blacksmith's hand in mid-act.

"There's no man in Flat Harbor," said Father, "who dares to match strength with me."

Jason only smiled.

Father tried to move his hand again, but Jason tightened his fingers almost imperceptibly, and Father cried out in pain.

Justice too cried out as if the pain had touched her. The two of them babbled in angry language as Father held his wrist, gasping. When Father could speak again, he ignored them, too. "I don't need them as guests, and I don't need you getting into forbidden things. They're going, and you won't have another thing to do with them until they're gone."

Jason and Justice left off their argument and heard the end of his speech. As if to stop the blacksmith, Justice took from her clothing a thin bar of pure gold; she bent it to show its softness.

Father reached for the gold and took it. Between two fingers he folded the bar flat, and with two hands folded it again, and tossed it against the front door. "This is my house, and this is my son, and we have no need of you."

Then Father led Lared from the room, unfed and unhappy, to the forge where the fire already was growing hot.

Lared worked there all morning, hungry and angry, but not daring to do anything but what his father asked. They both knew that Lared hated the work at the forge, that he had no desire at all to learn the secrets of smithing. He did what he had to, just the way he bore his share in the field—and no more. Usually that was enough for Father, but not today.

"There are things you'll learn from me," Father shouted above the roar of the flames. "There are things no half-witted strangers are going to teach you!"

They aren't half-witted, Lared said silently. Unlike Justice, however, when he held his tongue his words went unremarked. It was one of the things he did best, holding his tongue.

"You're no good at smithing, I know that, you've got weak arms like your mother's father, narrow shoulders. I haven't pushed you, have I?"

Lared shook his head.

"Pump harder."

Lared bore down on the bellows, pumped faster even though his back ached.

"And in the fields, you're a decent hand, and if you aren't big enough yet for a man's load, you're good at mushrooms and herbs and I won't even be ashamed of you if you end up a swineherd. God help me, I'd even bear having my son be the gooseboy."

"I'll be no gooseboy, Father." Father often made things out worse than they really were, for effect.

"Better gooseboy than a clerk! There's no work for a clerk in Flat Harbor, no need for one."

"I'm not a clerk. I'm not good enough at numbers, and I don't know but half the words in the book."

Father struck the iron so hard that it split, and he cast the piece that was in the tongs onto the stone floor, where it broke again. "Name of God, I don't want you not to be a clerk because you're not *good* enough! You're *good* enough to be a clerk! But I'd be ashamed to have a son of mine be no more useful than to scratch letters on leather all day long!"

Lared leaned on the bellows handle and studied his father. How has the coming of pain changed you? You're no more careful of your hands at the forge. You stand as close to the fire as ever, though all others who work near fire have taken to standing back far, and there's been a rash of calls for long strong sticks for spoons twice as long as anyone thought to want before. You haven't asked for longer tongs, though. So what has changed?

"If you become a clerk," Father said, "then there'll be nothing for you but to leave Flat Harbor. Live in Endwater Havens, or Cleaving, somewhere far.''

Lared smiled bitterly. ''It can't happen a day too soon for Mother.''

Father shrugged impatiently. ''Don't be a fool. You just look too much like her father, that's all. She means no harm.''

''Sometimes,'' Lared said, ''I think the only one who has a use for me is Sala.'' Until now. Until the strangers came.

''I have a use for you.''

''Do I pull bellows for you until you die? And afterward pull for whoever takes your place? Here's the truth, Father. I don't want to leave Flat Harbor. I don't want to be a clerk. Except maybe to read for a guest or two, especially late in the year, like now, with nothing to do but leather work and spinning and weaving and slaughter. Other men make up songs. *You* make up songs.''

Father picked up the wasted iron and put the pieces in the scrap pile. Another bar was heating in the forge. ''Pull the bellows, Lareled.''

The affectionate name was Lared's answer. Father's anger was only temporary, and he'd not bar him from reading, when it didn't keep him from work. Lared sang as he pulled the bellows.

''Squirrilel, squirrilel, where go the nuts?
In holes in the ground or in poor farmers' huts?
Steal from my barn and I'll string out your guts
To make songs with my lyre
Or sausaging wire
Or tie off the bull so he no longer ruts.''

Father laughed. He had made up the song himself when the whole village gathered in the inn during the worst of last winter. It was an honor, to have a song remembered, especially by your own son. Lared knew it would please his father, but there was no calculation in his singing. He *did* love his father, and wanted him to be glad, though he had no common ground with him, and was in no way like him.

Father sang another verse, one that Lared didn't like as well. But he laughed anyway, and this time he *was* calculating. For when the verse was over and the laughter done, Lared said, ''Let them stay. Please.''

Father's expression darkened, and he pulled the bar from the fire and again began to beat it into a sickle. "They talk with your voice, Lared."

"They speak in my mind," Lared said. "Like"—and he hesitated before saying the childhood word—"angels."

"If there are angels, why is the cemetery so full today?" Father asked.

"*Like* angels. There's no harm in it. They—"

"They what?"

They walk on water. "They mean no harm to us. They're willing to learn our language."

"The man knows ways to cause pain. Why would an angel know ways to cause pain?"

There was no good reason. Before yesterday no one had known what real pain was. Yet Jason could reach out his hand and stop Elmo the Smith with a subtle agony. What sort of man would even want to know such things?

"They can put thoughts in your mind," Father said. "How do you know they haven't put trust in your mind as well? And hope and love and anything else that they might use to destroy you? And us as well? Times are perilous now. Word is that upriver there was killing. Not just death, but killing yesterday. From such anger as had never been let out before. And here is a man who knows pain like I know the insides of iron."

And the sickle was complete. Father plunged it back in the fire, to let the iron know its true shape, and rubbed it on the hearthstone so it knew the earth, and would not offend at harvest time. Then he dipped it smoothly into the cistern, and the iron sang.

"Still," said Lared. He handed the whetstone to his father, to work an edge onto the iron.

"Still what?"

"Still. If they want to stay, how can you stop them?"

Father turned sharply. "Do you think I'd let them stay from fear?"

"No," said Lared, abashed. "But there's the jewel. And the gold."

"It's a low sort of man who changes his mind for the hope of wealth. Who's to say what gold and jewels are worth, if things get worse upriver? Will gold bring Mama back from the grave? Will it make Clany's flesh hold to her bones? Will it give the old clerk sight? Or heal the iron-bitten foot?''

"They've caused us no harm, Father, except that he reached out to protect me, when I sinned at his bidding.''

Father grew holy, thinking of the name Lared had offended by saying. "That's the name of God," said Father. "You're not supposed to learn it until you kiss the ice in your sixteenth winter.''

Lared, too, grew solemn. "You would turn away one who comes teaching the name of God?''

"The wicked can use God's name as well as God.''

"How can we ever know, then, unless we try them? Or should we cast away all men who use the name of God, for fear they're blasphemers? What name will God use, then?''

"Already you talk like a clerk," said Father. "Already you want them here too much. I'm not afraid of pain, I'm not afraid of wealth, I'm not even afraid of a man who blasphemes and thinks he does no harm. I'm afraid of how you want whatever it is they promised you—''

"They promised me nothing!''

"I'm afraid of how you'll change.''

Lared laughed bitterly. "You don't much like the way I am. What difference does a difference in me make?''

Father ran his finger along the sickle's edge. "Sharp," he said. "I barely touched her, and she cut me a bit.'' He showed the finger to Lared. There was a drop of blood on the finger. Father reached out and touched the bloody finger to Lared's right eyelid. Usually the rite was done with water, but it felt all the more powerful with blood. Lared shuddered—touch his left, and instead of a protection to Lared the rite would have been a fending, to drive Lared himself away. "I'll let them stay," Father whispered. "But all your winter work must come first.''

"Thank you," Lared said softly. "I swear it'll do no harm, but end up serving God.''

"All things end up serving God." Father set down the sickle on the bench. "There's another ready for a handlemaker. Blade's no good unless it fits somebody's hand." He turned and looked down on Lared—they were near the same height, but always he looked down to see his son. "Whose hand were *you* made to fit, Lared? Never mine, God knows."

But Lared's thoughts were all on Jason and Justice, and the work they had for him. He spared no thought, not now, for his father's pain. "You'll not let Mother invent more work than last year, just to keep me from them?"

Father laughed. "Nor will I." Then he touched Lared's shoulder and looked gravely in his eyes. "Their eyes are the sky," he said. "Beware of flying. It isn't the hunter's shot that kills the dove, but the fall to earth, they say."

So except for Mother's brittle silences and sharp remarks, Lared was unhindered that winter. From the first, even before the snowfall, he and Jason were every day together, every*where* together. Jason had a language to learn, he said, and he could earn more of Lared's time if he helped him in his work. So he came with Lared into the forest, searching for mushrooms before the first snow killed them all. And Jason had an eye for herbs, too, asking which was which yet knowing more of the answers than Lared, who had thought he knew them all.

"Are the herbs the same as here, where you come from?" Lared asked him one day.

Haltingly, Jason answered, "All worlds come are same ships from. Are come."

"From the same ships."

"Yes."

Lared had been puzzling out coincidences. "The world of Worthing, that the book of the Finding of the Stars talks about. Have you ever lived there?"

Jason smiled as if the question caused him secret pleasure and secret pain. "Seeing it. But *live* there, no."

"Does this world called Worthing have something to do with the name of God?"

Jason did not answer. Instead he pointed at a flower. "Did you eat this ever?"

"It's poisonous."

"Flower be—is poisonous." Jason broke the stem at the ground, and tossed the flower far away. Then he freed the soil around the root and brought it up. It was almost perfectly round

and black. "For winter eating." He broke it open. It was speck-
led black inside. "Water hot," he said, struggling for the word.

"Boil it?"

"Yes. What is going up?"

"Steam?"

"Yes. Drinking steam from this, it makes children." Jason
grinned as he said it, to show he didn't believe *that* particular
cure.

They walked on. Lared found a patch of safe mushrooms, and
they filled their bag. Lared kept up a constant chatter, Jason
answering as he could. They came to the boggy ground near the
edge of the swamp, and Lared showed Jason how to use his
quarterstaff to vault the fingers and arms of water. By the end
of the morning, Jason and Lared were running madly at the
water, plunging in the staves, and overleaping the stream without
getting wet. Except once, when Jason set the staff too deeply,
and it didn't come away when he reached the other bank. Jason
seemed at a loss for words, as he sat there covered with mud.
Lared taught him some of the more colorful words of the language, and Jason laughed.

"Some things is the same between languages," he said.

Lared insisted, then, that Jason teach him the words *he* used.
By the time they got home, they were both thoroughly bilingual
in cursing.

The cry of "Boat downriver!" came late in the day, at the
time when travelers would often put to shore and spend the night
in a friendly village. So Father and Mother and Lared and Sala
all ran to the dock to watch the coming boat. To their surprise
it was a raft, though the logging season wasn't till the breakup
of ice in the spring. And what seemed a large cook-fire was
much greater—one end of the raft itself was afire, right down to
the waterline.

"There's a man aboard!" shouted someone, and the villagers
at once put out in their rowboats. Lared was in a boat with
Father, whose strong arms brought them to the raft before any
of the others. The man was lying atop a pile of wood, surrounded by flame. Lared pulled himself across the short distance
between boat and raft, thinking to pull the man from the boat

before the fire reached him. But, standing aboard the raft, Lared saw that the fire had already reached him, that it was burning his legs; Lared smelled the flesh, the smell he knew from Clany's death. Lared staggered back to the edge of the raft, reached out and pulled the boat near enough to get in.

"He's dead," Lared said. Then the stench and the fear of having been aboard the flaming raft and the memory of flames rising from the man's naked flesh had Lared leaning over the edge of the boat, casting up his guts. Father said nothing. He's ashamed of me, Lared thought. He looked up from the water. Father had taken his hands from the oars and turned to signal the others to go back. Lared saw his face, how grim he looked. Is he ashamed of me, for being so afraid? Or does he think of me at all? Then Lared looked at the raft, clearly in view behind Father, though already growing distant as the mid-river current drew it on. As Lared watched, the arm of the burning man rose into the air, black and flaming; the arm stayed erect in the air and the fingers uncrumpled like paper in a fire.

"He's still alive!" Lared cried.

Father turned to look. The hand stayed up a moment more, than collapsed back into the pyre. It took a long time before Father again took the oars in hand and pulled for shore. In the bow, Lared could not see his father's face. He did not want to.

They had been so long without rowing in the current that they came to shore well downstream from the dock. Ordinarily Father would have worked the boat upstream in the almost currentless water near the bank, but this time he sprang from the boat and pulled it onto Harvings' gravel beach. He was silent, and Lared did not dare to speak to him. What could be said, after what they had seen? The people upriver had put a living man on a burning raft. And though the man had been silent, no sound of agony, the memory of Clany's death was too near; she had screamed into their minds enough to sear them again and again.

"Maybe," said Father, "maybe the heat made his arm rise, and him long dead."

That was it, thought Lared. They had seen the sign of life, but it was no sign of life.

"Father," shouted Sala.

They were not alone, after all. On a rise of ground above

Harvings' landing stood tall Jason, holding Sala in his arms. Only when Lared was halfway up the embankment did he realize that Justice was there too, curled around Jason's legs like a game animal freshly killed. But she was not dead; her body shook with weeping.

Jason saw the question in Lared's mind, and answered it. "She looked into the mind of the man on the boat."

"He was alive, then?" asked Lared.

"Yes."

"And you too looked into his mind?"

Jason shook his head. "I've been with men when they died before."

Lared looked at Justice, wondering why *she* had wanted to look at death so closely. Jason looked away. Justice raised herself partway from the ground, and looked at him as the words came into his mind: I am not afraid to know anything. But that was not all, was it? Lared was not sure, but he felt an overtone of meaning, as if she had really said, I am not afraid to know anything *that I have done.*

"You're so wise," said Father behind them. "What was that raft? What did it mean?"

The words of answer came to Lared, and he spoke them. "Upriver they have made pain into a god, and they burn the man alive so pain will be satisfied and go away."

Father's face went ugly with disgust. "What fool would believe such things?"

Again Lared spoke the words they gave him. "The man on the boat believed it."

"He was already dead!" shouted Father.

Lared shook his head.

"I say he was already dead!" Father stalked away, disappearing quickly in the scant moonlight.

When his footsteps died away, Lared heard an unaccustomed sound. Quick, heavy, uncontrolled breathing. It took a moment to realize that it was Justice, cold and immovable Justice; she was weeping.

Jason said something in their language. She answered sharply, and lifted herself away from him, sat up and bent her back so her head was clasped between her knees.

"She will stop crying," Jason said.

Sala wriggled in Jason's arms, and he let her down. She went to Justice and patted her trembling shoulders. "I forgive you," Sala said. "I don't mind."

Lared almost rebuked his sister for saying such silly, meaningless things to an adult—Sala was always saying inappropriate things until Mother's hand was nearly raw from swatting her. But before he could speak, Jason laid a firm hand on his shoulder and shook his head. "Let's go home," Jason said softly, and drew Lared from the hill. Lared looked back only once, and saw in the moonlight how Justice sat with Sala on her lap, rocking back and forth, for all the world as if it were Sala who wept, and Justice who comforted her.

"Your sister," said Jason. "She is good."

Lared had never thought of it before, but it was true. Slow to anger, quick to forgive: Sala was good.

For all their friendship in the field and forest, Lared still felt shy of Jason, and terrified of cold Justice, who did not want to learn the village speech. Jason and Justice had been there three weeks before Lared worked up the courage to ask even such a simple question as, "Why don't *you* ever speak in my mind, as Justice does?"

Jason deftly peeled the last shaving from the spade edge, and this time the iron blade-tip fit smoothly. He held it up. "Good work?"

"Perfect," Lared said. He took the spade and began to nail down the iron sheathing. "Why," he asked between blows, "don't you want to answer me?"

Jason looked around the shed. "Any other wood work?"

"Not unless you count smoking the winter's meat with the scrap wood. Why don't you ever speak in my mind?"

Jason sighed. "Justice does all. I do little."

"You hear what I think even when I don't speak, the same as her. You walked on the—walked where she did, just the same, the day I first saw you."

"I hear what I hear—but what you saw me do, *she* did."

Lared didn't like that, for the woman to be stronger than the man. It wasn't the way of Flat Harbor, anyway. What would it be like, if Mother had Father's strength? Who would protect him from her then? And would Mother work the forge?

Where I come from, Justice said silently in Lared's mind, *Where I come from men and women care nothing for strength, only for what you do with it.*

She had been listening in from the house, of course. Since she wasn't interested in learning the language, she often avoided their company, preferring to work at spinning and weaving with Mother and Sala, where songs were always being sung, and Sala would say whatever words Justice needed to say. Still, Justice was no less with them, just because her body wasn't there. And it annoyed Lared that he and Jason were never really alone together, no matter how far away they went, no matter how quietly they spoke. Justice even knew that it annoyed him, no doubt, and did it anyway.

As to what Justice claimed about her people, Lared was not surprised that they made no difference between the sexes. Where Justice and Jason came from people walked on water and learned to cause pain and talked to each other without opening their mouths. Why shouldn't they do everything else oddly, too? It was something else that interested Lared. "Where *are* you from?"

Jason smiled at the question. "She won't tell you," he said.

"Why not?"

"Because where she's from is gone."

"Aren't you from the same place?"

Jason's smile faded. "Where she's from, came from *me.* Where *I'm* from is also gone."

"I don't understand your puzzles or your secrets. Where are you from?" Lared remembered the falling star.

Of course Jason knew what was in his thoughts. "We're from where you think we're from."

They had voyaged between the stars. "Then why are you here? Of all the places in the universe, why Flat Harbor?"

Jason shrugged. "Ask Justice."

"To ask Justice, I only have to think. Sometimes even *before* I think, she knows. I wake up in the night and I'm never alone. Always there's someone listening in on my dreams."

We are here, said Justice silently, *for you.*

"For a blacksmith's son? Or a mushroom hunter? What do you want from me?"

"What you want from us," said Jason.

"And what is that?"

Our story, answered Justice. Where we're from, what we've done, why we left. And why pain has returned to the world.

"You have something to do with that?"

You've known all along that we did.

"And what do you need from me?"

Your words. Your language. Written down, simply, truthfully.

"I'm not a cleric."

That's your virtue.

"Who would read what I write?"

It will be true. Those who know truth when they see it will read it, and believe it.

"And what does it matter if they do?"

It was Jason who answered. "Our story won't bring burning rafts down the river."

Lared remembered the half-flayed man who gave his pain as a sacrifice to some imagined god. Lared wasn't sure yet whether Jason and Justice were good or evil—his very liking of Jason made him more suspicious sometimes than his dislike of Justice. But good or evil, they were better than torture in the name of God. Still, he couldn't figure out what need they had of him. "I've never written anything longer than a page, no one's read anything longer than my name, a million billion people in the universe, you still haven't told me why me?"

Because our story has to be written simply, so simple people can read it. It had to be written in Flat Harbor.

"There are a million places like Flat Harbor."

But I knew Flat Harbor. I knew you. And when all else that I knew was gone, where else could I go home?

"How could you know this place? When have you ever been here before?"

"Enough," said Jason. "She's told you more than she meant to."

"How can I know what to do? Can I write it? *Should* I write your story?"

Jason would not decide for him. "If you want to."

"Will the story tell me what it means? Why Clany died the way she did?"

The answer to that, said Justice, and to questions that you haven't thought to ask.

Lared's work began as dreams. He awoke in the night four, five, six times, ever more surprised to still see the split-log walls, the packed-earth floor, the half-ladder stairway that ran upward into the tiny guest rooms. Fire, barely contained within the chimney. A cat stretching before the fire. The sheepskins half-ready to be parchment, drying on their frames. The loom in the corner—of course the village loom was kept here. All this had been in Lared's eyes since infancy, and yet after the dreams it was strange. Strange at first, anyway, and then unpleasant, for compared to the world that Justice showed him in his sleep, Father's inn was filthy, disgusting, poor, shameful.

They are not from *my* memory, Justice told him. I give you dreams from Jason's past. Unless you live in his world, how can you write his tale?

So Lared spent his nights wandering the clean white corridors of Capitol, where not even dust dared to settle. Here and there the passageways opened into bright caverns, teeming with people—Lared had never seen so many people in his life, had not thought so many might exist. And yet in the dream he knew they were but a tiny fraction of the people of this world. For the corridors were miles from top to bottom, and covered the world from pole to pole, except a few patches of ocean, the only place where life renewed itself. There was some attempt to remember living worlds. Here and there among the corridors were little gardens, carefully tamed plants artfully arranged, a mockery of forest. A man could hunt mushrooms here forever, and find no life but what was planted and tended.

There were trains that flew through tubes connecting place to place; and in his dream Lared held a flexible disc that he inserted into flat holes to do everything—to travel, to pass through doors, to use the booths where people who weren't there talked to you and told you things. Lared had heard of such things, but they were always far away, and never touched the life of Flat Harbor. Now, however, the memories were so real that he found himself walking through the forest with the stride of a corridor-dweller, and the tracks of wild swine took him by surprise, for there were no impressions of the passage of living things on the floors of Capitol.

As the setting grew more familiar, his dreams began to be stories. He saw players whose whole lives were recorded for others to see, even what ought to have been done by dark of night or in the privy shed. He saw weapons that made a man come afire inside, erupting through the eyes like flames through spoilt cloth. The life of Capitol was always on the edge of death, precarious as an autumn leaf resting on a fence rail on a windy day.

Nowhere was the death of Capitol more clearly promised than in the catacombs of sleepers. Again and again Justice showed him the people lying down on sterile beds, having their memories drained away into balls of foam, and then waiting docilely as quiet servants injected death into their veins. Death in the form of the drug somec, death that only delayed itself while the frozen corpses waited in their tombs. Years later the quiet servants awakened them, poured back their memories, and the sleepers got up and walked around, as proud of themselves as if they had accomplished something.

"What are they afraid of?" Lared asked Jason as they stuffed sausages together in the butchery shed.

"Dying first."

"But they still die, don't they? Sleeping like that gives them not another day of life, does it?"

"Not an hour. We all end up like this." And he bound off another link of tight-stuffed gut.

"Then why? It makes no sense."

"It worked this way. Important people slept longer and woke up less. So they died hundreds of years later."

"But then all their friends died first."

"That was the point."

"But why would you want to live, if all your friends were dead?"

Jason laughed. "Don't ask me. I always thought it was stupid."

"Why did they do it?"

Jason shrugged. "How can I tell you? I don't know."

Justice answered into Lared's thoughts: There is nothing so stupid or dangerous or painful that people won't eagerly do it, if by doing it they will make others believe they are better or stronger or more honorable. I have seen people poison themselves, destroy their children, abandon their mates, cut themselves off from the world, all so that others would think they were a better sort of person.

"But who would think such cripples were better?"

"There were people who felt like you," Jason said.

But they never took somec, said Justice. They never slept, and so they lived their century and died and those who lived for the honor and power of sleep, thinking it was eternal life, they only despised the ones who refused somec.

It made no sense to Lared, that people could be such fools. But Jason assured him that for thousands of years the universe was ruled by people who lived only for sleep, who died as often as possible in order to avoid the sleep that would never end. How could Lared doubt it, after all? His dreams of Capitol were too powerful, the memories too real.

"Where is Capitol?"

"Gone," said Jason, stirring the spiced meat before funneling another handful into the casing.

"The whole world?"

"Bare rock. All the metal stripped away long ago. No soil left, no life in the sea."

Give it two billion years, said Justice, and maybe something will happen.

"Where did the people go?"

"That's part of the story you're going to write."

"Did you and Justice destroy it?"

"No. Abner Doon destroyed it."

"Then Abner Doon was real?"

"I knew him," Jason said.

"He was a man?"

"You will write the story of how I met Abner Doon. Justice will tell you the story in your dreams, and when you wake up, you'll write it down."

"Did Justice meet Abner Doon?"

"Justice was born some twenty years ago. I met Abner Doon some—fifteen, sixteen thousand years ago."

Lared thought that Jason, still uncertain of the language, had got the numbers wrong. Justice corrected him. The numbers are right, she said. Jason slept for ten thousand years at the bottom of the sea, and before that slept and slept and slept.

"You—used somec, too," said Lared.

"I was a starpilot," Jason said. "Our ships were slower then. We who piloted the ships, we were the only ones who had a need for somec."

"How old are you?"

"Before anyone lived here on your world, I was already old. Does it matter?"

Lared could not grasp it, and so he put it into the only terms he knew. "Are you God?" he asked.

Jason did not laugh at him. Instead he looked thoughtful, and considered the question. It was Justice who answered. All my life I called him God, she said, until I met him.

"But how can you be God, if Justice is more powerful than you?"

I am his daughter, five hundred generations from him. Shouldn't the children of God learn something in that time?

Lared took the finished chain of sausages from Jason's hands and looped it above the smoky fire. "No one ever taught me that God could make sausages."

"It's one of the little skills I picked up along the way."

It was afternoon already, and so they went back to the house, where Mother sullenly served them cheese and hot bread with the juice of the overripe apples. "Better than anything on Capitol," Jason said, and Lared, remembering clearly the taste of the tasteless food of Jason's childhood, agreed.

"Only one job left before your writing days begin," said Jason. "Ink."

"The old cleric left me some," Lared said.

"No better than mule piss," said Jason. "I'll teach you how to make ink that lasts."

Mother was not pleased. "There's work to do," she said. "You can't take Lared out on some foolish task like ink-making."

Jason smiled, but his eyes were hard. "Thano, I have worked in this village like your own son. The snow will be here soon, and you have never before been so well prepared. And yet I have paid *you* for my lodging, when by rights you ought to have paid me. I warn you, don't begrudge me your son's time."

"You *warn* me? What will you do, murder me in my own house?" She dared him to hurt her.

But he only needed to strike her with words. "Don't stand in my way, Thano, or I will tell your husband that he isn't the only one in this house who keeps a little forge. I will tell your husband which travelers you have had pumping the bellows handle for you, to keep your little fire hot."

Mother's eyes went small, and she turned back to cutting turnips into the supper soup.

Her docility was confession. Lared looked on her with contempt and fear. He thought of his thin body, his narrow shoulders, and wondered what traveler had sired him. What have you stolen from the chain of life? he demanded silently.

You are your father's son, said Justice in his mind. And Sala is his, too. Those who protected you from pain prevented bastards as well.

It was scant comfort. Cold and fearsome as Mother had always been, still he had never thought she was false.

"I'm learning the language very well, don't you think?" said Jason cheerfully.

"Go make your ink." Mother was sullen. "I don't like having you indoors here."

I don't much like to be here either, Mother.

Jason kissed Justice lightly on the cheek as he left. Justice only glared at him. Jason explained to Lared when they got outside. "Justice hates it when I make people obey me out of fear. She thinks it's ugly and not nice. She always used to make people obey her by changing what they wanted, so it didn't occur to them to disobey. I think that's degrading and turns people into animals."

Lared shrugged. Just so long as Mother let him learn how to make good ink, it didn't matter to Lared how Jason and Justice got it done.

Jason looked for a certain fungus growth on certain trees, and gathered them into one bag; he had Lared fill another bag with blackthorn stalks, though it cut his hands. Lared did not complain of the pain, because it gave him pleasure to bear it wordlessly. And as dark came on, and they were nearly home, Jason stopped and tapped a pine tree, which still had enough life in it to fill a little jar with gum.

The funguses they boiled and ground up and boiled again, then strained out the thin black fluid that was left. They crushed the blackthorn into it, and strained it again, and then boiled it for an hour with the pine gum. At last they squeezed it through fine linen, and ended up with two pints of smooth black ink.

"It will stay black for a thousand years, and readable for five thousand. The parchment will turn to dust before the ink is too faint to see," said Jason.

"How did you learn to make such ink?"

"How did you learn to make such parchment?" Jason answered, holding up a sheet of it that Lared had made. "I can see my hand through it."

"There's no secret to parchment," Lared answered. "The sheep wear the secret on their bodies till they die, and give it up when we butcher them."

That night Lared dreamed of how Jason met Abner Doon. How God met Satan. How life met death. How making met unmaking. The dream was given to him by Justice, as she remembered it from finding the memory complete in Jason's mind. Memories of memories of memories, that was what lay in Lared's mind the next morning, when with trembling quill he began to write.

3
A Book of Old Memories

Here is how Lared began his book:

"I am Lared of Flat Haven Inn. I am not a cleric, but I have read books and know my letters, ties, and bindings. So I write, with good new ink on parchment I made myself, a story that is not my own. It is a memory of my dreams of another man's childhood, dreams that were given me so I could tell his tale. Forgive me if I write badly, because I have little practice at this. I have not the elegance of Semol of Grais, though my pen longs to write such language. All you will have from me is the plain tale.

"The name of the boy I tell you of was Jason Worthing, then called Jase, without respect, because no one knew what he was or what he would become. He lived on a world of steel and plastic called Capitol, which now is dead. It was a world so rich that the children had nothing to do but go to school or play. It was a world so poor that no food grew there, and they had to eat what other worlds sent them in great starships."

Lared read it over, and felt at once pleased and afraid. Pleased that he could write so many words at once. Pleased because it did sound like the beginning of a book. And afraid because he knew how uneducated he was, knew that to clerics it would sound childish. *I am a child.*

"You're a man," said Jason. He sat on the floor, leaning against the wall, sewing the leather boots he had volunteered to make for Father. "And your book will be good enough, if you only tell the truth."

"How can I be sure I'll remember everything?"

"You don't have to remember everything."

"Some things in the dreams I don't even understand."

"You don't have to understand it either."

"How do I even know it's true?"

Jason laughed, driving the long, heavy needle through the leather and drawing the thread tight. "It's your memory of your dreams of Justice's memory of my memory of things that happened to me in my childhood on a planet that died more than ten thousand years ago. How could it help but be true?"

"What should I start with?"

Jason shrugged. "We didn't choose a tool, we chose a person to write our story. Start with the first thing that matters."

What was the first thing that mattered? Lared thought through the things he remembered of Jason's life. What mattered? Fear and pain—that's what mattered to Lared now, after a childhood virtually without either. And the earliest fear, the earliest pain that mattered, that was when Jason nearly lost his life because he did too well on a test.

It was in a class that studied the movements and powers of the stars, one that only a few hundred of the thirteen-year-olds of Capitol knew enough to take. Jase watched as the problems appeared in the air above his table, like little stars and galaxies he could hold in his hands. The questions were written in the air below the stars, and Jase entered his answers on a keyboard.

Jase knew all the answers easily, for he had learned well, and he grew more confident as it became clear the test was below his abilities. Until the last question. It was completely unrelated to the rest of the test. He was not prepared for it. They had not studied it in class. And yet as he looked at the problem, he thought he understood how the answer might be found. He began calculating. There was one figure that baffled him. He thought he knew what it meant, but did not know how to prove it, to be sure, to be exact. A year ago he would have called it a good guess and entered his answer. But this year had changed everything. He had a way of finding out what he needed to know.

He looked at the teacher, Hartman Torrock, who was gazing around the room. Then he shifted something in his mind, the way things shifted when his eyes suddenly focused on something far, when they had been seeing something near. It was as though he could suddenly see behind Hartman Torrock's eyes. Now Jase could hear his present thoughts as if he were thinking them himself—his mind was on the woman who had quarreled with him this morning, and whose body he wanted to cause pleasure to and cause pain to this night. It was an ugly sort of desire, to rule her and make her be like his own tongue, to speak only his thoughts, to disappear inside him when she was not in use. Jase never liked Hartman Torrock, but loathed him now. Torrock's thoughts were not pleasant scenery.

Jase quickly plunged deeper than Torrock's present thoughts, moved among his unthought-of memories as easily as if they were his own, finding Torrock's knowledge of stars and motions, seeking the meaning of the unfamiliar figure. And the exact figure was there, perfect to the fourteenth decimal place. Then he slipped gratefully from Torrock's mind and entered the result into the keypad. No more problems appeared above his table. The test was over. He waited.

His score was perfect, when it came. And yet a red glow appeared, and hung in the air above Jase's table. The red glow meant a failing score. Or a computer malfunction, or cheating. Torrock, looking worried, got up and came to him. "What's wrong?" asked the teacher.

"I don't know," said Jase.

"What's your score?" He looked, and it was perfect. "Then what's wrong?"

"I don't know," said Jase again.

Torrock went back to his own table and began talking quietly with the air. Jase, as always, listened to Torrock's mind. The mistake had been Torrock's. The last question should not have been on his test. It dealt with secrets that children should not learn until years later. Torrock had written it last night, meaning to append it to an examination he would give to his advanced students tomorrow. Instead he had added it to his beginning class today. Jase should not have been given the question at all; above all, he should not have been able to get it right. It was a sign of cheating.

But how could he cheat? thought Hartman Torrock. Who in the room knew the answer, except me? And I never told him.

Somehow this boy stole secrets from me, thought Torrock. They will think that I told him, that I broke my trust, that I am not fit to know secrets. They will punish me. They will take away my somec privileges. What has this boy done to me? How did he do it?

Then Torrock remembered the darkest truth about Jase Worthing: his father. What do you expect from the son of a Swipe? thought Torrock. He knew my secret because he is his father's son.

Jase recoiled from the thought, for it was his darkest fear. He had grown up with the horror of who his father was. Homer Worthing, the monster, leader of the Swipe Revolt, the foulest murderer in all history. He had died in space years before Jase's mother had decided to conceive a child. The Swipe war was over then. But the universal loathing for the Swipes remained, tinged with the memory of the eight billion people Jase's father had burned to death.

It had been nearly bloodless until then. In the seemingly endless war between the Empire and the Rebels (or the Usurpers and the Patriots, depending on which side you were on), both sides had begun using telepathic starpilots. The results were devastating—non-Swipes were helpless, and it quickly became clear to both sides that the Swipes, who could silently communicate with each other, might easily unite against both Empire and Rebels, unseat all government, take control of somec and therefore of the entire bureaucracy. As long as normal people could not tell what the Swipes had in mind, the Swipes could not, must not be given starships.

In fact the Swipe starpilots had been conspiring to end the war and impose peace on both sides. They thought, when both sides tried to remove them from their commands, that they could still bring off such a victory. So they seized their ships and declared both governments dissolved. In response, Empire and Rebels united, briefly, to exterminate the Swipes. At first the Swipe starpilots allowed themselves to be harried from here to there. Though Swipes were always killed as soon as they were captured, yet they tried to avoid causing too much harm, hoping at first for victory, later for compromise, at last for mercy. But the universe had no place for them; the Swipes must die. Homer was at the end of his last hope of escape. But in that moment he had chosen to destroy eight billion people rather than to die alone.

And I am his son.

All this came in a moment's memory to Jason Worthing. Hartman Torrock did not know what went on behind the mask of Jase's face.

"Blood test," Torrock said.

Jason protested, wanted to know why.

"Hold out your hand."

Jase held out his hand. He knew the test would show nothing. They were so smart, the ones who hated Swipes. They were sure they knew how the power to see behind the eyes was passed from mother to children, to lie dormant in daughters, to become active in sons. Jase's mother did not have the Swipe, and so Jase could not have it, *did* not have it. And yet he *was* a Swipe, *could* see behind the eyes. Someday, he knew, it would occur to someone that perhaps there was another way to be a Swipe, a way that might be passed from father to son, along with eyes as blue as a quepbird's breast. The gift to see behind the eyes had only come gradually to his mind, like the hair of manhood to his body. When he first realized what was going on, he feared that he was going crazy; later he knew that somehow the impossible had happened, and he had inherited his father's curse. That was terrifying enough—how much like his father, the mass murderer, was he? And yet the Swipe was not something he could refuse. He tried to be careful, tried to remember to pretend not to know the secrets he learned in other people's minds. The simplest way to do it, of course, would be not to look in their minds at all. But he felt like a cripple whose legs had just been healed—how could he not run, now that he had learned that it was possible? So in these months—or had it been a year?—he had grown more and more daring as he learned to better control and use his power. And today he had been careless. Today he had plainly known what he could not know by any other means.

And yet, he told himself, I did not *learn* it from Torrock's mind. I only *confirmed* it, clarified it. The shape of the answer came to me from my own thoughts.

Jase almost explained this aloud—I thought of the answer to the last question myself!—but he caught himself in time. Torrock had not yet told him aloud that he was worried about the last question. Don't be a fool, Jase told himself. Admit nothing, if you want to live.

The test result came in a moment, rows of figures scrolling up from the table and then slipping backward through the air until they faded out of sight, like sheep being led to the shearing shed. Negative. Negative. Negative. Jase had none of the signs of the Swipe.

Except one. He could not possibly know the answer to the question.

"All right, Jase. How did you do it?"

"Do what?" Jase asked. Am I a good liar? I'd better be—my life depends on it.

"The last question. We never studied it. I never so much as wrote down Crack's Theorem."

"What's Crack's Theorem?"

"Don't be an ass," Torrock said. He touched the keys and called up into the air the answer Jase had given to the last question. He made one set of numbers glow brighter than the others. "How did you learn the value of the curve of the straight line at the edge of light?"

Truthfully, Jase answered, "It was the only number that could fit there."

"To the fourteenth decimal? It took two hundred years to even know the problem existed, and years of work by the best mathematicians of the Empire to determine the value of the curve to *five* places. Crack only proved it to the fourteenth place some fifty years ago. And you expect me to believe you duplicated all this work here at your table in five minutes?"

The other students had been looking away from him, till now.

Now, to learn that he knew the value of Crack's Theorem and how to use it in a problem—now they looked in awe at Jase. Whether he cheated to get the value of the curve or not, he had known how to *use* it, when they were only just getting the hang of Newton, Einstein, and Ahmed. They hated Jase with all their hearts, and hoped that he would die. He made them all look so stupid, they thought.

Torrock too noticed the other students watching them. He lowered his voice. "I don't know how you got the value of the curve, boy, but if they think I wrote it down or taught it to you, which by God I did not, then it's my job, it's my *somec*, and God knows I get little enough as it is, one year under for three years up, but it's a *start*. I'm a *sleeper*, and you're not going to take it away from me."

"I don't know what you're talking about," Jase said. "I figured it out on my own. It's not *my* fault if you asked a question that made the value of the curve obvious."

"It was not obvious to fourteen places," Torrock whispered fiercely. "So get out of here, but come back tomorrow, there'll be questions to ask you, you and your mother and anyone else, because I *know what you are*, and test or no test I'll prove it and see you die before I let you ruin everything for me."

Jase and Torrock had never got along, but it still horrified Jase to have a grown man say in words that he wanted Jase's death. It frightened him, like a child that meets a rabid wolf in the forest, able to watch nothing but the streaming jaws, the foaming teeth, able to hear nothing but the low growl in the throat.

Still, he must pretend not to know what Torrock meant. "I didn't cheat, Mr. Torrock. I've never cheated before."

"There are only a few thousand of us on Capitol who know how to use the curve, Master Worthing. But there are millions of us who know how to notify Mother's Little Boys about a person who seems to show symptoms of the Swipe."

"Are you accusing me of—"

"You know what I'm accusing you of."

I know, said Jase silently, that you're frightened half to death of me, that you expect me to be like my father and kill you where you stand, small as I am, powerless as I am—

"Be prepared for questioning, Master Worthing. They'll know

how you learned to use the curve, one way or another—there's no honest way you could have done it.''

"Except figuring it out on my own!"

"Not to the fourteenth decimal.''

No. Not to the fourteenth decimal.

Jase got up and left the classroom. The other students were careful not to look at him until his back was to them. Then they stared and stared. The explosion had come, after all, from nowhere, out of silence, out of the tension of the test that *they* had all been struggling with. What have I done to myself?

He put his palm on the reader at the worm, and the gate chimed to let him through. As long as he was going home from school, there was no charge. The worm was not crowded at this hour, which made it more dangerous—at the levels where Jase and his mother could afford to live, the wall rats were bold enough to come out into the worm and take what they could. For safety, Jase walked forward from segment to segment as the worm rushed smoothly through its tunnel, until he came to a place where several people were gathered. They looked at him suspiciously. He was no longer a little child, he realized. He no longer looked safe to strangers.

Mother was waiting for him. He never found her doing anything when he got home—just sitting there, waiting for him. If it weren't for the fact that she still had her job, still earned what pitiful money they had, he could think she sat down across from the door the moment he left for school, and sat there the whole time until he came back. Her face looked dead, like a slack puppet. Then, after he said hello, after he smiled at her, the corners of her mouth twitched; she smiled, she slowly stood up. "Hungry?" she asked.

"Not much."

"Something wrong?"

Jason shrugged.

"Here, I'll call up the menu." She punched in the one-bark meal menu. Not much choice today—or ever. "There's fish or fowl or red meat.''

"It's all algae and beans and human feces," answered Jase.

"I hope you didn't learn to speak that way from me," said Mother.

"Sorry. Fish. Whatever you want."

She punched it in. Then she folded down the little table and leaned on it, looking across at Jase, where he sat on the floor in the corner. "What's wrong?"

He told her.

"But that's absurd," said Mother. "You can't have the Swipe. I was tested three times before they let me have Homer's—your father's child. I told you that when you were young."

"Somehow that doesn't reassure them."

And it didn't reassure Mother, either. Jase realized that she looked genuinely uneasy, frightened. "Don't worry, Mother. They can't prove anything."

Mother shrugged, bit on her palm. Jase hated when she did that, holding her hand palm up and gnawing on the fleshy part. He got up from the floor and went to the bedwall and folded down his bed. He swung up onto it and stared at the ceiling. At the spot on the ceiling tiles that Jase had known was a face since he was a child. When he was very little he had dreamed about that face. Sometimes it was a monster, come to devour him. Sometimes it was his father, who had gone away but still watched over him. When he was six Mother had told him who his father was, and Jase had known that he was right both times—it *was* his father, and his father *was* a monster.

Why was Mother so afraid?

Jase longed to look behind *her* eyes, but he never had before. Oh, her conscious thoughts, now and then, but nothing deep. He was afraid of the way she gnawed her hand, and sat slack-faced in the chair when he wasn't home, and knew the answer to every question he asked her and yet never seemed interested in anything—he was afraid, instinctively, that whatever was in her memories, he did not want to know it.

For he experienced other people's memories as if they were his own, and remembered them as clearly, so that once having dwelt in their minds for a time he could easily become confused about which things that he remembered were actually things that he had done. Many hours late at night he had lain in his bed, letting his mind wander, searching the nearby rooms—he did not know how to range farther than that with his listening, prowling gift. No one suspected his intrusions. They thought their thoughts, held their memories, dreamed their dreams as always, unaware of this spectator. In his memory, Jase was no virgin—with the prurience of childhood he had been man and woman in acts he did not think his neighbors had imagination enough to perform. In memory, Jase had beaten his children, killed a man in a riot on a lower level, stolen from his employer, quietly sabotaged the electrical system—all the most memorable, painful, exhilarating acts of the people whose minds he entered. It was the hardest thing about the Swipe, remembering when he awoke in the morning which things he had really done, and which things not.

He did not want his mother's memories to have such force upon him.

And yet she was too afraid, still gnawing at her hand there at the table, waiting for the commissary to send them supper. Why are you so afraid because someone has accused me of having the Swipe?

So he looked, and, looking, learned. She had married Homer Worthing before the rebellion, so she had rights. She had gone to sleep with somec, as starpilots' wives do, to be wakened when he returned. And one day, when her flesh burned from waking, when her memories were still newly returned to her head, the kind people in their white sterile clothes told her that her husband was dead. Outside the sleeprooms, some less kind people told her how her husband died, and what he had done in dying. She remembered having seen him only a few minutes ago, just before they bubbled her memory. He had kissed her good-bye, and she fancied she could still feel the pressure of his lips, and now he was dead, and had been dead a year before they thought it was safe to waken his widow; he was a murderer, a monster, and she hadn't had his child yet.

Why did you have a child, Mother? Jase looked for the answer, forgetting that his errand in her mind was to find out why she was so afraid. It didn't matter: his curiosity and her fear led to the same place. She wanted Homer's child, Homer's *son*, because Homer's father, old Ulysses Worthing, had told her that she must.

Ulysses Worthing had the same blue eyes that Jason saw each day in the mirror, those deep, pure, markless blue irises that looked like God had erased a spot of Jason and let the pure sky of a living world shine through. He looked at young Uyul, the girl his starpilot son had brought home to meet him, and she did not know what he saw in her that seemed to puzzle him so. "I don't know," said old Ulysses, "I don't know how strong you are. I don't know if there'll be much left of Uyul when she takes Homer into herself."

"Now, don't make her scared of me," said Homer.

I don't want to hear your voice, said Jason to his mother's memory of his father. I am no part of you, I have no father.

"I'm not afraid of you," Uyul said. But was she talking to Homer or Ulysses? "I might be stronger than you think." But what she thought was this: if I lose myself and become nothing but the woman half of Homer, that is fine with me.

Ulysses laughed at her. As if he could read her mind, he said, "Don't marry her, Homer. She's determined to be less than half a human being."

"I don't even know what this conversation means," Uyul said, laughing nervously.

Ulysses leaned close to her. "I don't care who or what my son marries. He doesn't ask my consent, and he never will. But listen tight, young lady. This is between you and me, not you and him. You will have his child, and it will be a son, and if it doesn't have blue eyes like mine, you have another until you have one that does. You won't leave me without inheritance, just because you're too weak to know your own name without Homer whispering it to you every night."

It made her furious. "It's none of your business how many children I have, or what sex they are, or what eyes their colors are. Colors their eyes are." She was furious that she had got her words twisted up. Ulysses only laughed at her.

"Never mind, Uyul," Homer said.

Hold your peace! cried the listening Jason.

"He's only pretending to be an impossible son of a bitch," Homer continued. "He's just testing to see if you can stand him."

"I can't," Uyul said, trying to make the truth sound like a joke.

Ulysses shrugged. "What do *I* care? Just have Homer's sky-

eyed son. And name it Jason, after my father. We've been cy-
cling those old names through the family for so long that—''

"Father, you're getting tedious," said Homer. So impatiently
he said it. So urgently. Jason wished, for just a moment, that he
could have been there, and listened to Homer's mind, instead of
getting only Mother's memory of it.

"What Homer is," said Ulysses, "I am, and Homer's child
will be."

Those were the words that Mother remembered. What Homer
is, I am, and Homer's child will be. Have a son with sky-colored
eyes. Name him Jason. What Homer is, I am, and Homer's child
will be.

"I'm not a murderer," Jason whispered.

His mother shuddered.

"But I do see all that Father—"

She rose and rushed toward him, knocking down the chair,
stumbling over it, rushing to put her hand across his mouth.

"Hold your tongue, boy, don't you know the walls are ears?"

"What Homer is," Jase said out loud, "I am, and Homer's
child will be."

Mother looked at him in horror. He named her worst fear to
her, that in posthumously obeying Ulysses's charge to her she
had unleashed another Swipe upon the world. "You can't be,"
she whispered. "Mother to son, that's the only way—"

"There must be other gifts to the world," Jase said, "than
those that reside in X chromosomes, only showing up when
paired with a stunted Y."

Suddenly she doubled her fist and brought it down like a hammer on his mouth. He cried out in pain; blood from his lips
rushed into his mouth as he tried to shout at her, and he choked.
Mother backed away from him whimpering, gnawing on the hand
that had just struck him. "No no no," she said. "Mother to
son, you're clean, you're clean, not his son but mine, not his
but mine—"

But in his mother's mind Jason saw that she looked at him
with the same eyes that had seen and loved her husband. After
all, Jason had Homer Worthing's face, that well-known face, that
face that frightened children in the textbooks in school. He was

younger, thicker of lip, gentler in the eyes, but he still wore Homer's face, and his mother both loved and hated him for that.

She stood in the middle of the room, facing the door, and Jason saw that she was seeing Homer, as if he had come back to her, as if he smiled at her and said, "It was all a misunderstanding, and I've come back to make you whole again." Jase swallowed the blood in his mouth and got off his bed, walked around Mother and stood in front of her. She did not see him. Still in her mind she saw her husband, and he reached out to her, reached out and touched her cheek and said, "Uyula, I love you," and she took a step toward him, into his embrace.

"Mother," said Jason.

She shuddered; her vision cleared, and she saw that it was not her husband she held, but her son, and his mouth was bleeding. She dissolved into sobs, clung to him, pulled him to the floor and wept upon him, touching his bleeding lips, kissing him, saying over and over, "I'm sorry, I'm so sorry you were ever born, will you ever forgive me?"

"I forgive you," Jason whispered, "for letting me be born."

Mother is insane, said Jason silently. She is insane, and she knows I have the Swipe, and if they interrogate her we are both dead.

He had to go to school the next day. If he stayed away he would be confessing; he would be begging them to come to his home, where they would find Uyul, who was nobody except Homer Worthing's wife—Uyul the monster's wife, that was the name he found inside his mother's head. I wish I had never looked, he thought again and again all night. He lay awake for a long time, and awoke often, always trying to think of a solution that was not terrifyingly desperate. Go into hiding, become a wall rat? He did not know how the people with uncoded hands survived on Capitol, living in the ventilation shafts and stealing whatever they could. No, he would have to go to school, face it down. They had no proof. He *had* answered the question himself. Pretty much. As long as his genes didn't show it, Torrock had no proof that he was a Swipe.

So he left his mother in the morning, and dozed in the worm on the way to school. He went to his morning classes as usual,

ate the free lunch that was usually his best meal of the day, and
then the headmaster came and invited him to his office.

"What about history?" Jase asked, trying to act unconcerned.

"The rest of your classes today are canceled."

Torrock was waiting in the headmaster's office. He looked
pleased with himself. "We have prepared a test. It's no more
difficult than the one you took yesterday. Except that I didn't
write the questions. I don't know the answers. Someone will be
with you all the time. If you could perform an act of genius
yesterday, surely you can do it again today."

Jason looked at the headmaster. "Do I have to? I was lucky
yesterday, I don't know why I have to go through this test."

The headmaster sighed, glanced at Torrock, and raised his
hands in helplessness. "A serious accusation has been made.
This test is—an allowable act."

"It won't prove anything."

"Your blood test is—ambiguous."

"My blood test was negative. It was from the time I was born.
I can't help who my father was!"

Yes, the headmaster agreed silently, it's hardly fair, but—
"There are other tests, and your genetic analysis shows—irreg-
ularities."

"Everybody's genes are different."

The headmaster sighed again. "Take the test, Master Worthing. And do well."

Torrock smiled. "There are three questions. Take as long as
you like. Take all night if you like."

Shall I take your secrets out of your memory and tell them to
the world? But Jase did not dare look behind Torrock's eyes. He
had to take this test with no knowledge of anything he should
not know. It might have been his life at stake. And yet even as
he denied himself any illegitimate knowledge, he wondered if it
might not be better to know as much as possible. To know what
the real object of the test was. He felt helpless. Torrock could
make him do anything, could make the test mean anything, and
Jase had no recourse.

At the table, staring at a pattern of stars moving in the air, he
despaired. Even the question made no sense to him. There were

two symbols that he didn't understand, and the movement of the stars was eccentric, to say the least. Who were they, to play God with his life?

They had been playing God with his life from the beginning. He was only conceived because of old Ulysses's command; Jason was not brought to life because of love, but because a half-mad widow followed someone else's dead ancient plan. Now, his life hinged on someone else's plan, and he couldn't even be sure that knowing what it was would help him to survive.

But despair led nowhere. He studied the stars and tried to understand the eccentricity; studied the figures and tried to eliminate possible causes.

"Do I have to answer the three questions in order?" Jase asked.

The headmaster looked up from his work. "Hmmm?"

"Can I answer these out of order?"

The headmaster nodded and went back to writing letters.

Jason went from question to question, one two three, one two three. They were related problems, building from bad to worse. Even the curve theorem wouldn't help. What did they think he was, a genius?

Apparently they did. Either a genius or a Swipe. If he didn't prove himself one, he could prove himself the other. So he set to work.

All afternoon. Torrock came in at dismissal time, and took the headmaster's place in the room. The headmaster left, and came back an hour later with dinner for all three of them. Jase couldn't eat. He was getting a handle on the first problem, learning things from the data on the second question that helped explain what was going on in the first. Before Torrock had disposed the tray, the first question was answered.

He fell asleep about eleven o'clock. The headmaster was already asleep. Jase awoke first, hours before school was supposed to start. The second question was still there, waiting for him. But Jason saw the answer at once, in a different direction from anything he had been pursuing. It meant a slight revision to the way he had understood the curve, but now it worked. He entered the second answer.

He tried for a while longer with the third question, but with what he had discovered on the first two, he realized that there were too many variables and he couldn't solve it with the present data. He could solve a few cycles in it, but that was all. So he entered what he could, called the rest unanswerable and closed the test.

There was a red glow above the table. Failure.

He woke up the headmaster. "What time is it?" the old man asked.

"Time to get somebody else to take tests for you," Jase said.

The headmaster saw the red glow and raised an eyebrow.

"Good-bye," Jason said. He was out the door before the headmaster was awake enough to do anything more.

His school was nested inside the university, and he went straight to Gracie, the university library. His student status would give him better access to Capitol's information system than he could get from public stations. However, he might not have much time. The red light at the end of his test might mean many things, and none of them were good. It might mean that he failed the test, and thereby "proved" to them that he could not have passed the first one without being a Swipe, and they would be looking for him to kill him. It might mean that he passed the test, but that they did not believe he could not have done it without being a Swipe. The truth was that neither the first nor second test proved anything. But if they thought it proved something, he was just as dead.

One thing might be. Mother believed that Jase's grandfather was also a Swipe, and certainly her memory of the event supported that view. If what Jase had was indeed a version of the Swipe that could be passed from father to son, and it had been going on long enough for Ulysses Worthing to know that it was hereditary, then there should be other Worthings with the same gift. Of course, the fact that Mother's Little Boys didn't know about it meant that all the others had succeeded in keeping their gift secret.

Row on row, hundreds of dusty pink plastic carrels with the grey-blue letter *C* of the Communications Bureau in prominent display. He had been here often enough before to know where the older students went, and where they didn't. He went to where they didn't, the older section without individual printouts in each booth—and where there weren't enough externals to play the most popular games. Jason had sat for hours playing Evolution, in which constant environmental changes forced the player to adapt animals to fit. He had gotten to the level where eight animals and four plants had to be adapted at once. Jase had a knack for it, but he wasn't here to play.

He carded the reader for charges, then palmed it for identification. The air over the desk went bright with directory entries. He flipped through it up, back, and to the left, until he got to the genealogical programs. He brought Genealogy: Relatives by Common Descent into the window and punched Enter. A much simpler menu appeared. He chose Male Relatives by Male Lines Only and entered his own name and code. Gracie identified him at once—his birth date and place appeared in the middle of the air, then settled slow as a dustflake toward the bottom. Above him, connected by a little line, was his father's name, and *his* father's name, and so on: Homer Worthing, Ulysses Worthing, Ajax Worthing, another Homer, another Jason. And spiraling around and out from the central column were all the cousins, hundreds of them, thousands of them. It was too much to handle.

Nearest five living cousins only, he entered.

All but five names disappeared. To his surprise, there were two near ones, and the next three were quite distant relatives, branching from his line more than fifteen generations back. Only the first two were close at all.

Full current address, he entered.

The nearest in blood was Talbot Worthing, a grandson of Ajax Worthing. But he lived on a planet forty-two light-years away. The other cousin was nearer in space: Radamand Worthing, a great-grandson of the first Homer. He was on Capitol, working as a government employee on the district manager level. Nice to know that a relative had done so well for himself. Jase asked for a printout. He heard the choke of a printer a few carrels away, and immediately went to get it, without signing off. On his way back he only happened to glance at the carrel he had been using.

"Attention: You are required to remain where you are until a proctor comes to your carrel and gives you further instruction.

Failure to comply will seriously endanger your academic standing.''

Right now Jase figured it wasn't his academic standing at stake. It was his life. If the test results were enough to call for the proctors, there was little hope the results would be benign. Fortunately, it would be a while before they could get permission to call for Mother's Little Boys—that was a power far above what the university could normally command. The Swipe would bring that power, of course. But it would take time.

If the test had convinced them he was a Swipe. How could he be sure? Whose mind could tell him the truth? He didn't know how to search at a distance, how to look for strangers that he couldn't see.

Cousin Radamand was far enough away that he was well under the curve of the earth; Jase took a deep worm, and in an hour he stood in the anteroom of the office of Radamand Worthing, supervisor of district 10 of Napa Sector.

"Do you have an appointment, young man?" asked the receptionist.

"I don't need one," said Jase. He tried to search for someone behind the door of Radamand's office, but without knowing who was there, or where in the other room he was, he hardly knew how to begin. As always when he could not see the person he searched for, he saw only flashes of random thoughts, connected to no one person, telling no particular story.

"Everyone needs an appointment, little boy." There was menace in her voice. Jase knew she was not to be trifled with. She looked decorative, but in fact she was trained to kill; Radamand kept a bodyguard in front of his door.

Jase studied her a moment, took a potent name out of her memory. "Would Hilvock need one? If he came wearing white?"

Her face went a deep red. "Never," she said. "How did you know?"

"Tell Radamand Worthing that his blue-eyed cousin Jason is here to see him."

"Do you think you're the first to pretend to be a relative of his?" But she stared at his pure blue eyes and he knew she did not doubt him.

"I'm the first to know how much money he makes from opening the foundation space to manufacturing. And child labor, since Mother's Little Boys have no eyes down there."

He did not take this from her mind. He had finally found his cousin in the other room. And now he could not so much as notice the woman who watched him. He could see only the memories in Radamand's mind. Radamand had the Swipe, all right; it was hereditary, all right; the question was if Jason would live to escape this place.

Radamand was wise—he knew there was profit in knowing secrets. District supervisor, that was all he was—but he knew so much about so many, had such a quiet reputation, that his power extended far into the heart of Capitol. And power breeds power, for the more you are believed to have, the more you have as others fear to cross you—Radamand knew that, too. Who could take him by surprise? He seemed to anticipate every move to thwart him. There were corpses here and there in Capitol that he had arranged for—but murder was not a thing that pleased him much. He took far more pleasure out of watching people who thought they were fearless as they learned to fear him, tasting the panic when they realized what was known about them, things that no one could know.

Worst for Jase was this: that Radamand was stronger than he was, that the mere memory of Radamand's will was stronger than Jase's present self. Radamand's memories inhabited Jason's mind as if they were his own. Jase tasted Radamand's delight in making others obey him, and it was as sweet to him as it was to Radamand.

As sweet to him, and yet there was Jase's own self, revolted at what he had done, at the murders he remembered committing, the lives he remembered having destroyed, and he could not bear to have such memories inside his head. How could I have done it! cried Jase silently. How can I undo what I have done!

He cried out. The receptionist was startled. He *was* a child, but a dangerous one, and all the more dangerous because of his seeming madness, to suddenly seem to be in pain like this. She got up slowly, walked to the door that led to Radamand.

Jase finally reached the bottom, the worst acts, the only murders Radamand had committed with his own hands. For Radamand knew that a man who profited from knowing other's secrets could not afford to have a dangerous secret of his own—not one, at least, that anyone else might know. And who would know that Radamand was a Swipe? Why, his own dear kin. As the first murder occurred to him, all the others had to follow. He killed his older brother on impulse, in the family's swimming pool; but from his father and younger brothers he could not possibly hide his guilt. They could see his memory of the act as well as he could. So he ranged through his house, killing every male that was kin of his, and using Gracie he located as many as he could find, all who had the pure blue eyes of the Worthing gift, and killed them. Evading arrest was easy—he had information to sell to powerful men about other powerful men, and made himself too valuable to lose; and for those not interested in buying or selling, he held their reputations hostage, and they dared not harm him. Only two of his kin with the gift were still alive. Talbot, who was on a far-off colony, and Homer, the starpilot who had made it impossible to be known as a Swipe and live. Homer, who had died in a holocaust of his own making. Radamand was safe. His hands were foul with his brothers', with his father's blood, but he was safe.

It did not occur to him that some thirteen years ago or so Homer's widow would choose to inseminate herself and bear Homer's son. Radamand was not expecting Jason. But when he knew that Jason lived—and worse, that Jason knew—

"Cousin," whispered Radamand from the door.

Jase saw the death in Radamand's mind and threw himself to the floor before the pellet was fired.

Radamand did not move to try again, not at once. Radamand was looking now into Jason's memories. Jase watched his own memories unfolding in Radamand's mind, saw that Radamand searched for only one thing: who knew that Jason was a Swipe. And in spite of himself Jase thought of his mother. And as he thought of her, he saw his memory of her knowledge pass through Radamand's thoughts, but not neutrally, no—it was overlaid with the decision to kill her also. Mother and son, they would die, because if once it was discovered that another sort of Swipe could be passed from father to son, it would be only a matter of time before Radamand was found.

The world would end if Radamand died—it would end, at least, for Radamand, and he cared for nothing else.

It was too much for Jason, to have to hold within himself memories of his mother with intent to kill her. He screamed and threw himself at Radamand, who dodged easily and laughed at him.

"Come, child. Try to surprise me."

How can I think of something that he doesn't know I've thought of? His only hope was not surprise at all; with an enemy who was more skilled than he in seeing behind the eyes, it was not quickness that would count. It was chess, and what stopped the checkmate would be check: force him to move another piece.

"You have no pieces," Radamand said. He was searching in Jase's mind for Jase's address, so he wouldn't have any trouble finding Jase's mother.

"Radamand Worthing is a Swipe," Jason said aloud. "So am I. It's hereditary, father to son."

Did Radamand's receptionist believe him? Indeed she did. Radamand had no choice. If he did not kill her, she would surely kill him—Swipes were the most loathsome creatures imaginable, and she could not possibly be trusted now. Jason was only a boy. He was no direct physical threat to Radamand. The woman was a killer, as he well knew. He dared not leave her behind him.

As Radamand fired a pellet at the receptionist, Jason fled. It would take time for Radamand to arrange things so that he wouldn't be charged with her murder. Was it time enough for Jason to escape?

From the office, yes. From Radamand's sector, yes. But Radamand knew his address, and would find him wherever in the world he hid. Even among the wall rats, Radamand had friends and would hunt him down.

And what could Jason do in return? If he denounced Radamand it was surely his own death, too. His only hope was to do what Talbot Worthing had done—go light-years away from Radamand, where he could not possibly be a threat.

There were two routes off Capitol that a boy of Jase's age could take. He could join the military, or he could go to a colony on one of the newly opened worlds. That would be far enough

away for Radamand, surely. And once enrolled in the Fleet or
the Colonies, even Radamand could not touch him—the administration of Capitol had no power in imperial services like those.

But he could not go directly to the Colonies. For if he did,
Radamand would find Mother, and she would die. He must act
to save her first. And the Fleet was not open to her, at her age.
Only the Colonies for Mother.

He had no choice but to go home now, at once. Yet Radamand
surely knew that Jason thought this way, and would be waiting
somewhere along the path, ready to destroy him.

At the thought of Radamand and death, his newly acquired
memories flooded back. He remembered his brother's face as he
broke his arm at pool's edge and then held him helplessly under
the water until he drowned. I have no brother, thought Jason.
But he remembered the brother, and his brother's death. And
pushing a knife into his sleeping father's eye. And loving it. And
could not bear the memories. Could not bear to be himself, with
such a past.

Not my past! he cried out to himself. It is not my past!

But the memories were too strong for him. He could not dis-
regard what he so clearly remembered having done. He wept
aloud in the worm as it hurtled through bedrock, skirting the
molten furnace of the world. It caused no particular commotion,
that he cried. They were used to weepers in the worm.

When Jase got home, Mother was angry. "What have you
been doing? The butler went off in the middle of the day and
said that you took a trip to the other side of the world! How will
we live through the month now? Half the food budget, in one
day—I should have restricted you, but you always—"

Then she realized his face was raw from crying, and she
looked at him in wonderment. "What's wrong?" she asked.

"You never should have given Homer Worthing a son," said
Jase.

Mother looked distractedly toward the butler, which still
showed a red alarm light. "It was naughty of you to run away
from school. The proctors called. They sealed the doors for a
while, till they were sure you weren't in here."

Jason immediately ran to the door and opened it, set a stool in front of it to keep it ajar. "Why did they say they wanted me?"

"Something about your answer to the third question."

The one that he missed.

"He said you knew things that you couldn't have known," said Mother. "You must be more careful, Homer. You must never know things that you couldn't possibly know. It makes people upset."

"I'm not Homer."

She raised her eyebrows. "He was a starpilot, you know."

"We have to leave, Mother."

"I don't like to leave. You go do whatever you must, and I'll wait here. That's what I like to do—wait here while you're gone. And then you'll come back to me. That's what I like. When you come back to me."

"If you don't come with me now, Mother, I'll never come back."

She turned away. "Don't threaten me, Jase. It isn't nice."

"If the proctors don't get me, Mother's Little Boys will! I have a man after me, trying to kill me, and he's very powerful, and he *will* succeed."

"Oh, don't be so serious, you're only a boy, Jase."

"He means to kill you, too."

"People don't go around just—killing people."

Jase exploded. "Everything they say about Swipes is true, Mother! Father killed billions of people, and Radamand Worthing is a killer, too! His own father and brothers and every cousin he could find—that's what Swipes are, is killers, and he knows I was coming here and he knows you know what I am and he means to kills us and he *will*! I'm a Swipe too, Mother! That's what you did when you had me—brought one more Swipe into the world."

She clamped her hand over his mouth. "The door is open, and other people might not know you're joking."

"The only way to save our lives is—" But she was not listening. She was only waiting. That was all that was in her mind—waiting for Homer to come back. Then everything would be all right. This was all too much for her to handle, and so she had to wait till Homer came back.

"Mother, he won't come here. We have to go to him."

She looked at him wide-eyed. "Don't be silly. He forgot me years ago."

But he knew that she believed him, in her madness. He could control her, because she believed him. "It means a long voyage."

She followed him docilely out the door. "Does that mean somec? Does that mean sleep? I don't like sleeping. They keep changing things while you're asleep."

"This time they promise that they won't."

All the way through the corridor Jase expected to be stopped by a constable, or even one of Mother's Little Boys—Radamand wouldn't hold back anything, he'd use all his power to find Jason and stop him. So it was almost with surprise that Jase found himself at the local Colonies station, and led his mother inside.

The room was cool, with a breeze machine going somewhere. One end of the room was given over to a scene near the brink of a cliff, surrounded by trees shedding their leaves in autumn. Far across a canyon was a slope think with brightly colored trees. "Earth Colony," whispered the room gently. "Return home again." Then the scene changed to a snowy hill, with skiers madly careening down the slopes. "Makor, the land of eternal winter."

"Where is he?" asked Mother.

"Catch stars on Makor, and bring them home as frozen light." The scene showed some of the fantastic crystals growing in the crevices of a cliff, with a climber making his way up to harvest them.

Jason left her looking at the crystal-hunter, and made his way to the man at the desk. "She's not herself today, but she wants to make a long voyage anyway."

The Colonies were not fussy. No one in his right mind would travel fifty light-years and wake up on a world where there was no hope of return, no hope even of somec, just work through the natural span of life to the end. "We have just the place for her."

"A place where you can walk around in the open," Jason said. None of those pressure-suit colonies for his mother.

"We have just the place. Capricorn. It's a yellow-sun planet, just like Capitol."

Jase looked behind the man's eyes. That was the assigned planet to push for the week—they needed more platinum and aluminum miners, and women to service them. Not what Jase had in mind. He searched the man's memories until he found a planet that would do. "How about Duncan?" asked Jason.

The man sighed. "Why didn't you tell me you had a tip from inside? Duncan it is." A place so good they haven't even had to terraform it.

Mother stood at his side. "Where are we going?"

"Duncan," said Jason. "It's a good place."

"You just have to sign these papers." The man began entering information at a keyboard. It was one of the ancient screen-view kinds. You'd think the Colonies could afford something better than *that*.

Name? Occupation? Parents? Address? Birthdate? As he demanded more and more data from her, Mother began to retreat from her illusion. Marital status? "Widow," she said. She turned to Jason. "He's not waiting for me, Jase. He's dead."

Jason looked her in the eyes, trying to think of an answer. This was not a good time for Mother to be sane.

The man smiled cheerfully. "And of course you're taking your son with you."

"Yes," said Mother.

In that moment Jason realized that he never intended to go. Even to save his own life, even though it was likely he would be arrested or killed the moment he left this office, he would not go to a Colony. Would not go off to the end of the populated universe and disappear. The Colonies were the only place his mother might be safe, but he had another alternative. The Fleet. In the Fleet he would be safe enough, might even become a starpilot. Like his father.

"No," said Jase.

"You're the legal guardian, according to this," said the man. "If you say he comes, he comes."

"No," said Jase.

"You're leaving me!" she cried. "I won't have it!"

"It's the only way to save your life," said Jase.

"Did you ever ask me," she said, "if I wanted my life to be saved?"

Jase knew his mother, better than she knew herself. "They put you under somec," he said. "For as long as the voyage takes."

It stirred all the old memories. All the sleepings and wakings. Usually to find Homer there. The last time, though, she awoke alone.

"I don't think so," she said. "I don't think I want to do it."

"I'll be there," he lied.

"No you won't," she said. "You mean to leave me. You plan to leave me, just like your father did."

It was unnerving. How could she know him so well, without the Swipe herself? But no, she didn't *know*, it was only her own fears. The worst thing in the world, to wake up and have him not be there. I am doing the worst thing in the world to her, for the second time.

"Just sign here," said the man. "Your personal code." He pushed a keypad across the desk to them.

"I don't want to do it," said Mother.

Jase calmly entered the numbers for her, taking the code out of her memory. The Colonies man was startled, but when the code checked out correctly on his screen, he shrugged. "Such trust," he said. "Now the lady's palm—"

Mother looked at Jason coldly. "The old lady's going crazy, so dump her off to another world, you miserable bastard, I hate you, just like your father I hate you, you bastard." She looked at the man. "Do you know who his father is?"

The man shrugged. Of course he knew. He had Jase's records up on the screen.

"He's his father's son, not mine."

"It's the only way to save your life, Mother."

"Who are you, God? You decide who's supposed to live and how?"

Like Radamand, thought Jason, again remembering the deaths of brothers he never had. But I do not use my gift to kill. I use it to save. I am not Radamand. I am not Homer Worthing. Yet he knew, from his mother's thoughts, that she loved Jase so much that she would rather die than lose him, than leave him.

"If you stay," he said coldly, "they will interrogate you."

"I'll tell them everything," she said.

"And that is why you have to go."

The Colonies man smiled. "Everything in the Colonies is in strictest confidence. No prosecutions, all crimes absolved—it's a fresh start, whatever it is you did."

Mother turned to him. "And do you erase the memories, too?"

Ah, yes, Mother. That's the question. How can we forget what we remember having done? How will I forget that to save your life I must destroy it?

"Of course not," said the man. "We dump the memories back into your head as soon as you come out of somec."

"Don't you love me?" Mother asked.

The Colonies man looked baffled.

"She's talking to me," said Jase. "I love you, Mother."

"Then why won't you be there when I wake up?"

Desperate, Jason turned to the one strategy he hadn't tried. The truth. "Because I can't spend my life taking care of you."

"Of course not," Mother said. "After all, I only spent *my* life taking care of *you*."

The Colonies man was getting impatient. "Your palm, lady."

She slapped her palm down brutally on the reader. "I'll go, you little bastard! But you're going with me! Sign him on, he's coming with me!"

"You don't want me with you, Mother," said Jase softly.

"Enter your number, please," said the man. The Colonies were used to getting unwilling people. He didn't care whether Jason went happily or not.

So Jase entered the man's own personal code. Of course it didn't check out. But Jase knew they printed the incorrect code on the screen, and the Colonies man recognized it.

"How did you—" began the man. Then his eyes narrowed. "Get out," he said. "Get out of here."

Jase was only too glad to obey.

"I hate you!" called his mother after him. "You're worse than your father, I'll hate you forever!"

May that hatred keep you alive, thought Jason. May that hatred keep you sane. You can't hate me any worse than I hate myself. I am Radamand. All that he could do, I could do. Haven't I killed my mother here today? Taken her out of the world. To save her life, yes. But then why didn't I go with her? I am Radamand, remaking the world, breaking and bending other lives to fit myself. I ought to die, I hope I die.

He meant it. He wanted to die. But even as he thought it, he scanned the minds of the people near him in the corridor. None was looking for him. He still had a chance to get away. And despite his feelings of despair, he would go on trying to escape until he succeeded, or until he was caught. So much for willing death.

But how could he get anywhere? The moment he palmed a reader he'd tell where he was. To eat, to travel, to talk to Gracie, anything he might do that was worth doing would alert Mother's Little Boys, and they'd find him. Worse, he was legally an orphan now, since his mother had irrevocably signed on with the Colonies. It made him a ward of the state, and he could legally be searched for and found by anyone, without the lengthy legal process of showing cause. Until he could get himself enlisted with the Fleet, he was vulnerable.

He used a booth and talked to Gracie, just long enough to get a directory and find the location of the nearest recruiting station. It was a good long worm ride to get there. Not as far as Radamand had been, but far enough. Did he dare?

His question was answered almost immediately. Leaving the booth, he again scanned the people near him—and one of them was one of Mother's Little Boys, coming to get him at the booth. He ducked into a crowd and left him behind. For once he was glad he was still small—he disappeared and turned a corner, all the while keeping the man's thoughts in his mind. Lost him, thought the man. Lost him.

But they were looking, and it had taken only a few minutes at the booth before one of Mother's Little Boys had reached him. He couldn't ride a worm. Even if he palmed the reader and immediately got aboard, the worm would hardly have finished acceleration before they got to him. So he had to walk. It was two hundred levels above him and four subs away. There was no hope of reaching there before tomorrow. In that time he would have nothing to eat—only water could be had without palming for it. And where would he sleep?

In one of the twenty-meter parks, under a tree. The lawn was artificial, but the tree was real, and the rough bark felt good on his hand; the needles pricked him but he needed the pain. Needed the pain so he could sleep, with his mind newly crowded with memories of what he never did, and what he had just done. His mother was not sane—he knew that better than anyone, having seen directly how she lost touch with reality, how she lived in the constant hope of Homer Worthing coming home. But how was he any less mad himself, with the vision of his dying brothers before his eyes? Why do I remember it this way? Why can't I see it as a story that happened to someone else? Why does my mother's face blend so easily into these memories? He could not separate what he knew he had done from what he knew he had not done. If he could shrug off Radamand's acts, then would he lose the guilt for what he had done to his mother? He was not willing to do that. Painful as it was, what he had done, he had done, and would not give up his own past, even at the cost of keeping someone else's. Better the madness of keeping Radamand within me than the worse madness of losing Jason.

So he slept with the prickling needles clasped lightly in one hand, the other hand resting on the bark of the tree. I am what I have done, he said to himself as he dozed off. But he awoke saying, I *was* what I did. I *am* what I will do.

It was a whole day's walk, up the endless stairs, not daring to palm the public elevators, along the corridors, taking a slidewalk when he could. He reached the Fleet recruiting station just before closing.

"I want to join," said Jase.

The recruiter looked at him coldly. "You're little and you're young."

"Thirteen. I'm old enough."

"Parents' consent?"

"Ward of the state." And without giving his name, he punched in his personal code, calling his data into the air above the recruiter's desk.

The recruiter frowned at the name. *Worthing* was a name not soon to be forgotten. "What, planning to follow in your father's footsteps?" he asked.

Jase said nothing. He could see the man wished him no ill.

"Good scores, strong aptitudes. Your father was a great starpilot, before."

So there were other memories of Homer Worthing. Jase probed, and found something that surprised him. The world that Homer destroyed had refused him permission to draw water from their oceans. They had kept him there until the Fleet could catch him. They were not wholly innocent. The Fleet did not hate Homer as the rest of the universe did. Jase had grown so used to being ashamed of who he was that he did not know what to do with this new information, except to hope there would be a place for him in the Fleet. Perhaps, at last, he had a patrimony.

But the recruiter only shook his head. "Sorry. I just applied you, and you've been rejected."

"Why?" asked Jase.

"Not because of your father. Code Nine. Something abut your aptitudes. I'm not allowed to tell you more."

He told Jase more whether he meant to or not. Jase was being refused entry into the Fleet because of his scores at school. He was too bright to be admitted to the Fleet without consent from the Office of Education. Which he would never get, since Hartman Torrock would have to approve him.

"Jason Worthing," said a man behind him. "I've been looking for you."

Jason ran. The man behind him was one of Mother's Little Boys, and it was arrest he had in mind.

At first the crowds in the corridors helped him. They were moving quickly, and Jase could dodge among them, moving faster than his pursuer, and always out of sight. Gradually the man chasing him was joined by more, until a half dozen were working their way through the crowd. He could not keep track of them all. It was too hard, to look out of their eyes and try to guess, from what they were seeing, where they were.

They caught him when the crowd was slow, for then he was too small and weak to force his way through. His size was no longer an advantage, the Swipe was no help to him, and he found himself sprawled on the ground with a savagely spiked shoe on his hand. Even so he was not afraid of pain: he ripped his hand away and, despite the agony of flayed skin and torn-open veins, he almost scrambled away into the crowd before they caught him, ankle and wrist, and cuffed and shackled him.

"Tough little bastard," said one of Mother's Little Boys.

"Why are you chasing me?"

"Because you ran. We always figure that anybody who runs should probably be caught." But he was lying. They had orders to take Jason Worthing alive, at all costs. Whose orders? Hartman Torrock's? Radamand Worthing's? Not that the answer made much difference. He should have gone to the Colonies with Mother. He had gambled everything on the chance of turning a foul future into something better; he had lost.

But it was neither Radamand nor Tork who came to take him into custody. It was a short, stout, balding man who ordered them to unshackle him, and to cuff them together. The invisible field kept their wrists within a meter of each other.

"I hope you don't mind," said his captor. "I wouldn't want to lose you again, after going to all this trouble. His hand is bleeding. Anyone have a healer?"

Someone passed a healer over Jase's hand, and the blood coagulated and the flow stopped. In the meantime, the short man introduced himself. "I'm Abner Doon, and I'm the closest thing to a friend you're likely to find in this world. I have every intention of exploiting you unmercifully to carry out my own plans, but at least while you're with me you're safe from Cousin Radamand and Hartman Torrock."

How much did this man know? Jase looked within his mind and saw: everything.

"I was asleep until you took that second test," said Doon. "But when you got half right a question whose answer wasn't known to but a handful of physicists, who weren't too sure themselves—well, the Sleephouse people wakened me. They have their instructions. I wouldn't have missed you for the world."

They went to an official highway, which Doon entered merely by palming the door, the way anyone else might board a worm. A private car was waiting. Jase was impressed, and willingly got inside.

"Who are you?" he asked.

"A question I've been trying to answer since adolescence. I finally decided I was neither God nor Satan. I was so disappointed I didn't try to narrow it down any further."

Jase probed his mind. The man was an assistant minister of colonization. He also believed he ruled the world. And, upon further examination, Jase realized it was true. Even Radamand, for all his machinations, would have been awed at what Abner Doon controlled. Even Mother—not Jase's mother, but Mother, the ruler of Capitol—even she was his pawn. It was not the world he ruled. He could twitch, and half the universe would tremble. And yet he was almost utterly unknown. Jase looked him in the eyes and laughed.

Doon smiled back. "It's flattering that I've had as much power as I have, for as long as I've had it, and yet a good-hearted boy can look into my heart and still laugh."

It was true. There were no murders in Doon's memory. Dwelling in his mind was not the agony that being Radamand had been. Doon did not live to shape the world to his convenience. He was shaping the world, but what he had in mind was not at all convenient.

"I've always wondered what it would be like to have a friend from whom I could keep no secrets," said Doon. "Have you noticed yet your stupid blunder at the Colonies office? You proved you were a Swipe to the counterman. Now I have to put him under somec and wake him up with a old bubble, so he doesn't remember it. It's very unkind of you to clutter up other people's lives that way."

"I'm sorry," said Jase. But he also knew that this was Doon's way of telling him that his mistakes were being covered for. He felt better.

"Oh, by the way, speaking of somec, your mother wrote you a note before she went under."

Jase saw in Doon's mind the memory of his mother handing over a paper, her face stained with tears, yet her lips smiling as Jase had not often see her smile. He clutched at the paper, read it despite the trembling of his hands.

"Abner Doon explained everything to me. About Radamand, and the school. I love you and forgive you and I think I won't be crazy anymore."

It was her handwriting. Jase shuddered in relief.

"I thought you'd want to know that."

Jase read the note again, and then they arrived. They went directly from the car into a short hall, and from the hall into a forest.

This was no park. The grass underfoot was real, the squirrels gamboling on the trunks of the trees were not mechanicals, even the smell was perfect, with not a hint of plastic in the air. The door closed behind them. Doon turned off the cuffs. Jason stepped away from him, looked up into a sky for the first time in his life. No ceiling. No roof at all. He was afraid he might fall. How could people stand to live without a roof overhead?

"Dazzling, isn't it?" asked Doon. "Of course, there *is* a ceiling—all of Capitol has a ceiling—but the illusion is well done, isn't it?"

Jase looked away from the sky and back to Doon.

"Why did you save me? What am I to you?"

"I thought Swipes didn't have to ask questions," answered Doon. To Jase's surprise, he was undressing, shedding clothing as he led the way deeper into the woods. They came to the largest open body of water Jase had ever seen in his life, nearly fifty meters across. "Swim?" asked Doon. He was naked now, and he was *not* stout. The bulk had come from protective clothing. Doon poked the armor gently with his foot. "There are those who want me dead."

Of course there were. Doon did not have Radamand's advantage of knowing other men's desires and secrets, to bribe and blackmail perfectly.

"My cousin Radamand will be one of them, as long as you keep me alive."

Doon laughed. "Oh, Radamand. He's due for his next sleep in the next few weeks. He's a loathsome sort of man, and he's not that much use to me anymore. I doubt he'll ever wake up."

Jase was horrified to realized that it was true. Abner Doon could cause the Sleephouse to kill a man. The one unshakable verity of life in Capitol was this: the Sleephouse could not be corrupted. And yet Abner Doon's influence reached even there.

"Swim?" asked Doon again, walking into the water.

"I don't know how."

"Of course not. I'll teach you."

Jase undressed and followed the man uncertainly into the water. He could see that Doon meant nothing but good toward him. Doon was a man that he could trust. So he followed Doon out until the water was almost to their necks. Doon and he were nearly the same height.

"Water is actually a very safe medium of locomotion," Doon said. Jase only noticed that it was cold. "Now here, my hand is against your back. Lean back against my hand. Now let your legs just come loose from the ground, just relax. I can hold you up."

Suddenly Jase felt very light, and as he relaxed he felt his body bobbing lightly on the surface, only the gentle pressure of Doon's hand under him to remind him of gravity.

Then the world turned upside down, Abner Doon had a back-breaking hold on him, and Jase's face suddenly plunged under the water. He gulped, swallowed; his eyes stung; he desperately needed a breath, and dared not take it. He struggled to come up, but couldn't break the hold. He struggled, he twisted, he tried to strike with his hands and feet, but he did not come to the surface until Doon pulled him up. And in all that time, Doon had meant nothing but good for him. Doon had intended no harm. If this is love, thought Jase, God help me—or is it that Doon is somehow able to lie to me, even in his own mind?

"Don't cough," said Doon. "It splashes water everywhere."

"What was that for?" demanded Jase.

"It was an object lesson. To show you what it feels like to be in something over your head."

"I already knew how it felt."

"Now you know even better." And Doon calmly proceeded with the swimming lesson.

Jase caught on quickly, at least to something as simple as a backfloat. The pseudo-sun was setting, and the sky turned gently pink. Jase lay on his back in the water, stroking the surface just enough to keep moving, just enough to stay afloat. "I've never seen a sunset before."

"Believe me, that isn't how sunsets look on Capitol. The sky of this planet is greasy and dank. Sunset topside is downright purple. Orange is noon. Blue sky is impossible."

"What does this place imitate, then?"

"My home world," said Doon. Jase caught his memories, and they were of the planet Garden. Indeed, this room was only an imitation of a tiny corner of the place. Jason could see Doon's longing for the rolling hills, the thick groves of trees, the open meadows.

"Why did you ever leave it?" asked Jase. "Why did you come *here*?"

Power is the only gift I have, thought Doon. Jason followed his thoughts. How to get power, how to use it, how to destroy it. A human being can only go where his gifts are useful. Capitol is the place where I must be. However much I hate it. However much I long to destroy it. Capitol is my dwelling place, at least for now.

Then, suddenly, Doon's thoughts changed. Jase heard him in the distance, getting out of the water. Jase tried to swim toward shore, but he was awkward and slow, and when he tried to stand the lake was too deep, and he only just recovered himself enough to return to the backstroke. Swimming—staying afloat, in fact—took so much of Jase's concentration, especially now that he was afraid—that he could spare little of his attention to probe in Doon's mind. That was why he taught me. That was why he brought me here. To distract me so I wouldn't know what he had in mind. So I couldn't predict his every move. He fooled me, and now what does he have in mind, what trap has he set for me?

When at last he reached the shore, Doon was disappearing through a door in the garden wall. Jase looked desperately into his thoughts, searching for danger, and found waiting for him Doon's knowledge of the Estorian twick. A small marsupial with teeth like razors. He saw Doon's memory of the little animal leaping at lightning speed onto the udders of a cow before the beast so much as noticed it was there. The twick hung there for a moment by its claws, then disappeared, boring upward and inward into the cow's body, blood gouting from the wound. The cow only then reacted, it had happened so quickly. It shuddered, ran a few steps, then dropped to the ground and died. The twick crawled slowly from the cow's mouth, panting and sluggish and bloated. Jase had read about twicks too and knew something of their habits. Knew too that twicks had wiped out the first colony on Estoria, and even now they were only restrained by ultrasonic fences that kept them confined to reservations.

Why was Doon thinking of Estorian twicks? Because he was releasing one into the park right now. The only prey the twick would want was Jase, and Jase was naked and unarmed beside the lake. Yet still in Doon's mind, Jase could find nothing but goodwill. That frightened him more than anything else—that Doon meant well for him, and yet had no idea how Jase would survive the attack of the little beast.

Already the twick was perched on a branch not twenty meters off. Jase stood absolutely still, remembering that twicks rely mostly on smell and sound and motion to identify prey. He tried, desperately, to think of a weapon. He pictured himself picking up one of the stones from the lake's shore, and as he tried to bring it down on the twick, the little animal would leap up and eat his hand in mid-stroke.

The twick moved. So quickly that Jase hardly saw the motion, except that now the twick was in the grass, and only ten meters off.

Jase's hand throbbed where it had been torn under his captor's boot. The smell of blood is on me, he realized. The twick will come for me whether I move or not.

The twick moved again. It was two meters off. Jase tried desperately to see into the animal's mind. It was not hard to get the fuzzy view the beast had of the world, but it was impossible to make sense of the welter of urges. He would not know what the twick meant to do until it happened. Jase could not use the Swipe, and had no other weapon.

Suddenly Jase felt an excruciating pain in his left calf. He reached down to pry the animal off. For a moment the twick clung, still boring into his leg; then it wriggled out and immediately was burrowing into the muscle of Jase's upper arm. The leg gushed blood. Jase screamed and struck at the animal with his left hand. Every blow landed, but it did no good.

I'm going to die, Jase shouted in his mind.

But his survival instinct was still strong, despite the terrible pain and worse fear. Like a reflex he realized that the twick would simply jump from target to target on Jase's body. It was only a matter of time until it hit a vital artery, or until it found the boneless cavity of his abdomen and devoured his bowels. But with each gram of flesh it ate, the twick would grow more sluggish. If Jase could only manage to stay alive, the twick would gradually lose its frenzied speed. But Jase too was growing weaker as the blood flowed out of him through two great wounds. And he had no weapon, even if the twick were slow.

He threw himself to the ground, trying hopelessly to crush the animal under the weight of his body. Of course the twick was uninjured—its skeleton was flexible, and it sprung back to shape as soon as Jase rolled off.

But it had stopped eating for a moment, was not attached to Jase's body, and it would be slower now. Jase scrambled to his feet and began to run.

With a wound in his leg, he was slower too, and before he got three steps away, the twick struck. But Jase's back was to it now, and the animal only dug into the muscles under the shoulder blade.

Jase threw himself to the ground, backward. This time the twick made a sharp sound and scurried a little farther away. Jase tried to run again, skirting the edge of the lake. This time he managed a dozen staggering steps before the twick clutched at his buttocks and began tearing at him again. Jase broke stride, fell to one knee. The lake was only a meter away. I can't swim with all these wounds, thought Jase. Oh well, the coldly intellectual part of his mind answered. Maybe the twick can't, either.

He crawled toward the water, dragging his left leg, for the twick had severed the great muscles of the thigh, and the leg would not respond to him, except with agony. Jase reached the water just as the animal struck bone.

It was impossible for Jase to float. He just crouched under the water, holding his breath forever, trying to ignore the agony pulsing from his buttocks, from his leg, from his arm, from his back. He could feel the twick burrowing along the edge of his pelvic bone. His analytic mind noted the fact that this was taking the animal away from the vulnerable anal areas. Muscles can heal. I can live. Muscles can heal. The repetition kept him underwater despite the pain, despite his lungs bursting for air.

The twick slowed. It emerged from Jase's body at the hip.

Immediately Jase grubbed it, fumbled for its neck. The twick was slow, and Jase had it by the throat, crushingly. Now Jase let himself rise from the water enough to take a breath, still holding the twick under. The air came like fire into his lungs, and he almost immediately fell forward into the water again. But he did not let go of the slowly wriggling twick. His hands, if anything, held it tighter. He struggled with his elbows and one good leg to drag himself toward shore again. The water became shallow enough that he could keep his head above the surface without trying to stand. The twick vomited and the water went black-red with Jase's undigested blood and flesh. Then, at last, the twick stopped moving.

Jase found the strength to fling the limp animal out toward the middle of the lake. Then he fell forward, onto the shore, his face slapping into the mud, his bleeding leg and buttocks and hip still under the water. Help, he thought. I'll die, he thought. After a moment he gave up trying to turn his thoughts into words. He only lay there, feeling the blood rush out of him, filling up the lake, touching every shore of the lake, until it was all red, all part of him, and there was nothing left in his body at all, nothing inside him now at all.

4
The Devil Himself

There were tasks, as winter came on, that books must wait for, even though Lared's bookwork was bringing money to the family. The coming of snow was not taken lightly, and all hands were needed to be sure of food and fuel enough for the season. Especially now, when they knew there was no protection; since the coming of pain, any dark thing was possible. So each day when Lared awoke he did not know whether today would be spent twitching his fingers to move a pen or bending his whole body into some heavy task. There were days when he hoped for one, and days when he hoped for the other; but regardless of what he hoped for, he worked hard at whatever the day required. Even when the story that he wrote was painful; even when the tale was held in memories of dreams that had been near unbearable when they came.

The first snowfall began late on the afternoon of the day Lared wrote the story of Jase and the battle with the twick. The snow had threatened all day; the sky was so dark that Jason had lit a candle at noon to light the page for Lared's work. But now that part of the tale was told, and Lared was already putting away the pen and ink when the sound of the tinker's cart could be heard above the ringing of Father's hammer in the forge. It was the old saying—the coming of the tinker is the coming of the snow. Actually, as everyone knew, Whitey the tinker came several times a year, but always arranged it so he'd reach Flat Harbor before the first hard snow.

Jason looked up from blotting the new ink on the parchment with a linen cloth, for Sala was stuttering up the stairs—both feet hitting each step, she was so short. "The tinker's come," she shouted, "the tinker's come! And there's snow on the ground today!"

It was worth a little rejoicing, that something in the world still worked as it should. Lared closed his penbox. Jason set aside the parchment. So small and fine was Lared's writing, so economical of words, that the first sheepskin was not yet full.

"It was good work for today," said Jason. "We've finished the first part. The worst part, for me, I think."

"I have to make up the tinker's bed," said Lared. "He stays the winter. He's a good bellows mender, and he can make a goatskin bag tight as a bladder."

"So can I," said Jason.

"You have a book to write."

Jason shrugged. "Looks to me like *you're* writing it."

Lared took two tick covers from the shelves in the attic, and together they ran through the innyard without bothering to put on jackets against the cold. The flakes were already falling, the little ones that had come twice before but didn't stick to the ground. They were sticking now, on the grasses and leaves, at least. They made their way into the haybarn, which was musty and crowded with the year's straw. Lared went unerringly to the bed straw, which was cleanest, and they began stuffing the ticks.

"The tinker gets two beds, and I get only one?" asked Jason.

"The tinker comes every year, and does his work for free, and pays nothing. That makes him kin." You'll never be kin, because Mother doesn't like you, Lared said silently. Knowing, of course, that he would be heard.

Jason sighed. "It's going to be a very hard winter."

Lared shrugged. "Some say it is, some say it isn't."

"It is."

"The worms in the trees are furry, and the greybirds flew on by us this year, going farther south. But who knows?"

"Justice and I checked the weather on the way in, and the winter's going to be very hard."

No one knew weather that far in advance, but Lared was long past surprise. "I'll tell Father, then. It's firewood time. I'll have to cut firewood, you know. And we always start at first snow. The trees always drop their sap by then."

"You need a rest from writing."

"The more I do, the easier it gets. Words come to mind easier."

Jason looked at him oddly. "But what do you think it all means?"

Lared didn't know how to answer without sounding foolish. He folded over the top of his tick. "Don't overstuff, it goes lumpy."

Jason folded the top of his, too. "If you put shadowfern in it, the fleas go away."

Lared made a face. "And where will we find shadowfern in the snow?"

"I guess it's a little late."

Now Lared had the courage to ask. "Doon is the devil, isn't he?"

"Was. He's dead now. At least, he promised me that he'd die."

"But was he?"

"The devil?" Jason heaved the tick over his shoulder like a collier with his sack. "Satan. The adversary. The enemy of the plan of God. The undoer. The destroyer. Yes. He definitely was." Jason smiled. "But he meant well."

Lared led the way back across the yard to the house and up to the tinker's room. "Why did he put you with the twick? Did he want you dead?"

"No. He wanted me to live."

"Then why?"

"To see what I was worth."

"Not much, if you had lost."

"Not much for a year afterward—it took a long time to heal,

and I still get twinges at my hip. Don't ask me to run long distances, for instance. And I sit a little slanted."

"I know." Lared had noticed that the second night, that Jason always leaned a little to the left in a chair. "I know something else, too."

"Hmm?" Jason cast his tick out along the bed first, and together they worked at smoothing it.

"I know how you felt, with Cousin Radamand's memories in you."

"Oh, you do?" Jason was not pleased. "That's why I insisted Justice give the story to you as dreams, instead of waking—"

"They're always too clear for dreams. They feel like memories to me. I wake up some mornings and see these split-log walls and I think—how very rich we are, to have real wood. And then I think, how very poor we are, to have a dirt floor. I reach out sometimes when I come to the door of Father's forge, to palm the reader."

Jason laughed at that, and Lared laughed, too.

"Most of all, I think, Sala and Mother and Father surprise me, just for being there. It's as if your memories are realer to me than my own. I like to pretend that I can see into their minds, the way I do in your memories. I look at their eyes, and sometimes I even think I know what they're about to do." Lared cast his tick over Jason's. "They never do it, though."

"I wish I had been like you," Jason said.

"I wish I had been like you," Lared answered.

"What Doon did, with the twick—I don't think he meant it this way, but it sorted out my memories. Coming so near to death, having so much pain, it does things to the way you remember the rest of your life. Nothing else seemed quite so real to me anymore. I still was not clean, mind you—I still felt guilty at what I had done to my own mother, at what I remembered having done in Radamand's past. But it didn't matter so much. I counted the days of my life from that moment. Before Doon, and After Doon. He had plans for me. He cleared my record of the blot that Torrock had put on it, he had Radamand's crimes made public—all but the Swipe—and my dear cousin was put on an asteroid somewhere. And then he made me a starpilot. Like my father."

"Justice hasn't given me any memory of that."

"She never will. We're trying not to clutter up your brain with things that don't matter. I became a starpilot the way everyone else does. I was just better at it than most. The hardest thing, though, was to make sure I always won my battles in ways that could be counted as clever thinking—not the Swipe. There I'd sit, knowing exactly what the enemy intended to do, and helpless to save as many lives as I might have, if I had been free. Always I had to wait a moment too long, see the enemy do a little too much, and people died to save my life. That's a problem for you, Lared. If I can save a hundred lives by making it obvious I have the Swipe, which would lead to my death, is that better than to save only fifty lives in order to hide the Swipe, so I can live to save another fifty, and another fifty, and another fifty?"

"That depends on whether I'm one of the fifty that gets saved either way, or one of the fifty that dies to save you."

Jason frowned. Together they cast the linen sheet over the ticks and tucked it in under them. "The tinker gets linen, and I have to sleep on wool."

"Wool's warmer."

"Linen doesn't itch."

"You didn't like my answer."

"I hated your answer. It doesn't depend on whether you'll live or die. It depends on what's *right*. And what's right and wrong doesn't come down to your personal preference. It never does. If it comes to what you personally prefer, then there's no right or wrong at all."

Lared was ashamed and angry. Angry because he didn't think it was right that Jason should make him feel ashamed. "What's wrong with wanting to live?"

"Any dog can do that. Are you a dog? You're not a human being until you value something more than the life of your body. And the greater the thing you live and die for, the greater you are."

"What did you live for, when the twick was eating you?"

Jason looked angry, but then he smiled. "The life of my body, of course. We're animals first, aren't we? I thought I would live to do something very important."

"Like make a bed for a wandering tinker?"

"That was exactly what I had in mind."

"You speak our language better than I do, now."

"I've spoken a dozen languages. Yours is just an evolved version of one I spoke very early in my life. My native language, in fact. All the patterns are there, and the words are changed in predictable patterns. This planet was settled from Capitol. By Abner Doon."

"When a child is very bad, they say, 'Abner Doon will come in the night and steal all your sleep.' "

"Abner Doon, the monster."

"Wasn't he?"

"He was my friend. He was a true friend of all mankind."

"I thought you said he was the devil."

"That, too. What would you call the man who gave you the Day of Pain?"

Lared remembered, as he did more and more rarely these days, the sound of Clany's screams, the blood pulsing from the leg of the man they carried upstairs, the death of the old cleric—

"You couldn't forgive him, could you?" asked Jason.

"Never."

Jason nodded. "And why not?"

"We were so happy before. Things were so good before."

"Ah. But when Abner Doon undid the Empire, unslept the sleepers, things were not good. Life was empty or miserable for almost every living soul."

"Then why didn't they thank him?"

"Because people always believe things were better—before."

Lared realized then that he had made a mistake. He had thought, from all his dreams, that Doon was Jason's enemy. Now he knew that Jason loved the man. It frightened Lared, that Jason Worthing loved the devil. What is this work I'm doing? I should stop at once.

Of course Jason and Justice heard this thought. But they answered not at all. Not even to tell him he was free. Their silence was the only answer that he got. Maybe I will quit, he decided. Maybe I'll tell them to go to some other village and find some other uneducated, ignorant scribe.

As soon as I find out what happened next, I'll quit.

* * *

Lared was the forester for Flat Harbor, and so he had to spend a week in the forest, girdling trees. Jason was coming along. Lared was not glad. Ever since he was nine years old, he had girdled the trees for the winter's lumbering. It meant days on end, wandering the woods that he knew better than any other in the village, seeing the old places made new and naked by winter, discovering where the animals were hidden, and above all spending nights alone in the wattle and daub huts he made himself each afternoon. No sound of anything but his own breathing, and then waking some mornings to see his breath like steam in the air, and other mornings to a thick fog in the woods, and other mornings to trackless snow hiding the ground from him, unmaking all the old paths, forcing him to make something new in the world just by walking forth from his night's hut.

But this year he would have Jason with him, because Father insisted.

"We've never had winter before, not like this," said Father. "In past years we've been—protected. This year we're like the animals—the cold can kill us, we can get lost, we can go hungry, a tool can bite us and who will be there to stanch the blood? You go nowhere alone. Jason is needed for nothing else, he can go, and so he *will* go." Father glared at Jason, daring him to argue. Jason only smiled.

It was not a job that needed two men. Lared had been watching the trees all summer, and knew which ones should be harvested this year. Such trees were almost never close enough together that Lared could point out one for Jason to girdle while he did another himself. And if they worked the same tree, Jason was always getting in Lared's way. By noon on the first day Lared made it plain that he did not want Jason there, and so Jason discreetly kept his distance. There was little snow on the ground, and that only in patches. Jason took to gathering mosses from trees and stones, sorting them into pouches in the woolen bag he had sewn for himself while Lared wrote. Not a word passed between them all afternoon. Yet Lared was always aware of Jason. He girdled the trees quickly, deftly, moving faster than he usually did. He knelt before the tree, and his chisel bit into the bark. He tapped it with the mallot and drove it all around the tree, then clawed the bark downward with the iron tool he had drawn for Father. Before Lared they had girdled twice, in two parallel lines around the tree. But that took twice as long as necessary—once there was a single cut, the bark could be clawed off far enough to be sure the tree was dead before harvest in the deep snow. Then, next year, new shoots would come from the stump. It was part of Lared's work each year to trim off the shoots, so they could be dried to shape and worked into stems and handles and frames on reed and wicker baskets. Nothing was wasted, and Lared was proud of how smoothly he worked, how quickly the job was done.

He worked with such concentration that the sun was already setting when he realized that he had not yet made the hut for the night's sleep. He had never done so many trees on the first day before. He had never had Jason Worthing watching him, either. Now he was well past the remnants of old first-day huts. He didn't want to go back for them. Nor would it be practical to go on to second-day huts—they were too far ahead, and he always scaled the rock cliff of Brindy Stream on the second day, in broad daylight—that wasn't a work for evening. So he would need Jason's help, making a new hut quickly, with no old wattles to start from.

No sooner had he thought this than Jason was beside him, silent and expressionless, waiting for instructions. Lared chose a good house tree, with a long low branch for the central beam, and near enough to a willow that it would not be inconvenient. Jason nodded and began using his own knife to cut the willow withes where they hung from the tree. Lared saw that Jason knew what he was doing, and could reach higher and cut longer sticks than ever Lared could. So after Lared had gathered the deadwood sticks for the wattle frames, he set to work making the daub at the edge of a stream. It was cold work, digging with a hand-spade in the muddy bank, and splashing water onto the soil with his wooden bowl. But he did it quickly, and by the time Jason had the withes woven together into large strong wattles, the mud was ready for daubing.

Jason brought over the wattles one at a time. He quickly learned Lared's way of daubing—taking a handful of large fallen leaves and scooping up the mud with it. They slapped the mud-covered leaves onto the wattle and left them there—the leaves made the wall thicker and warmer and more watertight than mud alone. Together they carried each finished wattle to the tree and leaned it against the beam. Because Jason had been able to cut such long twigs, the wattles spread out much wider than any hut Lared had ever made before—room for two men inside.

They cut saplings to strengthen the door, and hung on it the sheepskin Lared carried for that purpose. It was fully dark before they had a fire going out in front of the hut. They heated water and simmered the sausage so it would go warm into their bellies for the night's sleep. Lared went and washed the little pot, and when he came back Jason was already asleep on one side of the tent, leaving Lared with half the space to lay out his blanket and sleep. It was a fine hut, and Lared discovered that he didn't mind the sound of Jason's breathing beside him after all. They had not exchanged a word all day. The silence of the forest was complete, except for the noises of owls on the hunt, and a bearkin passing by.

As always on the first night of tree-girdling, Lared drifted off to sleep thinking, Why should I ever go back to Flat Harbor? Why don't I spend forever here?

That night he dreamed. And in his dream he was not Jason Worthing, the first time that he had not been given Jason's own life as a memory.

He was Abner Doon.

He sat before a table, and in the air before him was a world. Or rather, a map of a world, with nations marked out in different colors. He pressed keys, and different colors came onto the globe, and the world turned and showed him other faces, and as Doon studied it he understood that a thing of beauty was being wrought there. It was a game, of course, only a game, but among the players was one of true genius. Herman Nuber, said the computer registration of players. Herman Nuber, who at the moment was under somec, was the player who had taken the Italy of 1914 and played it into a position of world domination, with an empire of allies, client states, and outright possessions that was larger than anything Earth had seen till that point in history.

Nuber's Italy was a dictatorship, but one that was studiedly benign. In every client state and conquered territory, rebellion was ruthlessly suppressed but loyalty was lavishly rewarded, taxes were not high, local customs and freedoms were respected, and life for the computer-simulated populace was good. Rebellions profited nothing, and lost all, and so the government was stable, so stable that even inferior players, making stupid blunders while Nuber was on somec, even they could do little damage to Nuber's Italy.

Indeed, that was what had first drawn Abner to the game. He did not pay much attention to International Games, any more than he wasted time watching the endless lifeloops, with their tediously complete reproduction of the lives and loves of dull and oversexed people, in three dimensions and full color. He was busy building his own network of power, turning his office as assistant minister of colonization into the center of the world. But so many people were talking about Nuber's Italy. Nuber will be waking soon. Nuber will conquer the world this time. The bets were running high, but all the odds were on the actual date of the end of the game, not on whether Nuber could bring it off. Of course he could. Of all the players in the history of International Games, no one had ever started from so weak a position and built it into such a strong one in so short a time. Perfection, it was called. The ultimate empire.

Naturally, Abner had to see.

He studied it carefully for many hours, and all they had said was true. It was the sort of government that could stand forever. A new Roman Empire that made the old look transient and paltry.

Such a challenge, thought Abner.

And in his dream, Lared understood the thing of beauty Herman Nuber had conceived and brought to be, and he cried out in his sleep against the act that Abner planned. But the dream continued, for it was not in his control.

Abner Doon bought Italy. Bought the right to play that nation. It was expensive, because there had been some illegal speculation in the players market and the price had inflated, in order to force Nuber to pay bonuses in order to buy it. But Abner had no intention of forcing Nuber to pay anything. Abner never meant to sell Italy. Instead, he would use it as a test of what he planned to do in real life: he would see how well he could bring off the utter destruction of the order of the world.

He played carefully, and in his dream Lared believed he understood all that Abner did. He engaged in pointless wars and made sure they were badly generaled and stupidly fought—but not so stupidly that there were any crushing defeats. Just attrition, a slow wearing away of the army, of the wealth of the empire.

And within the empire he also began a quiet corrosion. Mismanagement and stupid decisions on industrial production; changes in the civil service to promote corruption; unfair, almost whimsical taxation. And the conquered nations were singled out for harrassment. Religious persecution; insistence on the use of the Italian language, discrimination against certain groups in jobs, in education; severe restrictions on what could and could not be printed; barriers to travel; confiscation of peasant land and the encouragement of a new aristocracy. In short, he did everything he could to make Nuber's Italy function much the way the Empire did. Only Abner timed and controlled things, watched carefully to be sure that the resentment built gradually, held off rebellions, kept them small and weak, biding his time. I do not want a few geysers, Abner told himself. I want a volcano that will consume the world.

The only thing Nuber's Italy had that Capitol lacked was Catholicism, a binding force, a common faith that bound at least the ruling classes together, ensured they looked out upon the world with a shared vision. The integrity of the Church, that was the one thing they trusted in the corrupt empire that Abner was giving them.

Like somec. Like the Sleephouse. The common hope and faith of all the ruling class of Capitol and the Thousand Worlds. To sleep, and thus live longer than the poor fools who could not qualify. The integrity, the incorruptibility of the keepers of the Sleephouse was the faith of all. If through my accomplishment I truly merit somec, I will have it. It can't be bought, it can't be demanded, it can't be cajoled, it can't be had by fraud. Only recognized achievement. It was the only thing that preserved the Empire of the Thousand Worlds, despite the rot that holed and softened it everywhere else. The faith in the final judgment of the Sleephouse, which measured men and women and gave them immortality, if they were worthy.

I will bring you down, thought Abner Doon, and Lared shuddered in his sleep.

It was only a matter of time, then, until Nuber's Italy became ripe. In the meantime, Herman Nuber awoke from his three-year sleep—a noble allotment of somec indeed, to sleep three years for each one year waking—a man could live four hundred years that way. But that was the esteem Nuber had won for himself, with such a creation as Italy.

Of course Nuber tried to buy Italy, so he could play. But Abner wouldn't sell. Nuber's agents were persistent, their offers princely, but Abner had no intention of letting Nuber save Italy. Nuber even tried to strong-arm him, sending hired thugs to frighten him. Abner had too much power in Capitol already, though. The thugs already worked for him, and Abner sent them back to Nuber with instructions to do to him what he had hired them to do to Abner. It seemed only just.

Except it was not just. Nuber could see what Abner was doing to his empire. He was no fool. He had spent seven years of his waking life—twenty-eight years of game time—building Italy into a phenomenon that would stand in the annals of International Games forever. And Abner was destroying it. Not clumsily, but deftly, with exquisite timing and perfect thoroughness. It was not enough to provoke rebellion and reorganization. Abner was provoking revolution and conquest that would erase Italy from the map, utterly destroy it so there was no hope that it would ever rise again. When Abner was through, he meant there to be nothing left for Nuber to buy and rebuild.

At last he judged the time was ripe. Abner did a simple thing, but it was enough: he exposed the secret corruption he had brought into the heart of the Church. The outrage, the loathing it caused tore away the last pretense at legitimacy, even decency, that Nuber's Italy possessed. The computer hardly knew how to cope with this, except with instant, overwhelming revolt. All the grievances in every nation were joined now with the anger of the aristocracy—all classes acted at once, and Italy was undone, the empire fragmented, the armies in mutiny.

It took three days, and it was over. There was no Italy left in the game.

Even Abner was stunned at how well it worked. Of course International Games used simplified patterns, but it was as close to reality as any game could be.

I will do it again, thought Abner. And the pattern unfolded in his mind. The seeds of universal revolution were already there, for the Empire was corrupt to the core, with only the hope of somec holding all in check. Abner's work, then, was to postpone revolution until he was ready, until it would all come at once, until revolution would not merely change the government, but undo everything, even cut the threads that bound world to world. Travel between the stars must end along with everything else, or his destroying would be in vain.

But here fate had been kind to Abner's plans—indeed, he suspected, things might have gone the way I wish them to without my intervention. That was the problem with manipulating reality: there was no way to find out what *would* have been. Perhaps I make no difference in the world. But then, perhaps I do. And so Abner began the slow process of corrupting the Sleephouse. Allowing quiet murders and manipulations through somec. Allowing sleep levels to be bought with money or power, allowing bubbles of memory to be tampered with or lost, allowing petty princes of crime or capitalism to think they could use the Sleephouse as they saw fit. When at last it all came out, the way somec had been misused, all the resentment would come at once, all hatreds would explode, with even the somec users themselves revolting against the Sleephouse, so that somec itself would be eliminated, even for the passage between the stars, even for the one legitimate use it had.

I can do it, Abner said, triumphantly.

But he was a man of conscience, in his way. He went to visit Herman Nuber, when it all was done. The man was stricken, to see his life's work undone for no purpose that he could understand.

"What have I ever done to you?" asked Nuber. He was a very old man, it seemed, or at last very tired.

"Nothing," said Abner.

"Did you win much, betting on the fall of Italy?"

"I had no wagers placed." The sums involved would have been petty, compared to what Abner already controlled.

"Why should you wish to hurt me, then, when it profited you nothing?"

"I did not want to hurt you," Abner said.

"What else, man, did you think it would do?"

"I knew it would hurt you, Herman Nuber, but that was a result I neither desired nor undesired."

"What did you want, then?"

"The end of perfection," said Abner.

"Why? What is it about my Italy that made you hate it? What low, small thing in your heart requires you to undo greatness?"

"I don't expect you to understand," said Abner. "But if you had taken this last turn, the game would have ended. The world of your game would have gone into stasis. It would have died. I was not against the beautiful thing you made. I was merely against it lasting forever."

"You love death, then?"

"The opposite. I love only life. But life can only continue in the face of death."

"You are a monster."

And Abner silently agreed. I am the monster of the deep. I am Poseidon, who shakes the earth. I am the worm at the heart of the world.

Lared awoke weeping. Jason touched his shoulder. "Was it as bad a dream as that?" he whispered.

Only gradually did Lared realize he was no longer in the plastic world of Capitol, but under the leaning wattles of a forest hut, with Jason leaning over him in the dim light coming from the edges of the sheepskin door. It was very warm inside the hut, which told Lared at once that it had snowed in the night, making a thick layer on their walls to keep in their bodies' warmth. Indeed, the wattles sagged deeply, and unless they unbuilt them soon they would break and not be usable for next year's huts. The urgency of the work took the dream from Lared's mind, or at least pushed it back enough that he could stop his grieving.

It was late in the morning when Lared brought up the dream

with Jason. Lared wanted the man beside him now, in the snow—it was cold hard work, and with Jason using the claw Lared could cut the girdle and go on to the next tree, leaving Jason to follow his tracks in the snow. Only when they reached the cliff were they together long enough to talk.

"We have to climb this?" Jason asked, looking at the snow-covered ledges.

"Or fly," said Lared. "There's a quick way, but it's too dangerous in the snow. We'll take the slanting crevice there."

"I'm getting old," Jason said. "I'm not sure I can climb it."

"You can," said Lared. "Because there's no other choice. You don't know the way back home, and I'm going up."

"It's sweet of you to be so careful with me," Jason said. "If I fall, will you climb back down to help me, or leave me as an offering to the wolves?"

"Climb back down, of course. What do you think I am?" And then his rage burst out. "If you ever send me a dream like that again, I'll kill you."

Jason looked surprised. How could he look surprised, when of course he knew all that Lared felt?

"I thought you'd understand Abner, if you saw that dream," Jason said.

"Understand him? He *is* the devil! He's the one who brought the Day of Pain! He found the world at peace, and beautiful, and he destroyed it!"

"He's dead, Lared. He had nothing to do with the Day of Pain."

"If he *had* been there, he would have done it."

"Yes."

"And he would have come here to gloat, to see how much we suffered at his hands, the way he came to Nuber!"

"Yes."

And then another realization more terrible than the first. "He would have come to see us, the way that you and Justice came."

Jason said nothing.

Lared got up and ran to the cliff and began to climb. Not the safe way, up the crevice, but the dangerous way, the quick way that he used when the rocks were dry and his feet were bare.

"No, Lared," Jason said. "Not that way."

Lared did not answer, just moved even faster, though his fingers had to fight for purchase and his feet kept slipping. Higher up the cliff, it would matter more, but Lared didn't care.

"Lared, I can find the safe way in your mind, you won't harm me by going this way, you'll hurt only yourself."

Lared stopped, clinging to the rock. "That's the only person that a good man would ever willingly hurt!"

So Jason began to climb up after him. And not the safe way, either. Step for step, he followed Lared up the most dangerous part of the cliff.

But Lared would not quit. He couldn't, now—going back down this way would be far more dangerous than going on. So he climbed, more slowly now, more carefully, brushing the snow from each handhold, each foothold if he could, trying to make the way clear to Jason, safe for him as he came up afterward. At last Lared lay at the top of the cliff, reaching down to help Jason up the last difficult clamber. They knelt beside each other on the brink, looking down over the forest below them. In the distance they could see the fields and cookfire smoke of Flat Harbor. Behind them the forest loomed as deep, as black and white as ever.

"More trees to girdle?" Jason asked.

"No more dreams of Doon," said Lared.

"I can't tell this story without him," Jason said.

"No more of his memories. I hate him. I don't want to remember being him. No more dreams of Doon."

Jason studied him a moment. Looking in my mind, aren't you! Lared shouted silently. Well, see how much I mean it! I would never do what Doon would do—

"Don't you understand, at all, why he did it?"

I don't want to understand it.

"Mankind is more than just these billions of people. Together we're all one soul, and that soul was dead."

"He killed it."

"He resurrected it. He broke it into little parts that had to change, to grow, to become something new. We used to call it the Empire of the Thousand Worlds, even though there were only some three hundred planets with populations. But Doon fulfilled the name for us—it wasn't all destruction. He sent out huge colony ships, spreading mankind farther and farther from Capitol, so that when the end came, when he destroyed Capitol and ended starships for three thousand years, there truly were a thousand worlds, like a thousand spider balls, each one teeming with its billion people, each one finding its own way to be mankind.''

And how many people were grateful to him? Were they as glad as Clany's mother, perhaps?

''It has been more than ten thousand years since then, and his name lives on as one of the devil's names. No, they weren't glad of it at all. Is the apple tree glad when you cut it off to graft it into the wild-apple root?''

A man is not a tree.

''As you are to the apple tree, Lared, Abner Doon was to mankind. He pruned, he grafted, he transplanted, he burned over the old dead branches, but the orchard thrives.''

Lared stood. ''There are more trees to girdle. If we hurry, we can make the third night's hut tonight, and save ourselves some wattling.''

''No more dreams of Abner Doon, I promise.''

''No more dreams at all. I'm through.''

''If you wish,'' Jason said.

But Lared knew that Jason agreed because he figured Lared would relent. And Lared knew that he was right. He would not dream of Abner anymore, but of Jason he would dream. He had to know how that child became this man.

So when the trees were girdled and they came home, two days earlier than usual because they had worked so well together, Lared went to his penbox and opened it, and cleaned the pens, and said, ''We write tomorrow, so give me dreams tonight.''

5
The End of Sleep

The tinker was a cheerful man, and he loved to sing. He knew a thousand songs, he liked to say, a thousand songs, and all but six of them were too filthy to sing in front of ladies.

Truth was he knew dozens, and if Sala's work was done, she'd sit at his feet and sing along with him—she had a memory for words and melodies, and her sweet voice with the tinker's piping tenor were a sound to hear, and upstairs where he wrote for hours each day Lared liked to hear them. Liked it so well that every now and then Jason would say, "The world won't end if you take a breath now and then," and they'd go downstairs and tool the leatherwork that always waited, while the women spun and wove and whispered and Sala and the tinker sang.

"Will you sing?" Sala asked Justice.

Justice shook her head and kept on with her weaving. She was not good with her hands, and Mother only let her do roughspun cloth, the sort of stuff that hardly mattered. The fine wool for shirts and trousers, that was done by cleverer hands; and above all Justice was never let to touch a spinning wheel. The village

93

women kept three of them, besides Mother's own, in the common room of the inn during winter—because there were no travelers, it was the gathering place for Flat Harbor. Each day when they bundled against the cold and came, the women each brought three good faggots for the fire and a pear and apple, or half a loaf, or a rind of cheese for nooning, and they made a feast of it. The men ate after, at a separate table, a hot meal that somehow seemed less cheery than the laughter from the cold table where the women ate. It was the way of things—women had their society, and the men had theirs. But poor Justice, thought Lared, she belongs to neither.

It *was* sad, for Justice made no effort at all to learn the language, and so while she understood everything—far more than anyone said, in fact—she never spoke a word to anyone, except through Sala or, occasionally, Lared—but usually Sala, for they were always together. Ever since Justice had tasted the pain of the burning man on the raft, from that time on Sala was Justice's comfort, her company, her voice. Of all the women, only little Sala seemed to love her.

So while Sala and the tinker sang, Justice listened intently, and Lared understood that Justice was, after all, capable of love. He could not see into her mind, as Jason could, to see she was drawn as much to the tinker as to Sala.

The tinker was a laughing man, of average height and profound but solid belly, and he alone did not treat Justice as if she were strange. Indeed, he must have made a point of making sure his eyes always included her as he looked from face to face around the room, that his ribald comments were directed as often to her as any other woman in the place; and Lared also understood if his smile seemed to fall on Justice more often than on any other woman. Justice *was* young, and none of her teeth had rotted, and she had a pleasant body and a face that in certain lights was beautiful, for all its sternness. The winter was long, and this woman seemed unattached, so why not try for her? Lared was old enough to understand *that* game. But the chance of playing heat the sheets with Justice—well, if the tinker did *that* he was more of a miracle worker than Jason. And I don't care *who* overhears my thoughts, I'll think what I like all the same.

"Think what you like," Jason said, "but Justice might surprise you. She's lost more in her life than *you* have, so she has a right to be stern—and a right to love whomever she likes, whenever she likes. Begrudge her nothing, Lareled."

To Lared's surprise, he *did* care who overheard his thoughts. Angrily he closed his penbox. "Do you *always* listen to my thoughts? When I strain over the hole in the privy, are you there, feeling what I feel? When my father takes me through the most sacred steps of a new man, will you be at his side, along with me?"

Jason raised his eyebrows. "I'm getting older, Lared. If I'm with you in the privy house, it's to recall how easy it is for a young man, compared to the work *I* go through."

"Well, stop it!"

"You don't know what straining *is*."

"*Stop it!*"

From downstairs came Mother's voice. "What's going on up there?"

"She's *your* mother," Jason whispered.

"I'm telling Jason that I hate him!" Lared called.

"Oh good," Jason whispered. "That will make everything so much easier."

But the frank answer turned away Mother's wrath. "At last you've come to your senses!" she called. "Will he go away now?"

"And will she give the jewel back?" Jason whispered.

"No he will not!" Lared called down the stairs. "He's not through studying how country bumpkins live." He closed the bedroom door and returned to the writing table. "Well, if you're ready to work, so am I."

"For your information, I have lived in far more primitive conditions than this. And loved it."

"Stay out of my mind."

"You might as well ask me to go through my days with my eyes closed, for fear I might see someone. Believe me, Lared, I've been inside some of the foulest minds you can imagine—"

"I know! You put the memory in *me*."

"Well, yes, that's right, we did. I'm sorry. It's the only way to tell the story."

"There are other ways to tell stories. You speak the language well enough, even if you can't write it. *You* tell the story. I'll copy down what you say."

"No. I've lied too often in my life. What *you* write will sound truthful. What *I* write is always in the language of lies. For someone like me, that's all language is *for*, to tell lies. I get the truth in other ways. Other people never get the truth at all."

"Well, I'm not going to dream of Abner Doon again, and we haven't finished his part of the tale, and so you're going to *have* to tell me at least a part."

"Where did we leave off?"

"The Estorian twick."

"That feels like forever ago!"

"We took a long walk in the woods."

"Well, no matter. Obviously I didn't die. It took half a year for the wounds to heal, and after that Doon arranged for me to be trained as a starpilot. I lived as a starpilot lives from then on. Somec kept me asleep and ageless while I traveled in deep space, and the ship woke me up whenever an enemy approached. No one ever killed me, and I killed a lot of them, and so I became very famous and popular, which meant I had a lot of enemies, and eventually they tried to kill me and so Doon sent me off as commander of a colony ship."

Lared spun the feathery tip of the quill between his lips. "You're right. I can tell the story better than you."

"On the contrary. *I* know which things are worth telling at length, and which things are best skipped over."

"There are some things you *never* explained."

"Like?"

"Like what happened on that second test they gave you. I remember every bit of how much you worried about it, and nothing of how it ended."

Jason strained to push the heavy needle through the leather of Father's new boot. "Whoever tans hides around here does a miserable job."

"He does an *excellent* job. His boot leather sheds snow and lets no water in."

"It also sheds needles."

Lared was feeling annoyed and impertinent, a delicious feel-

ing which he intended to indulge freely. "Keep trying and someday you'll be strong enough."

Jason got in the spirit of the quarrel and handed him the boot.
Lared took the needle and with a circular, twisting motion drove
it quickly and smoothly through the sole. He handed the boot
back to Jason.

"Oh," said Jason.

"The test," Lared reminded him.

"I passed it. But I couldn't have. Because the answer to the
second question had only been worked out by physicists at another university a few months before. And the answer to the
third question, which I halfway solved—well, *no* one had been
able to answer it at all. That alerted the computer. And the
computer alerted Abner Doon. Woke him up, because there was
a new thing in the world, a person that might be worth collecting."

Lared was in awe. "As a child you solved a question that the
scientists couldn't answer?"

"It's not as impressive as it sounds. Somec was killing phys-
ics and mathematics, just like it was killing everything else.
They should have solved both problems centuries before. But the
finest minds were quickly put on the highest levels of somec—
months awake for six years asleep. The only people awake long
enough to accomplish anything were the second-rate minds. Almost every nation does that to themselves, given enough time.
They make their great minds so secure, they bog them down so
much with being honored and famous, that they never accomplish anything in their lives. I was *not* a genius. I was merely
clever and awake."

"So Abner collected you?"

"He watched my moments through the computers and Mother's Little Boys. They could have caught me anytime. He saw
that I went to Radamand, he overheard our conversation—the
walls *were* ears—and he saw how I shipped my own mother off
on a colony ship. Ruthlessness in a child—he found it charming."

"You had no choice."

"No, but you'd be amazed at how often people who have no

choice act as if they had one, and lose everything because they could not bear to do what had to be done.''

"So then what happened?"

"No. Write what I've told you, and what you dreamed of Abner Doon—tell these stories, bare and clean, and then tonight you'll dream again."

"I hate your dreams!"

"Why? I'm not Doon."

"When I wake up I can't remember who is me and who is you."

Jason pointed to himself. "*I* am me. *You* are you."

"You never answer me."

"That was the only answer. Whatever is contained within your body, whatever acts your hands and feet performed, that's you. And if you remember my acts, then that is you, too."

"I never sent my mother to a world where I'd never see her again."

"No," Jason said. "No, you never did."

"Then why am I so ashamed of myself for doing it?"

"Because you have a soul, Lared. They found it out in early experiences with somec. Volunteers would go under somec, and lose their memories, and then when they were revived, they dumped someone else's memories into their minds. It worked fine with rats. But then, it's hard to think of a rat who would do something that another rat wouldn't mind doing. They woke up remembering a lifetime of performing acts that they could not bear to remember having performed. Why? They had no bench-mark to measure against—as far as they knew, it was their own life. But they couldn't bear to remember having made so many *wrong* choices. There was something that remained in a human mind even after somec had taken everything else, the part of you that says, 'This is the sort of thing I do,' and 'This is the sort of thing I do not do.' The part of you that names you. Your soul. Your will. All the old words.''

"And it lives after you when you die?"

"I didn't say that. It merely survives when somec takes everything else. If you would let me show you a story from Doon's own life—"

"No."

"Then I'll tell you. He loved a woman once. A bright and clever woman who was ruled by an invalid father and a spiritually crippled mother. All her life, this girl had bent and twisted her life to their bidding, because she loved them. It ruined everything, cut her off from everyone, except Doon, because he had his remarkable ability to understand human nature—without even the Swipe—and he saw her and knew what was locked away behind her parents' door. So he loved her. But she wouldn't leave her family to go with him."

"To marry him?"

"It was nothing like what *you* call marriage. But she wouldn't do it. She couldn't bear to leave her parents without the support she gave them—without her, they would have truly lived in hell. So she stayed. Fifteen years, until they finally died. And in that time she had become miserable, bitter, savage, and she was no longer interested in love, even when Doon came back to her and gave it to her. So he played a trick on her. Back when they were considering, uh, marriage, he had arranged for her to have her memory bubbled for storage, but she backed out before they ever gave her somec. He saved that bubble all those years, and now he put her under somec—he had corrupted the Sleephouse by then—and put the old memories into her head when she awoke. Then he told her what he had done—that she had cared for her parents to the end, but now she could go on with her life without remembering the years that had so embittered her."

"And so they lived happily?"

"She couldn't stand it. She couldn't bear to live without remembering every agonizing moment of her parents' decline. She was the sort of person who had to fulfill every bit of her responsibility, even if it destroyed her—she could not live without the memory of her own destruction. It wasn't the sort of thing she could do."

"Her soul."

"Yes. She made him put her full, true memories back into her. Even though it meant erasing the few good, happy months they had. The pain was more valuable to her than the joy."

"She sounds like the sickening kind of person Abner would love."

"You are so kindhearted, Lared. You have sympathy for everyone."

"Who would want to keep pain and throw away happiness?"

"A good question," Jason said. "Which you must answer before the end of this book. Now write these stories, and dream tonight."

"What will I dream about?"

"Don't you want it to come as a surprise?"

"No."

"You will dream of how Jason Worthing, the famous warrior and starpilot, ended up in command of a colony ship and lost a battle, for the first time in his life."

"I'd rather write that than the things you've told me to write today."

"Sometimes you have to tell the dull parts of the story so that the good parts will mean something when they come. Go on, write. Your father needs these boots before we go out lumbering next week."

"You're coming with us?"

"I wouldn't miss it for the world."

So Lared wrote, and Jason sewed. In the evening Father tried on his new boots and pronounced them good. In the night Lared dreamed.

Starpilots were young for a long time. On each voyage, which might take years, even at several times the speed of light, the pilot slept, only waking when the ship alerted him. It could be another ship, it could be planetfall, it could be some unexpected hazard or malfunction, but usually a pilot slept from three days after launch until three days before the voyage's end. It was rare for planetside duty to take longer than a few weeks. The result was that starpilots were at unbelievably high somec levels—an average of three weeks awake for every five years under. Only Mother, the Empress, slept more and woke less. No politician or actor had more prestige.

And of all starpilots, none was better known or more admired than Jazz Worthing, the hero of Ballaway, the darling of the trueloops.

Therefore, as Jason well knew, no starpilot was more hated

and envied, because no other starpilot so symbolized the Empire to those who loathed it.

So it was no surprise to him when he came to port at Capitol and found himself surrounded by people who hated him. What surprised him was that most of them planned to kill him. Things were getting out of hand. What had Doon been doing these last twelve years?

Only Capitol, of all the worlds, could afford a spaceport large enough for starships actually to land. It was part of the majesty of Capitol, the loops they sent out to every planet, showing the tugs lowering the starships into the gaping bays in the metal surface of the world. Almost every landing had *some* loopers there to watch. Jazz's landing had every looper, hired or freelance, who could get free of grisly murders or raids from wall rats. And crowds—

Thousands of people lining the tier on tier of balconies around the bay. Jazz knew they were there before the door broke open; without trying, he could feel their adulation. As always before he cracked the door he paused and asked himself, Do I need this? Have I come to live for this? And, as always, the answer was: No. I don't think so. I hope not. No.

His agent, Hop Noyock, greeted him as he stepped through the door. It was one of Hop's perks, to be featured on trueloops throughout the Thousand Worlds. It got him into an amazing number of parties while Jazz was gone. Hop was that rare creature, a starpilot's agent who didn't hate his client. After all, Hop had aged some dozen years since their relationship had begun, and Jazz had aged scarcely six months. Hop was going bald. Sagging a little in the belly. But he was loyal and intelligent and hard-working, a combination few agents ever achieved. Besides, Jazz liked him. He had grown up as a wall rat, and done well enough in the crawlspaces that he had the money and connections to buy papers and get into the corridors before he was eighteen. Doon had found him. Never met him, of course, but he was aware of him, and when Jazz decided he needed an agent to handle his Capitol business, Doon recommended him.

But Hop was taking no pleasure in the cheers of the crowd, not this time. Oh, he strutted and bowed and waved like the wall rat he was, but his heart wasn't in it. Jazz went into Hop's mind and found almost at once what was bothering him.

Hop had been wakened only two days before, when word reached the Sleephouse that his client was arriving. And they brought him a folded, sealed note. A memory slip, which the Sleephouse people kept on hand for the paranoid—people who thought of something after their memories were bubbled and before the drug and couldn't stand the thought of losing the idea. Hop had never used one before, thought they were foolish. But there it was, in his handwriting, a note that said, "Someone trying to kill Jazz. Warn."

Hop couldn't figure it out, and neither could Jason. How could he find it out just before going under? Did someone in the Sleephouse tell him? Absurd—they had no contact with the outside world, the monks and nuns of the god of sleep. What could they tell him? And no one else had access. Hop decided, therefore, that it must be that just before he slept he put together something that he had already known, combined facts so that he realized some plot on Jason's life. For the past two days he had been trying desperately to think of something he noticed on his last waking that might have been a clue. He had come up with nothing, and now Jazz was here, and he knew no more than the note he had written to himself.

Jazz knew something that Hop didn't know. He knew a man who could walk into the Sleephouse and tell something to someone whose bubble was finished, something that had to be written down. The warning came from Doon.

It was two hours before Hop could get away from the loopers long enough to tell Jazz about the note. By then Jason had already found a dozen people in the crowds around him who were in on one or another conspiracy to kill him. One was even armed. It was easy to evade him, and the others had cleverer plans than to pellet him in the presence of three hundred loopers.

"Don't worry," Jason said. "It's probably nothing."

"I hope you're right. But I don't write myself notes too often. It must mean something."

"How do *you* know how smart you are between bubbling and the somec? Nobody remembers."

"I'm always very smart."

It was the beginning of a hectic few days. Jazz couldn't go to his rooms at all—there was almost always someone waiting inside to kill him, and Jazz found out about several plots to lay traps for him. Finally, things came to a head at a party held by a former lifeloop star, Arran Handully, who had given up public fornication in favor of a life of ostentatious gentility. She was deep in one of the more dangerous plots to kill Jazz. For once, sitting against a wall with no one attempting to talk to him, Jazz had a chance to study the question of why all these murder plots were coming at once. He decided to do a little searching in depth. The mind of Arran Handully was convenient.

Jazz had to die—it was one of the foremost imperatives in her mind. But why? Here was where the surprise came: Jazz's death was the beginning of a coup. Not that Jazz had any political power, of course. Just that he symbolized all that Arran hated about Capitol, about the society that had driven the only man she had ever loved to suicide many years before. It was a charming and tragic story, the death of her lover, and Jazz found himself exploring her mind for the sheer pleasure of it, carelessly ignoring the dozen other threats at the party. While he studied her, she came up to him.

"Commander Worthing," she said.

"Call me Jazz," he said, using the charming smile that played so well on the loops. Of course, there were a few dozen clandestine loopers taking it all in, and Jazz knew enough to please his public, even when the loop was being taken illegally.

"And I'm Arran. You are something of an unexpected guest, Jazz. We didn't know you'd be in Capitol until yesterday. It was kind of you to come."

"The pleasure," said Jazz, "is mine. I have only seen one of your lifeloops, but it was enough to entrance me."

"Oh, which one is that?"

"I forget the name," Jazz said—he never knew it—"but it was one you did with an old actor named—named—ah yes, Hamilton Ferlock."

She felt stricken, but showed nothing. Ham Ferlock was the lover who had killed himself when she refused to break character on a twenty-one-day straight-through loop. It was cruel of Jazz to bring him up—but then, she was planning to kill him.

When? Why not now? A servant came with a single goblet of wine.

"No matter what we might plan," said Arran sweetly, "you are the guest of honor at any party you attend. I give you the cup of the night." She held a silver cup in her hand, and she held it toward his lips, for him to drink. The servant maneuvered closer, so he could take the goblet from the tray and put it to Arran's lips. Jason took the goblet, but refused the cup.

"How can I take such an honor at your hands?" he asked.

"I insist," she said. "No one deserves it more."

"What a remarkable woman you are, Arran. Such courage— to dare to poison me at your own party."

If he had been more watchful, he could have avoided this moment. But now the plots were coming together at once. More than a few of the guests at the party were armed; every exit was watched. The only person here who knew the secret ways out of the room was Arran herself, and they were all keyed to her palm. So he selected the most melodramatic of the would-be assassins, a young clothing designer who had created Arran's costume for the evening. Jazz stepped toward him. He was the murderer of choice, because he meant to be theatrical about it.

"Fritz Kapock," the young man said, to introduce himself. "How dare you accuse Arran Handully of such a foul crime?"

"Because it's true," said Jazz.

"Apologize, Jazz, and let's get the hell out of here," said Hop quietly.

"Rapiers or pellets?" asked Kapock. Oh, he meant to do it according to the rules, didn't he? Jazz laughed at him and accepted the duel with rapiers.

One thing led to another. Jazz didn't kill the young man, mainly because Mother's Little Boys arrived while the duel was in progress. No one had called them—Doon had sent them himself. So Abner is somehow responsible for all this sudden interest in my death. If only I were sure that Doon knows what he's doing.

Mother's Little Boys created enough havoc that he escaped, with Arran's unwilling help. Jazz had only one objective—to find Doon and point out to him that Jazz's love for him did not extend to a willingness to die for him. Along the way he shed Hop and

Arran, figuring they'd be safer away from him, and Hop knew well enough how to take care of himself. And at last he was face to face with Doon, beside the lake in his private garden.

"Very well done, to get away," said Doon. "Some of their plots were quite thorough. You were almost in danger several times."

Jason fingered the cut Kapock had given him on his arm. "What are you doing, Doon?"

"Oh, just isolating and bringing out the best people of Capitol. *You* can get inside their heads and find out who they are. I have to work out little tests like this."

"Next time just ask me."

"I look for things even you wouldn't be able to find."

"It shouldn't be too hard. Your test for the best people is whoever wants me dead."

"What do you expect? You're the foremost symbol of a detestable empire."

"I am what you made me. We're all what you made us."

Doon was genuinely hurt. "Surely you don't think I'm God, do you? I'm just one element in your environment, that's all."

"In theirs, maybe. In mine you're more."

"Because you love me so deeply?" asked Doon, mocking.

"Because the most important events in my life happened to you. The only woman who mattered to me was your little piece of unrequited love. All my best triumphs were your triumphs, all my strongest dreams were yours—"

"Not true."

"Of course it's true! Your memories are more present in my mind than my own!"

"And why is that?" asked Doon.

"Because you cared so much. You have such a strong sense of purpose, even when you don't even know what it is you're trying to accomplish—all your memories *mattered* to the person who went through the experience."

"And *your* own past? Is that nothing? Battles, struggles, fear, conflict—"

"What conflict? What fear? Except for one long moment with a little beast in your garden, Doon, I have never been afraid. A bit tense, to see how the game would go, but the outcome was never in doubt. In battle I could always hear the other fellow's plans as he thought of them, in conversation I always know the other person's hidden thoughts, I've never had to wonder or guess—''

"Your life is such a *bore*. Poor Jason."

"There are times when I wake up thinking that I'm you. I look around the inside of the ship and I think, why am I here? I look in the mirror and I'm surprised to see this face. This face is from the loops. This face is Jazz Worthing, but I remember very clearly, I am Abner Doon, I am the one who won the confidence of Mother herself and told her when it might be a good time to die—''

As he spoke, Jason looked in Doon's mind to see if indeed the time was up. Abner had wakened the Empress herself, had met with her, revealed himself to her many years ago. "I will wreck your empire," he told her. "I thought it only fair to let you know." She took it calmly, perhaps even happily, and gave her consent, on one condition—that he tell her when he was about to do it, so she could be awake to watch. Now Jason looked to see if he meant to tell her soon. To see if Doon was planning to end the Empire now.

"Of course not," said Doon. "I have too much to accomplish before that. Give me at least another hundred years."

What did he have to accomplish? He had been sending out colony ships for centuries now. But these that he was sending now, they were the ones that held his hope.

"Mankind is my experiment," said Jason. "Cut the threads that bind the stars together, and each world will spin on its own for a while. Perhaps thousands of years, until someone comes up with a stardrive that needs no sleep, and then we'll see what mankind has become in a thousand different cultures."

"That's *my* speech," said Doon.

"That's all right," Jason said. "You've been playing puppet with us all. My voice, your words."

"Are you angry?"

"Why me? Why am I singled out for the joy of being one of your twelve oddities?"

"I don't know."

"I know you don't know. I know what you know, and I know

what you don't know. I even know what you don't know that you don't know. I can find things in your head that you've forgotten ever knowing. You have been planning this for me for the fifty years that I've been gone, and you don't even know what you expect from it!"

"I'm sending you farther than I'm sending anyone else. I'm keeping no record that your ship was ever sent. Officially, all the traitors and conspirators going with you were executed. No one will look for you, not until they find the message that will be released a few thousand years from now. Your little world will have longer to develop than any other."

"What do you expect, evolution in a few thousand years?"

"Not evolution, breeding."

In Doon's mind, Jason saw himself as Doon saw him. With the eyes pure unflecked blue. Like his father's eyes, and *his* father's eyes.

"The stud for a world of Swipes, is that it?"

"*Sire* is the more delicate word."

"I wasn't raised on a farm."

"You and your family are an anomaly. Your gifts are far more reliable, far more extensive than any known strain of telepathy. Why not see what happens to it in isolation?"

"Then why didn't you isolate me? Why give me a colony full of people who have spent their last few wakings plotting to kill me?"

Doon smiled. "It appealed to my sense of proportion. It would be too easy for you to run a normal colony. It would hardly be enough to keep you awake all day."

"It's kind of you to keep me so alert."

Doon took Jason by the hair at the back of his neck and drew him down, drew him close, and face to face he said, "Surpass me, Jason. Do more than I have done."

"Is this a contest? Then why not start even? Three hundred and thirty-three colonists against one ship's captain—I don't like the odds."

"With you," said Doon, "no one is even."

"I don't want to go."

"Jason, you have no choice."

Jason saw that it was true. Doon had already given out more

than enough proof that Jason was a Swipe. He would be arrested the moment he left Doon's personal protection; if he tried to escape, where would he hide, when everyone on Capitol knew his face?

"The puppet," Jason said, "wishes to be free."

"You *are* free. Stay and die, go and live—you have your choice."

"What choice is that!"

"What do you expect, an infinite selection? To have a choice at all is to be free—even when the choice is between two terrible things. Which is most terrible, Jason? Which do you hate the most? Then choose the other and be glad."

So Jason chose to go; Doon had his way again.

"It's not so bad," Doon said. "Once you've gone, you won't have me manipulating things anymore."

"The only star on the journey through the night," said Jason. "It will comfort me as my colonists sharpen their knives in the darkness." Yet it was no comfort. To be without Doon, that was what frightened Jason most. Doon was the foundation for his life, for good or ill; ever since Doon had found him, Jason had known that nothing could go too wrong in his life—Doon was watching.

Now when he stumbled, who would lift him up? This was freedom after all, Jason realized, because from now on no one would save him from the consequences of his own acts. It wasn't freedom that I yearned for, was it? It was childhood that I wanted, and Doon is barring me from my refuge; he has been my father all these years, and now he's thrusting me away. "I'll never forgive you for this," Jason said.

"That's all right," Doon said. "I never expected to be loved." Then he smiled oddly, and Jason knew he was not as cheerful as he pretended. "But I love *you*," Doon said.

"I'm so much like you that to love me is purest narcissism." Jason was not trying to be kind.

"It's what isn't me in you that I most love," said Doon. "Where I have torn down, you will build up. I have made the chaos for you, and the world is without form, and void. You are the light that will shine on the face of the deep."

"I hate it when you say things you've been practicing up to say."

"Good-bye, Jason. Go meet your colonists—day after tomorrow they go under somec, and then you're on your way."

Lared put down his pen and sprinkled sand on the parchment to dry the ink. "Now I know why I wish you had never come here," he said.

Jason sighed.

"It's like you said. My strongest memories are yours."

"What I said was wrong," Jason answered. "Just because you remember me saying it doesn't mean it was true, or that I still believe now what I believed then."

"Sometimes I even forget and try to look into people's minds, and I can't, even though I remember doing it. It's like someone cut off my hand. Or burst my ears, or cut out my tongue."

"Still," Jason said. He held up the axe handle he was carving. "I cut the wood however I like, but it's the grain that decides the strength and shape of it. You can add and subtract memories from people, but it isn't just your memory that makes you who you are. There's something in the grain of the mind. They found it out from the start, when they tried dumping someone else's bubble into a person's brain. All his experiences, all his past—and the mind that came out of somec was empty, wasn't it? But the new memories wouldn't fit. He remembered only being this other person, he *believed* he was the other person, but he could not bear remembering it. It was not himself."

"What did he do?"

"They—there were several of them. They all went mad. There was nothing right in their past, how could they stay sane?"

"Will I go mad?"

"No."

"How can you be sure?"

"Because no matter how much of me you remember, me or anybody else, there is at the root of your mind a place where you are safe, a place where you are yourself, where your memories are right, and belong to you."

"But it changes me, to remember being you."

"And me," Jason said. "Do you think I'm the same man, knowing the insides of other people's lives the way I do?"

"No. But are you sane?"

Jason was startled, then laughed aloud. "No," he said. "God help me, but you ask the truest questions! Justice was right to pick you, you've got a mind like ice. No, I'm not sane, I'm utterly mad, but my madness is the sum of all the people I have known, and sometimes I think that I have known all the people in the world—at least all the kinds of people that it's possible to be."

He seemed so delighted, so exuberant, so glad to be himself that Lared couldn't help but smile. "How can all that fit inside your head?"

Jason held up the half-finished axe handle. "As tight as the handle in the axe. And there's still room to drive in a wedge or two. Always room for more, to set it tight."

The first heavy snowfall did not come, and did not come. "Bad sign," said the tinker. "It means the sky is saving up." And he climbed on the roof to mend the flashing around the chimney, and took out the flue and rebuilt it so it fit tight again, no leaking. "Do yourselves a favor with the doors and windows—make sure all the shutters are strong, and the doors fit tight, and caulk the walls."

Father listened to the tinker, went outside and looked at the bright cold sky, and announced that no other work mattered until the house was tight. The whole village then set aside their other work and closed their houses. The littlest children slapped more daub on the weak places of the walls, down low; doors were tooled to fit tighter; shutters were remade; and in a time of such work, Jason and Lared found themselves taken again from the work of pen and parchment. They did the ladder work together, fastening in place the shutters of the upstairs windows. Jason climbed the ladder the right way; Lared, who had always climbed like a cat, went up the ladder the wrong way, and quickly, and then perched on the sill of the beams that poked out of the wall of the house. He had no fear of falling.

"Be careful," Jason said. "There's no one to catch you if you fall."

"I don't fall," Lared said.

"Things have changed."

"I'll hold tight."

As they worked, Jason told stories. About the people of his colony. "I called them in, one by one, and while they sweated through interviews that meant nothing, I found out from their memories just what kind of person each was. Some were haters, the sort of people you'd expect to find in any conspiracy to kill. Others were merely afraid, others were dedicated to a cause— but I didn't care that much why they had wanted me dead. I needed to know more the purpose of their lives, what made them choose their choices."

Like Garol Stipock, a brilliant scientist-turned-engineer, who devised the machinery that could diagnose a planet from its ore to its weather in a few orbits. He thought of himself as an atheist, rejecting the strong, fanatic religion his parents had forced on him as a child; in fact, even as he worked hard to reject and break down any authoritarian system he could find, he was still the child who believed that God had definite ideas about what mankind ought to be, and Garol Stipock would give up anything and everything to try to achieve that ideal.

Like Arran Handully, who had devoted her life to entertainment, subsuming her own identity in her lifeloop role, living day after day, minute by minute, in the constant scrutiny of the loops, so that people could circle around a stage and watch her life from every angle. She was the greatest of the lifeloop actresses, and under it all was the desire for others to be happy— when she retired, she never missed the audience herself, for it was not her own need she had meant to satisfy when she performed.

Like Hux. A dedicated middle-level bureaucrat, on a two-up, one-down somec level. Everything he touched went smoothly, every job was accomplished on time and under budget. Yet despite the great esteem that superiors and underlings alike had for him, he had refused promotion after promotion. He was married to the same wife, had the same block of rooms, ate the same meals, played the same ballsports with the same friends, year after year after year.

"So why did he join a revolution?"

"He didn't know that himself."

"But *you* knew."

"Motives aren't remembered, especially the ones you don't understand yourself—I can't just find a place in his memory where all his unknown purposes are laid out for me to see. To others, to himself he seemed to have only one purpose in life: to keep everything the same, to resist change. But that need was just the outward face of what he wanted most: stability and happiness for everyone he knew. He was no Radamand, remaking the world to his own convenience."

As Lared worked, a face came into his mind, a lantern-jawed face with a hint of weakness around the eyes. Hux, he knew. Justice was showing him the pictures as Jason told the tale. Where are you, Justice? Working somewhere in silence, as always, listening to us talk, with almost never a word to say yourself?

"You're not listening," Jason said.

"You're not talking." Lared answered.

"Put in the pin, my arms are breaking holding this shutter."

Lared put in the pin. The shutter swung smoothly again. Together they set to fastening it down, top and bottom, and barring it from the outside. It was a north-facing window, and the northwest wind had torn shutters away before. Jason talked on as they drove the wooden pins that would hold the shutters closed. "Hux wanted an order of life in which all were reasonably content, and when it was found he didn't want it to change. He was no hypocrite—he willingly inconvenienced himself, sacrificed much in order to keep his corner of Capitol secure and stable. He was also bright enough to see how somec undid and destroyed everything. Separated families as they straggled their separate routes across the years, ended friendships as one went to the Sleephouse while the other stayed up, not having merited sleep—somec kept the Empire stable, but only at the cost of unbalancing almost every life it touched."

"So he wanted the Empire to go on without somec?"

"One of the few in my colony who didn't long for sleep. And then Linkeree—I remember them together because of what happened later. Link was as opposite to Hux as a man can be, on the outside. He had no friends, no close associates, no family.

He was the only person in my colony who had never been on somec in his life, except for the voyage from his home world. He had been confined in a mental institution for years before coming; his parents had been confusing, possessive, cruel, and exploitative—in cases like that it was usually the children who ended up being locked away. So Linkeree even believed himself to be half-crazy, a loner who loved no one and needed no one."

"But you knew better."

"I always know better. It's the curse of my life." Jason frowned. "If you don't hold on with at least one hand while you're balancing on only one foot up here, I'm going to throw you down myself to end the suspense."

"I told you I won't fall. What was the truth about Linkeree?"

"He had an overdeveloped sense of empathy. He could imagine other people's suffering, and felt it himself. His mother had used that against him all his life, torturing him with guilt for all the suffering of her life. The only thing that freed him was seeing what real suffering was." And again an image came into Lared's mind. But not a face this time. It was an infant lying in a clear place in tall, knifelike grass, left to starve or freeze or be devoured by the creatures of the night. With the image came a feeling of desperate compassion—I can do nothing, and yet I must do something or not be myself—and finally the image gave way to another, to a group of uncivilized tribesmen kneeling in a circle in the grass, taking the child's corpse apart in a ritual; I understand, the child must die for the sake of the tribe, the child's death means life. It was a moment of clear understanding for Linkeree, for in the infant he saw himself, torn and broken to keep his mother alive. I am not insane; she is the one who is mad, and I am suffering for her. But does she love me as these tribesmen love the infant they have killed? The answer was no, and so he left, escaped from his world and went to Capitol, a place where everyone looked for someone else to suffer for them. Linkeree was a living sacrifice; he suffered to expiate the guilt of all who touched him.

"Hold tightly when such a vision comes," said Jason. "I think we shouldn't do this when we're perched up here."

"I'm not so fragile as that," said Lared. But the infant stayed in his mind, lying there in the grass with savage insects hanging from its naked body.

"Linkeree was not a loner, after all. He was like Hux, in a way—all he cared about was other people. It made Hux sociable and stable; it made Linkeree shy and skittish; but I knew them both for what they were, and I said to myself, "These I will make my leaders. Because power in their hands would be used for the good of all, and not to please themselves. Or rather, if they pleased themselves they would please others as a matter of course, because they could not be happy in the knowledge of others who were miserable.""

"No one is that good," said Lared. "Everyone wants what he wants."

"You are that good," said Jason. "That's what goodness is, Lareled, and if there were no goodness in people, mankind would still be confined to loping across a savannah somewhere on Earth, watching the elephants rule, or some other more compassionate species."

"I don't know," said Lared. "I've never cared much about other people's pain."

"Because they didn't feel any. But you still hear a burned-up child screaming, you still feel a man's blood pumping from a wounded foot. Don't tell me you know nothing of compassion."

"What about you?" asked Lared. "Are *you* good?"

No, came the answer in his mind. It took a moment for Lared to realize that it was Justice who had answered, not Jason. No, Jason is not good.

"She's right," Jason said. "It's the whole meaning of my life, that I inflict suffering on others."

"Did you cause the Day of Pain?" asked Lared.

"It was not my choice," said Jason. "But I believe it was the right choice."

Lared did not say another word that afternoon, thinking how the man who worked beside him approved of what had changed in the world since the Day of Pain. And that night he dreamed.

Jazz awakened to see the lid of the coffin sliding back, the amber light winking at the edge of his vision. His bubble must have just finished dumping his memories back into his head, and his body was hot and sweating, as it always was when he came up out of somec. Push-ups, sit-ups, running in place made him alert and quick again.

Only then did he notice that it was not the amber light flashing in his coffin, but the red. Had it been red all along, or had it just changed? No time to decide the question now; in a moment he was at the controls, and the ship was telling him what it knew. An enemy ship had been hiding behind a planet, almost as if it expected his approach; two projectiles were already launched.

Even as Jason's fingers sent two of his ship's four torpedoes into space, his mind searched for and found the enemy captain, the mind controlling the missiles that dodged and pitched and weaved their way toward him. The missiles were far more maneuverable than Jason's massive colony ship, but Jason knew where the missiles were going, and moment by moment Jason drew himself farther out of the enemy's way. In the meantime, his own missiles homed in on the enemy, anticipating her attempts to dodge. For once Jason didn't care if anyone noticed that he knew things he could not possibly know, that he was a Swipe. He would not be going back to Capitol again, and so at last he could fight with his full ability.

Just before the enemy's ship exploded in a globe of light, the enemy captain knew that she would die, and in that moment she took grim satisfaction from the fact that even if she died, Claren would finish off the enemy.

Claren. She was not alone. Jason and his enemy had been concentrating on their duel, routing their missiles and their own ships; only now did he realize that there was another ship, still behind the planet, which had been using the first ship as its eyes to route its own attack. Jason's ship was tracking the enemy missiles, which were already near. Desperately Jason searched for Claren, the enemy who was so close to success. He found Claren just in time. Or it would have been just in time, except that Claren was no longer controlling his missiles—when the first ship blew up, he had lost his means of seeing and therefore controlling his missiles' flight. They were homing on Jason automatically, which meant their course was absolutely predictable and easy to dodge, except that Jason had wasted too much time looking for the captain's mind, and while he could avoid one missile, he could not avoid the other. It would strike him. Its high-intensity light would carve through his ship's armor; the skin of the ship would peel back from the wound and allow the missile to enter, to plunge into the core of the stardrive and there, gently, explode. A pathetic little explosion, really, but almost anything would upset the delicate balance of impossible forces, and the ship would explode.

Jason saw his future in a moment, and in that moment decided that he would prefer any alternative to utter destruction. The missile was too close from him to move his whole, massive ship out of the way. But the payload, a slender shaft projecting forward from the massive stardrive, *it* would not go off like a pent-up star if the missile struck and exploded there. Almost instinctively Jason swung himself into the path of the missile. Somewhere back along the kilometer-long tube behind him, the missile would strike, colonists would die, and Jason found himself hoping that the missile would kill only some of the people, and not harm the all-important animals and seeds and supplies and equipment at all.

Impact. The ship shuddered from the distant explosion; alarms went off on the control panels; but the explosion was far enough from the stardrive, shielded enough that the drive was able to cope with the disturbance, balance itself before an unstoppable reaction destroyed everything.

Alive, thought Jason. Then he set about killing Claren. The enemy remained out of sight behind a planet, but Jason used Claren's own eyes to track the missiles when they were in the lee of the world, in a place where Claren knew he would be safe, but the missiles came on as if they had intelligence of their own, as if they could read his mind, for wherever he dodged the missiles were already headed for his new course, and in a few moments he was dead.

I don't like knowing my enemy's name, thought Jason.

The damage was brutal, but not unsurvivable, or so it seemed at first. The 333 colonists were arranged in three parallel corridors at the back of the payload, each of the three corridors completely shielded from the others, to help protect against the whole colony being wiped out in such an event as this. One corridor was a total loss—it had been peeled open to space and the coffins had burst open and erupted with corpses. A second corridor seemed untouched—the bodies all lay peacefully within their coffins. But the controls had been seared as the missile canted into the ship, and none of them would ever be revived.

Still, the third corridor remained, and 111 people would be enough to start the colony; with the supplies and equipment unharmed, they would survive. They would accomplish less work the first year, but they would have all the more supplies on the ship to keep them going for a few more years, till things were up to speed. It was sad that so many had died, but the colony had not been undone.

So Jason thought, until he reached the very back of the payload, where the bubbles were stored in a carefully protected environment.

That was where the missile had actually exploded.

Fourteen bubbles had survived intact. Nine from the corridor that had exploded, four from the corridor whose residents would never wake up, and only one bubble from the surviving colonists.

Only one human being left. The others would be incapable of doing anything for themselves, remembering nothing, knowing nothing. How could he deal with 111 adult-sized infants? What good were people without minds?

He walked back through the surviving corridor and looked down into the coffins at the people who, though not dead, would never again be themselves. His good friend Hop Noyock, the actress Arran Handully, he touched each coffin and remembered what he had seen within each mind, Hux, Linkeree, Wien, Sara, Ryanno, Mase, I know what you will never know again—who you are, what you have done, what you meant to be. Now what are you, if I ever wake you up? You, Kapock, with your fierce, devoted loves, what lovers will you remember now? Their names were broken with your bubble, and your past is dead.

The only bubble that survived belonged to Garol Stipock. Jason studied his face as he lay in his coffin, sleeping. Are you the one that I should waken? The one person committed to undoing authority in any form? What sort of ally would you be? Anyone's bubble but yours, if the choice had been mine. Your childhood is the one I least needed to keep in living memory.

Jason swung the ship through its change of course, but when it was done he did not sleep. Instead he studied, dumped into his head the Empire's collective wisdom on the art of colonization. All the jobs took dozens of able-bodied women and men to make them work. He plunged deeper into the library, to the books rather than the bubbles, unscrolling them in the air over the control desk, trying to find out what he could teach infants to do, how many he could support by the labor of his own hands.

Many times he almost despaired. It could not be done. The high-level technology to farm and manufacture to create a modern society required many people with strong specializations. How could he hope to educate a hundred people from infancy to advanced specialties quickly enough that they wouldn't starve while they waited to grow up?

But gradually, inevitably, the answer came. The modern economy would be impossible, but an earlier life would not. A life with simpler tools that could be made by hand; a life from fields that could be plowed by people who had not learned their algebra but could drive an ox. I can plow an acre myself, plant and harvest it, to feed myself and a few others. Just a few at a time, until the first ones have developed enough to help me with the next ones.

The only drawback was that it would take years. The ship would preserve those he had not yet wakened, but each one he brought out would be utterly unproductive for some time, and during that time would still need an adult's portion of food, of clothing, of everything, and would require frequent attention and time-consuming care. The colony would never be able to sustain more than a few of these at a time, for the economy would always be marginal, farming as they would with hand tools and animal strength.

It would take years, but perhaps, if they learned quickly enough, Jason could leave them from time to time, return to the ship and sleep for a year or two, come back just to bring new colonists from the ship, just to check and make sure the colony was running smoothly. After all, these people had been carefully chosen—the best people of Capitol, Doon had said. If some of that ability survived, despite their loss of memory, it might work. And if a few of them showed exceptional leadership ability, I could bring them aboard the ship and put them under somec again, and preserve them for a time of great need. I could—

Then Jason realized what he was doing. Planning to create a colony of ignorant peasants, using somec to create an elite class, headed by himself, of people who would withdraw from the world and return to it, years later, without having aged. All that was detestable about somec I am already planning to use again.

But only for a time, Jason told himself. Only until the colony is firmly established, only until we've recovered from the missile that has so undone us all. Then I'll destroy somec, destroy the whole ship, sink it in the bottom of the sea, and somec will disappear from my planet.

It was the only way he could think of to form the colony at all. Even at that, it would require almost unbearable amounts of work from him, especially at the first. But it could be done.

Could be done, and might provide an opportunity no one else had ever had. A chance to create a society out of nothing. To create its social institutions, its habits, its beliefs, its rituals, to design them carefully with no need to compromise with old habits, old beliefs. I can make utopia, if I have wit enough; the power is in my hands, if I can only decide what the perfect society must be.

The idea grew, and he began to write of what he thought his world might be, until at last he realized that he was happy again, excited again for the future, more than at any time before in his life. The enemy's missile undid all of Doon's designs, and for the first time in his life Jason was truly on his own, without having to account to Doon or anyone else. If he failed now, it would be his own failure; if he succeeded, it would be success for him and for every generation that followed him in his world. And it will be my world, he told himself. By accident I have been made the creator; I am the one who will put the breath of mind into these men and women; let us stay in Eden this time, and never fall.

6
Waking the Children

The house was sealed; they could all feel the difference, lying in bed in the firelight. The drafts from under the door were almost gone, so Lared felt no urgency to hide behind the low walls of his truckle bed. The heat sometimes was so great that Sala would cast off her blankets in the night.

And still the snow did not fall. The cold whined out of the north, but the only snows were scattered, a few showers that blew into corners and clung to shingles.

"When it comes, it'll hide your head," said the tinker. "I've got me a weather sense, and I know."

In the night, Lared tossed and turned with the dreams that Justice took from Jason's memory and put into his mind. But it was different now. For some reason, when he awoke, he could not easily remember what he had dreamed.

"I'm trying," he told Jason. "I know it had something to do with plowing. You were doing it all wrong or something. You were trying to drive the oxen the way you lead a well-trained horse. You weren't much of a farmer then. Is that it?"

"Of course I wasn't much of a farmer," Jason said. "It was the first time I had seen dirt in my life."

"What's dirt? Dirt is dirt."

"I see," said Jason. "That's our problem. When I brought the oxen out of the ship and put them in their plastic barn, I had never set my hand on the back of a hot, sweating beast, never felt the play of his muscles under the skin. When I hitched the plow on them, I had to discover the tricks of the straight furrow and controlling the depth of the blade myself—none of the books taught me. The ox plow and the oxen were only sent along in case of a massive power failure. Who was alive in those days who knew how to use them?"

"Even Sala knows more than you did," said Lared. How was he supposed to take it seriously?

"It stays in my mind as magnificent, hard-won discoveries. It comes to you as clumsiness in tasks you do every year without thinking. No wonder you forget."

Lared shrugged, though in fact he felt like he had failed them somehow. "I can't help it. It's not as if I didn't try to remember. Find another scribe."

"Of course not," said Jason. "Why do you think we chose you? Because you were of this world, you knew what mattered and what didn't matter. I loved the work of the soil because I had never done it before, it was all new at a time in my life when I thought I had already done everything. To you it isn't new, it's drudgery. The little things I do while you write, the axe handles, the boots, the wickerwork, it's all pleasure to me; living here with you, after all these years to be part of a village again, I love it, but what does it matter to you? So don't write it. Don't write about how I worked as hard and fast as I could to earn an hour to go wandering through the forest, collecting herbs to test in the ship's lab. Don't bother with my first tastes of real food, the way I threw up at the taste of bread after so many years of predigested pap made from algae, fish meal, soybeans, and human manure. What's that to you?"

"Don't be angry," Lared said. "I can't help it that it doesn't matter to me. I'd remember it if I could. But who would want to read about it?"

"For that matter, who'd want to read about any of it? Lared, you dream of civilization, don't you—a life of comfort and safety, with time enough to read whatever you liked, and no one to turn you into a plowman or a blacksmith if you didn't want to do it. Yet what you do—herding the trees for harvest, shuttering the windows, making sausage and strawing the ticks—that is better than any other life I've lived or seen or even heard about.''

"Only because your life's never depended on it," Lared said. "Only because you're still just pretending to be one of us."

"Maybe so," Jason said. "Just pretending, but I know my way around the forest, and I do an axe handle as well as anyone I've seen here."

Lared was afraid when Jason was angry. "I mean then. You were pretending. You must have learned over the years."

"Yes," Jason said. "A little. Not much." He was twisting horsehair into a bowstring, and his fingers were quick and sure. "But I stole the skills from other men, who learned them better than I. I got inside them while they worked, and knew the feel of it without looking. I didn't earn it. I didn't earn anything in my life. I'm just pretending to be one of you."

"Did I hurt you?" Lared whispered.

"And that's another way I'm not like you. *You* have to ask."

"What did I say wrong?"

"You said nothing but the truth."

"If you can hear my heart, Jason, you know I didn't mean to hurt you."

"I know it." Jason tested the cord—it was fine and tight. "So. If we don't allow the farm and forest work into our tale, there wasn't much else. So what do we tell in the book you're writing?"

"The people—the ones who lost their memories—"

"It was the same as the farm work, tedious, filthy work. I just took them from the ship, a few a year, fed them, cleaned them, taught them as quickly as I could."

"That's what I want to know about."

"It's just like raising a baby, only they learned a lot quicker and when they kicked you it could really hurt."

"And that's all?" Lared asked, disappointed.

"It was all the same. It only interests you because you've never had a child," Jason said. "People who've had infants will know. The crying, the demands, the stink, and as they learn to get up and move on their own there's a lot of destruction and sometimes injury and—"

"Our babies have always got by without the injuries. Till lately."

Jason winced. Lared already knew that Jason bore some responsibility for the Day of Pain, and he took some satisfaction from Jason's silent confessions of guilt. "Lared, it was the only happy time of my life. Learning to be a farmer, and teaching the children as they learned. Don't despise it because you were born with what I only learned then. Can't you write that? Can't you write of a single day?"

"Which day?"

"No day in particular. Any day would do. Not the day I first took Kapock and Sara and Batta from the ship—I didn't know what I was getting in for, that autumn; with the harvest in, I thought the year's work was done."

"Winter's when the real work happens," Lared said. "Summer's harvest comes from winter's water."

"I didn't know that," Jason said. "Not that day, anyway. Not the time when I despaired, when they seemed to learn nothing, when I grew sick of their endlessly emptying bladders and bowels. Perhaps when I knew that it would succeed. Perhaps a day when I loved them. Find such a day, Justice, and give it to Lared in his dreams."

That afternoon the snow began to fall. The wind was harder than ever; they went out only to make sure all the animals were closed in the barns and stables, to make sure everyone in the village knew, and no children were out in the storm. That took the afternoon, and Lared felt a strange exhilaration in the danger of it, for they had treated him like an adult, letting him go from house to house, trusting him with the lives of some of the families because no one followed after him to be sure he delivered his messages. They have almost decided that I'm a man, thought Lared. I am almost on my own.

By suppertime there was no going out at all, for any reason. The wind was whipping the snow through the innyard, piling it up mountainously against the windward walls of house and barns and forge. Lared looked through the sliding shutter on the door—

even with so small an opening, the wind stung his eyes and made it hard to see. What he saw was the storm that the tinker had so long promised. There was never a calm in the wind, only an occasional slackening that would let the snow fall slightly downward, instead of seeming to fly straight across, level with the ground. It was impossible to tell how deep the snow was, after a while: he could see no buildings through the flying snow, had no reference point. Only when the snow drifted up against the door so high that it plugged the shutter hole, only then did he realize that there had never been such a storm in the village of Flat Harbor before. That night Lared went with his father into the cold attic, to see whether the roof beams could bear the weight. Afterward, he lay awake in bed a long time, listening to the wind whipping the house, prying at the shutters; listened to the snow press downward on the house, making the old timbers groan with the weight. He got up twice to put another log on the fire, to make sure the rising heat was stronger than the cold whistling down the chimney, or else the smoke would back into the room and kill them all.

At last he slept, and dreamed of a day in the life of Jason Worthing; he dreamed a good day, the day that Jason knew his colony would work.

Jason awoke to the lowing of the cows that needed milking. He had been up three times in the night with the new ones, just brought from the ship. Wien, Hux, and Vary, and they were trouble—with the first three on their own a little more, Jason had forgotten how much trouble they could be. Not that they needed nighttime feedings—their bodies were adult, after all, and not growing. They awoke because they did not know yet how to dream. Their minds were vast caverns, and they easily got lost; they had no store of images to guide them through the night. So they awoke, and Jason comforted them, calmed them.

The cows need milking and I must get up. In a moment I will.

How long till these new ones learn? Jason tried to remember back through the last months, the long winter, the longer spring as he tended Kapock, Sara, and Batta, doing his best to keep them safe, keep them learning, even as he struggled to ready the land, to plant, to grow a crop. But in the late spring they began following after him, imitating him, learning the work; it had not been long. Eight months and they were walking and talking and helping bear the burden of the work.

Jason knew enough of children, though he'd never had any, to know that they were progressing far faster than any infant. It was as if something in their brains that did not depend on currents of electricity kept a pattern; they learned to walk easily, in a matter of a few months; bowel and bladder control came soon, mercifully; their tongues found the tones of speech well enough. Learning their body from the inside was not as hard this time as it had been when they were very small. But it was little comfort during the months before they *had* learned, for no mother had had to contend with a six-foot infant crawling to explore in the night; and with bodies fully developed, Jason had to enforce strict rules about who slept where, and how they must stay dressed, and what may or may not be touched: it was hard enough to deal with them without a pregnancy. Jason meant to build a stable society, and that meant that the customs of marriage had to be firmly embedded in the patterns of their lives.

With Batta, Kapock, and Sara, that was already in the past, and still to come with Wien and Hux and Vary.

Jason sighed and forced himself to get up, to dress in the darkness. Only it wasn't as dark as it should be—light was coming in through the skylight. He had slept more than a moment, and the cows would be angry. Except that he didn't hear them lowing. They should be complaining loudly by now.

It was only when he opened the door and the light fell across the floor that he realized that the others weren't there. The new ones lay in their coffins—the sides kept them from falling out of bed—but the old ones were gone. Jason felt a thrill of fear as he thought of them down at the river. But no, they had been learning to swim, they could stay afloat, the current was weak this far into the summer—he should not be afraid. Should not be, but was: but they were not at the river, and as he walked around the plastic dome they called the House, he saw Kapock out in the vegetable field, hoeing along the rows of beans. He looked farther, and at the forest's edge there was Sara with Dog, letting the sheep out to graze beyond the edge of the fenced fields. He knew then where Batta would be, and walked into the barn.

She had already finished the milking, and was skimming the cream for butter-making. "You're just in time," she said, imitating a phrase that Jason often used, imitating even his intonation. "You're just in time. Let's curdle it." Oh, she was full of herself, but the work was well done, wasn't it? and Jason hadn't been there to help at all. So together they poured the buckets of skimmed milk into the wooden tub and set it in front of the heater to warm. Making curds in front of a solar-powered heater did not seem like such a contradiction to Jason. He knew that he would soon have to begin the use of open fire, but he dreaded it and figured to put it off at least another year. So it was radiant heat from a unit brought with the ship that kept the milk in the tub at the right temperature, and lactic acid saved from the belly of a slaughtered lamb that did the curdling, and bacteria carefully cultured from the ship's supply that began to grow in the milk to turn it, eventually, to cheese.

"We let you sleep," Batta said. "You were very very tired. The new ones were very bad in the night."

"Yes," Jason said. "Thank you. You've done very well."

"I can do it all," she said. "I know the way." So he only helped her when the job needed more than two hands, and told her nothing; when he was sure she knew the way he set about the simpler task of butter-making. With the curdling well under way Batta came to him, strutting a little, and smiled as she laid her hands on the handle of the churn. "Butter for summer sweet and cheese for winter meat," she said.

"You're a marvel," Jason told her, and he went back to the House to tend the new ones. He fed and diapered them, carried out the manure to the privy that he and the old ones used, and dropped the urine-soaked diapers into the tub, where the piss leached out for soapmaking later in the fall. Use everything, thought Jason, teach them to use everything even if it makes your civilized stomach a little sick. *They* have no such fine sensibilities. *They* can learn what matters and what doesn't. How many of the citizens of Capitol had thought nothing of adultery but shuddered at the sight of their own stools? The loops that showed defecation were considered far more pornographic than the ones that depended on interesting variations of sex. Capitol didn't need you, Doon, to make it fail. You only made it so somec would die with it—it was caving in before you came.

Kapock showed himself no mercy in the vegetable garden. Like Batta, he was working to earn Jason's approval, and he gave it gladly. Kapock had killed no table plants, and the weeds were well taken. "You've put food on the table today," said Jason. That was strong praise, for he had taught them what they had to know to survive: that every day's work had to put food on the table, that every hour of summer sweat was winter survival; and they believed him, though they remembered almost nothing of winter, and never doubted that there would be food enough to eat. Indeed there was—food enough on the ship to feed the four— no, seven—of them for a generation. But the sooner they were self-supporting, the better.

Jason looked in Kapock's mind, as the tall child hoed eagerly. He had few enough words to think with yet, but he had a strong sense of the order of things. He was the one who had thought of the day's surprise, to let Jason sleep while they did the work, and of course Kapock had chosen for himself the job he hated most, the one with endless repetition bent over in the hot sun. That was the order of things, to him: to do all that Jason taught them to do, without having to be asked anymore. He had taught them that was what it meant to be grown, that you did what must be done even when you didn't want to, even when it hurt, even when no one would know if you didn't do it. That was Kapock's project for the day, to be grown up in Jason's eyes.

But there was more. A sense of the future, too. And Kapock found a way to put it into words. "Will the new ones help tomorrow?" he asked. He had understood: as the new ones were, lying helpless in their coffins, he and Batta and Sara once had been; as he and Batta and Sara now were, the new ones would become.

"Not tomorrow, but in a few more weeks."

To Kapock that still meant an unmanageably long time, as far off as the mythical winter, but it was confirmation that he was right about the way things would go in the world. And so he dared another question. "Will I teach them everything?"

The question really meant, Will I become like you, Jason?

And Jason, understanding that, answered, "Not these new ones, but other ones, later ones, little ones, you'll teach them everything."

Ah, thought Kapock wordlessly. I will become you, which is all I want.

They took their noon meal together, without Sara because she was tending the sheep, and they wouldn't come in till late in the afternoon. Jason had never seen Kapock and Batta so happy, falling over their own words as they tried to tell each other all that they did, all the praise that Jason had given them, while Jason quietly moved among the coffins, feeding the new ones some of the cream saved out from the churn. Batta's new butter spoke for itself on the bread from last year's wheat. Last year's wheat, which Jason had planted and harvested himself, testing seven different seeds in this alien soil to find the ones that thrived best. No such loneliness again as when I plowed on the little tractor, and flew in the skiff to place the game animals in the forest, to stock the lakes with fish that my people could eat; I was far more free then to come and go as I liked, and I did not have to work half so hard as now, but I like this better, much better, the sound of their voices in my ears, the pleasure of seeing their joy in learning.

Together they strained the day's curds and wrapped it and put it under a stone to press it into cheese. Thirty other cheeses already growing strong and rank promised plenty to eat in the winter; Jason had been right to bring all but a few of the cows out from the ship, despite the trouble that they had caused him in building fences strong enough to hold them in.

I have done all this, thought Jason. I have come to a meadow by a river and turned it into a farm, with people and animals and food enough to keep all alive. And they are learning, they will someday know enough to survive without me—

It was the promise of future freedom, that they needed him less today than yesterday. It was also the warning of death.

Batta and Jason left Kapock to watch the new ones and went out to the edges of the unfenced fields to split last winter's logs for fence rails. It was hot, exhausting work, but before darkness forced them in from the field they had fenced another hundred strides—before summer was out they could let the pigs out into the forest to range and root, with a fence to keep them from the crops. Then the forest would feed them, and it would be one less drain on the resources of the little farm; the pigs would harvest the forest for them, and bring it back as bacon for the winter's eating.

Waste nothing. Harvest everything. The geese would glean after harvest, so the split grains would become roast meat late in the autumn. The sheep would eat the stubble and turn it into wool and ewe's milk and young lambs for next year's flock. The ashes from the wastewood burning would be used with urine and turned to soap; the guts of the slaughtered pigs and lambs would become strong threads for binding, or casings for sausages. Once it had been the daily life of every man and woman in the world, to turn everything into food or fuel or clothing or shelter; to Jason it was the dawn of creation, and everything he did was new.

Sara and Kapock had the supper ready. It was tasteless but good enough because Jason hadn't had to watch the cooking. They were serious about this today—twice as much had been accomplished as in any day since Jason took them from the ship. Batta even tried to feed the new ones. Hux spat it on her, and Wien bit the spoon, and she got angry and yelled at them. Kapock told her to be quiet, what did she expect from new ones? Sara shouted at Kapock to be nice to Batta, she was only trying to help. Jason watched it all and laughed aloud in delight. It was complete. They were a family.

"There," said Lared. "Is it what you wanted?"

"Yes," said Jason.

"I even tried to write it so cheese-making would sound wonderful. Anybody with half a brain can make cheese, you know. And sheep can jump over the kind of fence you were making."

"I know. I learned it before that summer was out, and we raised the fence."

"Human piss makes disgusting soap."

"The books didn't say that. Eventually we started leaching it out of the straw in the barns, the way you do it. We couldn't learn everything at once."

"I know," Lared said. "I'm just saying—you were as much

a child as they were. A bunch of big children. Like you were
five years old, and they were three, and so that made you like
God to them.''

"Just like God.''

Kapock came to him one night late in autumn, in the darkness
when the others were asleep across the room. "Jason,'' he said,
"did everything come out of the starship?''

He used the word *starship* but did not know that it meant a
thing that could move among the stars. It was just the word for
the tall, massive building an hour's walk from the House.

"Everything that you didn't help me build,'' Jason said. He
had been too careless in his use of the word *everything*, for
Kapock at once believed that somehow the land and the river
and the forest and the sky had come from the starship, too. Jason
tried to explain it, but the words were gibberish to Kapock.
What did *voyage* and *colony* and *planet* and *city* and even *people*
mean to him? Just an incantation that only Jason understood. It
remained his belief that everything had come from the starship,
and that Jason had brought the starship to this place. Later I'll
teach him, Jason thought, later he'll understand more, and I'll
teach him that I'm not God.

"And the new ones, did you make them?''

"No,'' Jason said. "I only brought them with me. They were
just like me, before we came. They slept all the way here. There
are more of them in there, sleeping.''

"Won't they wake up and be afraid, without you there?''

"No—they're asleep longer than that. The way the river is
asleep under the ice. The way the fields are asleep under the
snow. They won't wake up until I waken them.''

Of course not. Nothing wakes till Jason wakes it. Winter
comes when Jason wills it. And the people who sleep like the
river under ice, they come as Jason calls them. I also do as Jason
teaches, for I was also Ice.

The wind let up late in the afternoon. "Just a lull,'' said the
tinker. "Don't go far, and don't go alone.''

"Not far,'' said Father, "and Lared will come with me.''

They went out the south-facing kitchen window, bundled to

the eyes so that they climbed like clumsy infants. On the south side the snow wasn't quite so deep, though walls of drifted snow flanked the house left and right. The snow was still falling, straight down this time.

"Where are we going?" Lared asked.

"To the forge."

It was almost painful, the sound of their footsteps in the silence. For a while, between inn and forge, neither building was visible. Only the unfamiliar landscape of the drifts. Only his father, plowing awkwardly through the waist-deep snow ahead of him. Then the forge became a dark streak in the snow ahead, only the edge of the roof of it visible. Lared had never been outside in such weather before, but Father unerringly found the shallowest snow, avoiding the deep drifts that were higher than their heads.

A trick of the wind had put a drift in front of the south-facing door of the forge. They forced through it to the wide window in the top of the left-hand door; it opened inward, and the snow gave way, and they lowered themselves inside.

"Help me stoke the fire." It was still alive, from the day before. But what work was so urgent that they had to risk their lives in such a storm?

The answer came when Lared tried to close the window.

"The fire!" said Father. "And leave the window. The others need to see the light."

The others. Lared understood at once. They would make him be a man tonight. It was a great honor, to do it in such a storm as this, provided that the others came. And they did come, two by two, until eighteen men were crowded, sweating, into the hot smithy. They left a clear aisle from the open window to the fire of the forge.

"We stand," said Father, "between fire and ice."

"Ice and fire," said the others.

"Will you face the fire, or will you face the ice?"

What did it mean, to face one or the other? How could he pass a test if he didn't know what the question meant?

So he hesitated.

The men murmured.

Lared tried to imagine what they meant to do. Fire was Clany, dying in agony; ice was the snow outside, and no track to guide him home. Give me ice over fire anytime. But then he thought again: if I have to face two dangers, which would I rather have before me, and which behind? I will face what I fear most—perhaps that is the test.

"Fire," he said.

Many hands took him and faced him toward the fire. The bellows coughed. The cinders flew upward. The many hands took the clothing from him, until the fire seared his skin in front, and the wind from the door froze him behind.

"In the beginning," recited Father, "was the age of sleep, when all men and women longed for night and hated all the days of waking. There was among them one with power, who hated sleep, and all his ways were destruction. His name was Doon, and no one knew him until the Day of Waking, when there came a shout from the world of steel: Look at the man who has stolen sleep! Then the name of Doon was known everywhere, for the sleepers belonged to him, and there was none left who was not forced awake."

What would this have meant to me, wondered Lared, if I hadn't had Doon's face in my memory? All a mystery, all a myth if I hadn't known, but I *know* the truth behind it, I have spoken with Doon face to face, and I can tell you the way his eyes look when he knows you are afraid. I have also been Doon, and evil as he was, somec was worse.

"Then," said Father, "the worlds were lost in the light. They could not find the stars in the sky anymore. For five thousand years they were lost, until men learned to travel against the light, to travel so quickly they could do it without the sleep that Doon had stolen. Then they found each other again, found all the worlds but one, the world known by the holy name."

"Ice and fire," murmured the other men.

"Only here, between the fire and ice, may the name be spoken." Father reached out and put his thumbs on Lared's eyes. "Worthing," he said. Then he whispered, "Say it."

"Worthing," Lared said.

"It was the farthest world, the deepest world, and it was the place where God had gone to sleep when men awoke. The name of God is Jason."

"Jason," said the men.

"And the world was full of the sons of God. They saw the pain throughout the worlds, the pain of waking, the pain of fire and light, and they said, 'We will have compassion on the woken, and ease their pain. We are not Jason, so we cannot give them sleep, but we are the children of Jason, so we can keep them from the fire. We are Ice, and we will stand at your back, and hold the light at bay.' "

They know the end of the story, Lared realized. They know what became of Jason's world when he was done.

"Now," said Father, "they have given ice to us. But we remember pain! Here between the ice and fire, we remember—"

He stopped. The men murmured. "Remember," someone said. "Pain," someone whispered.

"It has *changed*," Father said. He wasn't reciting anymore. "It isn't the Day of Waking anymore, and it isn't the Day of Ice. It's the Day of Pain, and I won't let it go the old way."

The men were silent.

"We saw it coming down the river, what happens when you do the ice and fire now! And I said that day, we will not do it here!"

Lared remembered the man burning alive on the raft. From upriver, where there is still ice in the mountains. "What is supposed to happen now?" asked Lared.

Father looked sick. "We throw you in the fire. In the old days, we were stopped. Our arms would not do it, though we threw with all our might. We did it so we would remember the pain. And to test W-Worthing."

The men were still wordless.

"We saw what happened to Clany! We know that Worthing is asleep again! The Ice has no power anymore!"

"Then," said Clany's father, "give him ice."

"He chose the fire," said another man.

"Neither one," said Father. "We did it before because we knew there'd be no pain. Now we know pain and death."

"Give him ice," said Clany's father. "We did not make you speaker so that you could save your son."

"If we keep this alive then all our sons will die!"

Clany's father was on the edge of weeping—or was it the edge of rage? "We must call them back to us! We must wake them up!"

"We do not kill our children, even to waken a sleeping god!"

Lared understood it now. Naked, the boy-who-was-to-be-a-man was cast into the fire or out the window into the snow. He could see in the faces of the other men that they weren't sure what they wanted. There were many generations in this ritual. All the uncertainty since the Day of Pain was in their faces. And Lared knew his own value in their eyes. A bookish boy and so not trusted; not strong for his age and so not valued; the son of the most prosperous man in the village, and so not liked. They do not long for my death, but if someone is to die and wake the children of Jason they are willing for it to be me. And Father is shaming himself to save my life. If they consent to let me live, it will be because my Father begged, and he will never have his pride again in the village.

The fire is too much for me, thought Lared. But I can face the snow.

"Are the children of Jason in the fire or in the ice?" he asked.

He was not supposed to speak, but then nothing was supposed to happen as it had.

"They are Ice," said Hakkel the butcher.

"Then I will go into the ice," said Lared.

"No," said Father.

As if in answer, the wind howled outside. The lull in the storm was over.

"Tell me what to do, once I'm outside," said Lared.

No one was sure. The children of Jason had always stopped them before the end. "The words we say," said Father, "are, 'Till you sleep in ice.' "

"In the fire," said Clany's father, "we say, 'Till you wake in flame.' "

"Then I will go until I sleep."

Father put his hand on Lared's shoulder. "No. I won't allow it." But his eyes said, I see your courage.

"I will go," Lared said, "until I sleep."

No, said a voice in his mind. I will not save you.

I'm not asking you to, Lared answered silently, knowing he was heard.

Do not choose to die, said Justice.

"I will go until I die!" Lared shouted.

Their hands reached out to him like dozens of little animals, set to devour him. The hands lifted him, rushed him toward the window, and cast him out into the wind and snow.

The snow stung him, and as he struggled to right himself it got in his nose and mouth. He came up gasping and trembling, his legs weak under him from the shock of the cold. What am I doing? Oh, yes. Going until I sleep. There was enough light from the window to cast his shadow a short way into the snow— he stepped forward into his shadow. The wind caught him and he fell again, but he got up again and staggered forward.

"Enough!" cried his father, but it was not enough.

Until I sleep. Sleep was ice to them, in their story. There would be ice along the edges of the river. Not that far. I can run it in three minutes in summer. I must bring them ice from the river, I must take the cold and bring it back to them, the way Jason took the twick into his body and brought it out, and lived. From this night, if I live, Jason's memories won't steal me from myself.

No one will save you, said a voice in his mind. But he wasn't sure if it was Justice or his own fear speaking.

It wasn't far, but the wind was cruel, and it whipped along the river worse than anywhere in the village. Lared dug numbly in the snow until he uncovered stones that until yesterday had been half-buried in mud. Today it was already freezing, and he cut his clumsy fingers before he could persuade a sharp stone to rise into his hands. Then he knelt at the water's edge, where snow spilled out onto the new ice, and the ice reached arms out into the river. A few blows with the stone and the ice at the edge broke up; the water splashed and felt warm on his arms. He fumbled in the water to get hold of a large fragment of the ice, and then half crawled back up the slope of the bank.

He had the ice from the river, it was enough that he could go back and no one could say he failed, but the wind blew the snow into his face now, and as he staggered forward the world was nothing but dots of white coming toward him. He could not see the village, saw nothing but the snow around him, forgot where the river even was. A moment ago he could hardly hold the ice for shivering; now his body had forgotten it was cold.

Then, out of the endless points of snow, there came two shadows. Father, and Jason. It was Jason who led the way, but it was Father who put a blanket around him.

"I got to the river," Lared said, "and I got this ice."

"It doesn't even melt in his hands," Father said.

Together they lifted Lared and carried him through the snow. They shouted, and someone answered; someone also answered, faintly, farther on. It was a chain of men through the snow. Lared did not see the end of the chain. He slept in his father's arms.

He awoke trembling violently in a tub. Mother was pouring hot water on him. He screamed from the pain.

Seeing he was awake, she gave him the sort of sympathy he was used to. "Fool!" she shouted. "Naked in the snow! All men are fools!" She returned to the fire to heat more water.

She's right, said the voice in his mind.

"But so were you," whispered Jason.

The other men were there, their faces shifting in the firelight. The room was hot and it hurt to breathe, and Lared didn't want them to watch him that way. He ducked his head, turned to the side, turned back again, shaking his head back and forth slowly.

"Leave him," Jason said. "He got the ice for you, he came home asleep, he did all you said for him to do."

The men pulled on their heavy coats and capes, began to glove themselves.

"They say your name is Jason," said Hakkel the butcher.

"My name is Jason Worthing," Jason said. "Did you think Lared's father lied to you?"

"Are you," whispered Clany's father, "God?"

"I'm not," said Jason. "I'm just a man, getting old, wishing he had a family, and wondering why you are all such fools as to have gone from yours on a night like this."

They left through the kitchen window, guiding each other home through the darkness.

7

Winter Tales

It was not the worst storm they had ever had; the snow had been deeper in many a winter; but there had never been so bad a beginning to the winter. Everyone in the house kept saying it, over and over: "And this is only the first real storm." For three days the wind kept up, though after that first night the snow was only a few inches at a time, and they could get around enough in daylight to make sure the animals were fed and watered.

Lared did not get around, however. He lay in Father's own bed during the day, while the life of the house went on around him. The women of the village gathered on the third day, to resume the work of weaving. Though Lared was in the room with them, they did not much converse with him. He was feverish and didn't feel like speaking, and the others had such awe of him that they had little to say to him. After all, they had taken the storm without loss, and many suspected that it was because Lared had offered himself to the storm that it had been no worse than it was.

During the work, the tinker sang his songs and told his tales.

He was good for several hours' entertainment, but then there came a lull in the conversation, just the sound of the shuttlecock flitting back and forth in the loom. Then Sala got up from her needlework and walked into the middle of the room. She turned around twice, looking at no one, and then turned to face Lared, though he was not sure if she looked at him or not.

"I have a story of a snowstorm like this one. And a tinker."

"I like that," said the tinker, laughing. But no one else laughed. Sala's face was too serious. The tale she meant to tell came from someone else. Lared knew it was Justice. So did the others—they kept sneaking looks at Justice, who was doing coarse weaving with horsehair strands. She paid no attention to them.

"The tinker's name was John, and he came to a certain village every winter, to stay at a certain inn. The village was in the middle of a deep forest called the Forest of Waters. The name of the village was Worthing, because the name of the inn was Worthing. John Tinker stayed at the inn because it was his brother's. He lived in a room in a tall tower in the inn, with windows on every side. His brother was Martin Keeper, and he had a son named Amos. Amos loved his uncle John, and looked forward to winter, because the birds came to John Tinker. It was as if they knew him, and all the winter they were in and out of his windows; during the storms they huddled together on the sills."

Lared looked at the women in the room. They showed no reaction to the name, but there was a set to their lips and a steely look in their eyes that made Lared wonder if they too held that name as sacred.

"The birds came to him because he knew them. When they flew he saw through their eyes and felt the air rush by their feathers. When the birds were ill or broken, he could find the hurt place in them and make it well again. He could do this with people, too."

A healer. The name of Worthing. They knew then that Sala's story was somehow a story of the Day of Pain.

But Lared heard it a different way. This tale was from the story of Jason's world, but it came after everything that he had written in his book so far. Justice had given a tale to Sala that Lared had never heard before. Were they forsaking him?

"When he came to the village, they brought their sick to him, their lame, and he made them well again. But to do it he had to dwell inside them for a time, and become them, and when he left he took the memories with him, until the memories of a thousand pains and fears dwelt in him. Always the memory of pain and fear, never the memory of healing. So that more and more he was afraid to heal others, and more and more he wanted to stay with the birds. All they remembered was flight and food, mates and nestlings.

"And the more he withdrew from the people of the village, the more they feared and were afraid of him because of his power, until at last they didn't think of him as a man at all, even though he had been born among them, and he did not think of himself as one of them either, though he remembered almost all their agonies.

"Then came a winter like this one, and the snow was so deep in one terrible storm that it cracked the roof beams of some houses, and killed and crippled people in their sleep, and froze others so the sickness crept up their dead legs and arms. The people cried out to John Tinker, Heal us, make us whole. He tried, but there were too many of them all at once. He couldn't work fast enough, and even though he saved some, more died.

"Why didn't you save my son! shouted one. Why didn't you save my daughter, my wife, my husband, father, mother, sister, brother—and they began to punish him. They punished him by killing birds and heaping them up at the door of the inn.

"When he saw the broken birds he got angry. He had taken all the years of their pain, and now they killed the birds because he could not do enough of a miracle to please them. He was so angry that he said, You all can die, I'm through with you. He bundled himself in his warmest clothes and left.

"When he was gone, the storm came again, and pressed on every house, and tore at every shutter until the only house left unbroken by the wind and snow was Worthing Inn. To the inn the survivors came, then sent out parties to search for others who might be trapped in broken houses. But the storm went on, and some of the searching parties disappeared, and the snow was so deep that only the second-story windows could be used as doors, and many of the low houses were covered over and they couldn't find them.

"The fourth day after John Tinker left was the bottom of despair. Not a soul left alive that had not lost kin to the storm, saving only Martin Keeper, who had but the one son, Amos, who was alive. Amos wanted to tell the people, Fools, if you had only been grateful for what Uncle John could do he would not have left, and he would be here to heal the ones with frozen legs and the ones with broken backs. But his father caught the thought before Amos could speak, and bade him be silent. Our house stands, said Martin Keeper, and my son lives, and our eyes are as blue as John Tinker's eyes. Do we want their rage to fall on us?"

No one looked at Justice's blue, blue eyes, but everyone saw them.

"So they held their peace, and on the fourth night John Tinker came back, frozen from wandering in the storm, weary and silent. He came in and said nothing to them. And they said nothing to him. They just beat him until he fell, and then kicked him until he died, because they had no use for a god who couldn't save them from everything. Little Amos watched John Tinker die, and as he grew up and found strange powers within himself, like the power to heal and the power to hear and see through other people's ears and eyes and the power to remember things that had never happened in his life, Amos kept these powers to himself, and did not use them to help others, even when he knew he could. But he also did not use his powers to get revenge for John Tinker's death. He had seen the villagers' memory of John Tinker's death, and he did not know which was worse, their fear before they killed him, or their shame when he was dead. He did not want to remember either of those feelings as his own, and so he went away to another city, and never saw Worthing again. The end."

Sala broke from her trance. "Did you like my story?" she asked.

"Yes," said everyone, because she was a child, and people lie to children to make them feel better.

Except the tinker. "I don't like stories where tinkers die," he said. "That was a joke," he said. Still no one laughed.

That night, when everyone was asleep, Lared lay awake, bundled in blankets in his bed near the fire. He had rested so much these last few days that he could not sleep. He got up and climbed weakly up the stairs, and found Jason and Justice sitting awake in Jason's room, with a candle for light. He had thought to have to wake them. Why were they still up?

"Did you know I was coming?" Lared asked.

Jason shook his head.

"Why did you tell the tale to Sala?" asked Lared. "It's from after. It's from a time when Jason's descendants were getting much stronger than he was. It must have been hundreds of years."

"Three thousand years," said Jason.

"Which of you remembers it?" asked Lared. "Were you still there, Jason?"

"I was under somec, in my ship, at the bottom of the ocean."

"So it was you," Lared said to Justice. "You were there."

"She wasn't born for thousands of years after John Tinker died," said Jason. "But there's an unbroken chain. Every child at some point dares to penetrate his parents' memories. So generation after generation, some of the memories survive—the ones that each generation has found important enough to keep. It's not a purposeful choice—they just forgot what doesn't matter to them. I found the memory of John Tinker in Justice's mind. I've even looked back to try to find a memory of me." Jason laughed. "I suppose it's because my children only knew me for a little while, and what they found in my memory made no sense to them, I guess. I'm not there. I search for the oldest memories, and I'm forgotten. Just a name."

It was not Jason's reverie that Lared had come for. "Why did you give it to Sala, and not to me?"

Justice looked away.

"We were just quarreling about that when you came in," said Jason. "It seems that Sala *asked* her—why the Day of Pain had to happen."

"And that was the answer? The story of John Tinker?"

"No," said Jason. "It's the sort of answer you give to children. It doesn't explain the Day of Pain, it's part of another story. It belongs in another place in your book. The Day of Pain did not come because there was too much suffering for my children to handle all at once. My children did not run out of power to heal mankind's ills.''

Lared was determined to make Justice herself speak to him. "Then why did you stop?"

Justice still looked away.

"It is to tell that story," said Jason, "that we're writing our book."

Lared thought of how his book had been given to him, and remembered the tale that Sala told, and shuddered. "Did you give her that story as a dream? Did she see John Tinker die?"

That finally provoked Justice to speech. Into his mind she said, I gave it to her in words. What do you think I am?

"I think you are someone who sees pain and can heal it but walks away."

Lared did not have to be able to see behind the eyes to know that his words stung her.

"What," said Jason, "and if she walked in from the snow would you kick her to death? Wait until you understand before you judge. Now go to bed. You had your brush with death the other night, you've watched my survival in Doon's garden, that's what you wanted. No one helped you till you had accomplished what you set out to do. If I had found you and stopped you, or if Justice had warmed you on your way, so that you were never in any danger, what would it have meant, your hour naked in the snow?"

Lared did not say the answer, because it would have felt like surrender. Or apology. Did not say it, but of course they heard it anyway, and he went back down the stairs to sleep.

When he got there, he found his mother awake and waiting for him. She did not say a word, just covered him up and went back to bed. I am watched, he thought. Even my mother watches. That was a better answer than the one that Jason and Justice had given him. With that answer, he could sleep.

And when he slept, he could dream.

It was morning, and Kapock got up early to raise the fire. There was a new smell in the air. The others joked that with sheep around him all the time Kapock couldn't smell anything, but it wasn't true. He could smell everything, but everything smelled just a little bit like sheep.

The new smell was snow, a mere thumb-thick blanket on the ground. It was early. Kapock wondered if that was a sign of a hard or easy winter. What weather would Jason send this year, he wondered, for this was the first winter that Jason was not with them, the first winter that Kapock was the Mayor. I wish you would not go, Kapock had said. And if you go, I wish you would make Sara be the Major. But Jason said, "Sara is best at naming and telling tales, and you are best at knowing what is right and wrong."

It was true that Sara was good at naming. She made Jason tell her again about the Star Tower where the Ice People slept—she was the one who named it Star Tower. From the stories she decided that the place where they all lived on the north side of the Star River was Heaven City, and the huge river an hour's walk to the north was Heaven River, because it was as wide as the sky. And when she and Kapock took all the sheep across the Star River and lived there with them, Sara said in surprise one day, "We don't live in Heaven City anymore. We have a new place." And she promptly named it Sheepside.

Sara was good at naming, but Kapock wasn't very good at right and wrong. Jason could not be wrong, but Kapock was never sure what right and wrong were. Sometimes what he thought was right turned out to be right. Today everyone would know that he was right when he told them to make the thatch early, before it was even cold. Now every house was dry and warm inside, except the newest house, the one they were building for Wien and Vary. The early snow would make them all say, You were right.

But sometimes he was wrong. He was wrong when he tried to get Batta and Hux to marry. It seemed like the right thing. They were the last two of the first six Ice People—I had married Sara and Vary had chosen Wien. Hux thought it was a good idea. But Batta got angry and said, "Jason never told you to marry, did he?" and Kapock admitted she was right and he was wrong. Jason was never wrong, and so they were all disappointed that he was not as wise as Jason. This snowfall would help them trust him again.

Kapock remembered four winters in the world. The first was a very dim memory of light too dazzling to see—he remembered being afraid because the snow was much too large, and he fled back into the House. The second winter was better, because that was the winter when he and Sara and Batta lived only from the food they had worked to grow themselves, and it was the winter when Jason taught Hux and Wien and Vary to walk and talk.

The third winter was the winter when Kapock and Sara first lived in their own house across the Star River from Heaven City. Theirs was the first marriage and theirs was the first new house, and come summer theirs was the first child born. Sara named him Ciel.

But the fourth winter would be this winter, with Sara nursing Ciel and wanting Kapock not to talk so much, and Kapock was afraid. For now there was a problem in Heaven City that he did not know the right and wrong of.

It was the law that when there was a large work to do, all the people worked together. That was how they built new houses in two days, and how they harvested and harrowed, how they threshed and thatched, how they cut the winter's wood and cleared new fields. The tools belonged to all of them together, and so did the hours of the day.

So he did not know what to do when Linkeree asked him for an axe and a day. "What for?" asked Kapock. But Linkeree would not tell him. Kapock never knew how to talk to Linkeree, because Linkeree did not say much, even though he knew how. Linkeree was perhaps the cleverest of the Ice People from the second spring—he was the one who made the fish trap in the Star River, and no one taught him how, unless Jason did it secretly. It was Linkeree who first put berries in new wool so that five shirts were made blue. Linkeree was so strange that he never wore a blue shirt himself. Still, it did not take Jason to tell Kapock that Linkeree was different from the others, and in some ways better, and it made Kapock not want to argue with him, but to trust him to do right.

"Take the axe today," said Kapock, "but tonight you must chop your day's share of firewood."

Linkeree agreed to that and went.

But all day Hux was angry. "We all work together," he said,

over and over. "When Jason was here no one went off to do secret work." It was true. But it was also true that no one had ever before spoken against a decision of Kapock's, after it was made. And all day Hux kept saying, "It's wrong for Linkeree to change everything this way."

Kapock could not argue with him. He too felt uneasy with the change.

That was five days ago, and each day in the morning Linkeree asked for the axe, and each night he came back and did a good day's work while the others sang and ate and played games in First House, where the New Ones, who were just learning to crawl, would laugh and clap even though they couldn't yet speak. It was as if Linkeree were no longer one of them, as if he lived alone. And each day Hux would complain all day. Then at night when Linkeree came back, Hux would be sullen and watch Linkeree, but never said a word of complaint, and Linkeree didn't seem to notice how angry Hux was.

But yesterday Hux followed Linkeree into the forest, and last night he told Kapock what he had seen. Linkeree had built a house.

Linkeree had built a house, all by himself, in a clearing in the woods a half hour's walk from Heaven City. It was all wrong. Houses were built by everyone together, and they were built for a woman and a man who meant to marry. The man and woman always went in the door and closed it, and then opened every window and through each one shouted together, "We are married!" Kapock and Sara had been the first, and they had done this for the sheer joy of it; now everybody did the same, and you weren't married until you did it. But where was Linkeree's wife? What right did he have to have a house? The next marriage, as everyone knew, would be Hux and Ryanno. Why should Linkeree have a house? All he would have there would be himself. He would be alone, and far from the others. Why would he want that?

Kapock didn't understand anything. He was not as wise as Jason. He should not be Mayor. Sara and Batta were both wiser than he. They had both made up their minds quickly. Batta said, "Linkeree does what he likes. He likes to be alone and think his own thoughts. No one is hurt by it." Sara said, "Jason said

that we are one people. Linkeree is saying he does not want to
be part of us, and if he is not part of us then we are all less than
we were." They were both very wise. It would be so much
easier for Kapock if they had only agreed with each other.

This morning Linkeree would ask for the axe again. And this
time Kapock had to do *something*.

Sara came outside, bundled to protect her and little Ciel both
against the cold.

"Are you going to do something about Linkeree today?" she
asked.

So she had been thinking of it all morning, too. "Yes," said
Kapock.

"What are you going to do?"

"I don't know."

Sara looked at him in puzzlement. "I wonder why Jason made
you Mayor," she said.

"I don't know," Kapock answered. "Let's go to breakfast."

At breakfast Linkeree came to him, already holding the axe.
He did not ask. He just stood and waited.

Kapock looked up from his gruel. "Linkeree, why don't we
all take axes, and help you finish the house you're making?"

Linkeree's eyes went small. "It's finished."

"Then why do you need the axe?"

Linkeree looked around and saw that everyone was watching.
He fingered the axe. "I'm cutting trees to clear a field."

"We'll all do that next spring. We'll cut into the forest north
of First Field, up the hill."

"I know," said Linkeree. "I'll help you with that. May I
take the axe?"

"No!" shouted Hux.

Linkeree looked coldly at Hux. "I thought that Kapock was
the Mayor."

"It isn't right," said Hux. "You go off every day to do work
that no one needs you to do, and during the day no one sees
you, and during the evening no one talks to you. It isn't right."

"I do my share of work," said Linkeree. "What I do when
work is done is mine."

"No," said Hux. "We're all one people, Jason said so."

Linkeree stood silent, then handed Kapock the axe.

Kapock handed it back. "Why don't you take us to see the house you built?" he asked.

At that, Linkeree grew calmer. "Yes, I'd like to show you."

So they cleared up breakfast and left Reck and Sivel with the New Ones as they followed Linkeree eastward into the forest. Kapock walked in front, with Linkeree.

"How did you know I built a house?"

"Hux followed you."

"Hux thinks I am an ox, always to stay in my pen except when I'm needed to pull."

Kapock shook his head. "Hux likes things to stay the same."

"Is it so bad for me to be alone?"

"I don't want you to be sad. I'm sad when I'm alone."

"I'm not," said Linkeree.

The house was strange-looking. It was smaller from end to end than the other houses they had built, but it was taller, and there were windows up high, under the roof. And strangest of all was the roof itself. It wasn't thatch. It was chips of wood overlapping, and the only thatch was at the very top.

Linkeree saw Kapock looking at the roof. "I only had a little thatch, and so I had to do something to finish it. I think this will hold out the rain, and if it does, I won't have to make a new roof every year."

He showed them how he had put split logs across the tops of the walls and made a second-floor to the house, above the first one, so that the inside of the house was not smaller after all. It was a good house, and Kapock said so. "From now on," Kapock said, "we will put this second floor in all our new houses, because it makes more room indoors." Everyone agreed that this was wise.

Then Hux said, "I'm glad you made this fine house, Linkeree, because Ryanno and I are going to be married."

Linkeree was angry, but he answered softly. "I'm glad you and Ryanno are going to be married, Hux, and I will help you build a house."

Hux said, "There is a house, and Ryanno and I are next to need a house, so it is ours."

And Linkeree said, "I made this house myself. I cut the wood, I split and notched the logs, I cut the blocks for the roof and tied them all in place myself. No one helped me, and no one will live in this house but me.''

And Hux said, ''You used the axe that belongs to all of us. You used the days that belong to all of us. You ate the food that belongs to all of us. Your house is on ground that belongs to all of us. Your life belongs to all of us, and all of us belong to you.''

''I don't want you. And you don't have me.''

''You ate the bread that I helped grow last year!'' shouted Hux. ''Give me back my bread!''

Then Linkeree doubled up his fist, and with arms strong from lifting and pulling logs, he hit Hux in the belly, and hurt him. Hux wept. Such a thing had never happened before, and it did not take much wisdom for Kapock to see that this was wrong.

''What will you do now, Linkeree?'' asked Kapock. ''If you want to keep the axe all to yourself, and I say no, will you hit me? If you want to marry a woman, and she says no, will you hit her too until she says yes?''

Linkeree held his fist in his other hand, and stared at it.

Kapock tried to think. What would Jason do? But he could not be Jason—Jason would see into their minds and know what they thought. Kapock couldn't do that. He could only judge what people said and did. ''Words should be answered with words,'' said Kapock. ''A person is not a fish, to be beaten on a rock. A person is not a goat, to be whacked when it doesn't move. Words should be answered with words, and hits should be answered with hits.'' People agreed. It seemed fair.

Hux seemed willing to supply the vengeful blow himself, but Kapock wouldn't let him. ''If you hit him it would be the same quarrel going on. We must choose someone else to hit him, so that the blow comes from all of us, and not just from one.''

But no one wanted to do it.

At last Sara handed little Ciel to Batta. ''I will do it,'' she said, ''because it must be done.'' She strode to Linkeree and hit him hard in the belly with her fist. She was as strong as any man, from lifting sheep and making fences with Kapock, and Linkeree got the worst of it.

''Now for the house,'' said Kapock. ''Hux is right that it isn't fair for a man with no wife to have a house before he and Ryanno have a house. But Linkeree is right that it isn't fair for someone else to have a house that Linkeree built alone. Jason would know what to do, but he isn't here, and so I say that no one will live in this house until a house is built for Ryanno and Hux. We will build that house as soon as we can, but until then this house will stand empty." Everyone agreed that it was the right answer—even Linkeree and Hux.

But the snow melted that day, and that night it rained, and the ground was deep and wet. They couldn't build a house on such soft ground. And after four weeks of rain, the cold set in suddenly, and the snow fell thick, and they had to build a new barn quickly because there was danger that the animals would have no shelter if the barn roof broke. So instead of a house for Ryanno and Hux, they built a barn, with daub-and-wattle walls, and then the winter was too deep to build at all. "I'm sorry," Kapock said. "We couldn't help the weather, and the barn had to be built, and now it's too cold and deep to build a house—the snow won't be clear till spring."

Then Hux and Linkeree both grew angry. Hux said, "Why should Ryanno and I wait, when a house is built and ready for us!" Linkeree said, "Why should I have to stay here all winter, when the house I built for myself stands empty! I built my house, and I'm tired of waiting."

Kapock told them to be quiet, and said that it wasn't right for there to be an empty house. "But I don't know which of you should have the house. When Jason was here, people only got their own house when they married. He never gave a house to someone who wasn't going to be a family."

"No one ever built a house alone then, either," said Linkeree.

"That's true. So this is what I decide. The house belongs to Linkeree because he built it alone. *But*. It isn't right for one man alone to have a house, when Ryanno and Hux want to be married and have no house to be together in. So all this winter, until we can build them their own house in the spring, Ryanno and Hux will live in Linkeree's house, and Linkeree will live with us."

Everyone said that it was fair and right, except Linkeree, and he said nothing.

Ryanno and Hux went to Linkeree's house and shouted from the windows, even the little windows high up, but no one was quite as happy as usual because they knew it wasn't their true house.

That night, Linkeree lit the house on fire, and then shouted to wake up Hux and Ryanno so they could run outside. "No one will live in the house I built but me!" shouted Linkeree, and then he ran off into the snow. Hux and Ryanno walked barefoot in the snow to get back to First House, and Batta, who had learned the rules of healing, cut off two of Ryanno's toes and one of Hux's fingers, to save their lives.

As for Linkeree, he had stolen an axe and some food, and he was gone in the snow.

How could a man live alone in the snow, with no house and no friend? They were all sure that Linkeree would die. Hux raged that he should die, because of the finger he lost and the toes that Ryanno lost. But Batta said, "A toe is not a life," and in the morning she too was gone, with a pan and a dozen potatoes and two blankets made of blue wool.

Kapock was afraid now. Jason would come back and he would say, "How are the people that I left in your care?" And Kapock would answer, "All are well except Hux and Ryanno, who lost their toes and finger, and Linkeree and Batta, who ran off and died together in the snow." He couldn't bear to let this be that way. The toes and finger he couldn't help now. But Batta and Linkeree he could.

He left Sara as the Mayor, though she told him not to go, and he went off with a saw in his hand and a coil of woolen twine around his shoulder and a bag of bread and a cheese slung on his back. "If you die too, how will that help us?" Sara asked, holding Ciel up so Kapock would remember his child.

"I would rather die than have to tell Jason that I let Linkeree and Batta die."

So Kapock searched in the forest for three days before he found them, living in a cold wattle-and-daub shelter leaning against a hill. "We're married," they said, but they were cold and hungry. He gave them some of his cheese and bread, and then together they chose a place on firm ground, but in the shelter of a hill, and they cut switches from a tree and swept away the snow from a section of ground, and all afternoon Kapock and Linkeree and Batta felled and split logs. With the saw Linkeree cut shingles, and in three days the house was built. It was windowless and small, but it was the best they could do in the cold, and it was warm and dry enough inside.

"This house belongs to me as much as you," Kapock said when it was done.

"That's true," said Batta.

"I will give you my share of this house, if you will build Hux the same house you burned, the very house, and you must build it alone. Before you do one thing to make your house larger, you must build a fine house for Hux."

"I can only do that in the spring," said Linkeree. "The work's too fine to hurry it, or do it on soft ground in the snow."

"In the spring is soon enough."

Then Kapock went home, and all that winter he and Sara and Ciel lived in First House, with the New Ones, while Hux and Ryanno lived in Kapock and Sara's own house across the river. Every day Kapock and Sara would cross the river and care for the sheep, but whenever Hux and Ryanno wanted to give back their house, Kapock said no—while Linkeree and Batta had a house of their own, Ryanno and Hux would also have a house. Sara saw the wisdom of what Kapock was trying to do, and so she did not complain. And there was peace.

Jason had not said when he would return. For a long time Kapock hoped for him every day. But spring came, and fields were plowed and planted, and then summer, and trees were felled and houses built. It was near autumn when Jason came again. It was early morning, and Kapock and the dogs and Dor, one of last year's New Ones, were taking the sheep to a meadow in the hills southwest of Heaven City. Dor, who knew the way, was leading. Kapock brought up the rear, crook in hand, watching for stragglers. The sheep were drinking at a brook when he heard footsteps behind him. He turned, and there was Jason.

"Jason," Kapock whispered.

Jason smiled and touched him on the shoulder. "I've seen all that happened, all that was important enough for anyone to remember. And you've done well, Kapock. The quarrel between Linkeree and Hux, it could have destroyed Heaven City."

"I was afraid that everything I did was wrong."

"Everything you did was right, or as right as anyone could hope for."

"But I didn't know. I wasn't sure."

"No one ever is. You did what felt right to you. It's all we ever do. The way I did when I named you Mayor. It worked pretty well for both of us, didn't it?"

Kapock did not know what to say. "Yesterday my Ciel spoke. He called me by name. It's like you said, Jason—the little ones we make aren't as strong as your Ice People, but they learn, and they grow, just like the young lambs becoming rams and ewes. He said my name."

Jason smiled. "Bring all the people to the west end of First Field, under the arm of Star Tower, fourteen days from today. I'll come then, and bring New Ones."

"Everyone will be glad." And then, "Will you stay?" Stay, so I can be Kapock the shepherd again, instead of Kapock the Mayor.

"I will not," Jason said. "I'll never stay again. A few days, a few weeks if there's a need, but never longer than that. But I'll come every year on the same day, for a few more years at least, to bring New Ones."

"Do I have to be Mayor forever?" asked Kapock.

"No, Kapock. There'll come a time, not too many years from now, when I'll take you with me into the Star Tower, and leave someone else as Mayor. Someone else who doesn't want the job. I'll take you, and then someday, later, I'll bring you back, not a day older than you were before, and you'll see how the world has changed while you slept."

"I'll be Ice again?"

"You'll be Ice again," said Jason.

"And Sara? And Ciel?"

"If they earn it," said Jason.

"Sara will. And Ciel, I'll do my best with Ciel—"

"Enough. Your sheep are waiting. And Dor will wonder who I am. I don't think that he remembers me."

"Fourteen days," said Kapock. "They'll be there, all of them. There are nine houses now, and four children born, and five women growing big. Sara again, she's one of them—"

"I know all that," Jason said. "Good-bye."

He walked away, and left Kapock with the sheep and the dogs and Dor.

Dor's eyes were bright. "That was Jason, wasn't it!" he said. "He talked to you."

Kapock nodded. "Let's get the sheep to the hills, Dor." And he told him tales of Jason all the way.

Lared wrote the story as he sat in bed, with the parchment on a board on his lap. Everyone in the house saw him writing, and the women asked him to read it aloud. It was not really about Jason, and Lared saw no harm in it, and so he read the tale.

Before the end they all took sides, some saying that it was Hux in the right, and some saying that it was Linkeree.

When it was done, Sala asked, "Why did Kapock have to lose his house? He and Sara didn't do anything wrong at all."

Mother answered, "When you love people, you do whatever it takes to make them happy."

If that is true, thought Lared, why doesn't Justice protect us, the way she and the other children of Jason used to?

When Father came in from tending the animals, they told him the story too and then asked him the question Sala had asked. "He paid the price," Father said. "Someone has to pay the price." Then he turned to Lared. "As soon as the weather clears, we're taking the sledges out to bring home the trees you marked. We can't do it without you."

"No," said Mother. "He isn't well yet."

"I'll be ready," Lared said.

8
Getting Home

They set out at first light, twenty-two men with eleven teams of horses pulling sledges. Lared led the way, and this year, for the first time since he had begun to mark the trees, he was counted in the total of men. He had marked forty-four trees, four for each team. And Father rode beside him on the foremost team.

One by one they came to the trees that Lared had marked. Two men with axes and saws stopped at the fourth tree. They would cut it, then haul it back to the third tree, cut that and go back to the second, then to the first, and then home. Each team, with the surest foresters and the strongest horses saved for last, for they had the farthest to go to bring their timber home. Lared and Father would be last this time. They both had earned it.

Only six of them were still together at nightfall, when they had to make camp. They had brought wattles and poles on the sledges, enough to make a stable for the horses and a large hut for the men. It took only half an hour to set it up—they built the same structure every year, and they practiced doing it in the common field at Midsummer.

"Pretty proud of yourself," said Jason. "Oh, did I startle you?"

Lared finished cleaning himself with ice-cold leaves and snow. "You wouldn't know what it feels like. No one ever startled you in your life."

"Every now and then."

"What am I supposed to be proud of myself about?"

"Riding at the head of the company. And the way you pointed out the weakening at the top of the mast tree, so they agreed that you had to cut it this year, and not wait for it to be the best mast ever to float down the river—you were magnificent."

"Don't mock me."

"I wasn't. You earned it. Like my first solo in a cruiser. Rites of passage. I've lived a long time, that's all, and yet I still watch the young ones pass through into responsibility, before they realize that irresponsibility was better, and I can't help but love them for it. There's no better moment in your life."

"It was," Lared said, "until you pointed it out."

"Shall I show you how you looked?"

"What do you mean?"

In a moment he saw it before his eyes, supplanting his own vision: himself as Jason had seen him earlier in the day, talking oh-so-gravely with the older men. Only now he saw the half-veiled smiles. All very good-natured—they liked him—but still patronizing. He was still a boy pretending to be a man. And when the vision faded, he was ashamed. He walked away from Jason in the thickening darkness.

"I thought you'd had enough of wandering off in the snow," Jason called.

"You and Justice! You with your visions! Have you seen yourselves!"

"Always," said Jason, walking toward him.

"What do you gain from it? Making me ashamed?"

"Now look at it again."

"No."

But protest was meaningless. Again came a vision, but this time it was his own memory, with the way he felt at the time.

Riding at the head of the company, talking business with his father, explaining his decisions about each tree to the listening men. Only now there were his present bitterness and shame like tinted glass, coloring everything darker. He felt again the happiness he had felt all day. Only now he thought himself a fool, and was angry.

"Stop it!" he shouted.

"Lared!" His father's voice rang out from the distant camp. "Is something wrong!"

"No, Father!" Lared called back to him.

"Come on back, then. It's getting dark, if you can't see it!"

Lared could not answer, for again Justice put a vision in his eyes. The same memories of the same day, but this time not through Jason's eyes, nor through his own, but rather himself the way his father saw him. Constantly through the day as Lared spoke, Father saw that he was foolish, but also remembered him younger, remembered him as a child; remembered too himself on such a day. Remembered the boy who clung numbly to a chip of river ice, for the sake of honor or faith or manhood. The love and admiration were so intense that when the vision at last faded, Lared's eyes were filled with tears. He had never been a father, but he remembered fatherhood, and he ached for a little child that was gone forever, that he had never held, that had been himself.

"What are you doing to me?" he whispered.

A branch cracked overhead, and snow dribbled down near them.

"This is the last time," Jason answered.

The same scenes, in his own memory again. Only this time he saw himself more clearly than before. He no longer believed the happiness, of course, but neither did he believe the scorn. He saw himself as if from the distance of years. He saw that he was young, but he did not hold it against himself. He saw also that he was happy, but he did not wish that he still felt that way. He remembered too well the pain of discovering how foolish he had been. He saw himself more as Father had seen him, as a boy on a path of years, echoing childhood with every move, promising manhood also. And that combination of foolish happiness, shame, and love—meant something. Until then, the memories had meant nothing. But these visions of today had taken on a powerful resonance; his whole life trembled with it. And yet Lared could not think why this day should be so important, after all.

Jason leaned close to him, held him by the shoulders, almost in an embrace. "Were you happy before?"

"Before what?"

"Before we showed you how it really was?"

"Yes. I was happy." And the remembered happiness was somehow stronger than the happiness itself had been.

"And then what?"

"Angry. Ashamed." Was it the pain, then, that made the joy so strong? Was that Jason's lesson? Truth or not, Lared was not grateful. He did not like being carved into whatever shape suited Jason's purpose at the time, jammed in place and wedged like the handle of an axe.

"Now, Lared. What is it that you feel now?" asked Jason.

I've been wounded, and you're using the bloody place to teach me, and if that's what gods are supposed to do, then I wish there were no gods at all. "I don't want you near me." He ran from Jason toward the light of the cookfire.

As he ran, Justice spoke to him comfortingly in his mind. Joy, Lared. What you feel is joy. The happiness, the pain, the love. All at once. Remember it.

Get out of my mind! Lared screamed inside himself.

But he lay awake, remembering it.

"Lared," said Father, lying beside him. "We were all proud of you today."

Lared did not want to be lied to, and he knew the truth. "The others laughed at me.'

Father did not answer at once. "With affection, yes. They like you." A longer silence. "I didn't laugh at you."

"I chose the right trees."

"Yes, Lared."

"Then why did they laugh?"

"Because you were so proud of the first horse. They all rode the first horse once."

"They laughed because I was strutting like a cock in the chickenyard."

"Yes," said Father. "What are you, God? Must everyone always take you seriously?"

It sounded harsh, but Father's hand on his arm told him that it was meant kindly. "Like I said, Lareled. I was proud of you today."

Lared felt Jason's blue eyes burning inside his mind. I am alone with my father, Jason. Can't I be alone with him? He felt Justice haunting him, ready to put a veil across his sight and make him see whatever dream she chose. Because you give them to me, Justice, have I forgotten how to dream?

What are you, Jason? God, that's what you are. Going into and out of your starship, never aging as your people lived and died. A select few you took with you, and they too passed the time and stayed young. Kapock was taken up before his son was grown; Sara too left little ones behind. You gave them great prestige, and cut them off from all that they loved. They worshiped you, Jason Worthing, and what did they gain from it? Anyone can tell a lie to children, and win their love. It worked with me.

Ah, whispered Justice in his mind. So you don't like the way that they believed in Jason. You prefer doubt. You prefer those who know what Jason really is.

Lared remembered the one bubble that had been preserved. Garol Stipock. The one man who could remember Capitol, who knew that Jazz Worthing was mortal. A man who had once sought to prove it. You gave him his memory?

What do you do with another man's past? Jason rocked the case of Stipock's bubble in his hands. All of Stipock's past in his hands, and Stipock's living body hot with somec in the corridor, the last of the original colonists, waiting to be wakened.

Before the missile plowed this ship, I was full of plans, how I would deal with three hundred people who wanted to murder me. I had ideas, I remember. Keep them off balance, quarreling with each other, reliant on me for any kind of stability at all. I didn't need to do it after all. Now, instead of keeping them disturbed, I keep the peace. I find the best of them, the wisest, they serve a few years as Mayor and then I bring them here, I save them for when they're needed next. I never asked them to

think of me as God, but the prestige it gives to those I take into
the ship makes Heaven City a safe and stable people. Sixty years
so far, safe.

And stagnant.

He tossed the bubble gently into the air, caught it. Stipock
wasn't one of the haters. He hadn't wished for my blood, he
only wanted what Doon wanted: the breaking of the game. Stipock was one who did not believe. He had believed too much
religion as a child. I could not have created a society to gall him
more than this one, with their naive faith, their willing compli-
ance with authority. Why do you obey the Mayor? he would ask.
Because Jason isn't here, they would answer. Well, why do you
obey Jason? he would ask. Because he was the first. Because he
made us. Because everything obeys Jason.

Will you tell them, Stipock? Will you teach them all the ways
of Capitol? Teach them about stars and planets, bending light
and gravity? No, you're not such a fool as to think you can build
utter ignorance into true science. You'll see the oxen and the
wooden plows, the brasswork and the tin, the faith in Jason and
the peaceful trust in Jason's Mayors, and it won't be physics that
you tell them.

It will be revolution.

I would be a fool to wake you up with your memories. Just
one more New One, one more infant, the last of all, and you
would trust me as faithfully as you trusted in your parents' god,
until your disillusionment. But *I* would never disillusion you.
I'm what you longed for all your life—someone you could believe in. I know the thoughts of your heart, I never age, I come
and go as I like, I produce people from my tower and whatever
question you have, I can answer it, and you'll never know my
answer isn't truth. I'm the god that will not fail.

But if you have your memory, we will be enemies, and you
are the one I fear most of all. Without malice, without a lust for
power, not a rival for my people's faith, but an enemy of faith
itself. You will undo the stories that they've chosen to believe,
change the meaning of everything that happens. They're waiting
for you, as they wait in every generation of the world: the young,
the resentful almost-men and almost-women who want to move
into their parents' places. They were the built-in catalysts in

every culture I have found in the ship's computer. No society can stay the same, because the young ones have to *change* things, to show there's a reason for them to be alive. They're waiting for you to come and tell them not to believe.

Jason pressed the clear case between his palms. I will erase you, and you will be mine. No one will know it, life in Heaven City will be better because of it.

But he did not crush the case. He found himself walking back to Stipock's coffin, holding his memory, holding Stipock's childhood in his hands.

He tried to understand why he was going to do it. Some sense of fairness, some idea that you don't steal the past of a man? It was all right for it to happen accidentally, it was fine to take advantage of the thieveries of fate, but to do it deliberately would be murder, was that it?

But he had killed before, he had been inside a man's mind at the moment when Jason's missiles took him into the bright tunnel of death. He would do it in a moment, if he thought his people would be better for it. No moral scruples would stop him, if his children needed it.

His children. It was for them that he would put the bubble in its place, let it dump Stipock's life back into him. Jason did not even know what good would come of it. Perhaps it was that his people did not need good right now. Perhaps it was a taste of evil that they needed. Someone to do for his stable society just what Doon had done for Capitol. Trouble was, he never had found out how Doon's revolution had turned out.

Who is Mayor? Noyock? Poor Hop—what am I doing to you? Putting a rebellion in your city. Indeed, a rebellion in Noyock's own house. It was a troubling situation as it was. Noyock was here for his second stint as Mayor; he had slept forty years. He was still in his late thirties, physically, and his son Aven was older, in his fifties, going grey. Aven had guessed by now that Jason would not take him into the tower. How could he? Aven was a stubborn, vengeful man, the sort that would never do as Mayor. Now Aven was taking it out on Hoom, his youngest son, ruling him as cruelly as he would have ruled the city, given the chance, proving over and over again how right Jason was not to take him up. Hoom was another matter. He was Noyock again, he had ability, if his adolescence didn't ruin him.

Last year, when he had first realized how bad the situation was, Jason had toyed with the idea of taking Hoom from Aven's house. But the good of all was more important than the good of one—if he once violated the family, now in the third generation, the echoes would be heard throughout history. Hoom would pay for the safety of Heaven City. It was cruel, but necessary.

So why am I bringing Stipock out, if the good of the whole is more important than any individual? Jason hesitated again before starting to waken his sleeping enemy. How dare I do this, when I don't even know why I'm doing it?

Yet he knew that he must do it, and could only trust his own blind impulse. Any other mind he could probe and understand. With his own, he was as helpless as everyone else. For some reason, not in spite of but because of his love for the people of his city, he must let Stipock loose to do what he inevitably would do.

He depressed the levers, then leaned back against the other wall to wait for Garol Stipock to wake up. Now that he had committed himself to giving Stipock his memories, he had to figure out a way to explain to him why the colony was as it was, and why it had taken Jason sixty years to wake him.

It was almost sunrise when they brought the boat to shore. Stipock was almost naked and dripping wet and a little cold, and the others laughed at him as he shivered, but it was exhilarated laughter, and they loved him for what they had done this morning. Stipock had made a hobby of sailing on the great indoor lake of Sector ff3L, and it felt good to swim again, even if the river was a little silty. But it was not swimming and boating *again* that pleased him. The joy of it was its firstness: never before had a boat rested on the waters on this world; never before had these children seen a human being swim.

"You will *teach* us!" Dilna demanded. "If I'm going out on this boat again, I want to know how to swim!"

"If I can find time between road-building and shingle-cutting and answering your ridiculous *questions* all the time—" Stipock said.

Wix laughed at him. "If we didn't ask questions, you'd talk anyway. You're a talker, Stipock."

"But Hoom here is the only real listener."

Hoom smiled but said nothing. Just sat by the boat, holding the wood that he himself had worked and shaped to do what Stipock had said that it must do. There were few carpenters to match Hoom's handwork. He was slow, but when he was finished the boat was tight as a barrel, and scarcely needed the coat of gum they gave it. Stipock had thought of starting with a canoe, but it was too easy to spill from one, and the young ones couldn't swim. If he hadn't had Hoom as carpenter, he couldn't have done it.

"Well," said Dilna, "when do we hold a public demonstration?"

"Today," said Wix. "Right now. Let's call the whole of Heaven City to see us ride on the water like a woodchip."

Dilna poked at the boat with her toe. "It *is* a woodchip." She grinned at Hoom to show him that she meant no harm by it. He smiled back. Stipock enjoyed seeing how much he was in love with her. It was one of the best things about being with young people—everything was for the first time, everything was new, they were still young enough to believe in the future. No one had ever plucked them up from their life, thrown them into a colony ship, and sent them out to the edge of the universe in the power of a starship pilot who liked the idea of being God.

"I think we should wait to show everybody," Stipock said. "I'm supposed to meet with Noyock this morning. Let me talk to him about it. Besides, it isn't enough just to go out on the water with it. We have to *go* somewhere. The other side, I think. *Your* father should go with us, Hoom."

Why did Hoom look alarmed? "I don't think so," he said.

"Imagine meadowlands that went on forever. Room for millions of cattle to graze."

"Millions," said Dilna. "That's what I like best about you, Stipock. You always think small." Then, as usual, Dilna brought them all back to reality. "We have to get home now. It's morning, and people will wonder where we are."

Stipock left first, with Wix, because he could tell Hoom wanted to hang back and be alone with Dilna for a while. Wix took his leave as they crested Noyock's hill, and went on down into the city. Stipock walked up the dirt road to the house where Mayor Noyock lived.

It was hard for Stipock to take the Mayor seriously. He had seen him too often before, on Capitol, Jazz Worthing's oily, ubiquitous agent, getting into every loop, as if by appearing often he could become more than ten percent of a man. Everything was different here, of course. Hop Noyock had never been sycophant or a parasite, as far as *he* remembered, anyway. Stipock had seen the wound in the ship, the damaged coffins, the ruined bubbles. He knew that it meant a fresh start for everyone, to come into the world empty-minded again.

But not quite open-minded, after all. Because Jason was present in every part of the colony, Jason's mind was imprinted all over so-called Heaven City. Jazz Worthing, the starship pilot, had finally got what he longed for: absolute worship by backward, debased peasants. He had made no effort at all to teach them what the human mind was capable of. What the universe itself was like. Just a mumbo jumbo of religion, like an ancient emperor trying to convince his people that he was a god. Only Jason had done much better than most. He had the miracles to prove it. Only Stipock knew that his apparent agelessness was nothing but somec, that his wisdom was nothing but a decent education in Capitol's school system, that the miracles he wrought were all machinery hidden in the Star Tower—no, the colony ship, they've got me saying it, too.

Stipock knew what was in store for him. Jason had put his memory in place and let him come into the colony unfettered. Stipock could think of only one reason for such an act: the egomaniacal Jazz Worthing still needed an audience, still needed the people of Capitol to worship him. Stipock was the only person available to watch and then applaud. You'll get damn little cheering out of me, he told himself with anticipation. I've spent my life undoing pompous, dogmatic, self-serving tyrants like you, and I'll do it again. I'll do it the way I've done it every time before: with the truth. It's the one thing that the Jazz Worthings of the universe can't bear for long.

Stipock was not naive. He knew what he was up against. Sixty years of Jason's lies and miracles, his power and authority, had made this a rigid, powerful theocracy, with the Mayor like Jason's archangel standing guard at the tree of life. Jason still has the power of the rulers of Capitol: he still controls somec, and if he wishes he can leave me behind as he and his chosen servants skip like stones across the face of time. But while Jason slept, Stipock could do his own work of undoing. I will unweave your little fabric, Jazz, I will ravel it out before you wake again. Three years you've given me, or so you said, before you'll come again. See what I can do in that amount of time.

Jason had inadvertently given him a powerful tool. Because Stipock was the last of the New Ones, because he had let Stipock come from the ship walking and talking, with a store of knowledge and a vocabulary as elevated above the rest of the colony as Jason's own, some of Jason's aura of divinity had fallen upon Stipock. The most pathetically ardent of Jason's worshipers hardly dared argue openly with Stipock, his prestige was so high. It made him free.

Till now. No doubt Noyock had called him today to try to silence him. Well, Noyock, you can try. But already I have wakened enough people that your authority is shaken, and any punishment you try to measure out will only martyr me in the eyes of those who have realized the backwardness of Heaven City. I've taken the young people out on the water and shown them how to swim. They won't be trapped here between rivers anymore.

Still, Stipock was honest enough to admit to himself as he knocked at the door of Noyock's house that he was afraid. Noyock was not just a creature of Jason's shared prestige. It wasn't just the office of Mayor that made him powerful. Noyock had been Mayor before, for seven years, and on his own he had done much to change and improve the life of Heaven City. He was the one who had started the little villages miles away; he was the one who had divided up the land so each family farmed their own, and the common work was limited to road-making, lumbering, and harvest. The result had been much greater prosperity, a spurt of growth, and now, in his second term as Mayor, Noyock was still energetic, a good leader, with the trust and confidence of everyone whose trust was worth having. Including Stipock. Stipock's contempt for him as Jazz's agent did not make him blind to the fact that Noyock was a benevolent despot. Unfortunately, benevolent despots were the worst kind: it was so much harder to convince people they ought to get rid of them.

The door opened. It was Aven, Noyock's son. He greeted Stipock coldly. "Come in."

"Thank you, Aven. How are things going?"

"Your hair is wet," Aven said.

"It was in water,' Stipock answered.

Aven studied him for a measured moment. "You've built your boat, haven't you?"

"I'm not a carpenter," Stipock said. It was a stupid thing to say, he realized, for it instantly incriminated Aven's son. There was no better carpenter in Heaven City than Hoom. And from the anger in Aven's face, Stipock realized Hoom had lied when he said his father didn't mind all that much. The man looked capable of killing in his rage.

"Because my father built this house many years ago," said Aven, "before Jason took him into the Star Tower, I allow him to use two rooms upstairs to conduct his business as Mayor. That means I must permit any sort of scum to come into my house—but only long enough to walk up the stairs and into the Mayor's office."

"Things are going well for me, too," Stipock said. He waved cheerfully at Aven as he went up the stairs. Hoom was right—his father was as pleasant company as a boar in the woods.

Noyock's office door was open, and Stipock could see him, bent over a table, writing on a piece of sheepskin. Stipock thought of a paper mill, using rag and pulp, and decided there wasn't need yet for so much paper; nor were there people enough to spare from other work for such a task. Still, it might be worth teaching people how to do it. Parchment was so primitive, and only one fair-sized sheet of it from each animal killed.

"Oh, Stipock," said Noyock. "You should have said something."

"It's all right. I was thinking."

Noyock ushered him into the room. Stipock glanced at what Noyock had been writing. "The history," Noyock said. "Every month I take a few days to write what happened that was important."

"What *you* thought was important."

"Well, of course. How can I write what *you* thought was important? I'm not you. Jason settled that years ago—anyone who wants to can write a history. A few of them have. It's always interesting to compare them. It's like we lived in different worlds. But the Mayor usually knows more of what's going on. After all, what's important is usually a problem, and the problems always end up coming to the Mayor. It's been that way since the time of Kapock."

"There are some things you don't know about."

"Fewer than you think," said Noyock. "For instance, I know that you've been telling the children that Jason shouldn't choose the Mayor, that everyone ought to vote on it."

"Yes, I've said that."

"I've been giving that a lot of thought. And it occurs to me that if we did that, we'd usually choose someone that we liked. The trouble is, the Mayor has to make a lot of decisions that no one likes. Then no one will want him to be Mayor anymore, and so either we'd keep changing Mayors or we'd choose Mayors who govern very badly but never offend anybody. Now, before you start arguing with me, Stipock, let me tell you that those are just my thoughts of the moment, and I wonder if you'd be kind enough to think about them at least as long as I thought about your ideas before trying to answer them."

Noyock smiled, and Stipock couldn't help smiling back. "You're a clever bastard, you know."

Noyock raised an eyebrow. "Bastard? I wish you and Jason would write down all these words that none of the rest of us knows, so we can learn them."

"It's just as well. A lot of them aren't worth knowing."

Noyock leaned back in his chair. "Stipock, I've been very interested in what you've done in the six months since you've been here. You work hard at every task that's been put to you. No one calls you lazy, and no one calls you a fool. But I keep hearing complaints about you. Mostly from the older people. They're concerned because of the things that you've been teaching their children."

"I won't stop," Stipock said.

"Oh, I don't want you to stop," said Noyock.

"You don't?" asked Stipock, surprised.

"No, I just want to make it official. So they'll stop complaining about it. I want you to be a teacher all the time. I want it to be your work, the way the sheep are Ravvy's and the cattle are Aven's. I've calculated that we'll give you a plot of land and require your students to farm it for you. They'll pay in sweat for what you put into their heads."

Stipock was genuinely surprised—and puzzled. "You *want* me to teach them? Do you have any notion of what I say?"

"Oh, yes. You tell them how the world is a spinning globe, and the sun is a star. You tell them how sickness is the work of tiny animals, how the brain is the seat of the mind, and your story that Jason is only one of many who drive Star Towers through the sky has filled the children's mind with interesting speculations about what other worlds might be like, with all the miracles you talk about. It has little practical value, of course, but I'm not afraid of what will happen with the children thinking things that none of us have ever thought before. I think it's more to be encouraged than discouraged. But that isn't why I want you to be our teacher."

"Why, then?"

"You know things that will solve problems for us. You've talked of a water-powered mill to grind the grain—I want to build it, and I want you to teach some of the children the principles behind it so we can make more. You've talked of boats, so water-tight that we could cross the Great River and sail out to the ocean."

"You know about the ocean?"

"Of course."

"The children didn't."

"Those of us who have been in the Star Tower—Jason shows us the maps of the world, where the grasslands are, the forests, the metals hidden in the earth, the great rivers and the seas. He's shown us the computer and the pictures it draws in the air, he's shown us the coffins where the Ice People sleep. He showed me *you*, in fact, and warned me he might waken you this time."

"But you've told no one about it."

"There's been no need."

"But—they don't even know the shape and size of the world they live on."

"If they ask, I tell them. No one asks."

"Why should they ask? No one knows that you know."

"Well, *you* haven't kept your knowledge a secret, and that's all that matters now. Build your boats, Stipock, and take the children who adore you across the river. I'll help you—I can keep the frightened parents at bay. Start a new village there, with a river that only those who've learned to drive your boats can cross, and give these children a chance to become men and women without their parents breathing down their necks."

It was not at all what Stipock had expected. He had looked for a reprimand; he had come steeled for a quarrel. "Don't you realize how that will dilute your power, Noyock?"

Noyock nodded gravely. "I know very well. But Heaven City is growing larger all the time. Jason told me to separate my work and give bits of it to the best men and women for the job. I've put Worinn in charge of the building of firm roads, and he's doing well. Young Dilna is master of tools, since everyone knows she does fine metalwork better than anybody else. Poritil is harvestmaster and keeper of the grain—"

"And doing well. I didn't realize how new they were. I thought Jason set the system up."

"He suggested it. I only carried it out. But you—he didn't tell me what to do with you."

"But you said he warned you."

"That the children would follow you, and I was not to interfere, except—"

"Except?"

"That the peace and law of Heaven City must be maintained."

"And what does that mean?"

"That means that when you take the children across the river, Stipock, you will not teach them to disobey the law. I know more about the life of the Ice People than you think. Jason told us how they thought nothing of marriage, and coupled where they pleased, and killed their children—"

"I can see he gave you a neutral picture of it—"

"We need our sons and daughters, Stipock. I was here when

there were only fifteen of us, besides Jason. I was here when the first babies grew, before they were ever men and women. Now there are nearly a thousand. Now there are people who can spend all their working time at the forge or at the loom, so that those who are best at a job don't have to drop their work to weed the fields or shear the sheep. We're free now, to follow our desires. We do not need two or three or four separate cities, each one doing for itself what we could all do more easily together. We are too few for that. And Jason warned me of another thing.''

"What was that?" Stipock expected it to be something about him.

"War. Do you know the word?"

Stipock smiled tightly. "It was Jason's main line of work."

"The closest we've come to it was the burning of the house, back in the first year of Kapock. Jason told me stories of what it could be like. I believe him.''

"So do I."

"The seeds are there, Stipock. The seeds of war are in this house. My grandson Hoom hates his father, and my son Aven has done his best to earn that hate. Look among the younger ones, Stipock. Find the best of them. Not a hotheaded fool, like Billin. Perhaps Coren, though she tends to play favorites. Perhaps Wix—calm, not quick to anger. Or Hoom himself, though I fear he's learned too much of bitterness, and not enough of love. Before you take the children across the river, come to me and we'll name a Little Mayor for the other side.''

"No."

Noyock smiled. "You have another suggestion?"

"On the other side, if the new town is to be settled by the people who believe in me—and they aren't children, Noyock, not anymore—then we'll choose our leader *our* way."

"Interesting. Shall we compromise? Let's choose a Little Mayor for the first year, and after that year we can let the people choose a leader by their own voice."

"I knew you before, Noyock, knew who you were, at least."

"I don't want to hear about it. I have trouble enough being who I am now, without being troubled with thoughts of who I once was in another life."

"No, I didn't mean to dwell on it. I just wanted to tell you—
I never would have believed that you were the same man. Whatever else might be wrong with the way that Jason has things
going here, it's made a good man out of Hop Noyock."

"But *you*, Stipock, you *are* the same man you were before."

Stipock grinned. "And no better, is that it? Well, I'm good
enough for this—when the man in power is as flexible as you,
it's hard to hate you. But I can promise you that if you let me
do what you yourself have just proposed, in ten years the office
of Mayor will be elected, and the laws will be made by the
people of this place, and not by the dictates of a one-man judge
and king and legislator."

Noyock laughed and shook his head. "Not only do you use
words I've never heard of before, but you even pretend to be
able to see the future. Don't overreach yourself, Stipock. Even
Jason cannot see the future."

But Stipock knew that change would come, and knew that he
was giving shape to that change already. Noyock was giving it
to him as a gift. A town of his own, with a river between his
people and the Mayor; authority to teach as he saw fit, and begin
to modernize this backward place; and a promise of democracy
to come. I'll hold him to that, thought Stipock. And when Jason
comes back, he'll see what a little dose of truth and freedom
can do, even to the medieval society he created.

He took his leave of Noyock and opened the door to leave.
Downstairs he could hear shouting.

"Will you do what I forbid?"

And the sound of a blow.

"Will you do what I forbid?"

Silence. And another blow. A crash of chairs falling. "I ask
you, boy! Will you do what I forbid?"

From behind him Stipock heard Noyock emerge from his office and close the door. "I think your son is beating your grandson, Noyock."

"And I think you know the cause of it," said Noyock.

Stipock turned and answered sharply. "Hoom told me that he
had consent!"

"Are you so wise, Stipock, and yet you can't tell from his

face when a boy is lying? No, don't go downstairs. Not yet. It's between father and son."

From downstairs: "Will you do what I forbid? Answer, Hoom!"

Esten, Aven's wife, began to plead with her husband to stop hitting the boy.

"He's beating the boy. Is that part of what parents are allowed to do?"

"If the child is small, we take it away to save its life. But Hoom is old enough that he can't be beaten without his own consent. Listen—he's telling his mother to leave them alone. He doesn't want protection, Stipock."

"Answer me, little rutter!"

From downstairs Hoom cried out in pain. "Yes, Father, I *will* do what you forbid! I will sail on the river, I will go where I like, you were a fool to forbid it—"

"What do you call me! What do you—"

"No! Don't touch me again, Father! You've beaten me for the last time!"

"Oh, do you think you're a match for me?"

Noyock brushed past Stipock and headed down the stairs. "*Now* we step in," he murmured as he passed. Stipock followed him.

They got there just as Aven picked up a broken chair leg and began advancing on his son, who stood defiantly in a corner.

"Enough," said Noyock.

Aven stopped. "It's none of your affair, Father."

It seemed somehow pathetic that this fifty-year-old man called Noyock, who was fifteen years younger in appearance, *Father.*

"It became my affair when you laid a hand on the boy," Noyock said, "and it became an affair for all of Heaven City when you took a weapon in your hand. Is Hoom a badger that you need to kill to protect your herd of rabbits?"

Aven lowered the chair leg. "He threatened me."

"When you are striking him and he merely offers to strike you back, Aven, I think the threat is hardly out of line."

"What right do you have, as my father or as Mayor, to interfere with what goes on within my own home?"

"An interesting point," said Noyock, "to which I offer this

solution. Hoom, I have just asked Stipock to build boats, larger ones than the one that lies hidden at the river's edge.''

Noyock is a deep one, Stipock realized. He gave me no hint that he knew that we had already built a boat.

"You are the only carpenter to see that the boats are built well and safely. I am making it a project for the whole city, so the boats will belong to us all—but I place you in charge of the building.''

Hoom's eyes widened. "For my man's share?''

"For your master's share,'' answered Noyock.

"Master's share!'' cried Aven. "You might as well say he's not my son!'' It would have been bad enough to give Hoom a man's share, enough entitlement to food and clothing that he could have lived on his own. But a master's share was enough for him to build a house, and it freed him from a young man's constant liability to be called to road work or timbering. Indeed, Noyock had called it a city project, which meant Hoom would have the power to call others to work some part of the seven weeks of seven hours that each man and woman owed the city. Noyock had elevated Hoom above his father. It was Hoom's freedom from his father's house and his father's rule.

It was also Aven's humiliation before his son. And Noyock knew that he was doing it. "When you took that chair leg in your hand, Aven, you declared that he was not your son. I only finish properly what you so badly had begun. Stipock, these things take effect immediately—would you help Hoom take his clothing from his father's house, and let him live with you until he finds a wife or builds a house?''

"I will,'' said Stipock. "Gladly.''

Aven silently walked out of the room, brushing Esten out of the way. The woman came in and took her father-in-law by the hand. "Noyock, for my son I'm glad,'' she said. "But for my husband—''

"Your husband likes to wield authority he doesn't have,'' said Noyock. "I raised nine daughters and one son. I have concluded that I'm a better father of girls than of boys.'' He turned to Hoom. "What are you waiting for?''

Stipock followed Hoom up the stairs. It didn't take long to get everything that Hoom owned. Three shirts, two trousers, winter boots and a winter coat, gloves, a fur hat—it all wrapped easily inside the coat and made a bundle under Stipock's arm. Hoom took the only things he prized: the saw and the adz that Dilna had made for him, the work that Noyock had seen before he made her master of the tools. Stipock marveled at how little Hoom possessed, how little any of them owned. How pitiful—a carpenter forced to use tools of bronze, when there was iron to be had in the world, if only Jason cared to bring his colony out of the dark ages. That is the best gift I can give these people, Stipock thought. I can take them south to the desert land, where the trees have taproots two hundred meters long, I can take them there and let them mine the iron that lies locked in cliffs just waiting to be taken, the only iron in the world in easy reach, and I will give them tools and machines and bring them out of darkness into light.

Hoom stopped at the door of his room and looked back into it.

"A house of your own soon enough," Stipock said.

"It was this house I wanted to belong in," Hoom whispered. "He hates me now, and I'll never have a chance again to make it right."

"Give him time to see you as a man on your own, Hoom, and he'll come around, you'll see."

Hoom shook his head. "Not me. He won't forgive me." He turned his face toward Stipock and smiled. "I look too much like Grandfather, don't you see? I never had a chance here."

Hoom turned and walked away. Stipock followed him down the stairs and out of the house, saying to himself, Remember that Hoom sees more than anyone thinks he sees.

On the morning of Midsummer Day, Hoom and Dilna left their house, and with every other man and woman and child of Stipock's city, they climbed aboard a boat and let the southwest wind carry them against the current to the landing place at Linkeree's Bay. There were nine boats now, and Hoom had built them all; and because of his boats there were cattle grazing on the broken meadows to the north, and a new tin mine with a richer vein than any they had had before, and above all, Stipock's city, where Wix was Little Mayor because the citizens had voted for him themselves. All because Hoom could make a boat that was tight enough to hold water. He looked at the others, in his own boat, in the other boats strung out along the river, and he said to them silently, I gave this to you with my own hands. These boats, this river, the wind in the sails, they are who I am in Heaven City.

And Stipock gave them all to me, when he taught me how a boat could be.

And Dilna gave it all to me, when she made the tools that fit my hand.

And Grandfather gave it all to me, when he set me free of Father.

So in their way, they also made these boats. But between them and the water, I am. These boats are myself, and someday they will take me to the sea.

"You're quiet," Dilna said.

"I'm always quiet."

Little Cammar was nursing. "The wind over the water makes him hungry," Dilna said. "The wind makes me want to shout. But you—the water makes you still."

Hoom smiled. "Plenty of chances to shout today, when we vote."

Dilna tossed her head. "Do you think that it will pass?"

"Grandfather says it will. If all of us from Stipock's city come and vote for it, then it will pass. We'll have a council to make our laws, and I have no doubt, Dilna, that you'll end up a member of it, shouting at people to your heart's content."

Wix shouted from the tiller. "Stop talking and get ready for shore!"

Dilna started to pry Cammar's mouth away from her breast. Hoom stopped her. "You don't have to do every job, every time. There are enough of us to pull the boat ashore without interrupting Cammar's breakfast." Then he jumped over the side, rope in hand, and splashed ahead, pulling the boat into the channel it had dug for itself on previous landings. The others quickly joined him, and soon the boat was firmly aground. On *their* side of the river, they had built floating platforms tied to shore, and they moored the boats in the water, without having to get their feet wet. But the people on the Heaven City shore wouldn't build such docks, or even allow them to be built. "If you want to live across the water," they said, "you shouldn't mind getting wet." Just one more of the reasons why Grandfather's compromise had been so hard to reach—there had been so much vindictiveness over the two years that Stipock's city had existed. Petty things, like when a group of older people had demanded that Noyock not count road work and land-clearing on the Stipock side of the river against the seven weeks of seven hours. Father had been part of that. And the long quarrel over whether Dilna should be allowed to carry tools across the water—that had been Father's idea from the start, and he began it right after Dilna married Hoom. He couldn't bear the thought that Hoom would have children of his own, that Hoom was really free of him at last.

But you can't hurt me now, Father. I have Dilna for my wife, and Wix and Stipock for my friends, I have my child, my house, my tools, and above all, my boats. That was the one thing they hadn't argued with—when Hoom decided to locate his boatyard on Stipock's side of the river. "I hate the sight of the things," Father had said. "Build them under water, if you ask me."

They walked together up the road. Of course no carts were sent to greet them, and no horses. Hoom could almost hear his father saying, "They have horses and carts of their own on the other side of the river, why should they use ours?" But it was all right. They were all friends, or almost all, and the exceptions were tolerable. Billin, for instance, with his sharp tongue and his love for quarreling—but Hoom knew how to avoid him, most of the time. Today, for instance, Billin was off with the dozen or so friends who thought that he was wise. They walked behind the rest, no doubt plotting something absurd, like how to climb up into the Star Tower and bring Jason down, or some such thing.

At the crest of Noyock's hill they could look down the way they came and see their boats on the shore, then look the other way and see the Star Tower, rising still higher than they were, even here on the top of the hill, a vast, massive thing of stark white, so pure that in winter it almost disappeared, and now, in summer, it dazzled in the sunlight.

And at the foot of the Star Tower, there was First Field, where two and a half years ago, Jason had brought them Stipock. Stipock, who feared no one, not even Jason. Stipock, who had opened up the world to them. Stipock, who was even greater than Grandfather.

For an hour in First Field they talked again, as Noyock again explained to them all the agreement he had worked out over these last months, despite the quarrels, despite the ones who insisted that the only solution if the "children" would not come home was to divide the world at the river, and have no more to do with each other. The compromise was simple and elegant, like Dilna's tools: beautiful because they worked. All of Heaven City was divided into sections: Heaven City, Stipock's city, Linkeree's bay, Wien's forge, Hux's mills, Kapock's meadow, and Noyock's hill. Each separate group had some authority to decide their own way, and each would choose someone to sit in Council, where with the Mayor they would decide the laws, and try offenders, and decide disputes between the towns. "We are too many now," said Noyock at the end, "too many for one man like me to know everyone and decide everything. But even with these changes, *because* of these changes, we are still one people, and when Jason returns after harvest, he will find that we found a way to settle our differences without hatred, and without division."

It was a hopeful speech. It promised much, and it was plain that Noyock believed in it. Hoom believed it, too.

Then the vote was taken, and Billin and his friends voted with Aven and the others who hated Stipock's city, and the compromise failed.

The meeting broke up in chaos. For an hour afterward, the people of Stipock's city quarreled and argued. It was finally clear that Billin would settle for nothing less than complete separation, and when he took to calling Wix a dog because he always barked when Noyock told him to, Wix declared the meeting over and started up the hill. Hoom and Dilna at once followed him, with Cammar in Hoom's arms. So it was that they were the first to crest Noyock's hill, the first to see the ships on fire.

They cried out and called the others to help, but it was too late. Many of them worked, trying to get water up onto the boats, but it was too late, and the fire burned too hot for them to get very close, and Hoom never bothered at all. He just sat on the shore, Cammar in his lap, watched the flames dancing above the water, and thought, You have burned me up, you have killed me on the water, Father and whoever helped you bring the flame. You have undone all that I have ever done, and I am dead.

Hours later, exhausted, their boats mere skeletons of blackened wood along the shore, they all watched the sun go down and talked dispiritedly of what they ought to do.

"We can build new ships," Dilna said. "I'm still the master of tools, and Hoom still knows how it's done. You know that Noyock will allow us. Our enemies can't stop us!"

"It takes three months to build a ship."

"The cows will go unmilked," someone answered.

"The gardens will go to seed."

"The cattle on the meadows will go wild."

"Where will we live for the months of building?"

"With our parents?"

And then, amid the weary, hopeless anger, came Billin's voice. "Where in Jason's law is our protection? We trusted Noyock, but he didn't have the power to save us, did he? If we're to be protected, then we must protect ourselves!"

Wix tried to silence him. "It was you that did this, voting against us."

"Do you think that made a difference? They planned this before the meeting ever began. Fice and Aven, Orecet and Kree—they knew that this would be their one chance, the one time that every one of us would come, that all our boats would be here, and no one back in Stipock's city to sail across and bring us home. They burned our only road home. And I say we ought to answer them in kind!"

For once, Hoom agreed with Billin. What else was there to do? Nothing would undo the harm that this had done them. It was Father again, just when I thought that I was free.

The talk got wilder and angrier as the night came on. They built fires on the beach, and their friends from Heaven City came to them and offered food and beds for the night. One by one the families went away, leaving behind only the angriest, only those who still cared to hear Billin talk of hate and vengeance.

"Come with me," Dilna said. "Roun and Ul have offered us a place to sleep, and Cammar and I need the rest."

"Then go," said Hoom.

She waited for a while longer, hoping he would come. But he stayed, and finally she left, and at last there were only a dozen of them gathered at the fires on the beach, and the moon was setting in the west, so the darkest of the night was soon to come.

It was then that Hoom finally raised his voice to be heard.

"All you do is talk," he said to Billin. "All you do is talk about how they'll pay. I say we answer them as simply as we can. They used fire to steal our homes from us. What right do they have to sleep content in their own homes, after what they did to us?"

"Burn Heaven City?" Billin asked, incredulous. Even he had not thought of something as insane as that.

"Not Heaven City, fool," Hoom said. "Were they all consenting to the fire? Justice is all I want. It was my father who did this, you know it's true, my father who hated me so much that he would burn my boats."

So they pried off boards from the half-burnt boats, water-soaked on one end, easily alight on the other, and carried them a roundabout way up the hill, so they'd not be seen from the city. Hoom led the way, because the dogs knew him.

But someone was awake and waiting for them as they passed behind the stables, where the horses stamped at the smell of fire.

"Don't do this," Noyock said.

Hoom said nothing.

Noyock looked past him to the others. "Don't do this. Give me time to find those who burned your boats. They'll be punished. We'll turn all the resources of Heaven City to build new boats for you. It won't take months, but weeks, and in a few days Stipock assures me we can have a small boat so a few of you can cross and tend the animals."

It was Wix who answered him—at heart he still hoped for compromise, probably. "What sort of punishment will *you* give the ones who did this?"

"If we can be sure who did it, then the punishment is in the law—they lose their property, and all they own is given to you."

Billin spat. "And of course all you have to do is ask who did it, and they'll step right forward, won't they?"

Noyock shook his head. "If they won't admit it, Billin, then Jason will be here in four more months. You will have long since gone back to your homes, and he will settle it. I promise you, he'll have no tolerance for what they did. But if you do this tonight, he'll have no more tolerance for you. What kind of justice is this? What if you burn the house of an innocent man?"

"He's right," someone murmured. "We don't know for *sure*."

But Hoom said, "If we burn *this* house, Noyock, I think it won't be an innocent man who suffers."

"It'll be an innocent woman, then, your mother. And me. I live there."

Billin laughed. "That's all he's thinking of. His own roof."

"No, Billin. I'm thinking of you. Tonight all Heaven City is outraged, their sympathy is with you. But if you come and burn a house in the night, you'll lose every friend you have, because they'll all be afraid that sometime in the night *their* house will burn, too."

Hoom took Grandfather by the shirt, and pushed him back against the stable wall. "Don't talk anymore," he said.

"It's the Mayor," someone whispered, aghast that Hoom would touch him.

"He knows who it is," Billin said. "Hoom doesn't have the courage." And Billin stepped up, pushed Hoom aside, and struck Noyock a blow in the jaw, jamming his head back into the wall. Noyock slumped and fell to the ground.

"What are you doing!" Wix demanded.

Billin whirled on him. "What is Noyock to us?"

"Stipock told us that if we strike a man, then his friends will only strike us back. No one said anything about coming to blows, like children playing in the grass."

Hoom didn't hear any more of the argument. He took a sheaf of long straw from inside the stable door. The horses looked in fear at the torch in his hand. "Not for you," he murmured, and strode from the stable to the house. The others fell silent when they saw him go, and some of them, at least, soon followed him. Hoom went in through the kitchen door, set the straw and some of the cookfire wood near the curtains in the big room with the table. The room where Aven had struck him for the last time. He did not hesitate—when the kindling was ready, he put the torch to it. The flames erupted at once, and the curtains soon caught. It was hot enough that Hoom had to step back right away, and step back again a moment later. The fire quickly caught on the timbers of the house, and the smoke rushed along the ceiling toward the opening of the stairs.

Wix stood behind him. "Come on, Hoom. We've got fires well set outside, too—it's time to give the alarm to them."

"No," said Hoom.

"We didn't bargain to kill anybody," Wix said.

Father killed *me*, Hoom answered silently.

"Your wife and son are alive," Wix said. "Don't let it be said that someone besides you gave the alarm to save your mother's life. Don't let it be said that you wanted your father dead."

Hoom shuddered. What was I doing? What am I? He ran to the foot of the stairs and shouted, "Fire! Fire, wake up! Come out!"

Wix joined in the shouting, and when no one came from the rooms upstairs, they ran up. Smoke must be seeping through the floors, Hoom realized—it was already thick in the hallway, and there was smoke coming through the tops of the bedroom doors. He ran to his father's room and opened the door. His mother was staggering from the bed, coughing, brushing smoke away with her hands, trying to see. Hoom took her, led her out, rushed her down the stairs. The other end of the house downstairs was all aflame. "Who else is in the house?" Hoom demanded.

Mother shook her head. "Just Aven and Biss."

"Father wasn't in bed," he said.

"I made him—I made him sleep somewhere else," she said. "He burned your boats," she said. Then all at once she realized. "You set this fire! You burned my house!"

But by then he had her out the door. He rushed back in. Wix had Biss and was carrying her down the stairs. "Where's Father!" Hoom shouted.

"I didn't see him!" Wix shouted back. Hoom pushed by him and ran back up. Flames were already lapping around the edges of the stairwell, and the door of his parents' bedroom was bright with flame. The fire was spreading faster than Hoom had expected. He could see the flames coming in from the windows now, spreading across the ceilings of each room in turn. Father wasn't in his own room, wasn't in Biss's—of course not, you fool, Wix would have seen him!—wasn't in Noyock's room.

"Come down, Hoom! He isn't there!" Wix shouted from downstairs.

Hoom ran to the head of the stairs. The stairway itself was on fire, at the edges.

"Come down before it's too late!" Wix was standing at the front door. The porch was also on fire now.

"Is he down there?"

"If he were in the house he'd be awake by now!" shouted Wix.

So they hadn't found him. He must be here. Hoom opened the door of Noyock's office. The flames leapt out at him when he opened the door, singeing his hair, catching his pants on fire. But he didn't stop to beat out the flames. Only one room left—his own. He forced his way down the little hallway, kicked in his door. This room hadn't caught fire as badly as the others, but it was thick with smoke. His father lay coughing on the floor.

"Help me," he said.

Hoom took him by the hand and tried to drag him to the door, but Aven was too large and heavy for him. So he took him under the arms and tried to lift him. "Get up!" he shouted. "I can't carry you! Get up and walk!"

Aven finally understood, and staggered to his feet, clung to his son as he led him from the room. Hoom rushed him as fast as he could toward the stairs, but as they passed the open door of Noyock's office, Aven pulled away from him. "The history!" he shouted. "Father will kill me, Father will kill me!" He staggered toward the door. The pages of the history were already curling with flame. Hoom tried to hold him back, shouted that it was too late, but Aven only knocked him down and stumbled into the room. Hoom got up again in time to see the flames reach out to greet Aven as he clutched at the parchments and screamed and screamed. "I'm sorry!" he cried. He turned to face Hoom through the doorway, his clothing all afire, and screamed again, "I'm sorry!"

Then he fell backward onto the burning floor, just as someone grabbed Hoom by the ankle and pulled him to the stairs. Desperate hands took him and carried him outside. But all Hoom could think of was the sight of his father in the fire, clutching the burning parchment, screaming, "I'm sorry" as the flames uncovered his heart.

Lared awoke sobbing, his father holding him close, whispering, "It's all right, Lared. Nothing's wrong, Lared, it's all right."

Lared gasped at the sight of his father's face, then clung to him. "Oh, I dreamed!"

"Of course you did."

"I saw a father—a father dying, and I was afraid—"

"Just a dream, Lared."

Lared breathed deeply, tried to calm himself. He looked around and saw that the other men were also awake, looking at him curiously. "Just a dream," he explained to them.

But it was not just a dream. It was a true story, and a terrible one, and when the other men finally looked away, Lared gripped Father's hand and held it to his lips and whispered, "Father, I love you, I would never harm you."

"I know it," Father said.

"But I mean it," Lared said again.

"I know you do. Now go back to sleep. It was a terrible dream, but it's over now, and you didn't hurt me, whatever happened in the dream."

Then Father turned away, curled back under his blanket to sleep again.

But to Lared it was no dream. What Justice put into his mind came with too much clarity to be dismissed as mere madness of the night. Lared knew now how it felt to watch his father die, knowing that he caused it. And then, with her unsurpassed ability to intrude in his thoughts when Lared wanted her the least, Justice asked him, Did you know you loved your father before now?

To which Lared answered fervently, I hope I die before you make me dream again.

At sunrise Lared felt spent from the night's experience. He felt shy now before the other men—they had seen him vain as a cock yesterday, and tearful as a babe last night. This morning he was quiet, speaking little, embarrassed now to be in the lead with the others watching him.

Above all, to Jason he said nothing. Rather he stayed with his father, spoke to him when he needed to, and kept the pure blue eyes out of his sight.

At noon, Lared and Father mounted their horses to leave the last team behind. Jason would not be put off then. "Lared," he said.

Lared looked at the harness of his horse.

"Lared, I remember it, too. Before you dreamed your dreams, I have dreamed them all."

"Only because you wanted to," Lared said. "I never asked to see."

"I was given eyes. If you had them, would you leave them closed?"

"He has eyes," Father said, puzzled.

"Let's go now, Father," Lared said. They rode in silence past each of the last four trees in turn, until they reached the hut that Jason and Lared had built the last night, not all that long before. There was the final tree, girdled and ready for cutting.

And suddenly Lared was afraid. He did not know why. He simply felt—unprotected. Exposed. He stayed close to his father, following him when it had no purpose, even when his father went back to the sledge for another axe, because the one he used was too light for him, and kept twisting when it hit the tree.

Finally, Lared had to speak, just to calm his fear. "What if there weren't any iron in the world? Or so far away we couldn't get it?"

"I'm a blacksmith, Lared," Father said. "Those words are like telling a woman she's barren."

"What if?"

"Before iron, people were savages. Who would live in such a place?"

"Worthing," Lared said.

Father stiffened, rested on his axe for a moment.

"I mean the world, the planet. The iron only came shallow enough to find it in one place in the world. A desert."

"So you go to the desert and dig it out. Cut wood."

Lared swung his axe and made a chip fly. Father swung in turn and made the tree shudder.

The tree fell, and together they hacked away limbs, and rolled and levered it onto the sledge. It was not a mast tree; it was not so heavy that the horses had to be used just to pull it into place. By nightfall they had the second tree as well, and then they lay down to sleep in the hut.

Lared did not sleep, however. He lay awake, staring into darkness, waiting for the dream that he knew would come. Whenever he began to doze, he pictured Aven in his mind, Aven burning like paper in the forge. He did not know whether it was his own memory of the dream, or Justice putting it in his mind afresh. He dared not sleep for fear of worse dreams, though he did not know how he might stop Justice even if he could stay awake forever. It was not a rational decision to stay awake—it was pure dread, dread of the woman waiting in the night to take his mind from him and make him be someone else and do another man's acts. I would die for my father, I would never harm him.

Sleep never came, and neither did the dream. For once they had done precisely what he asked. They told him nothing, they showed him nothing. But waiting for it cost him rest, and at first light his father, thinking him asleep, poked him to wake him up. Now, with his father awake, now suddenly Lared felt himself able to sleep; and once he could dare to do it, his desperate body demanded it. Sleep. He staggered through the morning rituals, the hitching of the team; he almost fell from his horse when he dozed. "Wake up, lad," Father said, annoyed. "What's wrong with you?"

Chopping at the third tree invigorated him somewhat, but he was still not alert. Twice Father had to stop him. "You're cutting too high here. Bring it down, we don't want the branches to get caught up in other trees and never fall."

Sorry, Father. I thought I was cutting where you said. Sorry. I'm sorry.

And when the tree was ready to fall, it tipped the wrong way and tangled up, as Father had warned.

"Sorry," Lared said.

Father stood looking upward in disgust. "I don't see what's holding it up as it is," he said. "There's hardly a branch touching, if you look closely enough. Go bring the team, unhitch the team and bring them here, we'll have to pull it down."

Lared was still unharnessing the horses when he heard the crash of the tree falling.

"Lared!" cried his father. Lared had never heard such pain in his father's voice.

His left leg lay fully under a great branch of the tree; his left arm was pierced by a smaller one, which drove in at the great muscles of the upper arm and passed clear through, snapping the bone so the arm bent upward like another elbow at the break.

"My arm! My arm!" Father cried.

Lared stood stupidly, unable to understand that something was expected of him. Father's blood seeped out on the snow.

"Lever it off me!" Father cried. "It's not such a big tree, son! Lever it off me!"

Lever. Lared got the lever quickly from the sledge, got it into place, and heaved. The tree rolled up and away from Father, and with his good arm he struggled to slide away, but the balance of the tree was still wrong, and it rolled back down again. This time it caught only his foot, and didn't fall so far, so that there was little new pain. "Lared, stop the bleeding," Father said.

Lared tried pressing on the break in the arm, but the blood came too quickly. The bone was in tiny fragments there; the arm was so soft all the way through that there was nothing to press against. Lared knelt there in a daze, trying to think what else to do.

"Cut if off, you fool!" Father screamed. "Cut it off and tie off the stump and burn away the end of it!"

"Your arm—" Lared said. To cut off a blacksmith's arm, either arm, was to take the forge from him.

"My life, you fool! An arm for my life, I'll pay it!"

So Lared stripped the sleeves off his father's arm, then took an axe and this time struck accurately, taking off his father's arm just above the break. Father did not scream, only gasped. Lared used the torn-off shirtsleeve to tie the end so at last the bleeding stopped.

"Too late," Father whispered, his face white with pain and cold. "I've got no blood left."

Don't die, Father.

His eyes rolled back in his head and his body went limp.

"No!" Lared shouted angrily. He ran to the lever and this time forced the tree upward hard enough that it achieved a balance and stayed off his father's body. He dragged his father away, closer to the sledge. The leg was broken, but nothing had pierced the skin there. It was the stump of arm that made Lared so furious. There was nothing that had prepared him to see his father's body so mutilated. Those were the arms that went in and out of the fire—

Burn the stump of the arm. But there was no point in that if Father was dead. I should see if he's dead or not.

He was breathing, and there was a weak pulse in his throat.

But the wound was not bleeding now. It was more important to get him home than to do anything else. Muddled as his thinking was, Lared still knew that. It took him fifteen minutes to lever yesterday's trees off the sledge, and another quarter hour to get his father in place, his body bundled and covered with every blanket, then tied in place. Lared mounted the right-hand horse, the lead horse, and the sledge lurched forward.

Once they were under way, Lared realized he wasn't sure which way to go. Ordinarily he would follow the smoothest path home, which mean retracing their route. But they had gone far out of their way, leading the others to their trees. By far the shortest journey would be to go direct. The only trouble was that Lared didn't know the way for sure. On foot he could get home with no trouble. But he couldn't be sure of finding a path that was smooth and wide enough for the sledge.

He could not decide. His mind refused to clear. At last all he could think of was that home was closer if he left the path. As long as he stayed alert, as long as he kept in mind the way the forest was in summer, he could find a safe, quick route. He might yet save his father's life.

But he could not stay awake. Now, with the steady rhythm of the horse's walk, the hiss of the sledge over the snow, the endless whiteness of the winter forest, he could not concentrate on anything, kept waking to find his face pressed against the horse's neck. Desperately he clung to the horse and urged it on, faster and faster, crying out against himself. Why didn't you sleep last night! You've killed your father! And Aven's face loomed against the whiteness of the day, Aven stood in every bright place, clinging to the burning parchment, his clothes awash with flame.

Help me, he cried silently. "Help me!" he screamed aloud.

Of course Jason was watching. Of course Justice heard. But what they sent him was not a miracle, but another dream. He watched the snow ahead of him, he guided the horses among the trees, but it became sand, and his mouth dry and thirsty, and he was Stipock at the end of his dream of steel.

It was time for the rains to come, and the water in the cistern was getting low. Three jars had been broken in the last month, and now the memory of so much water spilling over the sand haunted Stipock.

Haunted him all the more because at last they had reached the iron. Carving into the cliff face with bronze and stone tools, they had penetrated some twenty meters into the rock. He thought it would be closer. Perhaps he had chosen the wrong spot. But the waiting had taken its toll. If they had found iron at once, it would have been too easy, it would have meant little. So it was just as well that the first year of their colony they spent most of their time turning the streams into ditches to make the sand produce food, and hacking at the ironwood trees a few miles away to bring down logs for their wooden houses. Heaven City had been generous with their tools, and Jason had brought more than a year's supply of ship's food when he flew them down to the southern desert. All had looked promising.

Except that even then the dust had choked them whenever they ran; even then there was always a thin film of dust on the top of the water, settling into deeper and deeper mud at the bottom, so that they learned not to stir the water in the cistern or the drinking pots. And the second year, when Hoom and Wix and Billin took their turns leading the diggers into the rock, then the dust was always in the air, until they became accustomed to filth, to white streaks in blackened faces, to the coughs at night as the diggers took their gritty breaths.

And now drought. The rains were due. The winds had come

on schedule, whipping sand and dust along the plain in gusts.
Here the wind was visible, and Stipock shielded his eyes,
squinted and watched each wall of wind as it came, dark as a
wave of the sea. The rains were due, and they had stuck iron;
for rain, they would have been grateful. But the iron was nothing. The iron was useless stone.

"We can't eat it," Billin said, standing on the pile.

The others listened wordlessly. A dust devil whipped by,
skirting the heap of ore.

"We can't drink it."

Stipock grew impatient. Usually at these meetings he held his
tongue, let the younger people reach their own conclusions, and
only stepped in with advice if they became deadlocked. But he
knew where Billin was leading, and it would be the end of them,
the end of the hope of bringing steel to Jason Worthing's world.
"Billin," he said, "we can't drink words, either. If you're going
to list the useless things in the desert, you might include those."

They laughed, some of them. Even Billin smiled. "You're
right, Stipock. So I won't make a speech. Don't all thank me at
once."

They laughed again. We aren't finished yet, thought Stipock,
if they can still laugh.

"You know that I went south for ten weeks. But since I came
back, I've told no one what I saw. No one but Stipock. He asked
me not to say anything because it would distract you from the
work. But now I think, since we do things by vote here, that you
ought to decide for yourselves what you do and do not want to
hear."

They wanted to hear about his journey south. Stipock bowed
his head and listened to the tale again. He went up the stream
into the hills, where the ironwood grew thicker and taller, where
some animals lived; and then up through a pass in craggy mountains, and when he reached the other side, the world changed.
There was not an exposed rock without moss, thick grass sprang
up underfoot, the soil was moist, and as he walked down the far
slope, the forest became unimaginably thick. Fruits that he had
never seen before grew from the trees. He tried some of them,
and they were good—he dared not try too many, for fear one
would be poisonous and so he could never return to tell the rest.

"And it was that way all the way down the river to the sea. All the way to the sea I went, where the sand is only in a ring around a bay, and water comes in pure streams down to the beach, and fruits and roots are so plentiful that you could eat forever and never have to farm at all. I'm not making that up. We've had enough disappointment. I wouldn't promise more than is there. It rained four of the five days, downpours so heavy the sea splashed with the raindrops, but it was over in an hour and the sun was bright again. You know it's true! I left with five days of food, and came back ten weeks later. I was tired and hungry, but not ten weeks' worth of hungry. There's food there! And Stipock knows it. Stipock knew all along that those lands were there. I say we should go there. I say we should live there, where there's plenty to be had. It doesn't mean giving up on the iron. We can send an expedition back here every year, well stocked with food and tools. But our families won't have to eat this dusty bread all year, they won't have to live with hunger every hour of every day. We can wash in the sea and be clean, drink from clear streams—"

"Enough, Billin," Stipock said. "They get the idea."

"Tell them that it's true, Stipock. They don't believe me."

"It's true," Stipock said. "It's also true that for half the year terrible storms come and ravage the shore, raising huge waves, with winds that kill. That's a danger. But there's a worse danger. And that is the danger that in a place where you don't have to work hard and think keenly to stay alive, you'll forget how to work and forget how to think."

"Who can think with his tongue thick as a stone in his mouth?"

"What Billin says sounds like perfection. But I ask you to stay. The rains are late, but they'll come soon. We aren't starving yet. There's still water."

They said little, but when the meeting was over, they agreed to stay.

As always, that night Stipock and Wix ate with Hoom and Dilna because otherwise they would have had to eat alone. "Why haven't either of you married?" Hoom asked from time to time. "I highly recommend it."

But Wix and Stipock never answered. Stipock never answered

because he didn't know why—he had never married on Capitol, either. Perhaps he was so much of an anarchist that he didn't want the government of a wife and children. Stipock knew much better why Wix didn't marry. It was because he already loved a woman, but the woman was Hoom's wife.

It was an open secret in the iron colony: when Hoom took his shift at the rock, leading his diggers deeper into the cliff, Wix called upon Dilna where she worked with the tools, or Dilna visited him in his house. People were busy at their work; no one was watching; perhaps they thought they were undiscovered. Stipock confronted Wix one day and said, "Why are you doing this? Everyone knows."

"Does Hoom know?"

"If he does, he doesn't show it. He loves you, Wix, you've been his friend since you used to sneak out of his father's house together. Why are you doing this?"

Wix wept with shame and vowed to stop, but he didn't mean it, and he barely hesitated. As for Dilna, Stipock did not even ask her. When she was with Hoom it was plain she loved him—he was a good father, a loving husband. Yet she did not bar her door to Wix. With Bessa and Dallat asleep, and Cammar outside playing or working in the sand, she took Wix into her bed like a thirsty man takes water. Once, when Stipock came to the house and found them together, she looked at him with eyes that begged him to forgive. That surprised him—he had seen so many adulteries on Capitol that it did not strike him as a sin anymore. Yet she wanted absolution. Forgiveness without repentance. Stipock could hear his father give the sermon: the coin of sin is pleasure, but the pay that comes is death. Watch out for death, Dilna. If you keep on with this, you'll surely die. Of course, you'll die if you live a chaste life, too. The beauty of chastity is that when death comes, you'll regard it as a blessed relief.

"They won't stay long now," Wix said, "if it doesn't rain soon."

"I know it," Stipock said.

Hoom broke the bread, and it crumbled like the sand outside the door. He smiled grimly and passed the dish. "Take a handful of bread. Also swallow an ironwood seed—there's soil enough in our bellies for it to grow."

Dilna poured the crumbs on her tongue. "Delicious, Hoom. You're definitely the best cook in the family."

"That bad, is it?" Hoom took a mouthful of water and swished it in his mouth, tasting it as if it had been palatable. When he finally swallowed, he looked disappointed that it was gone. "Stipock, I have to go, too. The children—we've got to do something before we run out of water, or it'll be too late, they'll not have the strength to go anywhere. It already dries them out, the sun and wind dry them, and they walk around here as if they were thinking of dying. We can't stay."

Dilna looked angry. "We came here for a purpose, Hoom—"

"I'm sorry," Hoom said. "Once these dreams of machines that could move themselves, and tools that could bite through bronze like butter, I thought that was all I wanted with life. When Jason sent us away from Heaven City to dig this iron, I was glad. But now that it comes to a choice between the future of the world and the future of my children, the choice goes the other way. For me there's no world without Cammar and Bessa and Dallat. They're asleep in there right now, and for me all that matters in the world is that they wake up tomorrow, and every tomorrow from now on. You and Wix, you have no families, you can decide for yourselves. And Dilna, she has courage that I can't find. But I am a father and that's all that matters to me now, with only four inches of water left in the cistern."

Stipock thought of Aven's house burning like a vast torch on the top of Noyock's hill, remembered Hoom screaming and screaming all night, so that they could hear him from Heaven City to Linkeree's Bay. They all thought it was the pain of burning, and it was true that he had heavy burns. But it was his father that he called for, hated Aven that he pleaded with. And now his fatherhood meant more to him, apparently, than motherhood to Dilna.

"I know what you're thinking," Dilna said. "You're thinking I don't love my children."

"It never crossed my mind," said Stipock.

"But I do love them. I just don't want to see them growing up to be useless and lazy and stupid. I am what I do. I'm a toolmaker. But what if they live in a place where they need no tools? Where they don't need clothing or shelter or—what would they be then? I won't go south. Stipock is right.''

Wix nodded. ''I'll wait for the rains too, as long as I can. And then I'll go. But not south. The way I see it, it's time to go home.''

They took that in silence for a while. Stipock watched them eat, watched them savor their water, watched them remember Heaven City and the boats on the water.

''We could make a boat from the ironwood trees,'' Dilna said, ''and go out to sea, and let the water carry us home.''

Stipock shook his head. ''There's a falls five hundred meters high well down the river, when the river flows at all. And even if we made it out to sea, we can't drink the seawater. It has salt in it.''

''I don't mind a little salt.''

''It has so much salt that it makes you thirstier and thirstier, and the more you drink the more you want until you die.''

Hoom shrugged. ''That means we walk.''

''It's a long way,'' Stipock said.

''Then let's hope it rains,'' said Hoom.

It didn't rain. The winds shifted to the west, but didn't move northwest; there was no water from the sea, but now the sand and dust became much worse than ever before. The dust seeped into every crack. It was millimeters deep on their beds and bodies when they woke in the morning. Children choked on it and cried out. After two days of it, one of Serret and Rebo's younger twins died.

They buried him in the sand during one of the brief lulls in the wind.

The next morning the dessicated body was in the open, the skin flayed away. The wind, in one of those cruel tricks of nature, carried the baby up against the front door of his family's house. Serret had to shove to get the front door open in the morning; his screaming once he saw what had jammed it closed brought everyone out of their houses. They took the body from him, tried to burn it, but the wind kept putting the fire out, and finally they carried it out into the desert to the lee of their settlement and let it lie there for the wind to carry it away.

That night they did the same with two more children, and

then carried Wevin's body to the same place after her baby tried to come four months early.

Billin went from house to house in the morning, his face muffled against the wind, and said, "I'm going today. I know the way. In three hours we'll be among the ironwood trees. By nightfall we'll be in a place with water. I'll wait there for three days, and then whoever is with me, I'll take them through the pass. Next year we'll come back to dig for iron. But this year we'll leave while our children are alive."

An hour later they huddled together in the lee of Billin and Tria's house, carrying their precious skin-covered jars of water, carrying or leading children. Stipock did not argue with them or try to make them stay. Nor did he listen to them when they whispered, "Come with us. We don't want to follow Billin, we want to follow you. You can keep us together, come with us."

But he knew that in a land where life was easy, no one could keep them together except with magic or religion, and he wasn't much with either—he wasn't cynic enough for the trickery of the first, or believer enough for the latter. "Go," he said. "I wish you well." They moved off into the desert at mid-morning, the wind whipping across their path, erasing their footprints almost before they were made, the sand whipping out from under their feet with every step. "Live," Stipock said.

For three more days, Stipock, Wix, Hoom, Dilna, and the children survived by living in the mine, sealing it off as best they could by tearing apart an empty house and rebuilding the walls at the mine entrance. At the back of the mine, in the darkness, they could breathe more easily. On the third day, they awoke to the sound of rain.

They ran to the entrance, tore away the wall, and caught their first glimpse of hell. It was as if the whole sea had fallen on them. The ground was all mud, and the houses themselves were sliding along the gentle slope as the mud flowed slowly toward the river. Yesterday the river had been dry. Now it was a torrent, well over its banks.

"Rain," said Wix. "Should we stay?"

It was a bitter joke. Wix and Hoom plunged out into the rain, which soaked them by the second step, and they went from house to house, gathering up what they could salvage before the houses were swept into the river. As it was, they barely made two trips each before the river lapped out to carry the huts away. Then they watched from the mine entrance, glad that it sloped upward so they were in no risk of drowning. They drank and drank, filling and refilling the same jars. Well back from the mine entrance they poured water over the children, washed them and let them play naked on the blankets. They had never been so clean, it seemed, and the sound of their laughter made the rain joyful.

Until the storm ended. The sun came out within minutes, and before nightfall the ground was baked and cracked. A few sticks remained of one house, all the rest were gone. The river continued to flow well into the night, but by morning it was back down to a mere trickle, a few stagnant ponds.

The heap of iron ore was gone. It had been too close to the river.

There was no need for discussion. They had little food and only the water in their jars and water bags. It was madness to go anywhere but south. So they went east, following Stipock's memory of the maps that Jason showed him. Cammar walked, and Hoom and Wix each carried a child. Dilna and Stipock carried their pitiful belongings. A few blankets, an axe, a few knives, crumbly bread, clothing. "We need clothing and blankets," Stipock warned them, "because it's going to be cold a few times on the way home."

Now, on the journey through the desert, it was harder for Wix and Dilna to pretend they did not love each other. Sometimes, in their weariness, they would lean on each other as they walked on. Stipock watched Hoom at such moments, but he only held Bessa or Dallat and walked on, perhaps singing or telling a story to the child. Hoom is not blind, Stipock decided. He sees but chooses not to see.

Before night the dust began to rise again, and Stipock led them south into the shelter of the ironwood forest. The next day they moved eastward among the trees, and the next day did the same, until they came to a broad riverbed heading northeast. It flowed, not strongly, but with water they could drink. So they followed its course for five days through desert and occasional grassland to the sea.

One of the days along the river, Stipock crested a hill and

stood beside Hoom and saw what he was watching: Wix and
Dilna embracing. It was just for a moment; they must have
thought they were far enough ahead not to be seen; or perhaps
they didn't care anymore. It was not passionate but weary, their
embrace, like a husband and wife long married and returning to
each other for familiar comfort. It occurred to Stipock that this
might well be more galling to Hoom than if they had looked
furtive and eager.

Hoom stepped down from the rise, and the lovers were suddenly out of sight behind a low ridge of dirt. "I thought," said
Hoom with a self-deprecating laugh, "I thought that of the two
of us, she felt *that* way toward *me* "

Stipock set his hand on Hoom's shoulder. Little Bessa breathed
hotly on his hand. "They both love you," he said. It was inane
to think that such words would comfort Hoom.

To Stipock's surprise, however, Hoom smiled as though he
needed no comfort at all. "I've known since we lived in Stipock's city. It began not long after we were married. Before
Cammar was conceived."

"I thought—that it began here."

"I think it was something they couldn't help. It was here that
they stopped trying to hide it. How could they?" Hoom held
Bessa tightly to him. "I don't much care whose seed it was that
grew. I'm the one who hoed, and I will harvest. These children
are mine."

"You're a kinder man than I am."

Hoom shook his head. "When Jason was with us, before he
brought us here, and I was trying to take the blame for my
father's death, he said to me, You are forgiven as you forgive
Wix and Dilna. I do, you know. It's not a lie. I had already
forgiven them before Jason said that. And because I knew that I
had no blame or hate for them, I believed Jason when he said
there was no blame or hate to hold against me, either. Will you
tell them that? If I should die sometime before the journey's
through, will you tell them that I forgive them, that it's all right?"

"You won't die, Hoom, you're the strongest of us—"

"But *if*."

"I'll tell them."

"Tell them that it's true. That I meant it. Tell them to ask Jason if they doubt it."

"Yes."

Then they crested the low ridge, and Wix and Dilna were there resting, playing with Cammar, trying to pretend that they were only friends weary from the journey.

From the mouth of the river eastward until they finally reached the isthmus leading north, it was the worst desert they had yet crossed. Stipock warned them, and they filled their water jars and water bags and drank from the river for two days until they could hardly bear to drink. "Keep this up and we can all piss and float home," Wix said, and they laughed. It was the last time they laughed for a while. The desert was longer to cross than Stipock had thought. The smooth and sandy beach gave way to cliffs and crags. There was as much vertical and horizontal travel, and each day Stipock insisted that they drink less and less. They ran out of water anyway, except for the little bit they had saved for the children. "It's not that far," Stipock told them. "There are streams on the isthmus, and it isn't far." Indeed, from the tops of hills they could look across the sea and catch a glimpse of land going northward, a coastline leading toward the land of pure water.

It was too far, though. They buried Bessa under a pile of rocks before dawn one day, and walked on more slowly, even though their burden was lighter by her scant weight. That night they reached an oasis of sorts, and drank the foul-tasting water, and filled their water bags and jars again. They thought they had made it. An hour later all were vomiting, and Dallat died of it. They buried him by the poisoned pool, and weakly walked on, emptying their jars and bags along the way through the sand. They did not weep. They hadn't the water in them to make tears.

The next day they reached a clear spring in the side of a hill, and the water was good, and they drank and didn't get sick. They stayed at the spring for several days, building back their strength. But now their food was getting low, and with full jars and bags they set out again.

Two days later they reached the top of a rocky rise, and stopped at the edge of a cliff that plunged nearly a kilometer, almost straight down. To the west they saw the sea, and to the east another sea, the water winking blue in the sunlight of early morning. At the bottom of the cliff the land funneled into a narrow isthmus between the seas. The isthmus was green with grass.

"Do you see the green down there, Cammar?" asked Hoom. The boy nodded gravely. "That's grass, and it means we'll find water, and perhaps something more to eat."

Cammar looked annoyed. "If we were going where there was food, why didn't you bring Bessa and Dallat? I know they were hungry."

No one knew how to answer, until Hoom finally said, "I'm sorry, Cammar."

Cammar was a forgiving child. "That's all right, Papa. Can I have a drink?"

They found a way down the cliff before noon; it was not sheer, but broken with many possible paths. They slept on the grass that night, and in the morning, for the first time in years, they awoke to a world that was wet with dew. Only then, with Cammar throwing wet grass at them, only then did they cry for the ones who died.

Lared shook himself, looked around. The horses were stopped facing a thicket. Behind him Father was moaning softly. It was afternoon. Lared could not remember any of the journey until now. Where was he? He looked behind him at the trail left by the sledge. It wound well enough among the trees. Had he guided the horses? Or had he slept? All he could remember was the desert, and Hoom and Wix and Dilna, and the children dying, and how at last it looked like life. But Father was moaning on the sledge behind him. Lared dismounted and walked stiffly back to see him.

"My arm," Father whispered, when he saw Lared. "What happened to my arm?"

"A branch broke clear through it, Father. You told me to cut it off."

"Ah, God," cried Father, "I'd rather die."

Lared had to know where they were. He walked back into an open area, found the rise of the mountains to the south. He was still headed in the right direction. But he couldn't picture this place in the summer. It looked all new to him. And if it was new, it meant he must have drifted far to the south, so far that he was in forest that he didn't wander in. Or perhaps he had passed Flat Harbor entirely.

Then, suddenly, he felt something shift in his mind and he recognized where he was. The clearing he was standing on was a pond, that's why it was so unfamiliar. He was on thick snow over the ice of the pond. There was the low mound of the beaver house. Somehow, in his sleep, in his dreams, he had followed the right course. Only the thicket stopped the horses, and it was a simple matter to turn them and follow the course of the frozen stream for a while, leading the horses to bring some life back into his own legs.

"Lared," Father called out. "Lared, I'm dying."

Lared did not answer. There was no answer to that. It was probably true, but it didn't stop him from pushing on. The trees opened into meadow, and he mounted again. And again the snow and the sound and the movement dazed him, and Justice brought him onward with a dream.

Stipock was tired. They had been climbing every day for a week, rising into the highest mountains in the world. Nowhere near the peaks, of course, but still fighting through incredible country. These were fairly old mountains, with many rolling hills—but the rolls were steep and high, and many times what looked from a distance to be an easy stroll turned out to be hands-and-knees climbing up the face of what lacked only two or three degrees to be a cliff.

Now they crested another grassy hill, with higher, craggier mountains on either side; but this time, instead of another, higher hill beyond, there were only lower hills, and clearly visible beyond them was an endless sea of deep green.

The others had reached the top before him. Cammar was running around in erratic circles—the child had energy left to spare—while the others contemplated the scene ahead.

"I feel like I'm falling," Dilna said. "It's been so long since anything ahead of us was down. Are we almost there?"

"More than halfway, now, and the worst behind us. No more desert. We should reach a large river soon, and we follow that for a long, long way. We might build a raft, and float down until it meets with a river nearly as large from the south. Then we go north, straight north, and cross low and gentle mountains, and soon we'll strike the Star River and follow it on home.''

"No," Wix said. "Tell me that we only have to go down this slope and Heaven City will be there. The world should not be any larger than this.''

"How do you keep the map in your head like that, Stipock?''

"I studied the map in the Star Tower. Searching for iron. I once thought of leading an overland expedition. I didn't expect Jason would be willing to fly us there.''

"Will they be glad to see us?'' Dilna asked. "We didn't leave under happy circumstances.''

Stipock smiled. "Do you really care how glad *they* are? We've had our stab at trying to build a perfect place. The climate was bad and the goal was all wrong. It isn't iron that makes a civilization." He thought of Hoom, loving his children and tolerating the intolerable between his wife and his friend. That is civilization, to bear pain for the sake of joy. Hoom grew up before I did, Stipock realized. He found out that if you try to eliminate the pain from your life, you destroy all hope of pleasure, too. They come from the same place. Kill one, you've killed all. Someone should have mentioned that to me when I was younger. I would have acted differently when Jason put me in his world. I was the devil, when I might have been an angel if I tried.

"People," Dilna said.

"What?''

"Civilization. People, not a metal, not a parchment, not even an idea.''

Wix eased himself to a sitting position on the grass, then lay back. "Stipock, admit it! All your talk of Jason being just a man was sham. You and Jason are both gods. You made the world together, and now you're here just to see what use we're making of it. And to impress us with miracles.''

"Mine haven't been too impressive so far.''

"Well, it takes a while to get in practice. Like chopping wood. The first few strokes are never right. That's when people lose

legs and feet, the first few strokes, when they aren't accustomed
to it.''

"A clumsy god. Well, I confess it. That's what I am." He
was about to say, And so are you, but a piercing scream interrupted them, and they jumped to their feet. "Cammar!" Hoom
shouted, and they quickly saw that he wasn't on the crown of
the hill. They ran in different directions; Stipock went to the
northwest brow of the hill, and saw with hope that there were
depressions marking small footprints in the grass; then saw, with
horror, that the running steps had carried the child, unsuspect-
ing, to the brink of a cliff. For once the roundness of this country
had failed. There was a mark of scraping at the very brink, torn
grass where Cammar had clutched. If we had been watching, if
we had been near, we might have saved him before he fell.

"Here!" Stipock called.

As the others ran up, Cammar's voice came from below the
edge of the cliff. "Stipock! Where's Papa! I'm hurt!"

Hoom ran along the edge of the cliff, out to an angle where
he could see. "Cammar! Can you see me!"

"Papa!" Cammar cried.

"He's just over the brink, on a ledge. Almost in reach!" Hoom
shouted, and he ran back to them. "I can reach him. Stipock
and Wix, hold onto my legs. Dilna, stay near the edge to help
me with him when we get him near the top. Don't lean out,
though. The edge isn't too secure."

His confidence, his air of authority calmed them all. It will
turn out all right, thought Stipock. It only vaguely occurred to
him that this was Hoom's blind spot, that he might not be willing
to believe that saving his son was impossible. Still, the child was
alive. There were piles of stone in the desert for the other two;
Dilna was pregnant again, but the unborn child could not compare with Cammar, the oldest and the last now alive. They had
to try, even at risk of their own lives.

Hoom lay on his back, not on his belly—it was an admission
that Cammar was so far down that he could not be reached by
a man bending at the waist, only by a man bending at the knees.
Stipock gripped his leg and together he and Wix lowered him
backward over the cliff

"Almost there!" Hoom shouted. "Just a little farther."

"We can't," Stipock said, because they were already so close to the edge themselves that he had to double his legs up under him to keep them from dangling over the edge. Stipock only had Hoom by the ankle now, and his grip was none too sure. But somehow they lowered him another few centimeters.

"Almost! A little farther!"

Stipock was going to protest, but saw that Wix was grimly moving closer to the edge. Of all people, Wix cannot fail to help Hoom save his son, Stipock knew that, and so he began to carefully adjust his grip to allow him to lower Hoom a little more.

Then, suddenly, Hoom screamed, "No, Cammar! Don't jump for me! Stay there, don't jump for me!" And then a high-pitched child's scream, just as Hoom kicked powerfully, lunged downward, pulling his leg out of Stipock's grasp.

By some miracle Wix held on, crying out in the pain of the exertion. Dilna held onto Wix to keep him from falling over, too. Stipock could not get near enough to help Wix hold onto Hoom; he could only help Dilna in her effort to keep him from following Hoom over the edge.

"We could use a miracle now," whispered Wix.

"Cammar!" cried Hoom, his voice echoing among the mountains. "Cammar! Cammar!"

"He doesn't even know that he's in danger," Dilna said, panting and whimpering from grief and terror and despair. Stipock knew the feeling. They were safe. They had come this far, they were surely safe now. Something was very, very wrong with the world.

Then Wix screamed and his fingers gave way and Hoom slipped over the edge. They heard him strike ground; they heard him strike again. Not far away. Not all the way down. But definitely, definitely out of reach.

Dilna screamed and struck at Wix. Stipock got above them, pulled them both until they came up with him, up away from the lip of the abyss. Only when he was sure they would not accidently follow Hoom, only then did he shout "Hoom! Hoom!"

"He's dead, he's dead!" Dilna cried.

"I tried to hold him, I really tried!" Wix sobbed.

"I know you did," Stipock answered. "You both did. Neither

of you could have done more. You did the best you could." Then
he called again for Hoom.

This time Hoom answered, sounding exhausted and afraid.
"Stipock!"

"How far down are you!" Stipock called.

Hoom laughed hysterically. "Far. Don't come down. You can't
get here. Can't get down or up."

"Hoom," Dilna said. But her voice was not a shout, it was
a prayer.

"Don't try to come after me!" Hoom shouted again.

"Can you climb up at all? Or down?"

"I think my back is broken. I can't feel my legs. Cammar is
dead. He jumped for my hands. I touched his fingers, but I
couldn't hold him." Hoom wept. "They're all gone, Stipock!
Do you think I'm even now?"

Stipock understood what he meant: trading his children's lives
for his own guilt at the death of his father. "This isn't justice,
Hoom. It doesn't come out even."

"It must be justice!" Hoom cried. "It sure isn't mercy!" A
pause. "I can't hold on for very long, I think. Just my arms
holding me."

"Hoom, don't let go! Don't fall."

"I thought of that already, Dilna, but it's going to happen
anyway—"

"No!" Dilna shouted. "Don't fall!"

"I tried to hold on to you!" Wix shouted.

"I know. It was Stipock who let go, the old turd. Stipock, do
your miracle now."

"What miracle?" Stipock asked.

"Make us clean."

Stipock took a deep breath, and then he spoke, loudly, so
Hoom could hear him, too. "Hoom told me that if he ever—if
something happened to him—"

"Yes, go on!" Hoom shouted.

"That he has known since before Cammar was conceived.
And he loved you both anyway. And loved the children. And
he—forgave. I believe him. He has no anger in him."

Dilna was weeping. "Is it true?"

"Yes," said Hoom.

Wix turned over and lay facedown in the grass and cried like a child.

"I'm going to let go now," said Hoom.

"No," said Dilna.

So he didn't let go. But there was nothing to say, nothing to do. They just waited at the top of the hill, listening as Wix cried, listening to the birds calling each other in the canyons.

"I have to let go now," Hoom said. "I'm very tired."

"I love you!" Dilna cried.

"And I!" shouted Wix. "I should have died, not you!"

"*Now* you think of it," Hoom said. Then he let go. They heard him slide a little, and then heard nothing at all.

"Hoom!" Dilna called. "Hoom! Hoom!"

But he didn't answer. He never answered.

So after they spent themselves in tears, they got up and took their burdens, they climbed carefully down the safe slopes, and made their way out of the mountains into the great forest. They found the river, built a raft, and the three of them floated for weeks, it seemed, they lost count of days.

They wintered north of the river, and Dilna's child was born. She thought of naming him Hoom, but Stipock forbade it. She had no right to saddle the child with her guilt, he said. Hoom had forgiven them, they owed no debt to him, the child should not be forced to remind them. So she named him Water. And in the spring they crossed the mountains and entered Heaven City, where they were greeted with rejoicing.

"Lared," said Jason.

Lared awoke. He was on horseback. Villagers were all around him. "Lared, you brought your father home."

Lared turned to look at his father on the sledge behind him. Justice was bending over him. Sala stood beside her, nodding. "He's alive and probably won't die," she said, her voice calm and almost adult-sounding. "Cutting off his arm saved his life."

"He told me to," Lared said.

"Then he told you well." The words were strange, coming from his younger sister. Strange to her too, for suddenly it was as if the water had poured from a goatskin bag. She began to cry. "Father! Father!" And she knelt on the sledge and held her father and kissed his face. He awoke then, opened his eyes and said, "He took my arm, damn the boy, he took my arm."

"Never mind," Jason whispered to Lared. "He's not himself."

"I know," said Lared . He slid from the horse, stood shakily on the ground. "The day went on forever. Take us home."

It was less than a kilometer back to the village. Jason had cut loose his team, abandoning the sledge, and rode down the whole path, alerting all the timbering crews. They too unharnessed the horses and rode on quickly, gathered along the six men who had already brought their logs home, and only just got to where Lared had brought his father.

"Did Justice guide me?" Lared asked. "I dreamed the whole way here. Stipock and Hoom and—"

"She sent you the dream, but she didn't guide you. How could she? She doesn't know the way."

"Then how did I get here?"

"Perhaps there's more in you than you thought."

Jason helped him through the door of the inn, where Mother hugged him tightly, savagely, and then demanded, "Is he alive!"

"Yes," Lared said. "They're bringing him now."

Then Jason helped him to his truckle bed, which waited ready by the fire. He lay there trembling while four men carried in the mutilated body of the blacksmith. He was unconscious. Jason set to work at once, boiling herbs and dressing the stump. While Father was still unconscious, Jason set the leg and splinted it.

All the time, Justice sat in a chair, watching. Lared watched her from time to time, to see if she winced at his father's pain. She showed no sign of noticing. No sign that she knew that she could heal him with a thought, could even restore his arm. Lared wanted to shout at her. If you can heal it, and don't, then you consent to it!

She did not speak into his mind. Instead, Sala came to him and touched him on the forehead. "Don't torment me, Lareled," she said. "Think of Hoom and Cammar and be glad you're home."

He kissed his sister's hand and held it for a while. "Sala, please say your own words to me."

Almost at once Sala began to cry. "I was so afraid, Lared. But you brought Father home. I knew you would."

She kissed his cheek. But then it suddently occurred to her. "But Lared, you forgot to bring his arm. How will he beat the iron, without a hand to hold it?"

Then Lared wept softly, for Father, yes, and for himself, and tears for Hoom and Cammar, for Bess and Dallat, for Wix and Dilna and for Aven, for the innocent and guilty, for all the pain. I never knew I loved Father till he lay there at the brink of death. Perhaps I never *did* love him, until he was nearly gone. It seemed a very powerful thought, until it occurred to him that Justice probably put it into his mind. At that he went to sleep. He could not escape them, and the price of trying was too high. He had somehow got home, and he had kept his Father alive somehow, and that was enough for now, he feared nothing now, not even dreams; no, not even sleep.

9
Worthing Farm

Father lay in bed, sleeping like death for several days. But whenever anyone asked how he was, Sala answered, "He'll be fine."

Fine, thought Lared, good as new, but with his left arm missing and a memory of his son, staggering like a drunken man, chopping at the tree like a child; I took his arm, and not because I swung the axe to cut it off—there'd be no blame in that, God knows—but because I made the tree fall wrong, I made it hang in the branches of the other trees.

He tried not to blame it on Jason and Justice. Forcing me to have dreams of fathers dying, so that I lay awake in terror of it, and so caused my father to as much as die. Was this in their design from the start? Did they show him Aven's death so that he would maim his own father? What then does Hoom's death mean? What fall is in store for me? But when he thought like that, he would become ashamed, because it was the dream of Stipock's journey home to Heaven City that had kept him moving when on his own he could never have brought Father home.

The others in the village wanted to make much of him. Lared, the treeherd who saved his father's life and brought one-armed Elmo home on an unknown path. The tinker kept threatening to make up a song about the deed, and the other men, who had been so amused at him before, now treated him with unfeigned respect. With awe, in fact, falling silent when he entered the room, asking his opinion as if he had some unusual wisdom. Lared took all these changes courteously—why should he rebuff their love?—but each kindness, each honor galled him, for he knew that rather than praise he should have blame.

He hid from them in the book. There was much to write, of Stipock, Hoom, Wix, and Dilna, he told himself. So he closed himself in Jason's room all day, writing and writing. He came down for meals, and to do the work that must be done with Father lying deathlike on his bed, but even that became unnecessary, for Lared began to find that whatever job he thought that he must do, Jason was already doing when he got to it. Lared had nothing to say to Jason, just walked away. Obviously Jason was hearing the need to do the job from Lared's own mind, and then rushing to do it so that Lared would get back to the book. Lared even wondered sometimes if they hadn't plotted out the entire thing so that he would spend more time writing. Very well, he thought, I *will* write, as quickly as I can I'll write, and finish the book and send you and it away as far from me as possible.

One day, when the snow was falling thick outside and the house was full of the smell of sausage frying, Lared bent over the table and wrote at last of the death of Cammar and Hoom. He wept as he wrote it, not because of the dying, but because of the forgiveness Hoom gave to Wix and Dilna as he died. Jason found him there; Lared resented his coming in—Jason, at least, couldn't plead the excuse that he didn't realize Lared didn't want him there.

"I know you don't want me here," Jason said. "But I *am* here, all the same. You've written all you know so far."

"I want no more dreams from you."

"Then I have delightful news. You've finished all the tales I have that are worth seeing for yourself. I will tell you how I ended my time with my people, and then—"

"And then I give you the parchment and you go away."

"And then Justice will give you the memories that my own descendants preserved through all the generations. Like the tale of the tinker."

"I want no more dreams and tales."

"Don't be so angry, Lared. You should be glad of the dreams you've had. You might take a lesson from Hoom, for instance, and instead of punishing yourself and me and Justice for your father's injury, become as generous as Hoom and forgive us all."

"What do you know and understand of Hoom?" said Lared.

"You forget that I'm the one who sent my mother off to a colony against her will. Very much the way you cut off your father's arm. You have in you the memory of every pain I've suffered in my life. You loved Hoom the more for knowing him— why not me?"

"You are not Hoom."

"Yes I am. I'm Hoom and everyone else whose heart I've had in me. I've been so many people, Lared, I've felt so much of their pain—"

"Then why do you cause more? Why don't you leave me alone?"

Jason struck the wall behind him with the butt of his fist. "Why don't you realize that I feel even what you're feeling now, you fool! I know you and I love you and if I could spare you one bit of this, if I could ease your burden and still accomplish what must be done—"

"Nothing *must* be done! You only *want* to do it."

"Yes, that's right. I want to do it the way you want to breathe. Lared, for thousands of years my children watched all the worlds of men, protected you all from pain and suffering. In all that time, Lared, in all those years there *never* was a Hoom! Do you understand me? A Hoom or Wix or Dilna is impossible in a universe where actions have no consequences! Why do you love Hoom, if not because of what he did in the face of suffering? Without the suffering, what was he? A clever carpenter. Without his father's beatings all his life, without the face of his father haloed in the flames, without his wife's adultery and the deaths of Bessa, Dallat, and Cammar—yes, without the touch of Cammar's fingers as he leapt and fell, what would there he in Hoom to make you love him? What would there be of greatness in him? What would his life have meant?''

Jason's passion shocked Lared. He had been so calm for all these weeks, it made his rage the more fearsome. But Lared would not be put off, even so. "If you could ask Hoom, I think he would gladly have forgone the greatness if he could have lived his life in peace.''

"Of course he would. Everybody would prefer that everything go smoothly for them. The worst bastards in the world are those who devote their entire lives to making sure things go smoothly for themselves. Individual preference has nothing to do with what I'm saying.''

"That's plain—you've never been one to go out of your way to do good for other people, except when you need them to do something to further your grand design.''

"Lared,'' Jason said, ''people aren't individuals, even though we all think we are. Even before I came, what did you know of yourself, except what your family told you? Their tales of your childhood became your vision of yourself; you imitated your father and mother both, learned what it means to be a human being from them. Every pattern of your life has been bent and shaped by what other people do and what other people say.''

"So what am I then, a machine that echoes everyone around me?''

"No, Lared. Like Hoom, you have in you something that makes a choice—something that decides, This is me, this is not-me. Hoom could have become a murderer, couldn't he? Or he could have treated his children as his father treated him, couldn't he? It's that part of you that chooses that is your soul, Lared. That's why we couldn't dump one person's bubble into another's mind—there are some choices you cannot live with, you cannot bear remembering that you did this thing, because it is not the sort of thing you do. So you aren't just an echo. But you are part of a cloth, a vast weaving; your life forces other people to make choices, too. The men who honor you for saving your father—don't you realize that it gives meaning to *their* lives, too? Some might be jealous of you, you know—but they are not. They love you for your goodness, and that also makes them good. But if there were no pain, if there were no fear, then what does it matter that we live together, that our lives touch? If our actions have no consequences, if nothing can be bad, then we might as well die, all of us, because we *are* just machines, contented machines, well oiled and running smoothly with no need to think, nothing to value, because there are no problems to solve and nothing we can lose. You love Hoom because of what he did in the face of pain. And because you love him, you have become him, in part, and others, knowing you, will also become him, in part. It's how we stay alive in the world, is in the people who become us when we're gone." Jason shook his head. "I tell you all this, but you don't understand."

"I understand, all right," Lared said. "I just don't believe you."

"If you understood it, Lared, you'd believe it, because it's true."

Then Justice spoke in Lared's mind: Jason tells you only half the truth, and that is why you don't believe.

Jason must have heard her too, because his face went dark with anger, and he slumped down and sat on the floor and whispered, "So I'm not human; so be it."

"Of course you're human," Lared said.

"No, I'm not. Justice knows me better than any living soul. It's what she told the Judges: I am not human."

"You have flesh and blood like any man."

"But no compassion."

"That much is true."

"I *feel* what other people feel, but I have no pity for them. I saw the universe without pain and I said, This is foul, undo it, and then I chose to remain in it because I prefer to live here, surrounded by fear and suffering, I would rather live in a world where there can be agony like Hoom's—so that there can be a man like Hoom. I would rather live in a world where a man does a mad thing like walking naked through the snow just for the sake of honor, or where a blacksmith chooses and says, Take my arm to save my life, or where a woman sees her husband come home one-armed and almost dead and goes that day to tell her lover, I will never come to you again, for now if my husband learned of this, he would believe I hated him because he wasn't whole.''

Lared held the quill tremblingly in his hand. ''I hate you.''

''Your mother was a woman, and nothing more. She had no face until the Day of Pain.''

''We were happier without faces, then.''

''Yes, and the dead are the happiest of all. They feel no pain, they have no fear, and the best sort of human is the one most like a river, flowing wherever it's carried by the slope of the land.''

''You're glad for other people's pain, that's what you are. That's why you came here—to relish it.''

The words stung. ''Think of me what you like,'' Jason said, ''but now tell me this: which of all the dreams I've given you would you like to forget? Which of them would you like to have taken completely out of your mind, as if it had never happened? Which of these people do you wish you had never known?''

''You,'' said Lared.

Jason looked as if he had been hit. ''Besides me. Who would you like Justice to remove from your memory, the way you scuff out a drawing in the dirt?''

''You've done enough to my memory. Leave me alone.''

''You fool. What do you think all your protection *was* but changes in your memory? You tell me to leave you alone, but you hate me because we have done exactly that. Which do you want, boy—to be safe or to be free?''

''I just want to be alone.''

''As soon as I can, Lared, I'll let you be as alone as your heart desires. But we have a book to finish. So listen and I'll tell you all the rest of the story that's mine to tell. No dreams—your precious memory will be undisturbed. Are you ready?''

Lared set down the pen. ''Make it quick.''

''Do you want to know what happened to Stipock and the others?''

Lared shrugged. ''You'll tell me what you want.'' He knew he was infuriating Jason all the more; it was what he wanted.

''Wix and Dilna married, of course. I took them both into the Star Tower, and they each served several terms as Mayor. I made Stipock write a few books on machinery and fuels and general knowledge—something that future generations could build on. Then I took him into the ship as well, and he was Mayor twice. He married and fathered eleven children before I took him, though. At the end of three hundred years there were some two million people in Heaven City. Though it wasn't a city like Capitol—maybe twenty thousand people lived in the city proper. They were spread well onto the northern plain, and south into the forests and mining country clear to the headwaters of the Star River, and already there were some who had gone to live at the mouth of Heaven River. They were all one culture and one language and one people, and I decided that they had foundation enough. They had learned all that I could teach them, and so I brought out all the people I had saved in the Star Tower, and chose some few dozen among those who had never gone under somec, and I sent out colonies year by year, five thousand people at a time. Stipock sailed in ships to the land where his mining effort had failed before; Kapock and Sara went overland with two thousand sheep to crop the grasslands east of Stipock's desert; Wien the bronzesmith went to the mountains of the northeast, and Wix and Dilna led their people eastward. Noyock sailed westward to the islands, where his cattle were fenced only by the sea. Linkeree and Hux each founded cities at opposite ends of the Forest of Waters, on the river that Stipock, Wix, and Dilna rafted on their journey home. Those are all the ones you know— there were many others. And the one colony I didn't wish to send—Billin's people in the islands of the south. As I heard it, they became uncivilized rather sooner than the rest. But the peace I established wasn't permanent, not anywhere. There was commerce and there was war, exploration and concealment; lies were told and truth was left forgotten. Still, every people in every land remembered the golden age of Jason, the time of peace. People have a way of longing for lost golden ages. *You* know about that.''

"It isn't you I miss," said Lared.

"When the last of the colonists left Heaven City, I raised the starship from its resting place in First Field. It wasn't fit for flight among the stars, but that hardly mattered. I put it into orbit and then I went to sleep. For fifty years.''

"Perched like God in the sky," said Lared, "peering through the clouds to see how the world got on."

Jason went on as if Lared hadn't spoken. "It was only when I awoke that I began my real work. After all, I hadn't tried to make a utopia—all I had done, really, was teach the people how to work and prosper and live with the consequences of their acts. I had some other business to attend to. I was feeling and looking nearly forty, now, and I had had no children. And Worthing's world, Lared, was going to be a place where my gifts would grow and develop and perhaps become something more than I had made them.

"So I took a landing craft and some equipment, and chose a place beside the West River in the densest part of the Forest of Waters, a place where no highways would go, at least not until the world filled up, which I doubted would be soon. I set off a circle ten kilometers across, and marked it with an inhibitor."

"I don't know the word."

"I know you don't. It sets up an invisible barrier that's very uncomfortable for an intelligent being to cross. Birds fly through it. Dogs and horses are a bit annoyed. We had no dolphin problem, for obvious reasons. I embedded the inhibitor in a stone, and lasered an inscription on the stone:

> **WORTHING FARM**
> *From the stars*
> *Blue-eyed one*
> *From this place*
> *Jason's son.*"

"I can see you were determined to stop this nonsense of people worshiping you," Lared said.

"I didn't start it—you know that, Lared. But I could use it, couldn't I? Already every colony had legends of Jason, who took the Star Tower into heaven, but someday would return. I only had to change that a little. I went to Stipock—the nation of Stipock, since Garol had already died. His grandson, Iron, was the Mayor of the place. I didn't tell them who I was, just asked for a place to live. But they weren't blind—it's hard to hide my eyes. Stories sprang up at once, and people came to see me, but

I never admitted being Jason. I only lived there six months, but in that time I told some stories. Enough to tell the world to look for the coming someday of my son, and to give them some reason not to hate and murder my children if they found them. You must remember that I had lived half my life—more than half, then—in fear of being called a Swipe and killed.

"At the end of six months I married Iron's daughter, Rain, and took her north with me, to Worthing Farm. Oh, did I mention? I never told my people the name Worthing. I only gave the name to Worthing Farm, and only told it to an inner circle in Stipock. They were my watchers, to protect the world in case one of my children should be a Radamand—it was, after all, in the blood.

"I took poor Rain with me to Worthing Farm, and we had seven children, and it was the happiest time of my life. But I'm not like Hoom, Lared. I loved my children, but I loved them less than I loved other things. I was like my father, I suppose, or perhaps like Doon—I had work to do and things to learn that I valued more than love. You're the one that's right, though. It's as you said—I have no heart." Jason smiled cruelly. "At the end of ten years—and to me, remember, Lared, this was a year ago—I put the gate of the inhibitor in her hand and taught her how to use it, and then I left. I had to know what would come of things. How the world would end. So I said good-bye to Rain and told her that it was vital that she only leave Worthing Farm when it was time to choose a husband or a wife for one of our children. No child with these blue eyes would ever be allowed to leave. And any child who did not have these eyes was to be sent away at adulthood with whatever inheritance the farm could spare."

"What a happy family it must have been," Lared said, "with the children prisoners."

"It was cruel and miserable. I thought they would never keep it up. I was just trying to give them time, perhaps three or four generations to establish themselves in some numbers before they went out and put themselves at the mercy of the world. Someone would rebel, I was sure, and steal the gate, open the inhibitor and leave it open. How was I to know how patient they would be? Perhaps it lasted so long because I told Rain that each keeper of the gate, before she died, must name a daughter or daughter-in-law to own the gate after her, and control the ins and outs. When I founded my little family, remember, my particular gift was passed from father to son, linked to sex. I had no way of knowing that would change—and it didn't, for a long, long time. So the gate passed from one woman to the next, women who did not have this gift, whose only power in their families was the gate itself. They handed down the gate for a thousand years. For a thousand years only the children stayed who could look behind the eyes. What I didn't count on was that many of those who were cast out, simply went beyond the inhibitor's range and started farms, and it was their daughters who became the wives of Worthing. After a while the inbreeding became quite intense. It changed the power as it doubled and redoubled. It also made them brilliant and intense, weak and sickly, frightened of the world and conscious, always, of the invisible wall and the stone in the middle of the farm. I should have foreseen it, but I didn't. I gave them powers beyond anything men had conceived of except in their dreams of God; but I also made them less than human in their hearts. The miracle is not that they grew powerful. The miracle is that when they finally left Worthing Farm, any of them had any humanity at all."

"And where were you, while your beautiful family grew up?"

"I went back up to the starship, and got everything ready, and then took the ship down to the bottom of the sea. I would only waken when the world had technology enough to notice I was there and bring me to the surface. Or when the rest of mankind discovered my little world, and woke me. Either way, I thought that would be a good time to wake up. I never doubted that I'd waken. I didn't know it would be fifteen thousand years, of course, but I would have done it anyway. I had to know how things would end."

Lared waited. Apparently Jason was finished. "Is that it, then? I'll write it in an hour, you can take the book, and then you can leave here and never disturb us again."

"I'm sorry to disappoint you, Lared, but it isn't the end. It's only the end of the part of the story I can tell. Justice will give you dreams for all the rest."

"No!" Lared shouted, and he got up from the table, knocking it over, spilling the ink across the floor. "Never again!"

Jason caught him by the arm, spun him back into the middle of the room. "You owe us, you ungrateful, self-pitying little bastard! Justice dreamed you home. You owe us your father's life."

"Why doesn't she just change me, then, and make me *want* to endure these dreams?"

"We thought of that," Jason said, "but we're forbidden to do that in the first place, and in the second place it would change who you are, and anyway, you've told us not to play with your mind. There aren't many more dreams, Lared, because we're nearly finished. Besides, the dreams aren't so clear now. They're not memories of direct experience, as Stipocks's were, from him to me to you. These memories were passed on through generations of my family, just the bits and fragments that each new generation found to be vital enough to remember. What you'll dream tonight is the oldest memory that survived. A thousand years after I left them, and this is how they finally ended their imprisonment."

"Don't give it to me in the night. Tell me now," said Lared.

"This one must be seen in memory. If I tell you, you won't believe or understand it."

There was a knock at the door. It was Sala. "Father's awake," she said. "He isn't very happy."

Lared knew that he must go downstairs, but dreaded facing his father. Father knows what harm I did him. He could see all too clearly in his memory the way Father's arm looked, impaled and crushed on the end of a broken branch. He could remember all too well the feel of the axe as it cut through flesh and split the bone. I did it, Lared said silently. I did it, as he went down the stairs. I did it to you, as he stood beside his father's bed.

"You," Father whispered. "They say you brought me home." Lared nodded.

"You should have left me, and finished what you began."

His father's cold hatred was more than he could bear. He ran upstairs and threw himself on Jason's bed and wept for grief and guilt. He wept until he fell asleep, and Jason didn't wake him when he saw him there, but slept on the floor himself so Lared could have his dream.

* * *

Elijah held the plow as the oxen pulled, making straight furrows across the field. He did not look to the left or the right, just followed as steadily as if he and the oxen were all one animal, the same beast. It was almost true, for Elijah's mind was not on his plowing. He was seeing through his mother's eyes, his old mother's mind, watching as she committed the unspeakable act.

"There are flecks of black in Matthew's eyes," she said. Her eyes, of course, were brown, since she was a child of over-the-wall. "He isn't one who has to stay. He has to leave."

Wants to leave, that's all, wants to go away because he hates this place and hates *me* because I am stronger than he is, he wants to get away from *me* to over-the-wall, but it is forbidden. His eyes have flecks of black in them, but Matthew has the power of Worthing nevertheless, and so must stay; he has *one* power, whatever else he lacks: he has the power to shut me out. He has the power to keep me from peering in his mind. In all of Worthing, in all of time that anyone remembers, never has there been a one who had the power to close himself to our Worthing eyes. What does he hide? How dare he keep secrets? He must stay, he must stay—we want no one in the world whose children might have power to close us out. He must stay.

As Mother took the gate from its place above the fire, Elijah called silently to all the others. Come. Mother means to use the gate. Come.

And so they came, all the blue-eyed men of Worthing, all their wives, all their children. Silently, wordlessly, because they had so little need of speech. They gathered at the low stone wall that marked the edge of Worthing. They were waiting when Mother came to let Matthew go.

"No," said Elijah.

"The decision is mine," said Mother. "Matthew isn't one of you. He can't see the way you see. He doesn't know the things you know. Why should I make him live here with you, like a blind man in a world of sight, when out there in over-the-wall he's like everyone else?"

"He has a power, and his eyes are blue."

"His eyes are bastard, and the only power he has is privacy. I wish to God I had it, too."

Elijah saw himself through Mother's eyes, felt the fear she felt of him, but still he knew she would not bend. It made him angry, and the grass grew dry and brittle beneath his feet. "Do not betray the law of Worthing, Mother."

"The law of Worthing? The law of Worthing is that I am keeper of the gate, and the decision is mine. Which one of you will dare to take the gate from me?"

No one, of course. None of them would dare to touch the gate. Defiantly she squeezed it and held it open. They felt it as a sudden inward silence, the absence of a noise they had always heard before but never noticed till it ended. The gate was open, and they were afraid.

Matthew started forward, carrying his inheritance—an axe, a knife, a scrip that held a cheese and a loaf of bread, a water bag, a cup.

And Elijah stood in front of him, to block the way.

"Let him go," said Mother, "or I'll leave the gate open every moment of every day, and your children will climb the wall and wander off, and Worthing Farm will become the same as over-the-wall! Let him go or I will do that!"

Elijah thought then to take the gate from her and give it to another woman who would keep the law, but when the others saw that thought in his mind they forbade him, and said that they would kill him if he did.

You are all unworthy, Elijah said in silence. You are all cursed. You all will be destroyed because you consented to her breaking of the law. Then in silent rage Elijah stepped aside and let his brother go. Then he walked back to the field. Behind him, the grass where his feet had stepped went dry, and withered, a small trail of death. Elijah was angry, and there was death in him. He saw his mother notice this, and it pleased him. He saw that his cousins and his uncles also were afraid. There has been none like me in Worthing until now. Worthing has given me such power now, at the time when the law was broken by a woman who did not understand the danger of her most-beloved son. Worthing made me at the time of trouble, and I will not let Matthew leave here without punishment. The law will not be broken without revenge.

He did not decide what his revenge would be. He merely let

his anger grow. Soon Mother began to shrivel like the grass, her skin drying and flaking off her, her tongue thick in her mouth. She drank and drank, but nothing could quench her thirst. Four days after Matthew left, she handed the gate to Arr, Elijah's wife, who did not want it; handed the gate to Arr and died.

Arr looked at her husband in fear and said, "I don't want this."

"It is yours. Obey the law."

"I can't bring Matthew back."

"I don't expect you to."

And in her mind Arr said, She was your mother.

And into her mind Elijah put his answer: Mother broke the law, and Worthing is angry at her. Matthew also broke the law, and you will see what Worthing does.

But nothing seemed to happen as the days went by. Matthew did not go far—he walked among the people of over-the-wall, the cousins and sisters and aunts with all their families, and the ones whose eyes were not the blue of Worthing, and he persuaded many of them to come away. Elijah could not know what Matthew planned, only what he told the others. He spoke of building a town, where he would keep the inn, a place ten miles to the west, where the north road crossed the river and travelers often passed. We will learn something of the world of men and women, he said. And of all blasphemies, this was the worst: as he laid the foundation of his inn he named it Worthing.

There is only one Worthing in the world, and that is Worthing Farm.

It took two months before they realized how terrible Elijah's vengeance was going to be. For in those weeks no rain fell, and the sun beat down mercilessly every day. A stretch of pleasant weather became a dry spell, and a dry spell became a drought. No cloud came over the sky, and the heavy mustiness of the air was gone, the air was dry as desert. The people's lips chapped and split; the dry air hurt like a knife to breathe it; the river fell, and hidden sandbars became islands, and then peninsulas, and finally the river did not flow at all. The trees of the Forest of Waters went greyish green, the leaves hung limply from the branches, and in the fields of Worthing Farm, despite the wells they dug and the water that they hauled from the slackening river, the seedling crops went brown, went black, and died.

It was the work of hate, of Elijah's anger; even he had not realized he could do so much.

And as the days went on, the people and animals began to weaken. They came to Elijah then, and pleaded with him. You have punished us all enough, they said. Our children, they said. Let it rain. But Elijah could not do it. He had never decided that the rain should stop; he had only filled himself with anger, and he could not cease to hate just because he was asked to; not even because he wanted to.

He wasn't even sure that he had done it. He heard travelers telling Matthew in his fine new inn that droughts like this came every now and then, but usually in Stipock across the sea. It was natural enough, and it would end soon with a great storm that near tore roofs from houses and drowned the world—it happened every century or so, to renew the world.

Others said it was just chance. Storms passed to the south; there was no drought in Linkeree, far to the west, or eastward in Hux. Even the West River flowed strong and bold from Top of the World down past Hux, only to dry up when it reached the area of the drought. "I'd say you're in the center of it here," the travelers would say. "But it's just chance."

The children began to sicken, and because the water was saved for them, the animals began to die. The squirrels dropped from the trees and lay dead in the field. The rats died under the houses, and the dogs tore at them to drink their blood and live another hour. The horses were found stiffening in the stall, and the oxen staggered once or twice, and dropped.

If it is me, I wish to stop. If I have caused it, let it end. But no matter how often he said it, or even shouted it aloud, the drought only deepened, the heat grew worse, and now in distant corners of the forest men and women patrolled to kill anyone who lit a fire; even cookfires were forbidden, because the slightest spark could burn the Forest of Waters from end to end. And wagons rolled over the Heaven Mountains or upriver from the sea or down from the Top of the World, filled with water jars and water barrels, to buy a farm for a barrel, a house for a jar, a child for a cup, and a woman's virtue for a swallow of it. But water was life, so worth the price.

The cousins and uncles came to Arr and said, Use the gate and let us go. We must go where the water is being sold. Even if we must sell Worthing Farm, we'll do it to save our lives.

But Elijah raged at them. What were their lives, compared to Worthing Farm?

And in return they threatened him with death, until one of them said that whatever Elijah had done to the world, he must be left alive to undo it.

What are you waiting for? they finally said. Kill us now or let us go—or does it please you to watch us die?

As for Elijah's wife, Arr, and their sons John and Adam, they had no more to drink than anyone else. But it was as if they sucked moisture from the air, or perhaps sank taproots deep into the earth, for their breath did not rattle in their throats and their lips and noses did not bleed and they did not scream for water in the night before they died. Even those who lived over-the-wall did not suffer so badly, for they could sell their souls for water, and survive. Nothing, however, passed the wall of Worthing Farm.

One day Elijah heard Arr planning to use the gate and let the water sellers in. But Elijah knew the hearts of all the cousins and the uncles, and he knew that if the wall were opened they would all leave, all do as Matthew had done, and Worthing Farm would die.

It's dead anyway, they answered him. Look at the desolation. You have killed it.

But he did not open the gate, and he could not wish away the drought.

So on a day of maddening grief, those who survived began to carry all the corpses and lay them on the ground in front of Elijah's door. The babies and the children, the mothers and the wives, the old men and the young men: their parched corpses were a monument in the yard before Elijah's house. He heard them planning it and forbade them. He screamed at them but still they went on. And finally his rage at them was murder, and they died, adding their own fresh bodies to the pile they had made, and there were none left alive within the walls but Elijah's own family.

In an agony of hatred Elijah cursed them for having provoked him. I never wanted you to die! If you had stood beside me and kept my brother here—

And as he railed at the dead, they began to smolder, they began to burn; flames erupted from their abdomens, their limbs were crisp as tinder, and the smoke leapt up into the sky. When the flames were at their brightest, Arr ran from the house and flung the gate into the fire, where it exploded almost at once, the fire was so hot. And then she threw herself among the bodies of her friends and neighbors, whom her husband had made her kill: she blamed him for it with the passion in her heart, because he had not let her use the gate to set them free.

It was only then, in utter anguish, that Elijah wept. Only then that he himself gave water to the world. And as he cried, while his sons watched the awful fire, there came a cloud in the west, so small at first that a man's hand held out from his body could cover it. But Matthew Worthing saw it from the tower of his inn, the tower that he had built to rise above the treetops so he could see Worthing Farm. Matthew saw the cloud and shouted to the people of his new village, Look, water!

And their hope for rain came into Elijah's mind like an earthquake, and he gasped with the power of it, and he too longed for water with all their longing, and his own besides; and with all the force of his anger and his guilt and his grief at what he had done, all that together in him called for the rain. The cloud grew, and the wind came up, and the brittle branches of the trees began to shatter in the wind; thunder pealed out and lightning raced across the blackened sky, and the rain began to fall like seas upon the forest. The rivers filled almost at once, the ground was torn and stripped, the trees caught fire from lightning but the rain soon put the fires out.

Then through the eyes of the villagers, Elijah saw the one fire he was glad of. The tower of Matthew's inn began to burn, with him in it; but Matthew raised his hand and the fire went out, vanished as if it had never been. I was right, thought Elijah. I was right, he lied to us, he had more power than to shut us out, I was right, I was right.

When the storm died away Worthing Farm was desolate; even the corpses had been swept into the torrent of the river. The gate was gone, which meant the wall was also gone; Elijah had nowhere else to go now, but to take his sons, leave Worthing Farm, and go west ten miles to his brother's inn, and beg forgiveness from him for the great harm he had done the world. But I was right, he said to himself, even as his brother galled him with his kindness and cruelly named him half owner of Worthing Inn. I was right, and Mother should have kept you in.

But he never said it aloud. Said, in fact, almost nothing for the rest of his life. He even held his tongue when Matthew took Elijah's sons into the street and said to them, "See that sign? That says Worthing Inn. That's all that's left of Worthing now, you and your father, and me and my wife and our children yet to come. We're all that's left of Worthing now, thank God. It was a prison, but at last we're free."

Lared woke in darkness, to find Jason kneeling beside his bed. "Justice told me the dream was over," he said. "Your father calls to you."

Lared got up and went down the stairs. Mother was bending over Father, holding a cup to his lips. Lared wanted water too but didn't ask. Father's eyes had caught him.

"Lared," Father said. "I had a dream."

"So did I," said Lared.

"In my dream, I saw that you blamed yourself for this." He raised his stump. "I dreamed that you thought I hated you. By Worthing I swear it isn't so. There is no fault to this, I hold you blameless, you are still my son, you saved my life, forgive me if I said a thing to make you take the blame upon yourself."

"Thank you," Lared said. He went to his father and embraced him, and his father kissed him.

"Now sleep," said Father. "I'm sorry that I had them wake you, but I couldn't bear it if you went another hour with such feelings in your heart. By Jason, you're the finest son a man could have."

"Thank you," Lared said. Then he started for his truckle bed, but Jason led him up the stairs instead. "Tonight you've earned a better bed than that miserable straw bed by the fire."

"Have I?"

"You had the memory of Elijah Worthing in you, Lared. It's not a pleasant dream to have."

"Was it true? There was a drought like that in Stipock's colony, and it ended with the sort of storm, and no one made it happen."

"Does it matter? Elijah believed that he caused the drought and caused the storm. The rest of his life was shaped as if it were true—"

"But *was* it true?"

Jason pushed him gently down onto the bed and covered him with blankets. "Lared, I don't know. It's the memory of memory. Did all the people of Worthing die that way? Certainly there were no others in the world with my blue eyes, except those they could trace to Matthew and Elijah, but perhaps all the rest were hunted down and killed. As to the storm, there's no one now who can control the weather. But Justice can do other things, things with fire and water, earth and air. Who's to say that once there might not have been one man of all my children who could cause a drought like hell itself, and a storm like the end of the world. Certainly there's never been such hate as his. Never in all the memories I've see has there been such hate."

"Compared to him," Lared whispered, "my hate for you is love."

"And so it is," said Jason. "Go to sleep."

10
In the Image of God

Father was out of bed now, but no one was rejoicing about it. He was foul to be with, stamping around the house with his crutch under his one arm, leaning like a tree in a hard wind, snapping at everyone when he spoke at all. Lared understood why he was so short-tempered, but it didn't make it any easier. Gradually Lared found himself more interested in being upstairs in Jason's room, working on the book, while others found their own strategies for avoiding him. The women stopped coming to the inn for their work; the tinker started visiting from house to house; soon only Mother and Sala and Justice were left in the empty downstairs of the inn. And even Mother avoided him, forcing him to be alone more and more, and his rage and shame grew, for he blamed it on his mutilation that no one came near him if they could help it.

Except Sala. She haunted him. If Mother made her sweep, Sala would soon be sweeping near Father's bed, where he lay brooding; if she played with her mannikins, they danced the May at Father's feet, where he rested by the fire. At such times

Father would watch her, and it would keep him quiet for a time. But then he would try to do something—put a log on the fire, grind the pease for the week's porridge—and she would be there also, taking the other end of the log as he struggled with it, brushing back the hard pease that he spilled; and then he would grow savage, railing at her for a clumsy fool and ordering her away. She went, and in a moment returned, quietly, and stayed always within reach of him. "If you don't want trouble," Mother whispered to her once, "stay away from him."

"He lost his arm, Mama," Sala answered, sounding for all the world as if she thought he had mislaid it somewhere.

One evening as the tinker returned to the inn for supper, and Lared came down from upstairs, Sala said to Father, loudly, "Papa, I dreamed of where your arm is!"

There was no talking then, as they waited for Father's rage. But he surprised them: he only looked calmly at her and said, "Where is it?"

"The trees have it," she said. "So you must do as trees do, and when they lose the end of the branch, they grow it back."

Father whispered, "Sarela, I'm not a tree."

"Don't you know? My friend can tree you and wood you." And she looked at Justice.

Justice looked wordlessly down at the table in front of her, for all the world as if she hadn't understood a word. For a long moment they all stood there, looking at Justice. Then Sala began to cry, "Why is it forbidden!" she said. "It's my papa!"

"Enough," said Mama. "Sit to eat and stop your crying, Sala."

Father sat gravely at the head of the table, laying down the crutch beside him. "Eat," he said. And he began lifting the spoon to his mouth, again and again, to finish the meal as quickly as he could.

Jason had not been at table, but of course it was no accident that he came in now. He walked to Father carrying tongs from the forge and a bar of iron. "Somehow," he said, "this is supposed to become a scythe."

Mother took in her breath sharply, and the tinker looked at his plate. Father, however, merely studied the bar of iron. "It's too short for a scythe."

"Then I need you to find me a bar that *will* do."

Father smiled wryly. "Among all your talents, Jason, are you also a smith?" Father touched Jason's upper arm, which was strong as a man's arm should be, but slim as a child's compared to Father's.

Jason touched his own arm and laughed. "Well, we have a chance to see if a man gets an arm like yours from hammering, or hammers well because he has the arm."

"You're not a smith," said Father.

"Then perhaps I can, with both hands, serve as the left hand of a smith."

It was a bargain, and Father was good at bargaining. "What's to gain for you?"

"Little to gain, except good company and something to do that's worth doing. Lared is writing things now that I never knew. He doesn't need me."

Father smiled. "I know what you're doing, Jason. But let's see if it will work." He turned to Sala. "Perhaps I can have two arms where I used to have one."

He got up from the table and put on his layers of coats and scarves; Jason helped him, and did not get shouted at once, because he knew just when Father wanted help and when he didn't, and just how much to do.

Lared watched them leave, thinking: I should have been the one to stand beside him at the forge. But I must write Jason's book, and so he takes my place beside my father. Yet he could not convince himself to be angry, or jealous, or to grieve. He had never longed to be a smith. He was almost relieved that someone else would stand with Father before the fire.

In a half hour they all heard the welcome sound of the hammer ringing in the forge, and Father cursing at the top of his lungs. That night Father stormed through the house, raging about muddleheaded fools who can't handle anything right and a scythe that will never be good for harvesting anything but hay. Father was interested in something again, and life would be bearable for the family.

And in the night Lared dreamed an ancient memory of a boy who lay in bed discovering the hearts of men.

* * *

John snored softly beside him, his breath sour from the night's cheese, but Adam was content to let him sleep. As long as John had lain awake, Adam couldn't go exploring. Now he could send his mind away to wander with no fear of John distracting him.

Adam had found this power only a few weeks before. He had been stalking a squirrel, to kill it with a thrown rock, and as he crept slowly forward he kept saying silently to the animal, Hold still, hold still. Squirrels had always held still for him longer than for any of the others—he thought it was because he was so stealthy. But this time the squirrel did not so much as twitch, and when Adam threw the stone and it missed, the squirrel did not scurry up the tree. It still sat, still waited until Adam came right up to it and picked it up and beat it against the tree. It never moved at all.

He played with the boys at the swimming hole. They had always ducked each other in the water, played at drowned man; Adam could do it better now, and when Raggy swam under the water, he made him think that up was down until the air was a knife in his lungs. Then he let him up. Raggy came out of the water crying, terrified, and would not go in again whatever the boys said. But once Adam had done it to enough of the boys, they grew afraid and said there was a monster in the water, and they wouldn't swim anymore.

That was all right. Adam had grown into other amusements. Now he lay awake at night, and went exploring in the minds of the villagers of Worthing Town. Enoch Cooper first, because Adam was doing a thing to him each night when he went at his wife. Last night he had made him go limp as a leaf just before the end. Tonight he stayed with him for an hour, never letting him finish, until his wife, who was long since satisfied, begged him to quit and go to sleep. Oh, Enoch Cooper did swear and call on Jason, and he couldn't sleep for the tightness of his groin.

Then Adam found Goody Miller, who kept cats. Last night he made her favorite hiss and scratch at her, so she cried herself to sleep. Tonight he made her hold the cat's head under the millstone. In the old days it would have been the crushing of the cat that Adam relished, but there was far more pleasure now in being inside Goody Miller's mind as she screamed and grieved over the cat. "What have I done to you! What have I done!"

And Raggy—he was always fun to do things to, because for so long he had bossed them all in whatever game they played. He got Raggy to stand out of his bed, take off his nightgown, go to Mary Hooker's place beside the river and stand at her door, playing with himself, until her father opened it and drove him off with kicks and curses. Oh, this was a grand night.

In the back of his mind, each person that he did things to became a little dry corpse, and he added it to a growing pile of corpses at the door. Is that good, Papa? Is that enough?

He made Ann Baker think that there were little spiders on her breasts, and she scratched and tore at them until they were a mass of blood and her husband had to bind her hands behind her.

Is that enough?

Sammy Barber went to his shop and filed his razors flat.

Is that enough?

Veddy Upstreet nursed her baby in the night, and suddenly the child refused to breathe, no matter what she did.

Stop.

Wouldn't breathe no matter—

"Stop."

Adam opened his eyes, and there stood Father in the doorway. John stirred beside Adam in the bed. "Stop what, Papa?" asked Adam.

"What you have came to you from Jason. Not for this."

"I don't know what you're talking about." In the Upstreet house, the baby breathed again, and Veddy wept in relief.

"You are no son of mine."

"I'm just playing, Papa."

"With other people's pain? If you do this again I'll kill you. I ought to kill you now." Elijah held a knotted hemp in his hand, and he dragged Adam from the bed, pulled his nightgown up over his head and arms, and began to beat him.

From the bed, little John cried, "Papa, stop! Papa, no!"

"You're too softhearted, John," Father said, grunting from the force of the blows he gave. Adam writhed in his grasp, so the rope struck him on the back and belly, hip and head, until Adam did what he had never dared to do, and made his father hold *still*.

And Elijah held still.

Adam pulled free of his father's grasp and gazed in wonder at him. "I am stronger than you," he said. Then he laughed, despite the pain of the blows his father gave him. He took the hemp from his father's hand and raised his father's nightgown over his head. He tapped his father with the hemp.

"No," whispered John.

"Hold your tongue or I'll do you, too."

"No," said John aloud.

In answer Adam struck his father across the belly with the rope. Elijah did not so much as flinch. "See, John? It doesn't hurt."

"Why doesn't Papa move?"

"He likes it." He kicked his father in the groin with all his strength. Again not a sound; but the blow overbalanced him, and Elijah toppled over backward, lay helpless and unmoving on the floor, looking for all the world like one of the corpses on the pile. What are you doing, Papa, lying on the pile? Do you want to burn with Mama? Are you dry? Adam kicked and beat and stamped and John screamed, "Uncle Matthew! Uncle Matthew!" And suddenly Adam felt himself flying across the room, slamming into the leathers hanging on the wall.

Uncle Matthew stood at the top of the cellar stairs. "Get your clothing," Matthew said.

Adam tried to make him hold still, just like Elijah, but he couldn't seem to find Uncle Matthew's mind. Suddenly he felt himself burn up inside, so that he clawed at his belly to let the fire out. Then he felt his eyes melting, dripping down onto his cheeks, and in terror he screamed and tried to push them back in place. Then his legs began to crumble like a sugar man, and he lurched closer and closer to the floor; he bent over and watched the pieces of his face fall off and lie shriveling on the floor, ears and nose and lips and teeth and tongue, his eyes last like jelly, only now he looked up from those eyes at his empty face, just blank and featureless skin with a gaping hole for his mouth, and he saw the mouth suddenly fill from inside, and out came his heart, and then his liver, and then his stomach and bowel as his body emptied itself, until he was light and empty as a flourbag in spring—

And then he lay on the floor, weeping and pleading for mercy, for forgiveness, for his body back the way it was.

"Adam," John said softly from the bed, "what's wrong with you?"

Adam touched his face and everything was there, as it should be; he opened his eyes, and he could see. "I'm sorry," he whispered. "I'll never do it again."

Elijah was crying where he sat now, leaning against the wall. "Ah, Matthew," he wept, "what have I made here? What monster have I made?"

Matthew shook his head. "What harms have you done to Adam that you haven't also done to John? The child is what he is—he eats what you feed him, but he turns the food into himself."

Then Elijah realized something, and smiled despite his pain. "I *was* right. You are one of us, just as I said."

"Please don't do it again," Adam whispered.

"You and your father," Matthew said. "Neither of you knows what your power is for. Do you think Jason made us to live forever on a farm, Elijah? Or to play cruel pranks on people who can't protect themselves? I am watching you now, both of you. I'll have you do no more harm. You have both done enough harm in your life. Now it's time that you began to heal."

Adam lived at Matthew's inn for two more years. Then, on a day when he could bear it no more, he fled empty-handed, stole a boat and went downriver to Linkeree. On the way he searched backward, looked in Worthing Inn until he found his uncle's son, little Matt, a baby just learning his first words. He made the baby speak aloud: "Good-bye, Uncle Matthew." And then he killed it.

He waited for the answering blow from Matthew's mind, but it never came. I am beyond his reach, Adam realized. I am safe at last. I can do what I like.

He made his way to Heaven City, the capital of the world. Adam was safe on every road, for who could even think of harming him? And he was never hungry, for so many people yearned to give him food. In Heaven City he waited and watched. This much he had learned from Uncle Matthew: his power would not be used for games. He had read the stone in the middle of

Worthing Farm, as all the blue-eyed children read it: "From the stars blue-eyed one, from this land Jason's son." I am the first to leave the Forest of Waters. I am Jason's son. I will not be content with a plot of ground, or even with an inn. The world should be enough for me.

And bit by bit, the world came to him.

Came to him in the shape of a girl, not so little anymore, the granddaughter of Elena of Noyock. She haunted the palace, always just out of sight, holding still in a corner, under a stair, by a curtain. It was not that she was unsupervised. Some of the servants were probably detailed to keep an eye on her. But it didn't matter much. No one cared that much about her, for she had a younger brother, and Noyock's rulers were succeeded by the eldest male. Elena of Noyock was merely guardian, in favor of her grandson, Ivvis. What was Uwen, the daughter, the invisible? When Adam first came to live at Elena's palace, he noticed her, determined that she was nothing, and ignored her.

So a year had passed, in which Adam had made himself indispensible to Elena of Noyock. He had risen quickly, but not suspiciously so—no higher or faster than native genius might make a young man rise. Now Elena sent him to conduct delicate negotiations for her—he always seemed to extract the very most that could be won from any situation. Now Elena had him choose her servants and her guards, for the ones he chose were loyal and served well; he was never deceived. And when he told her what her enemies were planning, his information always turned out to be correct. Elena prospered. Noyock even prospered. Above all, Adam prospered. Everyone watched him as he made his way through the chambers and porches of Heaven City. Watched him with envy, or hatred, or admiration, or fear.

Except for Uwen. Uwen watched him with love. Whenever Adam noticed her, he noticed that. Saw in her memory that she came sometimes to his room at night, as he lay alone on his mat in the darkness. In the night she studied him, when he was alone and when he was not alone, studied him and wondered how this man from nowhere had managed to be powerful, to be noticed, to be somebody, when she, the daughter of a lord, granddaughter of Elena of Noyock, she had never been noticed at all. What do you do, she wondered? How do you know what you know? How do you say what you say?

But by the time Adam noticed that Uwen was asking these questions, she had the answer. Adam was the enchanted man. Adam was the man of wood from the forest. She knew all the old tales. Adam was the Son of God. When he climbed the stairs to the third floor to go to bed one night, she was leaning on the banister at the top. Not hiding anymore. It was time, she had decided, to be seen

"What did you do, Adam Waters?" asked Uwen. "For a living, I mean. Before you came here." She perched on the banister above the steep drop down the stairwell.

"I looked for little girls who wanted to die, and I pushed them down stairwells," said Adam.

"I'm fourteen years old," said Uwen, "and I know your secret."

Adam raised an eyebrow. "I have no secrets."

"You have one very big secret," said Uwen. "And your secret is that you know all the other people's secrets."

Adam smiled. "Do I?"

"You listen all the time, don't you? That's how *I* find out secrets. I listen. I've seen the way you pay such close attention to everyone who comes to our house. Mother says you are very wise, but I think you just listen."

"We wouldn't want people to think I'm wise, would we."

Uwen entwined herself into the rails like a weed grown up through a picket fence. "But when you listen," said Uwen, "you even hear what people didn't say."

Adam felt a thrill of fear. In all his maneuvering to rise through the ranks of diplomats and bureaucrats in Heaven City, no one had guessed his secret until now. How many people had he whispered to, who had recoiled in fear and said, "Who told you? How did you know?" But none had said, You even hear what people didn't say. Already Adam imagined Uwen's death. It would annoy her grandmother, but not seriously. The child was not particularly useful until she could be married to political advantage. It was not as if the child were loved. Adam felt no debt to Elena of Noyock. He had benefited her as much as she had him, and that made them even; he did not owe her his life itself. And it *was* his life at stake. For if people once guessed that instead of controlling a network of informers, as they all supposed, Adam Waters had only his own mind supplying him his secrets, then everyone he had blackmailed would be out to kill him, and Adam would be dead within a day. My life or yours, Uwen. "How could I hear them?" asked Adam.

"You lie on your back in bed," said Uwen, "and you listen. Sometimes you smile, and sometimes you frown, and then you wake up and write letters, or go make visits, or tell Grandmother, 'The governor of Gravesend wants this much and no more,' or 'The bank of Wien has let all its gold slip away to build the highway, and they're buying at a premium now.' It gives you power. You're going to rule the world someday."

"Don't you know that if you tell people such things, someone might actually believe you, and then my life would be in danger?" I could make the banister break right now, but the fall might not kill her.

"I don't tell secrets. I'll never tell yours, if you do one thing."

I could make her erupt into flames from the inside out—it would be thorough, but perhaps too flamboyant. "You were a cute little girl, Uwen, but you're becoming something of a fart as you get older."

"I'm becoming an unusually interesting young woman," said Uwen. "And if you're planning on killing me, I've already written everything down. All my proof."

"You don't have any proof. There's nothing to prove."

"As Grandmother always says, innuendo is everything in politics. It's much easier to be believed when you're telling people that a powerful young man is really a monster."

The banister creaked and began to crack.

"I love you," said Uwen. "Marry me, get rid of my brother, and Noyock will be yours."

"I don't want Noyock," said Adam. The banister began tilting backward.

"You wouldn't dare," said Uwen. "I'm second in line to the throne of Noyock. I can help you."

"I can't think how," said Adam.

"I know things."

"Everything you know, I know," said Adam.

"I would be the one person," she said, "that you could tell the truth to. Don't you ever wish that you could tell the truth to somebody? You've been in Heaven City for five years now, and you're just about to play for everything, and when it's done what will you have to do with yourself?"

The banister righted itself. "You'd better get off that," Adam said. "It isn't safe."

She unwound her legs from the rails and clambered off, then walked to Adam where he stood leaning on the wall; she walked to him and pressed herself against him and said, "So you'll marry me?"

"Never," said Adam, putting his hands behind her, holding her close to him.

"You want to marry power, don't you?" she said, lifting her skirt and guiding his hand to rest on her naked hip.

"You aren't the heir. Your brother Ivvis is."

She lifted his tunic too and began to fumble with his codpiece. "I don't *have* to have a brother."

"Even if you had no brother, Noyock isn't strong enough for what I want to do. You will never be powerful enough." He checked the servants and made sure none of them had the slightest desire to come up to the third floor of Duchess Elena's Heaven City palace.

She looked angry. "Then why did you let me live?"

He lifted her up, his hands behind her thighs, and carried her into her room. "Because I like you."

Adam was very careful with her. He could feel everything she felt, knew what she enjoyed, what she did not enjoy, when she was unready, when she was eager, when she needed passion, when she needed gentleness. He was her only memory of lovers; the other women he had taken were too cluttered with faces in their minds, names to cry out in the moment of delight. Uwen had only him. She would never need anyone else. "You love me," she whispered.

"Whatever you need to believe," said Adam, "is fine with me."

Adam was in no hurry. There was little suspense in the final outcome. Heaven City was not like Worthing Farm. Here there was no one to undo him, no one whose power matched his or surpassed it. When he was challenged to a duel here he knew that he could win, and did, until the challenges stopped. When someone thwarted him he could easily move them aside. He could flatter almost anyone, and when he tired of that, he could frighten or seduce or, ultimately, strike down whoever stood in his way.

Except Zoferil of Stipock. Zoferil was a woman of honor and deep faith, who alone of all the rulers of the world had never lied and never would. When she could not speak the truth she said nothing, and when she did speak the truth her words were knives that cut to the heart of all hearers. They feared her, even those whose armies were larger, because they knew that the people of Stipock truly loved Zoferil as she loved them, and would die for her, and she for them; they could not get her to conspire with them in any dishonorable thing, and so she remained aloof from all their plans, a constant threat because if she brought her army into any war it would easily swing the balance. Without her as an ally there was always the risk that she would be an enemy. People of every nation said, Jason must love the land of Stipock, because he gave them Zoferil.

"I will have Zoferil's power and I will have her love," said Adam. "She is mine."

"She's an old lady and you'll never love her," said Uwen.

"But with Stipock and Noyock both mine," said Adam, "the rest of the world will slip into place quietly."

"Noyock isn't yours," said Uwen. "It's Grandmother's."

Adam didn't need to argue. Didn't need to say, *she* is mine, and you are mine, and your little brother Ivvis is also mine. Everyone was his; Uwen simply knew it, that's all, and it gave her a sense of freedom, to at least be aware of her possession.

Elena of Noyock grew old, and her son Ivvis was only twelve years old; with the weight of future death on her, she felt a need to name a regent—Adam was her choice, of course. She died soon after when her ship was lost at sea. Adam was a scrupulous regent, protecting the child-magister from all harm, teaching him studiously to be a man of virtue. At the court of the Heaven King they watched how the young man grew, a model of what a ruler ought to be; and in a world where regents more often had to be removed by bloodshed than by law, Adam surprised them all by turning power over to young Ivvis two years before the law required, because the boy was ready to be magister in his own right. The world admired how gracefully Adam stepped back at once into his role as one adviser among many. No one thought it anything but a fortunate coincidence that this happened just as Zoferil's eldest daughter and, sadly, only surviving child came of age. No one but Uwen.

"If you can kill off Gatha's brothers, why couldn't you kill off mine?" demanded Uwen. "And why didn't you just keep the power, when you had it?"

"Doesn't it occur to you that sometimes I like to win things by merit, and not by secret compulsion?"

"You'll never compel *me*."

"I never had to."

"She's not as beautiful as I am. What does Gatha have, that you want to marry her and not me?"

"For one thing," said Adam, "she's a virgin."

Uwen kicked at him, and Adam laughed at her as he went to call on Zoferil.

"All my sons have died during these last few years," said Zoferil to Adam. "I would have hoped that, if they lived, they would each have become a man like you. Adam, it is time for my daughter to have a husband, and the desire of her heart is like the desire of mine: that you be my son, and help her rule Stipock after I am gone."

"I would say yes at once," said Adam, "but I cannot deceive you. I am not what I seem."

"You seem to be the best and wisest and most honorable of men," said Zoferil.

"No," said Adam. "I have deceived the world and disguised myself all these years."

"Who are you, then, if you are not Adam Waters?"

"My true name is Worthing. I think you know the name."

"Jason's son," whispered Zoferil.

"I thought before you gave me your daughter, you ought to know."

"You," she whispered. "For a thousand years the secret rite of the men and women of Stipock has called upon the sacred, holy name of Worthing, Jason's son. When I saw your eyes like a perfect sky, I wondered. When I saw your virtue like the purest of all men, I hoped. Now, Adam Worthing, now I know you, and I beg you to take my daughter and my kingdom both, if only you think us worthy."

She crowned him with the crown of iron, and put the iron hammer in his hand, and he vowed that never a sword would come from the forges of Stipock, as all the philocrats of Stipock had sworn before him. All the world looked to him in love or jealousy, and the people of Stipock honored him as if he had been born among them.

Adam had some mercy. He waited to unmask himself until Zoferil was dead.

Then, with a pathetic plot of Wien and Kapock as his excuse, Adam sent the armies of Stipock and the fleets of Noyock to bring blood and terror to every kingdom of the world. Adam's enemies could not stand against him. Their armies could not find him until he stood behind them; their own guards turned against them and assassinated them; and within three years, for the first time since Jason had taken the original Star Tower into heaven, all the world was ruled from Heaven City, and Adam named himself Jason's Son, the true Heaven King.

Even then there were still some who loved him. But through the years of his misrule they learned what he truly was. How could he pursue power now, when there was no more power to be had in all the world? He plumbed the secrets of death and pain by torturing and killing while tasting the experience in his victims' mind. He broke great men and women, and impoverished great families. He took his pleasure with the virtuous daughters of noble houses and then sold them out for whores. He took as much in taxes as he could, and more, so that famines came to lands whose harvests had been good; when the desperate people begged for food at any price, he bought them as slaves to build his monuments. It was as if he set himself the task of proving that he was so powerful that even when everyone in the world hated him, he could still rule them, could still keep his power. His wife, Gatha, wept to see what he had become; his mistress, Uwen, urged him on, for she loved the pleasures of power even more than Adam did. In Heaven City she built the Star Tower the same size and same shape as the one described

as Jason's own, and sheathed it in silver, and the bodies of five
thousand dead were buried under it. And any who spoke or acted
against either of them were ingeniously undone for all the world
to see, for all the world to hear their screams. I am God Himself,
Adam said at last, and there was no one who dared to say that
he was not.

But Adam lived in fear. For he had sent an army to a certain
village in the Forest of Waters, and they had killed all the in-
habitants and brought their heads to him, and he had looked
from head to head, the eyes sewn open, and not one of the eyes
was pure as the sky, and not one of the faces belonged to Father
Elijah or Uncle Matthew or Brother John; not one of the faces
seemed even to be kin. Somewhere in the world there was someone, he knew it, someone who could see into his mind. And
yet, like Matthew, they could hide their minds from him. He
dreamed at night of the way that Matthew poured his face upon
the ground, and woke up screaming, and then searched the minds
of those around him, trying to find one who might have seen a
blue-eyed man, who might have heard of someone who had
power to rival his own.

Poor me, thought Adam. There is no pleasure for me in the
world, so long as I have not found and killed my kin.

"Jason's son," said Lared scornfully. "This is what came of
all your plans?"

"You've got to admit that as a breeding experiment it worked
out beautifully. More power than I dreamed could come of what
I had. I can't control other people's thoughts or actions. All I
can do is see through their minds and memories. And don't
believe that he's as singularly monstrous as the dream says. This
came to you through too many people who loathed him. He was
the devil, the Abner Doon of Worthing's world. I suspect he
lived in a cruel time, and differed from other rulers only in that
he was far more successful in exercising his power. The tor-
tures—I suspect he didn't invent them, though he didn't refuse
to use them, either. He was a very bad man, but by the standards
of his time I think he wasn't monstrous. But then, I may be
wrong. Write him as you dreamed him, and your tale will not
be lies."

"What about the others—his father and uncle and brother?"

"Oh, his father died of despair soon after he left. His brother—
you know the tale. His brother became a tinker and a healer and
a lover of birds. As for Matthew, his baby, Little Matthew, did
not die. In the thirty years of Adam's rise to power, Little Matthew grew, and had a son named Amos, and inherited the inn
when his father died. After the death of John Tinker, which
happened the year of Adam's wedding to Zoferil's daughter,
Matthew and Amos went away to live in Hux, near the place
where the West River flows out of Top of the World. They became merchants."

Amos looked out the window of his tower onto the streets and
rooftops of Hux. He always lived in a tower and worked in a
tower, and left seed for the birds at the sills of every window.
They came to him all winter, all summer, and he never failed
them. Sometimes, with the birds fluttering about his tower, he
could pretend that he was worthy of his uncle John Tinker, who
lay in a grave at Worthing.

"You remember Uncle John," said Amos.

"Not myself," said his youngest daughter, Faith. It was her
way, to try to make picky differences in words.

"You remember my memories of him."

"He should never have let them have power over him. He
should have changed them."

Ah, Faith, sighed Amos. Of all my children, will you be the
first that could not bear the burden that we have taken on? "Oh?
And what would he have made them, then?"

"He would have made them stop. Hurting him. He didn't have
to let them hurt him."

"They've paid with their lives," said Amos. "Their heads
were all cut off and taken away to Stipock City, for Jason's Son
to view them."

"And he," said Faith, "he is another one we ought to stop.
Why should we allow a man like that to—"

Amos touched her lips with his finger. "John Tinker was the
best of us. Infinite patience. None of the rest of us has it. But
we must try."

"Why?"

"Because Jason's Son is also one of us."

He watched her face. Since childhood there had not been much that could surprise her, but this was the most painful and dangerous of secrets, and so the children were not shown until they came of age. But are you of age, Faith? Or will we have to put you into the stone for safekeeping, for the sake of the world? To ourselves we must be crueler than cruel, so that to the world we can be kind.

"Jason's Son! How can he be one of us? Whose child is he? You have seven sons and seven daughters, and Grandfather has his three and eight, besides you. I know all my brothers and sisters, all my nieces and nephews, and—"

"And hold your tongue. Don't you know that all your brothers and sisters are watching their little ones, to be certain that they do not overhear us? We can't take too much time for this. I have much to explain, and there is little time."

"Why so little time?"

"Because Adam and his children are asleep," said Amos, "but soon they will waken, and you must be decided before they do."

"What do you want me to decide?"

"Hold your tongue, Faith, and hear me, and you will know."

Faith held her tongue, even as she probed for answers in her father's mind.

"Foolish child, don't you know that I can close my mind to you? Don't you know that this is what makes us different from Adam and his children? He has no guard in his mind against us, but we can shut him out. Power for power we match him, but we can also keep him out. It makes us stronger than he is."

"Then why don't we throw the bastard out!" cried Faith. "He has no right to rule the world!"

"No, he has no right. But who has a better? Who will take his place?"

"Why does the world need to be ruled at all?"

"Because without rule there is no freedom. If people do not walk within their appointed path, and obey a law, and unite themselves to say a single word, at least from time to time, then there is no order in the world, and where there is no order there is no power to predict the future, for nothing can be depended on, and where the future cannot be known or guessed at, who can plan? Who can choose? There is no freedom, because there is no rule. Must I teach you the lessons that I taught you from your infancy?''

''No, Father, you don't need to teach me anything.''

''If you've learned it already, why are you such a fool? Why did you strike down Vel when she quarreled with you in the street?''

Faith immediately looked defiant. ''I hardly touched her.''

''You made her remember, for just a moment, the grief she felt at her mother's death. You took the worst hour of her life and gave it back to her, just because she said something you didn't like. You did to her the worst thing in the world, and only for your petty vengeance. Tell me, Faith, what is the difference between Jason's Son and you, that you think you should rule in his place?''

''A hundred thousand dead, that's the difference.''

''He killed more because he had more power. Take his power, and won't you be the same? There is more at stake here than you think, Faith. When Father and I first came here, we understood for the first time how much power we really had, as Adam must have realized when he went to Heaven City more than a generation ago. We could make people lend us money and then forget that we owed it to them; we could make our debtors pay us first; we could buy properties whose owners didn't think they would ever sell. We could be very, very rich.''

''You *are* rich.''

''But no one is poorer because of it,'' said Amos. ''We stole from no one. We only made new land where there was none before, and found gold where it was hidden in the earth, and above all made the city safe and prosperous, so that all who lived here did well. There are no poor in Hux, Faith. You've never known it any other way, but I tell you that is our achievement. It is our achievement every day.''

Faith looked narrowly at him. ''What do you gain?''

''John Tinker doesn't reproach me with his death,'' said Amos. ''John Tinker's birds still come to me.''

''That's not a reason.''

''Yes it is. He lived his life and did no harm.''

"And look what it got him."

"Death. But we've learned from him."

"Yes—don't let them near you."

"No. Don't let them know. Uncle John could have healed them to his heart's content, and never would have tasted their resentment if they hadn't known he was the healer. So the people of Hux look at the countinghouse of Matthew and Amos and see nothing but a prosperous business with what seems like half a hundred blue-eyed children constantly about. They don't know that their children live through childhood because of us, their cows give milk and do not sicken and die because of us, their marriages remain unbroken and their contracts all are kept, because somewhere in this house, always, there are two or three or five or half a dozen of us listening, watching, making sure this city is safe from pain—"

Faith shook her head and smiled. "I know what you are. You think that *you're* Jason's children."

Amos shook his head. All the other children had nodded, had understood. They had done nothing to deserve their gift; it was a stewardship; the city had been given into their care, and they must keep it safe. "In all the history of this world," said Amos, "there has never been a happier place than this, the city of Hux, under our care. Mothers no longer fear childbirth, because they know that they will live. Parents are willing to love their children, because they know the children will survive to be adults."

"And yet you still let Jason's Son rule the world."

"Yes," said Amos. "Your very desire to destroy him, Faith, tells me that you are more kin of his than kin of mine. Child, today is the day I ask you, Will you protect the secret and keep the covenant? Will you use your gifts only for healing, never for vengeance, punishment, or harm?"

"What about justice?" demanded Faith.

"Justice is the perfect balance," said Amos, "but only the perfectly balanced heart can be just. Is that you?"

"I know good from evil."

"Will you take the covenant?"

She did not need to answer. He knew her answer from the fact that she closed her mind to him. When she said, "Yes," it only made it worse.

"Do you think that you can lie to *me?*"

She tossed her head defiantly. "Jason's Son is a wound in the world, and I'll heal it. If that's keeping the covenant, then I'll keep it."

"And plunge the world into war again."

Faith got up. "The world is in pain, and one little city is all that you can think about. What good is Hux's happiness, while the world is ground down?"

"It takes time. The children growing up now—then there'll be enough to reach out farther, accomplish more—"

"I won't be part of this," said Faith. "I'm a match for Jason's Son, and I will take his place."

"Will you?" asked Amos. "I hope that you will not. But for the world's sake, Faith, we must put you in the stone."

She did not know what he meant.

But she knew when they took her out into the wilderness, up into the foothills of the mountains, to a place where the living rock cropped out and lay smooth and flat as the sheets on a virgin's bed. "What are you doing to me?" she demanded, for being violent-hearted, she feared violence.

We have to know, said Amos silently, who you are.

"After all these years, and you don't know me?"

We can know your memories, and we can know our memories, but how can we know your future? How can we know how much evil can dwell comfortably in you? The seeds of destruction are there—will they take root, and will you crumble away the rock at the heart of the world?

"What will you do to me?"

Why, we'll make you someone that you are not, and learn from that who you are. We'll float you over the stone, where you're cut off from all life; make you part of the stone, so you're cut off from your own flesh; and then see how much of Adam Worthing you can be.

"Will I die?" Faith asked her father.

I've gone into the stone myself, and came out whole. I did it—we did it because only in the stone can we set our memories aside and let someone else's whole mind enter into ours; I floated the stone, and brought each of Adam Worthing's children, one by one, into my mind, to judge them.

"And did they fail?"

Failure would have been not to know them fully. I did not fail. We know them now from the inside out.

"Were they good people?"

As much as I am good, they are good, because their whole memory could fit into my mind and did not drive me mad. So now you will float the stone, and put yourself out of yourself into the living rock, and take another mind into your own.

"Whose?"

That's your choice, Faith. You may take mine. Or you may take Adam Worthing's. Whichever will be most like you. Whichever you think least likely to destroy you.

"How can I know? I don't know either of you. Not really."

That's why we float the stone. It's more than remembering someone else's memories. It's becoming someone else, and measuring his life against your own soul. If the person is too different from you, then you will die.

"How do you know? Who floated the stone and died before?"

Elijah. He was the first. When Adam ran away, when Adam murdered and ran away, Elijah floated the stone and searched for him. And found him. Young Adam was so monstrous that it killed the old man.

"But Father—didn't you say that you had floated the stone for Adam, too?"

No. Only for his children.

"And for me? Would you float the stone for me?"

Faith, I would do it for you if I thought that I would live.

"Do you think that you're so different from me, then? That I'm as monstrously evil as Jason's Son?"

I think that his memories can dwell in your heart better than mine can. I think that if you had a perfect memory of every act and every choice and every feeling I have had in my life, child, that it would drive you mad and you would never find your own self in the stone, and you would die.

"Then I'll take Adam into me. But I'm not a fool, Father. I know what this means. If I can be Adam Worthing, then I am not worthy, by your standard. And if I can't endure him, then I'll be justified, but unfortunately I'll also go mad and die."

That's why the choice is left to you

She took the memory of floating the stone from her father's mind: he opened the memory to her, so she could see. Then, wearing nothing between her and the naked stone, she lay down on it and did exactly what she remembered that her father did.

It was Father who worked on the stone, Father who knew how to make it flow, cold as water, smooth as water, so that she sank backward into the liquid stone and floated on the cold face of the world.

And as she lay there, letting herself seep into the stone, letting her memories flow away, the others guided her to Adam Worthing. They were gentle with Adam, so that he would not know what was being done. They could not be kind to her.

So Faith became Adam Worthing, from his childhood up, from the first terror in his cellar room at Worthing Inn, through each vicious act, each seizure of power, each undoing of other men and women, each slaughter on the battlefield, each massacre of innocents for the sheer joy of doing it.

And when it was done, and she had borne the weight of his terrible past as if it were her own, and it had not driven her mad, she wept with shame, and let herself flow back into herself, and wished that she had died upon the stone.

The others looked at her coldly and turned away. Only her father did not turn from her, and he was weeping. "I couldn't do it," he said aloud.

In his unguarded mind she saw his failure: when it was clear that she could bear to be Adam Worthing, it was his duty to let the liquid stone solidify, and hold her there; to kill her, and keep her memories imprisoned in the rock, rather than to let her live and become another Adam in the world.

"It isn't true," she said. "It isn't just. I can bear him, but I could bear you, too. I'm not like him, not wholly. I'm like him, too. Father, you won't regret it, that you let me live."

But he did regret it. They all regretted it, until Faith could hardly bear the shame of it, that she was still alive. I am not like him, she said to herself, over and over. They're wrong about what the stone means.

They were not wrong, though. She knew it, deeper than all her silent protests, she knew that the judgment was just. It took her months of living as a pariah in her father's house, but at last she understood that, yes, all the malice of Adam's life fit easily into her heart, with room left, still. Room for more.

But where is it written, where was it said that I can't change?

The others were never glad to talk to her. They shared with her no tales of their work in healing all the wounds of Hux. But they also could not stop her from watching, from letting her mind wander through the city and see how each wound, each grief, fear was healed. This is how it's done, she saw; all my instincts were to break, but this is how the broken heart is made whole again.

And when she was confident of herself, she went to Adam Worthing.

She went to Adam Worthing, not in the mind, but in the flesh. She had kept her mind closed to the others; they did not know where she had gone. It hardly mattered—they would not miss her if she died, and as for any danger from Adam, she would not let him know where the others were, or that they even existed. But even if he did know, even if her act endangered everyone, she would do it. For she had taken Adam Worthing into herself, and knew where he was broken, and hoped to heal him, if it was in him to endure the healing.

She half expected them to follow her, to stop her, but when they didn't she realized bitterly that they were probably glad that she was gone. Down the West River to Linkeree, then by sea to Stipock City. She made her way easily from wharf to city, from city to castle, from castle to the palace on the red rock cliff overlooking the sea. She knew the words to say to get past every guard and every servant. Until she stood in the anteroom of the court of Jason's Son. She sat calmly and waited as the people came and went for audiences with the Son of God.

"You're too late," said the tired-faced woman beside her.

"For what?" asked Faith.

"To stop him," she said. "You should have come years ago."

The woman was worn, and the elegant clothing could not hide the emaciation. She was dying.

"And he could heal you, if he would."

"Healing isn't what he does." She lifted her chin defiantly. "But I had what I had of him and it was better than the world gives."

"Uwen," said Faith, naming her.

"He knows you're coming," said Uwen.

"Does he?"

"He's known for all these years. Always waiting. I saw it in him. I was good at watching. Always looking southward from Heaven City, or northward from here, toward the village he destroyed in the Forest of Waters. You come from there, don't you? You can tell me. I won't whisper a word." She smiled. "He knows your heart already. He does that, you know. He knows your heart."

So there was no surprise in her coming. It hardly mattered. She knew Adam better than Adam knew himself. She was not afraid of him. "I'll go in now," she said to Uwen.

"Have you come to kill him?" asked Uwen.

"No."

"Will he love me, when you're through?"

"You're dying, aren't you?"

Uwen shrugged.

Faith reached into her, found the sickness, and made her whole.

Uwen said nothing, just sat and stared at her hands. Faith got up and walked into the hall. The guards did not so much as think of stopping her. She saw to that.

She knelt before the white-haired Son of Jason on his throne. "I've been waiting for you," Adam said.

"I didn't send word ahead. I think we've never met," said Faith.

"She comes with eyes as blue as mine, as blue as my children's eyes, and when I look behind those eyes I see nothing. There was a man once who hid from me. I'd kill him if I could. I'll kill you too if I can."

Behind her she heard the footsteps of the soldiers, the whisper of metal rising through the sheath.

She stilled the soldiers with their own memories of the fear of death.

"I know you," she said to Jason's Son. She froze him with the memory of Uncle Matthew standing at the door, the image he had feared most, all his life—the man who could undo him, treat his power like the strength of a squirrel, all quickness but no force in it. And while he sat transfixed, she went into his memories and changed them.

Some things would be possible, and some would not. She could not change his ravening appetite for power, or the fear of failing that gnawed at him—that was deeper than memory, that was part of the shape of himself. But she could make him remember controlling those appetites and fears, refusing to be ruled by them. In his memory now he never killed, though he was tempted to; never seduced, never bullied, never tortured, though the opportunities had come. And when the blood was too thick and deep for her to scrub it out of Adam's memory, she gave him reasons why these acts were not sheer exercise of power. Reasons why each was necessary, why each was good, in the long run, for the people.

And when she was done with him, he was no longer an irresistible tyrant jaded by so many crimes that he hardly noticed them and destroyed by mere habit. Now he was a ruler who feared nothing but his own desires, and avoided his lust for cruelty with the same fear that once he had devoted to the memory, now lost, of Uncle Matthew.

No, not lost. For his memories, the most vivid of them, lived in Faith's own mind. The stone had given her back herself, but nothing could take from her Adam's past.

They were surrounded by people, courtiers and bureaucrats who had come to marvel at the sight of the blue-eyed tyrant and the girl who stood before him, matching him gaze for gaze, hour after hour, in utter silence, while they hardly breathed. What power did she have over Jason's Son? What death would this result in? Who would suffer?

But then it was over, and Adam smiled at her and said, "Go in peace, cousin," and she turned and walked away and they did not see her again, and Adam forbade them to look for her.

It was a clumsy job she did—for years afterward there were curious lapses in Adam's memory, and sometimes he rebelled against the life of self-restraint that he believed that he had led. But on the whole, he was healed, and all of Worthing's world knew it, bit by bit. The monster in the Son of Jason had been tamed, the world could bear his rule.

Amos was waiting for her when she returned to Hux. He met

her at the city gate, and walked with her out into the orchards that organized the hill into neat columns and rows. "Well done," he said.

"I was afraid," she said, "that you would stop me."

He shook his head. "We all hoped for you, child. Only you of all of us could understand him well enough to heal him. If you had failed, we would have had no hope short of killing him, and that would taint us forever."

"So I was part of your plan from the start?"

"Of course," said Adam. "There are no accidents in the world anymore."

Faith thought about that for a while, trying to discover why she was sad that the accidents, the agonies were over. It is part of the Adam in me, she finally decided, and put it behind her, and worked with the others to spread the healing influence of Worthing farther and farther out into the world. I will heal the world, and there will be no more accidents anymore.

"The story's almost dull from there on, Lared. Stories of good people doing good works are never very thrilling. For the first many hundreds of years Adam's descendants used their powers to learn the true needs and desires of their subjects and make sure they had good government and were treated kindly; in the meantime, unknown to Adam's family, the descendants of Matthew and Amos watched an ever-growing portion of the world, sparing them from pain, removing from their minds the memory of grief, healing the sick, calming the angry, making the lame walk and the blind see. Then, in the Great Awakening, they made themselves known to Adam's kin, and the groups joined their work together, and intermarried. By the time they woke me and brought me up from the bottom of the sea, every living soul on Worthing was descended from me. They conquered the world by marriage.

"When the starships came at last from the other worlds, they saw it as the challenge their power had been created for. They began to watch all the worlds of men. The ships came back to worlds like yours, and told of what they had found on Worthing's world, the lost colony, and how it meant the end of pain. That's when the ritual of fire and ice began here, Lared. And since that day *nothing*, nothing in all the universe of men, has changed."

Lared sat at the writing desk, tears dropping onto the page. "Until now," he said. "Your children could have made all mankind their slaves, but they chose to be kind instead—why did they undo it all? Why did they stop? Why are you glad of it?"

"Lared," Jason said. "You don't understand. They *did* make all mankind their slaves. They just kept them happier than any master did before."

"We were not slaves. And my father had two arms."

"Write the story that you know so far, Lared. We have to finish soon—winter's almost over, and they'll need you in the forest and the fields again. Finish the book, and then I'll leave you as you wanted me to."

"How much more is there, after this?"

"One more dream," said Jason. "The tale of a man named Mercy and his sister, Justice. And how between them they undid the pattern of the universe. Maybe when it's over, you'll not hate me anymore."

11
Acts of Mercy

The wind was out of the southeast, warm and dry. The ice on the river broke up in the night; great rafts of ice floated downstream all day. The snow was still white with flecks of ash from the forgefire, but underneath it Lared heard the running of water. He tossed a bale of hay into every stall, forked it loose, and checked the sheep for lambing. The time was getting near for more than one of the ewes. And hard as the winter had been, there was still hay enough from last summer to last two more months. A good year for crops and animals. Not so good for men.

The tools stood ready for the summer's work; soon it would be time to spade and ditch the hedges and take the faughter to the peasepatch and the harrow to the fields. Today is warm enough, Lared decided, and he let the geese out into the yard. It was a measure of how much had changed since fall that he didn't even think to ask Father if it was time.

Mother was pregnant. Mother was going to have a little baby and Father was certain it was his. Well, it might be, Lared

thought. I wonder who her lover is? It occurred to him to wonder
if it might be the tinker—Mother liked him well enough. But
no, he had no opportunity. Indeed, when did anyone have time?
With the women always visiting and Father never far away, how
could it be at home? And Mother ran no errands, except when
she worked in company of other women at some clothwork or
to carry grain to the mill—

The miller? Surely Mother could not prefer him to Father.
No, impossible.

"That's not a very worthy line of thought," said Jason.

Lared turned to him. He stood in the doorway of the barn,
silhouetted in the sunlight. "I'm going out to mark the hedges,"
Lared said. "Do you know the work, or does Father need you
in the forge?"

"I need you at the book," Jason said. "That's spring work
you're thinking of, and the book's not done."

"The spring work needs doing in the spring. That's why we
call it spring work. It's spring, and so I'm doing it. Whatever
the value of whatever you paid to Father and Mother, it isn't
worth a winter with no crop. Starving to death is possible these
days, you know."

"I'll come with you to the hedges."

They each took sawhooks with them, and walked the rows.
The snow was wet and slippery underfoot, and the south-facing
slopes of the hedgebanks were plain mud, the snow already gone
from them. Lared stopped at a plant that was broken from the
weight of the winter's snow, so it lay over half into the hedge-
road. "You hardly need to mark one like this, but you do it
anyway," Lared said. "When they come along to do your rows,
sometimes they're tired and they don't much like the landmaster
by then, and anything without its twist of straw gets left, even
though they know they have to do it over." He plaited a straw
on the outmost branch and they went on, cutting off branches
that were broken from the stem, marking plants that needed to
be rooted or moved back into line.

"Mother's pregnant," Lared said. "I know you know it, but
I thought you might be able to tell a bit about the father."

"Same as yours."

"Is that the truth?"

"Yes," Jason said. "Justice says so. She knows how to tell. In the old days, she would have stopped it being born if it were a bastard. It was one of the ways they kept life simpler."

"Why should she have a child at all? She has two."

"With no premature death before the Day of Pain, Lared, what would have happened to the world if every couple had more than its two? All the women who aren't virgins or too old are pregnant, Lared. Most of their children will survive. But look forward to a hundred children underfoot before two years are out. You'll have to make this land produce much more, or some will die."

"The way it used to be" Lared said. "I'm an expert now on how things used to be. I think I've lived more in your history than I've lived in my own life."

"I know you have. Has it changed you?"

"No." Lared stopped walking and looked around him. "No, except the hedges have no mystery anymore. I know there's nothing on the other side. When I was a child I used to wonder, but not now."

"You're growing up."

"I'm getting old. I've lived too many lifetimes this winter. This village is so small compared to Heaven City."

"That's its greatest virtue."

"Think that Star Haven would have need of a country-born scribe?"

"You write as well as any man."

"If I can find a man to help Father at the forge, or perhaps another blacksmith to take his place there, and let him run the inn—then I'm going. Maybe not Star Haven. There are other places."

"You'll do well. Though I think you'll miss Flat Harbor more than you think you will."

"What about you? When you leave? Will you miss this place?"

"More than you know," said Jason. "I've come to love it here."

"Yes, you would. A nice place to find pain."

Jason said nothing.

"I'm sorry. It's coming on spring and Father hasn't got his

arm and even with you helping at the forge it isn't the same. The farm is on my back now, and I don't want it. It's your fault, you know. If there were any justice, you'd stay and bear the burden of it yourself.''

"Oh, no, not at all," said Jason. "Sons have always taken over when their fathers faltered, and daughters have always done the same for mothers. This is the natural way now. This is justice. What you had before was pure mercy. You never did a thing to deserve it, so don't complain now that it's taken away.''

Lared turned away from him and went on up the hedge. They worked in silence till the job was done.

When they got home, Father was in the big copper tub, taking a bath. Lared saw at once that he was angry to see him. He couldn't understand why—Lared had seen Father bathing naked since he was as little as he could remember, Mother pouring the hot water into the tub and Father crying out, "What, do you want to boil my balls off?" Then Lared saw how Father tried to hide his stump behind his body. He must have waited for his bath till Lared was gone hedging, and because of Jason's help Lared had come back too soon. "Sorry," Lared said. But he didn't leave the room. If he had to hide forever from his father's bath, he'd soon be afraid to come indoors, and Father would bathe but once a year at most. Instead Lared walked to the kitchen and took a crust of old bread from the bin and dipped it into the porridge simmering before the fire.

Mother slapped playfully at his hand. "Will you rob the dinnerpot, and the porridge not yet half cooked?''

"It's already delicious," Lared said, his mouth full. Father had stolen porridge that way a thousand times before. Lared knew that Mother wouldn't mind.

But Father minded. "Keep your hands out of the food, Lared," he said gruffly.

"All right, Father," Lared said. No point in arguing. He'd do it again, and Father would get used to that, too.

Father arose from the tub, water dripping. Almost at once Sala, who had been playing silently nearby, ran to him and looked up at the naked stump. "Where are the fingers?" Sala asked.

Father, embarrassed, covered the stump with his hand. It was sadly funny, that he made no effort to hide his loins, but only tried to hide what wasn't even there.

"Hush, Sala," Mother said sharply.

"There should be fingers," Sala said. "It's spring."

"There'll be no new growth on this stump," Father said. And now, the shock of it over, he took his hand away and began to towel himself with a thick wool cloth. Mother came over to towel his back, and on the way she gave Sala a push. "Run along, Sala. Go away."

Sala cried out as if in terrible pain or grief.

"What is it? I didn't push you so hard, girl."

"Why didn't you do it!" Sala screamed. "Where is it!"

Only when Justice appeared at the foot of the stairs did they realize what Sala meant. Sala ran to her. "You can do it! I know you can do it! So where is it? You said you loved me! You said you loved me!"

Justice only stood there, looking at Father, who held the towel in front of him. Then, defiantly, he thrust the towel into Mother's hands and stepped out of the tub toward Justice. "What have you promised the child?" he asked. "In our house we keep our promises to children."

But Justice didn't answer. As usual, Sala did. "She can put an arm back where you lost it," Sala said. "She told me in my mind. I've dreamed of it, I saw it open like a flower, all five fingers back again."

Jason stepped between them.

"Stay out of this, Jason. That woman's been living like a ghost in my house all winter, I want to know what she promised to my daughter."

"Put on some trousers," Jason said.

Father looked at Jason coldly for a long moment, then reached for his longshirt and put it on.

"Justice didn't promise anything to Sala. But Sala still saw— what Justice would like to do, if she weren't bound."

"Put a hand back on my stump? Only God could do that. And God is gone."

"That's right," Jason said.

"How does Sala know what that woman thinks? Or does she talk when they're alone?"

"When one of Justice's people loves someone, she can't hide her thoughts from them. She never meant to deceive your daughter, or to disappoint her. What Sala saw is forbidden."

"Forbidden. Bound. But if she weren't bound and forbidden, does she have the power to heal my arm?"

"We came here," Jason said, "to write a book, with Lared's help. He'll finish it tomorrow, and then we'll go." He walked to Justice and pushed her gently back up the stairs. Sala stayed at the bottom step, crying. Father pulled his trousers on, and Lared sat before the fire, watching the flames trying to escape up the chimney, always dying before they quite made it out.

Mercy was the firstborn, and a boy; Justice was his sister. Their mother had known them well in the womb—their names fit them. Mercy could not bear it for another to suffer anything; Justice was sterner, and insisted on fairness and equity regardless of the cost.

Justice's name was not just decorative; it was the path that pulled her through the wilderness of childhood. For almost as soon as she could walk and burble sounds, she began to reach into the memories of those around her, or the memories were forced on her against her will. Father, Mother and the thousand other lives that dwelt within their minds, all the other *I*'s, all the events of their lives that mattered enough to be held in memory, and somehow in all this Justice had to remember who she was, which memories were hers. She herself was so small, her life so slight, that for a long while she was lost. What brought her out into a sane world, knowing who she was, was that need to set things to rights, to make things balance, to have all right things rewarded, all wrong things done away.

She also emerged from childhood with a yearning to be more like Mercy, her compassionate brother. In ways they were alike— they both lived in dread of undeserved suffering. But Mercy's desire was to bear the misery himself, to simply take it from the sufferer. Justice, on the other hand, sought to find the cause of it, to strike it at the root. She had to know the why of everything. It was a trial to her teachers. Mercy was able to become a Watcher at a very early age, because he had a keen sense of other people's pain, and soon mastered the technique of healing it. Justice, on the other hand, kept getting distracted from the main task. Her teacher wondered to her once, What if it should turn out that you are not a Watcher? There are other works to do, which must be done.

I will Watch, said Justice silently, because Mercy Watches.

So she left behind the games of childhood still unready for Watching, and spent her youth perched in the trees of the School, bending herself to a task that came so easily to Mercy, that was such agony for her. She dwelt in his mind as often as he would let her, to try to discover what it was that made him so quick to sense a hunger and satisfy it, so good at finding pain and healing it. But it was no particular skill that she could find. Until at last she realized that it was this: Mercy loved at once anyone he knew, and cared more for their joy than for his own. Justice, on the other hand, loved almost no one, but instead measured each person against the standard of what that person believed was right and wrong. Few people were good by such a measure, and Justice's love was not easily given. So when she tried to Watch, she had to learn it as an unnatural skill, and she was twenty years old before she finally left the Schooltrees and was taken into Pools.

By that time all her childhood friends had been Watching for years, and Mercy was already a master, entrusted with the Watching of a world for a third of every day. Still, Justice did not condemn herself for being so slow. She was just even with herself; she knew she was succeeding at a task she was not suited for, and so the price she had to pay was higher.

She passed her trial hour on a day, and on the next day went to Pools for the first time to Watch alone. She came to Gardens, shed her gown to dress herself in wind, and found a Pool with room for her. Gently she lowered herself to her knees in the shallow water, then lay forward until her face was flat on the smooth pebbles. Toes, belly, breasts, and face were in the cold water; heels, buttocks, back, and ears were in the breeze that scattered tree-cotton across the surface of the water. She did not breathe, but that was almost second nature now; how many hours as a child had she hung upside down from a tree branch, learning to close off her body and free her mind to wander among the stars.

Because she was so new, she was allowed to Watch only a village on a primitive world that still shunned electricity, had not yet turned to steam. It was a little place beside a river, with one inn, whose keeper was also the blacksmith—that's how small the village was.

She came to the village in the last hour of night, so there were no waking eyes for her to see through. Instead she coasted the currents of life itself, the dim wash from the serene and stupid trees, the frantic energy of the nightbirds, the beasts of dawn looking for water or salt. She thought, in such an hour as this, that Watching would be joyful.

Just as hunger awoke the first child of the village, she felt a hand on her shoulder. It was Mercy, she knew at once. She did not lift her face from the pool, for Watchers never do. Gently his fingers pressed up and down her back, to say, This is life, you are alive now. She did not need to make any answer to tell him that she heard. But he was not through. Of course he could not speak into her mind—her mind was closed to any thoughts but those of the village that she Watched—so he spoke to her in words, aloud. She hardly knew his voice, or perhaps it was the water that made it strange to her. "They say that Justice is bright and beautiful, and she brings equity behind her eyes. They say my sister is dark and terrible, for she can live with truth."

The words chilled her like his breath on her wet cheek. She dared not leave the village long enough to look into his mind, even if it were open to her. But there was something final in his words, and it made her afraid. He was bidding her good-bye, and she could not understand it.

Or is it a test? On the first full day alone, do they try all new Watchers by giving them dreadful words from the one they love the best? If it is a test, I will not fail it. She kept her face in the water, kept her mind among the villagers, and Mercy went away.

Justice began to have eyes to see with, sleepy, rubbed eyes as cows and ewes were milked and porridges were stirred over hearthfires. Everything was wood and wicker, pottery and leather—it was an old place, a once-lost place, where the machines did not help the Watchers in their work. Here the horses pissed hot in their stalls, dust seeped unfiltered into houses, children let caterpillars crawl up their arms, and one Watcher had to care for each town, so many things could harm them.

A child began to choke on a sausage. The parents looked up, uncertain what to do. Justice spasmed the child's diaphragm, ejecting the sausage onto the table. The child laughed, and thought of doing it again, but Justice let his mother scold him, and the child stopped. Justice had no time to waste with games at the breakfast table.

The cobbler sheared off his thumb along with the leather he was cutting. He was not used to pain, and screamed, but Justice took the pain from him, made him pick up the half-thumb from the bench and put it back in place. It was a simple thing to grow vein to vein, nerve to nerve, and then reach into his mind and take away the memory. She also made his wife forget she heard the sound of terror in his cry. What you do not remember, did not happen.

There was anger, which she calmed. There was fear, which she comforted. There was pain and injury, and she healed all. Disease could not take root, for she quickened the body's power to purify itself. Even hunger could not last, for everyone wanted to work hard in the morning, as Justice spread vigor through the village with the dawn, and soon the fields were dotted with workers, and bench and barrel, forge and oven had its worker in place.

In the afternoon an old man's heart stopped beating. Justice quickly did the death check. It would take more than three minutes' work to heal him; he had no children under twenty; his wife was healthy of mind and heart; and so he would be allowed to die. Instead of healing him, Justice brought his son to his house, the thirty-year-old innkeeper with blacksmith's arms. She kept the young man's mind a blank; he did not recognize the old man, merely picked him up and carried him out to the burying place, where friends were waiting with a hole half-dug. Within the hour the old man was laid into the ground. The men who dug the hole would remember the burying, but they remembered it as long past, a year ago, and they had long since got over the grief of the old man's death.

On his way back home, Justice put into the mind of the dead man's son all the joyful moments of his childhood in his home, a generous eulogy; but he believed that he had only walked to his grandfather's year-old grave today, to remember him on the anniversary of his passing.

The dead man's widow blankly packed up all she owned and moved into her son's inn, where she was given a bed in the wall downstairs not far from the fire, with her grandson near her in a truckle bed, and her granddaughter across the room. She was long since past grieving, or even feeling strange to live with her daughter-in-law. Everyone was comfortable with each other by now, and life went smoothly on, with Grandfather a beloved memory and no grief to darken their days.

She tended wombs, to be sure the right ones were filled and the rest stayed empty; she came to the aid of the girl who decided it was time not to be a virgin, and made it a pleasure to her, despite the boy's overeagerness. And at last night came to the village, and the Sleep Watchers touched her gently and told her she was through. Good work, they said silently, and Justice lifted her face from the pool hot with pride, cold from the breeze on her wet face and body. It was noon on Worthing, and the skin of her back and buttocks and thighs was hot and brown. She let the breeze dry her, saying nothing to the other Watchers who had shared Pool with her.

She walked into Garden, and then allowed herself to breathe, letting the air come like snow into her throat. She untied her hair and let it fall over her shoulders. Five more days of Watching, and if she did well they would let her cut her hair. She would be a woman then, her test completed.

She found her clothing and put it on. Only then did her friend Grave come to her, and tell her the news.

They've found God, he said silently. In his starship at the bottom of the sea. He's asleep, but we can wake him if we want. One thing is certain, though. He's just a man.

Justice laughed. Of course he's just a man—we knew that, didn't we? We *are* his children.

No, Grave told her. Just a *man*.

And she understood now that Jason Worthing, the father of their race, did not have their power after all.

Oh, he could see behind the eyes, but he couldn't *put* anything there, he couldn't *change* anything.

Poor man, thought Justice. To have eyes, but then no hands to touch with, no lips to speak with. To be dumb and motionless in the mind, and yet see—what torture it must have been. Better to leave him sleeping. What will he make of us, his children, if he's such a cripple among us?

There are those, said Grave silently, who want to waken him anyway. To have him judge us.

Do we need judging?

If he is strong enough to bear the disappointment of not being as powerful as we are, then they say we ought to waken him and see what he can teach us—what other man is living who knew the universe *before* we began to Watch? He can compare, and tell us if our work is good.

Of course it is. And if he is too weak to bear inferiority, then we have only to change his memory and send him somewhere else.

Grave shook his head. Why wake him, if we only mean to take away his memory? What good, then, were all his centuries of sleep?

When a man is grieved or sick or weak, we heal him.

He has memories that are otherwise lost to the world.

Then learn his memories and heal him.

Justice, he is our father.

Then it comes to special cases, and that is unjust. Bring him up because he is alive, and heal him if he is in pain. There's no reason to determine first if it would cause him harm or not. Especially since we could not find *that* out unless we float the stone—

And she realized then what Grave had hoped to hide from her, at least for a while longer, that they had already decided to float the stone while she was Watching, and that her own brother Mercy was to do it.

Justice waited for no other thought from Grave; she ran at once to the Hall of Rock. All she could think of as she ran was that Mercy had come to bid her good-bye, had known even then what he meant to do, and had not told her. It was not because she was in Pools; he had waited till she was there before coming to her, so she would not try to stop him. But she must stop him, for to look into the mind of the dead meant death or madness.

Of course Mercy would say, Let me be the one. Here I am, let me—he would gladly give his mind or his life to dwell within the mind of God.

When Justice got there it already was too late. Only she, of all who were not at that moment Watching, only she had not been told of this. Everyone else was gathered, here or at the other Halls of Rock, and they already waited inside Mercy's mind. He lay on his back on a flat rock, his arms spread out to hold him as the stone softened under him, let his body sink gently. The breeze began to ripple the surface of the stone, as Mercy arched his back and let his head sink downward into the stone, down until his whole head was immersed.

She had no choice, then, but to join the others, as if she were a willing participant in this act—could not bear to be the only one who was not with him in his sacrifice.

As she looked beneath the stone, she felt within her a familiar mind. It was her mother, and she said, Welcome, Justice.

How could you let him! cried Justice in her anguish.

How could we not, when he wanted so much to do it, and it needed to be done?

It isn't fair for him to give all, when I give nothing.

Ah, said Mother silently, so it comes to fairness after all. You want to match your brother pain for pain.

Yes.

You can't. Even if you wanted to, you could not float the stone. It takes more compassion than you were born with—there are few of us who could. But you can help us, all the same. You know Mercy better than anyone. When the mind of God is in him, you better than anyone can tell us how much of himself is Mercy, and how much is Jason Worthing. And with your perfect sense of measure, you can tell us when the ordeal is done, and from you we can learn what we should do.

I do not consent to this.

But if you do not help us, you may be letting Mercy give himself in vain.

So Justice was not merely an observer, but the leader of all the world as they Watched in Mercy's mind.

Mercy dwelt now at the bottom of the sea, inside a cold and silent chamber where a mind had lived. Now the memories were in an unfathomable bubble, and Mercy had to go into the brain where they once had lived and dwell there, strike out all his own memories and all that he had learned from everyone else, and see what his mind did in the space where Jason once had been. If all went well, he would become Jason, and from him they could learn what Jason would do when he awoke, how he would respond; but it was always less than perfect, this technique, because no one had ever been able to drive out all of his own memories, and leave the dead man's mind alone. Always there was something of the floater left, to distort the result. Justice's work was to measure the distortion, and to compensate.

But there was no distortion. They had not counted on how little Mercy loved himself. There was no memory, however deep, that he had to cling to to survive. There was no part of him that had to live on, no matter how much he willed to die. So as Justice searched for Mercy in the cold liquid granite, she found nothing. Only a stranger in Mercy's place. Only Jason Worthing, a poor crippled man who could see but could not speak.

It was already a long, long time, and still she had not found her brother. Where is he, demanded Mother. You must find him, for he can't go on much longer.

At last Justice cried out in despair, He isn't there, he's gone.

And in awe at Mercy's perfect gift, all of Worthing withdrew from Mercy's mind at once, having learned from Jason all they needed to know. Justice opened her eyes in time to see the stone go solid again, with Mercy's head still inside, his back arched, his hands clutching the surface. For a moment it seemed that he moved, that he was alive, still trapped and trying to get out. But it was only an illusion, caused by the pose he died in. His flesh was not flesh now, but also stone, and he was gone.

Justice searched inside herself for the balance, the perfect balance that should be there, but it was gone.

Lared stood over Justice's bed where she pretended to be asleep.

"You were giving me dreams," he said. "You are not sleeping."

Slowly she shook her head, and he saw, by the light of the candle that he held, tears seeping from the corners of her eyes.

Before he could speak to her again, there was a hand on his shoulder. He turned, and it was Jason. "She Watched our village, Jason."

"Only the once," he said. "After her brother floated the stone, she never Watched again."

"But I remember that day. I saw myself in her memory, I saw her go inside me and it was as if I understood myself whole for the first time. Nothing that you showed me before, nothing was—"

"Everything else came from lesser minds than hers. What she sees, she understands."

"All these months she's been with us, and I never knew her, never guessed. *She* is God, not you."

"She was the least of the gods, if you want to call them that. But then, at the end she was the greatest. She came to know me, you see. She insisted that she be the one to tend me when they raised me from the sea. I remember waking, with my ship going crazy with warnings—something was moving the ship, and it wasn't anything the poor ship's computer had met before. When we rested on the surface of the sea, I opened the door, and there was Justice, standing on the water in front of me, looking back at me with eyes as blue as mine, and I thought, My daughter. It was only a few days to me, then, since I left Rain and the children in the Forest of Waters. And this was what they had become. She hated me, of course."

"Why? What had you done?"

"It was unfair. She knew that. But it made her the fairest judge of what I might have to teach them. If anyone had reason to disbelieve and doubt me, it was Justice. She showed me everything; they even let me watch them Watch, so that I saw through their eyes what they were doing in the world. It was beautiful, and kind, a world full of people devoting themselves to nothing but the service of mankind. I cursed them and told them that I wish I had been castrated at the age of ten before I spawned any such thing as them. I was quite upset, as I remember. And, as you can imagine, so were they. They couldn't believe that I loathed so much what they were doing. They could not understand, even though they could see into my mind, why

I was angry. So I showed them. I said, Justice, let me take from you all memory of your brother's death. And she said—''

"No!" cried Justice from her bed. The word was not in Lared's language, but he needed no translation to understand it.

"Hypocrites, I said to them," said Jason. "You dare to rob mankind of all its pain, yet treasure your own agonies. Who Watches you?"

"Who Watches you?" cried Jason.

No one, they answered. If we ever forgot our own pain, how could we care enough to protect *them* from *theirs*?

"Did you ever think that however much they railed against the universe or fate or God or whatever else, that they might not thank you for stealing from them all that makes them human?"

And they saw in Jason's mind the things he treasured most, the memories that were strongest, and they were all the times of fear and hunger, pain and grief. And they looked into their own hearts, and saw what memories had endured through all the ages of time, and they were memories of struggle and accomplishment, sacrifices like Mercy when he floated the stone and gave a perfect offering of himself, agonies like Elijah Worthing when he watched his wife cast herself upon the flames, even cruel Adam Worthing with his terror that his uncle would find him and punish him again—these had lasted, while the simple contentment had not. They saw that this was what had made them good, even in their own eyes; and because they had left the rest of man no evils to overcome, they had robbed them of the hope of greatness, of the possibility of joy.

Full agreement did not come at once. It came only gradually, over the weeks and months. But finally, because they could see themselves through Jason's eyes, they decided that mankind was dead as long as they Watched, that men and women would only become human again with the possibility of pain.

"But how can we live?" they asked, "knowing of all the suffering that will come, knowing we can stop it, and yet withholding ourselves? That is more suffering than *we* can bear; we have loved them all too long and well."

And so they decided not to live. They decided to finish what

Mercy had begun, the perfect offering. Only two people in the world refused.

"You people are crazy," Jason said. "I wanted you to stop controlling everything, I didn't ask you to kill yourselves."

Some kinds of life are not worth living, they answered mildly. You're too uncompassionate to understand.

And as for Justice, she refused to stay because she wasn't worthy to die in Mercy's cause. It would be giving her more value than she was worth.

But you'll have to live among the people in their suffering, they said. It will destroy you, surely, to see their grief and yet not save them.

Perhaps, said Justice. But that is the price that Justice pays; that will balance me with Mercy, in the end.

So Jason and Justice took a starship to the only world outside of Worthing that Justice had ever known, as behind them the world of Worthing tipped inward toward its sun and spiraled down to die in fire.

Justice heard the deaths of a hundred million souls and bore it; felt the horror of the Day of Pain in Flat Harbor, and bore it; felt Lared's hatred as he learned of her power and that she yet did nothing, and bore it.

But now, lying on her bed, it was Sala's grief that struck too deep, Sala's suffering that she could not bear. She gave that moment to Lared as he watched, let him see her from the inside even at the moment of her pain.

"You see," said Jason, "she is not like me. She isn't uncompassionate, after all. There's more of Mercy in her than she thought."

12
The Day of Justice

Lared and Jason stood at Justice's bedside, and for the first time Lared did not fear her and did not hate her; for the first time he understood what lay behind her choice, and though he thought that it was wrong, he realized it was not Justice's fault.

"How could they decide wisely," Lared whispered, "when they only had your mind to judge by?"

Jason shrugged. "I didn't lie to them. I only showed them the way things seemed to me. Remember, Lared—they didn't just take my word for it. It was only when they saw that they were taking away from others what they would not willingly give up themselves, that what mankind was missing then was the only thing that was worth remembering about the time before—"

"That's fine," Lared said, "if you stand above mankind in a tower, looking down. But here, Jason, when you have the power to heal, and do not heal, I call that evil."

"But *I* don't have that power," Jason said.

At that moment someone screamed downstairs. Screamed in

pain, again and again. It's Clany, thought Lared. But Clany's dead.

"Sala!" he shouted, and flew down the stairs, Jason after him.

Father was braving the flames to pull Sala from the hearthfire. There was no part of her that was not afire. Lared did not hesitate, but plunged his hands into the fire and together he and Father pulled her out. The pain of his own burnt flesh was excruciating, but Lared hardly noticed, for Sala writhed in his arms, screaming over and over, "Justice! Justice! Now! Now!"

"She was in the fire already when I woke!" Father said frantically.

Mother kept reaching frantically for her daughter, but shied away each time before she touched the charred flesh, lest she somehow add to Sala's pain.

Lared thought for a moment that her eyes were closed, but then realized that they were not. "She has no eyes!" he cried. And then he looked at the foot of the stairs and saw Justice standing there, her face a mask of anguish.

"Now! Now! Now!" cried Sala.

"How is she alive?" cried Father.

"God in heaven, not three days!" cried Mother. "Not like Clany, let her die now, not three days!"

And then Father and Mother were pushed aside, and Justice seized Sala, tore her from Lared's arms, and gave a wail so terrible that Lared could not stop himself from crying out at the pain of hearing it.

Then silence.

Not even Sala crying.

She is dead, thought Lared.

But then, as he watched, Sala blinked her eyes, and they were bright again, not the empty sockets Lared had seen a moment ago. As he watched, he saw the burnt skin flake from her body, leaving a pale, smooth, perfect layer of unburnt, untouched, unscarred flesh.

Sala smiled and laughed, threw her arms around Justice and clung to her. Lared looked down at his own arms, and they were healed, then reached out to Father and touched the bud of fingers blossoming on the stump where once his arm had grown. In only a few minutes the arm was whole, as strong as ever.

Justice sat on the floor, Sala in her arms, weeping bitterly.

"At last," Jason murmured.

Justice looked up at him.

"You're human after all," Jason said.

You *are* good, Lared said to her silently. I was wrong. You are so good that you could not stop yourself, with the test that Sala set for you. There is more mercy in you than you thought.

Justice nodded.

"You didn't fail," Jason said aloud to her. "You passed." And he leaned down and kissed her forehead. "You wouldn't be my daughter if you had made any other choice."

For the small village of Flat Harbor, the Day of Pain was over. It would not be as it was before. Justice played no tricks on memory, and death itself she would not hinder, but the pain was at an end in Flat Harbor, and would be as long as she lived.

It was a spring day, and the snow was gone. The men and women were out among the hedges and the fields, replanting bushes that the snow had moved, harrowing the stubbled fields, getting ready for the plow.

The last of the logs were bound together in a raft, to be floated down the river to Star Haven, where they would fetch a good price, especially the great mast tree in the middle of the raft. Jason and the tinker stepped aboard. The raft shifted slightly, but did not rock for long. It was sturdy, and the tent they had pitched already in the middle of the raft would make a pleasant house for the two-week river journey. The tinker had his pots and pans, his tin and all his tools carefully arranged with floats in case the raft broke up—he could not afford to lose all that. Jason carried only one thing with him, a small iron-bound chest. He opened it only once, to be sure all nine closely written sheets of parchment were neatly rolled and stacked lightly within.

"Ready?" asked the tinker.

"Not quite yet," said Jason.

They waited for a moment, and then Lared came running onto the bank, carrying a hastily packed bag over his shoulder and shouting, "Wait! Wait for me!" When he saw that they were still against the shore he stopped and grinned foolishly. "Got room for one more?"

"If you promise not to eat much," said Jason.

"I decided not to stay here. Father's arm is whole, and they don't need me much, they never did, and I thought you might need someone along who can read and write . . ."

"Just get aboard, Lared."

Lared stepped carefully into the boat and set down his bag beside the iron chest. "Will they use a printing press and make a real book of this?"

"If they don't, they won't get paid," said Jason, and he and the tinker poled the raft away from shore.

"It's a good thing to know they'll all be safe," Lared said, looking back at the villagers in the fields and hedges.

"I hope you don't think that you'll be safe with *me*," said Jason. "I may be getting along in years, but I intend to live. I intend to sleep as little as possible, for one thing. And I hope you remember how many things there are that I cannot do."

Lared smiled and opened his bag to reveal four cheeses and a smoked shoulder. "It's going to be a terrible life, I know," he said. He cut off a strip of meat and gave it to Jason. "Still, I'll take my chances."

Tales
of
Capitol

To Jay A. Parry,
who has read everything
and made it better

No child can be understood without knowing the parents; no revolution can be understood without knowing the *ancien régime*; no colony can be understood without knowing the mother country; no new world can be understood without knowing the old world that went before.

Here are tales from the world of Capitol, the society built of plastic, steel, and somec, all of it supposedly eternal, all of it doomed to crumble. These stories will show you why—and how—Abner Doon set out to hasten the day of destruction.

13
Skipping Stones

Bergen Bishop wanted to be an artist.

Because he said so when he was seven, he was promptly given pencils, paper, charcoal, watercolors, oils, canvas, a palette, an exquisite assortment of brushes, and an instructor who came and taught him once a week. In short, he was given all the paraphernalia money can buy.

The instructor was smart enough to know that when one hopes to make a living teaching the children of the rich, one learns when to be honest and when to lie. Thus, the words *the child has talent* has often passed his lips before. But this time he meant them, and it was difficult to find a way to make the lying words now express the truth.

"The boy has *talent!*" he declared. "The boy *has* talent!"

"No one supposed that he hadn't," the boy's mother said, a bit surprised at how effusive the teacher was. The father said nothing, just wondered if the instructor thought he'd get a bonus for declaring it with such fervor.

"*That* boy has talent. Potential. Great potential," the teacher said (again), and Bergen's mother, finally grown weary of the effusion of praise, said, "My dear fellow, we don't mind a bit if he has talent. He may keep it. Now come again next Tuesday. Thank you."

Yet despite his parents' unconcern, Bergen applied himself to learning to paint with some vigor. In a short time he had acquired technique well beyond his years.

He was a good-tempered boy with a strong sense of justice. Many young men of his class on the planet Crove used their serving-men as whipping boys. After all, since brothers were out of fashion one had to have *someone* to pick on. And the serving-men (who were boys the same age as their masters) learned very early that if they defended themselves, they would soon face far worse than their youthful master could mete out.

Bergen, however, was not unfair. Because he was unquarrelsome, he and his serving-man, Dal Vouls, never had harsh words or blows. And because he was fair, when Dal shyly mentioned that he too would like to learn to paint, Bergen immediately shared his equipment and his instructor.

The instructor didn't mind teaching the two boys at once—Dal was obedient and quiet and didn't ask questions. But he was too aware of the possibilities for added income not to mention to Bergen's father that it was customary to give an added stipend when there were two pupils instead of one.

"Dal, have you been wasting the instructor's time?" Locken Bishop asked his son's serving-man.

Dal remained silent, too afraid to speak quickly. Bergen answered. "It was my idea. To have him taught. It doesn't take the teacher any longer."

"The teacher's dunning me for more. You've got to learn the value of money, Bergen. Either you take the lessons alone, or you take them not at all."

Even so, Bergen forced the teacher ("I'll see you're fired and blackballed throughout the city. Throughout the *world!*") to let Dal sit quietly to one side, just watching. Dal didn't set pencil to paper in the sessions, however.

When he was nine, Bergen tired of painting and dismissed the teacher. He took up riding this time, years before most children did, but this time he insisted and his father purchased two horses; and so Dal rode with Bergen.

It's too easy to depict childhood as an idyll. Certainly there were some frustrations, some times when Dal and Bergen didn't see eye to eye. But those times were buried in an avalanche of other memories, so that they were soon forgotten. The rides took them far from Bergen's father's house, but there was no direction in which they could ride and leave his father's land and return home the same day.

And because Bergen was able to forget for hours at a time that he was heir and Dal was only a contracted serving-man, they became friends. Together they poured hot wax on the stairway, which nearly killed Bergen's sister when she slipped on it— and Bergen stoically took the full blame, since he would be confined to his room and Dal, if caught, would be beaten and dismissed. Together they hid in the bushes and watched as a couple who had ridden nude on horseback copulated in the gravel on the edge of a cliff—they marveled for days at the thought that *this* was what Bergen's parents did behind closed doors. Together they swam in every untrustworthy waterhole on the estate and started fires in every likely corner, saving each other's lives so often they lost track of who was ahead.

And then, when Bergen was fourteen, he remembered that he had painted as a boy. An uncle visited and said, "And this is Bergen, the boy who paints."

"His painting was just a childish whim," Bergen's mother said. "He outgrew it."

Bergen was not accustomed to getting angry with his mother. But at fourteen, few boys are able to accept the word *childish* without wrath. Bergen immediately said, "Did I, Mother? Then why is it that I still paint?"

"Where?" she said, disbelieving.

"In my room."

"Show me some of your work then, little artist." The word *little* was infuriating.

"I burn them. They aren't yet representative of my best work."

At that his mother and the uncle laughed uproariously, and Bergen stomped off to his room, Dal a shadow behind him.

"Where the hell is it!" he said angrily, hunting through the cupboard where the art supplies had been.

Dal coughed. "Bergen, sir," he said (at twelve Bergen had halfway come of age, and it was the law that he had to be called *sir* by anyone under contract to him or his father), "I thought you weren't using your painting stuff anymore. I've got it."

Bergen turned in amazement. "I wasn't using it. But I didn't know *you* were."

"I'm sorry, sir. But I didn't get much chance to try while the instructor was coming. I've been using the materials ever since."

"Did you use them up?"

"There was a good supply. There's no more paper, but there's plenty of canvas. I'll get it."

He went and got it, brought it into the big house in two trips, being careful to use the back stairways so Bergen's parents wouldn't see. "I didn't think you'd mind," Dal said, when it was all brought back.

Bergen looked puzzled. "Of course I don't mind. It's just the old biddy's taken it into her head that I'm still a child. I'm going to paint again. I don't know why I ever quit. I've always wanted to be an artist."

And he set up the easel at the window, so he could see the yard below, dotted with the graceful whiptrees of Crove that rose fifty meters straight up into the air—and then, in a storm, lay over completely on the ground, so that no farmer of the Plains could ever be free of the worry of having a whiptree crash against his house in the wind. He began with an undercoat of green and blue, and Dal watched. Bergen hesitated now and then, but it came back quickly, and, in fact, the long separation from art had done him no harm. His eyes was truer. His colors were deeper. But still—an amateur.

"Perhaps if there were more magenta in the sky under the clouds," Dal offered.

Bergen turned to him coldly. "I'm not through with the sky."

"Sorry."

And Bergen painted on. Everything went well enough, except he couldn't seem to get the whiptrees right. They kept looking so brown and solid, which wasn't right at all. And when he tried to draw them bent, they were awkward, not true to life. Finally he swore and threw the brush out the window, leapt to his feet and stormed away.

Dal walked to the painting and said, "Bergen, sir, it isn't bad. Not at all. It's good. Just the whiptrees."

"I know about the damned whiptrees," Bergen snarled, furious at his failure to be perfect in his first attempt in years. And he turned to see Dal taking swipes at the canvas, quick strokes with a slender brush. And then Dal turned around, and said, "Perhaps like that, sir."

Bergen walked up to the canvas. The whiptrees were there, by far the most lifelike, most dynamic, most *beautiful* thing in the painting. Bergen looked at them—how effortless they seemed, how effortlessly Dal had stroked them into the painting. This was not how it should be. It was *Bergen* who was going to be the artist, not Dal. It was not just or right or fair that Dal should be able to paint whiptrees.

And in anger Bergen shouted something unintelligible and struck out at Dal, catching him a blow at the side of his head. Dal was stunned. Not from the force of the blow, but from the fact of it.

"You've never hit me before," he said, wonderingly.

"I'm sorry," Bergen said immediately.

"All I did was paint the whiptrees."

"I know. I'm sorry. Hitting servants isn't the kind of thing I do."

And now Dal's surprise turned to fury. "Servants?" he asked. "For a moment I forgot that I'm a servant. I saw us try our hands at the same task and I was better at it than you. I forgot I was a servant."

Bergen was frightened at this turn of events. He hadn't meant anything by his statement—he just prided himself on not being an uncontrolled master.

"But Dal," he said innocently, "you *are* a servant."

"That I am. I must remember that in the future. Not to win at any games. To laugh at your jokes even when they're stupid. To let your horse always be a little faster. To always agree that you're right even when you're being a fool."

"I've never wanted anyone to treat me like that!" Bergen said, angry at the unfairness of it.

"That's the way servants treat their masters."

"I don't want you to be a servant. I want you to be my friend!"

"And I thought I was."

"You're a servant *and* a friend."

Dal laughed. "Bergen, *sir*, a man is *either* a servant *or* a friend. They're opposite directions on the same road. Either you're paid for service, or you do it for love."

"But you're paid for service, and I thought you did it for love!"

Dal shook his head. "I served for love, and I thought you fed and clothed me for love. I felt free with you."

"You are free."

"I have a contract."

"If you ever ask me to break it, I will!"

"Is that a promise?"

"On my life. You aren't a servant, Dal!"

And then the door opened, and Bergen's mother and uncle came in. "We heard shouting," his mother said. "We thought there was a quarrel."

"We were having a pillow fight," Bergen said.

"Then why is the pillow neatly on the bed?"

"We finished and put it back."

The uncle laughed. "What a regular housemaid you're raising, Selly."

"My Lord, Nooel, he wasn't joking. He still paints." They walked up to the painting and looked at it carefully.

Finally Nooel turned to Bergen and smiled, and put out his hand. "I thought it was just bluster and blow. Just a teenager spouting off. But you've got talent, boy. The sky's a bit rough, and you need some work on detail. But whoever can paint whiptrees like that has a future."

Bergen could not take credit unfairly.

"Dal painted the whiptrees."

Selly Bishop looked furious, but smiled sweetly at Dal nonetheless. "How nice, Dal, that Bergen lets you play with his paintings." Dal said nothing. But Nooel stared at him.

"Contract?" Nooel asked.

Dal nodded.

"I'll buy it," Nooel offered.

"Not for sale," Bergen said quickly.

"Actually," Selly said sweetly, "it's not a bad idea. Think you might want to develop the talent?"

"It's worth developing."

"The contract," Bergen said firmly, "is not for sale."

Selly looked coldly at her son. "Everything that was bought can be sold."

"But what a man loves enough, Mother, he'll keep regardless of the price he's offered."

"Loves?"

"Your mind is disgusting, Selly," Nooel said. "Obviously they're friends. Sometimes you can be the worst bitch on the planet."

"You're too kind, Nooel. On *this* planet it's an achievement. After all, there's the empress."

They both laughed and left the room.

"I'm sorry, Dal," Bergen said.

"I'm used to it," Dal answered. "Your mother and I haven't ever gotten along too well. And I don't care—there's only one person here I care about."

They looked at each other closely for a short time. Smiled. Then dropped the subject, because at fourteen there are few gentle emotions that can be openly borne for very long.

When Bergen turned twenty, somec came to their level of society.

"A brilliant stroke," Locken Bishop said. "Do you know what it means? If we qualify, we can sleep for five years at a time and wake up for five years at a time. We'll live for another century beyond what we would have otherwise."

"But will we qualify?" Bergen asked.

His parents laughed uproariously. "It's pure merit, and the boy asks if his family will qualify! Of course we'll qualify, Bergen!"

Bergen was quietly angry, as he usually was with his parents these days. "Why?" he asked.

Locken caught the edge in his son's tone. He turned authoritarian, and pointed at Bergen's chest. "Because your father provides jobs for fifty thousand men and women. Because if I went out of business, half this planet would reel under the impact.

And because I pay more taxes than all but fifty other men in the Empire.''

"Because you're rich, in other words," Bergen said.

"Because I'm rich!" Locken answered angrily.

"Then, if you don't mind, I'll wait to go on somec until I qualify by *my* merit, and not by my father's."

Selly laughed. "If I waited until I qualified on my own, I'd *never* get on somec!"

Bergen looked at her with loathing. "And if there were any justice in the world, you never would."

It surprised Bergen, but neither his mother nor his father said anything at all. It was Dal who spoke to him, later that night, as the two of them sat together putting finishing touches on art pieces—Dal a miniature in oils; Bergen, a massive, almost mural-sized portrait of the houses on the estate as he thought they ought to be, with the house much smaller and the barns large enough to be of some use. And his whiptrees were beautiful.

Weeks later, Bergen slipped off and paid the examination fee and tested high enough in basic intelligence, creativity, and ambition that he was given the right to go on somec for three years and off for five years. He would be a sleeper. And he did it without money.

"Congratulations, son," his father said, more than a little proud at his son's independence.

"I notice you've scheduled it so you wake up two years before us. Time to play around, I imagine," Selly said, looking and sounding more bitter than ever.

Dal said only one thing when he heard Bergen was going on somec. "Free me first."

Bergen looked startled.

"You promised," Dal reminded him.

"But I'm not of age. I can't for a year."

"And do you think your father will? Or that your mother would let him? My contract lets them forbid me to paint, or lets them own anything I produce. They could make me clean the stables. They could make me cut trees with my bare hands. And you won't be back for three years."

Bergen was genuinely distressed. "What can I do?"

"Persuade your father to give me my freedom. Or stay awake until you come of age and can give me my freedom yourself."

"I can't forfeit the somec. You have to use it when you get it. They only have so many openings a year."

"Then persuade your father."

It took a month of constant badgering before Locken Bishop finally agreed to release Dal from his contract. And the contract had a stipulation. "Seventy-five percent of your income above room and board comes to us for five years or until you have paid us eighty thousand."

"Father," Bergen protested, "that's gouging. I would have freed him eleven months from now. And eighty thousand is ten times what you paid for his contract in the first place—and you didn't pay it to *him.*"

"I've also fed him for twenty years."

"And he worked for it."

"Worked?" Selly interrupted. "He just played. With you."

Dal spoke, softly enough that they quieted down to hear him. "If I give you that, I won't be able to get enough money to take the somec merit examination."

Locken set his jaw. "That makes no difference. It's that or you stay under contract."

Bergen put his face in his hands. Selly smiled. And Dal nodded. "But I want it in writing."

The words were soft, but the effect was electric. Locken rose to his feet, towering over Dal, who was seated. "What did you say, boy? Were you saying you expected a Bishop to make a written contract with a bastard contract worker?"

"I want it in writing," Dal said softly, meeting Locken's fury with equanimity.

"You have my spoken word, and that's enough."

"And who are the witnesses? Your son, who'll be asleep for three years, and your wife, who can't be trusted alone with a fifteen-year-old servant boy."

Selly gasped. Locken turned red, but stepped back from Dal. And Bergen was horrified. "What?" he asked.

"I want it in writing," Dal said.

"I want you out of this house," Locken answered, but his voice had a new emotion in it—hurt and betrayal. Of course,

Bergen thought: if Dal really meant that, and Mother certainly isn't denying it, of course Father is hurt.

But Dal looked up at Locken with a smile and said, "Did you think that territory where you trod would always belong to you?"

Now Bergen refused to understand. "What does he mean, Father? What is Dal saying?"

"Nothing," Locken insisted, too quickly.

Dal refused to be stopped. "Your father," he said to Bergen, "plays the strangest games with five-year-old boys. I always urged him to invite you to join in, but he never would."

The uproar didn't die down for an hour. Locken kept uselessly pounding his left fist against his thigh, as Selly gleefully attacked him to take the opprobrium for her own dalliances from her shoulders. Only Bergen could honestly grieve. "All those years, Dal. This was happening all those years?"

"To you I was a friend, Bergen," Dal said, forgetting to say *sir,* "but to them I was a servant."

"You never told me."

"What could you have done?"

And when Dal left at the end of the hour, he had the agreement in writing.

When Bergen woke from his first time under somec, he learned from a kindly man in the Sleeproom that his father had died only a few days after Bergen had left home, and his mother had been murdered by a lover two years later. The largest estate on Crove, besides the emperor's, was now Bergen's.

"I don't want it."

"Along with it, you should know," said the kindly man, "comes a five years under and one year up somec privilege."

"I'd only have to live one year in every six?"

"It's the Empire's way of expressing the value of certain large forces in the economy."

"But I want to paint."

"Paint then. But unless you want to visit your parents' graves, the managers of your businesses are doing a remarkably good job, according to the government auditors, and you can go back under to complete your two years of entitlement."

"I have someone I want to see first."

"As you wish. We can put you back under any time within the next three days. After that, you have to complete your year up, and you will have lost two years of sleep."

Bergen spent the first two days trying to find Dal Vouls. He finally succeeded when he remembered that Dal would still be bound by the contract with his father—the executors of the estate were able to locate him because he was sending in occasional draughts to complete the seventy-five-percent clause.

Dal opened the door and his face lit up with immediate recognition. "Bergen," he said. "Come in. It's been three years, then, hasn't it?"

"I guess so. Dal, it feels like yesterday to me. It *was* yesterday. How have you been doing?"

Dal pointed to the walls of the flat. Forty or fifty paintings and drawings hung there. For twenty minutes there was little conversation except "This; I like this" and "How did you manage that?" And then Bergen, thoroughly awed, sat on the floor (there was no furniture) and they talked.

"How is it going?"

"Sales are fairly slow. I don't have a name yet. But people do buy. And the best of it is, the emperor has decreed that all government offices are to be moved to Crove. Even the name of the planet is changing. To Capitol. It seems that if all goes well, every damn planet's going to orbit politically around Crove. And that means customers. It means people who know art instead of the military and commercial bastards who've had a stranglehold on money on this planet since time began."

"You've learned how to talk in long sentences since I last saw you."

"I've felt freer."

"I brought you a present." Bergen handed him the release from the contract.

Dal read it, laughed, read it again, and then wept.

"Bergen," he said, "you don't know. You don't know how hard it's been."

"I can guess."

"I haven't been able to take the examination. Heaven knows, I've hardly been able to live. But now—"

"More than that," Bergen said. "The examination costs three thousand. I brought it." He handed the money to his friend.

Dal held the money for a few seconds, then handed it back. "Your father is dead, then."

"Yes," Bergen said.

"I'm sorry. It must have been a shock to you."

"You didn't know?"

"I don't read papers. I don't have a radio. And my draughts were never returned."

"Contracts are contracts, the executors figured. Trust my father not to free his contract servants in his will."

They chuckled wryly in memory of the man, whom Dal had last seen three years ago, whom Bergen had last seen yesterday.

"Your mother?"

"The bitch died in heat," Bergen answered, and this time there was emotion. Dal touched his hand. "I'm sorry." And it was Bergen's turn to weep.

"Thank God you're my friend," Bergen said at last.

"And you mine," Dal answered.

And then the door opened and a woman walked in carrying a child that couldn't have been a year old. She was startled to see Bergen there. "Company," she said. "Hello. I'm Anda."

"I'm Bergen," Bergen said.

"My friend Bergen," Dal introduced them. "My wife Anda. My son Bergen."

Anda smiled. "He told me you were bright and beautiful, and so our son had to be named after you. He was right."

"You're too kind."

The conversation was good after that, but it was not what Bergen had expected. There couldn't be the banter, the in-jokes, the delightful gutter talk, the insults that Bergen and Dal had known for years, not with Anda there. And so they parted with friendship in the air—but a hollow feeling in Bergen's stomach. Dal had refused his gift of the examination fee, and accepted only his freedom. He would share that freedom with Anda.

Bergen went back to the Sleeproom and used the rest of his new entitlement.

* * *

When he awoke the next time, things had changed. With Crove now called Capitol, there was an incredible building boom. And Bergen's companies were deeply involved.

The building was haphazard, and Bergen began to realize that it wasn't enough just to throw buildings into the air. Capitol would be the center of trade and government for hundreds of planets. Billions of people. He could conceive of it eventually becoming one vast city. And so he began to plan accordingly.

He set his architects to planning a structure that would cover a hundred square miles and house fifty million people, heavy industry, light industry, transportation, distribution, and communication. The roof of the building had to be strong enough not only to handle the takeoffs and landings of landing craft, but also to cope with the weight of the huge starships themselves. It would take years to design—he gave them the obvious deadline of his next waking after five years of sleep.

And then he spent the rest of the year lobbying with the bureaucrats to get his plan, already taking shape, adopted as the master plan for the planet. Every city designed the same way, so that as the population boomed, the cities could link up floor to floor and pipe to pipe and form a continuous, unbroken city with a spaceport for a roof and its roots deep in the bedrock. When his time was up, he had won—and the contracts almost all went to Bergen Bishop's companies.

He did not forget Dal, however. He found him by his paintings, which were now gaining some note. It was difficult to talk, however.

"Bergen. The rumors are flying."

"Good to see you, Dal."

"They say you're stripping the planet right down to the bedrock and putting steel on top."

"Here and there."

"They say it's all supposed to interlock."

Bergen shrugged it off. "There'll be huge parks. Huge tracts of land untouched."

"Until the population needs it. Right? Always that reservation."

Bergen was hurt. "I came to talk about your painting."

"Here then," Dal said. "Have a look." And he handed Bergen a painting of a steel monster that was settling like pus onto the countryside.

"This is repulsive," Bergen said.

"It's your city. I took it from the architect's renderings."

"My city isn't this ugly."

"I know. It's an artist's job to make beauty more beautiful and ugliness uglier."

"The Empire has to have a capital somewhere."

"Does there have to be an empire?"

"What's made you so bitter?" Bergen asked, genuinely concerned. "People have been tearing up planets for years. What's getting to you?"

"Nothing's getting to me."

"Where's Anda? Where's your son?"

"Who knows? Who cares?" Dal walked to a painting of a sunset and shoved his fist through it.

"Dal!" Bergen shouted. "Don't do that!"

"I made it. I can destroy it."

"Why'd she leave?"

"I failed the merit test. She had an offer of marriage from a guy who could take her on somec. She accepted."

"How could you fail the merit test?"

"They can't measure my paintings. And when you're twenty-six years old, the requirements are higher. Much, much higher."

"Twenty-six—but we're only—"

"*You're* only twenty-one. I'm twenty-six and aging fast." Dal walked to the door and opened it. "Get out of here, Bergen. I'm dying fast. In a couple of your years I'll be an old man who isn't worth a damn, so don't bother looking me up anymore. Get on out there and wreck the planet while there's still a profit in it."

Bergen left, hurt and unable to understand why Dal should suddenly hate him. If Dal had only taken the money Bergen offered two years before, he could have taken the test when he could still have passed it. It was his own fault, not Bergen's. And blaming Bergen for it wasn't fair.

For three wakings, Bergen didn't look Dal up. The memory of Dal's bitterness was too harsh, too hurtful. Instead Bergen concentrated on building his cities. Half a million men were working on them, a dozen cities arising simultaneously on the plain. There was plenty of land left undisturbed, but the cities rose so high that the winds were broken and the whiptrees died. How could anyone have known that the seeds had to fall to the earth from no more than a meter off the ground, and that without wind strong enough to bend the trees all the way to the ground, the seeds would fall too far and break and die? In fifty years the last of the whiptrees would be gone. And it was too late to do anything about it. Bergen grieved for the whiptrees. He was sorry. The cities were already filling up with people. The starships were already coming in to land at the only spaceport in the galaxy large enough and strong enough to hold them. There was no going back.

On his fourth waking, however, Bergen learned that he had been promoted to a one year up, ten years down somec level, and he realized that if Dal still wasn't on somec, the man would be in his mid-forties, and in the next waking would be getting old. Bergen was only in his mid-twenties. And suddenly he regretted having stayed away from Dal for so long. It was a strange thing about somec. It cut you off from people. Put you in different time-streams, and Bergen realized that soon the only people he would know would be those who had exactly the same somec schedule as he.

Most of his old friends he wouldn't mind losing. After all, he had survived losing both his parents in his first sleep. But Dal was a different matter. He hadn't seen Dal for three waking years, and he missed him. They had been so close up till then.

He found him by simply asking a man with exceptionally good taste if he had ever heard of Dal Vouls.

"Has a Christian ever heard of Jesus?" asked the man, laughing.

Bergen hadn't heard of Jesus or Christians either, but he got the point. And he found Dal in a large studio in a tract of open country where trees hid the view of the eight cities growing here and there in the distance.

"Bergen," Dal said in surprise. "I never thought I'd see you again!"

And Bergen only looked in awe at the man who had been his boyhood friend. What had been only four years for Bergen had been twenty for Dal, and the difference was staggering. Dal had a belly, was now an impressively stout man with a full beard and a ready grin (this is not Dal! something shouted inside Bergen). Dal was prospering, was friendly, was, it seemed, happy, but Bergen couldn't stop thinking of this stranger as an older man to whom he should show respect.

"Bergen, you haven't changed."

"You have," Bergen answered, trying to smile as if he meant it.

"Come in. Look at my paintings. I promise to stand aside. My wife says I could hide a mural, I'm getting so fat. I tell her I have to be large enough to hold all my money on a single belt." Dal's laugh boomed out, and a middle-aged woman appeared on a balcony inside the studio.

"You make my cakes fall, you break glasses, and now you have to shout loud enough that the birds' nests are falling from the eaves!" she shouted, and Dal lumbered over to her like an amorous bear and kissed her and dragged her back.

"Bergen, meet my wife. Treve, meet Bergen, my friend who returns like a bright shadow out of my past to tie up the last of my loose ends."

"Until we buy you new clothes," Treve complained, "you *have* no loose ends."

"I married her," Dal said, "because I needed someone to tell me what a bad artist I am."

"He's terrible. Best in the world. But still Rembrandt returns to haunt us!" And Treve punched Dal in the arm, lightly.

I can't stand this, Bergen thought. This isn't Dal. He's too damn cheerful. And who's this woman who takes such liberties with my dignified friend? Who's this fat man with the grin who pretends to be an artist?

"My work," Dal said, suddenly. "Come see my work."

It was then, walking quietly along the walls where the paintings hung, that Bergen knew for sure that it was Dal. True, the voice at his shoulder was still cheerful and middle-aged. But the paintings, the strokes and sweeps and washes of them, they were all Dal. They were born in the pain of slavery on the Bishop estate; but now they were overlaid with a serenity that Dal's paintings had never had before. Yet, looking at them, Bergen realized that this serenity had also been there all the time, waiting for something to bring it out into the open.

And the something was obviously Treve.

At lunch, Bergen shyly admitted to Treve that, yes, he was the man who built the cities.

"Very efficient" she said making short work of a cappas-flower.

"My wife hates the cities," Dal said.

"As I remember, you don't love them either."

Dal grinned, and then remembered to swallow what he had been chewing. "Bergen, my friend, I am above such concerns."

"Then," his wife interjected, "those concerns had better be strong enough to support a great amount of weight."

Dal laughed and hugged her and said, "Keep your mouth shut about my weight when I'm eating, Thin Woman, it ruins the lunch."

"The cities don't bother you?"

"The cities are ugly," Dal said. "But I think of them as vast sewage disposal plants. When you have fifteen billion people on a planet that should only have fifteen million, the sewage has got to be put somewhere. So you built huge metal blocks and they kill the trees that grow in the shadows. Can I reach out and stop the tide?"

"Of course you can," Treve said.

"She believes in me. No, Bergen, I don't fight the cities. People in the cities buy my paintings and let me live in luxury like this, making brilliant paintings and sleeping with my beautiful wife."

"If I'm so beautiful, why never a portrait of me?"

"I am incapable of doing justice," Dal said. "I paint Crove. I paint it as it was before they killed it and named the corpse Capitol. These paintings will last hundreds of years. People who see them will maybe say, 'This is what a world looks like. Not corridors of steel and plastic and artificial wood.' "

"We don't use artificial wood," Bergen protested.

"You will," Dal answered "The trees are nearly gone. And wood is awfully expensive to ship between the stars."

And then Bergen asked the question he had meant to ask since he arrived. "Is it true that you've been offered somec?"

"They practically forced the needle into my arm right here. I had to beat them off with a canvas."

"Then it's true that your turned it down?" Bergen was incredulous.

"Three times. They keep saying, We'll let you sleep ten years, we'll let you sleep fifteen years. But who wants to sleep? I can't paint in my sleep."

"But Dal," Bergen protested. "Somec is like immortality. I'm going on the ten-down-one-up schedule, and that means that when I'm fifty, three hundreds years will have passed! Three centuries! And I'll live another five hundred years beyond that. I'll see the Empire rise and fall, I'll see the work of a thousand artists living hundreds of years apart, I'll have broken out of the ties of time—"

"Ties of time. A good phrase. You are ecstatic about progress. I congratulate you. I wish you well. Sleep and sleep and sleep, may you profit from it."

"The prayer of the capitalist," Treve added, smiling and putting more salad on Bergen's plate.

"But Bergen. While you fly, like stones skipping across the water, touching down here and there and barely getting wet, while you are busy doing that, I shall swim. I like to swim. It gets me wet. It wears me out. And when I die, which will happen before you turn thirty, I'm sure, I'll have my paintings to leave behind me."

"Vicarious immortality is rather second-rate, isn't it?"

"Is there anything second-rate about my work?"

"No," Bergen answered.

"Then eat my food, and look at my paintings again, and go back to building huge cities until there's a roof over all the world and the planet shines in space like a star. There's a kind of beauty in that too, and your work will live after you. Live however you like. But tell me, Bergen, do you have time to swim naked in a lake?"

Bergen laughed. "I haven't done that in years."

"I did it this morning."

"At your age?" Bergen asked, and then regretted his words. Not because Dal resented them—he didn't seem to notice them. Bergen regretted the words because they were the end of even the hope of a friendship. Dal, who had painted beautiful whip-trees into his painting, was an older man now, and would get even older in the next few years, and their lives would never cross meaningfully again. It was Treve who bantered with him like a friend. While I, Bergen realized, I build cities.

When they parted at evening, still cheerful, still friends, Dal asked (and his voice was serious): "Bergen. Do you ever paint?"

Bergen shook his head. "I haven't the time. But I admit—if I had your talent, Dal, I'd find the time. I haven't that talent, though. Never did."

"That's not true, Bergen. You had more talent than I."

Bergen looked Dal in the eye and realized the man meant it. "Don't say that," Bergen said fervently. "If I believed that, Dal, do you think I could spend my life the way I have to spend it?"

"Oh, my friend," Dal said, smiling. "You have made me sad, sad, sad. Hug me for the boys we were together."

They embraced, and then Bergen left. They never met again.

Bergen lived to see Capitol covered in steel from pole to pole, with even the oceans encroached upon until they were mere ponds. He once went out in a pleasure cruiser and saw the planet from space. It gleamed. It was beautiful. It was like a star.

Bergen lived long enough to see something else. He visited a store one day that sold rare and old paintings. And there he saw a painting that he recognized immediately. The paint was chipping away; the colors had faded. But it was Dal Vouls's work, and there were whiptrees in the painting, and Bergen demanded of the storekeeper, "Who's let this painting get in such a condition?"

"Such a condition? Sir, don't you know how old this is? Seven hundred years old, sir! It's remarkably well preserved. By a great artist, the greatest of our millennium, but nobody makes paint or canvas that stays unmarred for more than a few centuries. What do you want, miracles?"

And Bergen realized that in his pursuit of immortality, he had got more than he hoped for. For not only did friends drop away and die behind him, but also their works, and all the works of men, had crumbled in his lifetime. Some had crumbled into dust; some were just showing the first cracks. But Bergen had lived long enough to see the one sight the universe usually hides from mankind: entropy.

The universe is winding down, Bergen said as he looked at Dal's painting. Was it worth the cost just to find that out?

He bought the painting. It fell to pieces before he died.

14
Second Chance

By the age of seven Batta was thoroughly trapped, though she scarcely recognized it until she was twenty-two. The bars were so fragile that to most other people they would not have existed at all:

A father, crippled in a freak tube accident and pensioned off by the government months before Batta was born.

A mother, whose heart was gold but whose mind was unable to concentrate meaningfully for more than three minutes at a time.

And brothers and sisters who, in the chaos and depression of the mindless, will-less home, might have come unstuck from the fabric of adjusted society had not Batta decided (without deciding) that she would be mother and father to her siblings, her parents, and herself.

Many another person would have rebelled at having to come home directly after school, with never an opportunity to meet with friends and do the mad things through the endless corridors of Capitol that occupied the time of most adolescents of the middle class. Batta merely returned from school and did home-work, fixed dinner, talked to Mother (or rather, listened), helped the other children with their problems, and braved the den where Father hid from the world, pretending that he had legs or that, lacking them, he had not diminished in worth. ("I fathered five damned children, didn't I?" he insisted from time to time.)

But all was not bleak. Batta loved studying, was, in fact, not far from being a genius—and she indulged herself enough to go to college, largely because she got a scholarship and her mother believed in taking advantage of every free thing that came.

And in college there was this one young man.

He was not far from being a genius too—from the other side. Batta had never known anyone like him (she didn't realize that she had hardly known anyone at all) but a crazy friendship grew up that ranged from gift-wrapped presents of dissected thwands from Basic Zoology to hours of silence together, studying for examinations.

No held hands. No attempted kisses. No fumbling experi-mentation in the dark.

Batta was unsure of what it was like and whether she would want it (she always imagined her mother making love to a legless man), while she wondered if Abner Doon ever thought of sex at all.

And then college ended, degrees were granted—hers in phys-ics, his in government service—and they stopped seeing each other and the months went by and she was twenty-two and it suddenly occurred to her that she was trapped.

"Where are you going? You're through with college, you don't have to go to class anymore, do you?" her mother asked plain-tively.

"I thought I'd take a walk," Batta answered.

"But Batta, your father *needs* you. You know he's only happy when *you're* here."

Which was true. And Batta spent more and more hours inside the three-room flat until one day, almost a year after graduation, a buzzer.

"Abner," she said, more in surprise than in delight. She had almost forgotten him. Indeed, she had almost forgotten that she had a college education.

"Batta. I haven't seen you. I wanted to."

"Well," she said, turning around for him to see her but knowing she looked terrible even as she did it, "here I am."

"You look like hell."

"And you," she said, "look like a specimen that they forgot to dissect."

They laughed. Old times, old magic. He asked her out. She refused. He asked her to go for a walk. She was too busy. And when her father called her out of the room for the fifth time since he had arrived, he decided the conversation was over and had left the apartment before she returned.

And she felt more trapped than ever.

Days passed, and in every day something different happened as the other children grew older (and married or didn't marry but left home anyway), but looking back, Batta felt that the days were all the same, after all, and the illusion of variety was just her mind's own way of keeping itself sane. And at last, when Batta was twenty-seven and a virgin and lonely as hell, all her brothers and sisters were gone and she was alone with her parents.

That was when Abner Doon came again.

He had not been on somec either, she noticed to her surprise as she showed him into the living room (same battered furniture, only older; same color walls, only dirtier; same Batta Heddis, only deader) and he sat, looking her over carefully.

"I thought you'd be on somec by now," she said.

"So did everyone. But there are some things that can't be done while one sleeps the years away. I can't go on somec until I'm ready."

"And when will that be?"

"When I rule the world."

She laughed, thinking it was a joke. "And when they find out I'm Mother's long-lost daughter kidnapped by gypsies and kept by space-pirates, they'll make me Empress after her."

"I'm going on somec within the year."

And she didn't laugh. Only looked at him carefully and saw the way worry and work and, perhaps, cruelty had worn certain lines in certain places and given him an expression that made his eyes seem deep and hard to plumb. "You look like you're drowning," she said.

"And you look like you're drowned."

He reached out and took her hand. She was surprised—he had never done that. But the hand was warm, dry, smooth, firm— just as she had thought a man's hand ought to feel (not like Father's claw) and she didn't take her hand away.

"I saw how it was when I came before," he said. "I've been waiting till you were free. The last of your loving siblings left a week ago. Your affairs should be in order. Will you marry me now?"

Three hours later, they were halfway across the sector in a modest-seeming apartment (only seeming—computers and furniture came, literally, out of the walls) and she was shaking her head.

"Ab," she said, "I can't. You don't understand."

He looked concerned. "I thought you'd prefer the contract. It's so much safer for everyone. But if you'd rather we kept it informal—"

"You don't understand. Five minutes before you came I was praying for something like that to happen, anything to get me away from there—"

"Then come away."

"But I keep thinking about my parents. My mother, who can't manage her own life, let alone Father's, and Father, who does his best to rule everyone and only I can keep him under control and happy. They need me."

"At the risk of being thought trite, so do I."

"Not much," she said, waving her hand to indicate the paraphernalia that proved that he was a man of power and wealth.

"This? In fact, Batta, this is all part of a much grander plan. A direct line leading to something rather fine. But I'd rather share it with you."

"You *are* a romantic idiot like all the other adolescents," she laughed. "Share it with me, nonsense. What makes you even think you love me?"

"Because, Batta, every now and then my dream fails to keep me warm."

"Women are rather inexpensive."

"Batta isn't even for sale," he reminded her, and then he reached out and touched her as she had never been touched, and she held him as she had never held anyone. For two hours everything was new, every flutter, every smile.

"No," she whispered as he was about to end her long sexual solitude. "Please no."

"Why," he whispered back, "the hell not?"

"Because if you do, I'll never be able to leave you."

"Excellent," he said, and moved again, but she slid away, slid off the bed, began dressing.

"You have very poor timing," he said. "What's wrong?"

"I can't. I can't leave Mother and Father."

"What, are they so loving and kind to you?"

"They need me."

"Dammit, Batta, they're grown-up people, they can take care of themselves."

"Maybe when I was seven, they could," she said, "but by the time I was twelve they couldn't. I was dependable. I could do it. And so they lost all their pretenses at adulthood, Ab. I couldn't go off and be happy knowing they'd disintegrate, having to watch them."

"Yes you can. Knowing that if you don't, *you'd* disintegrate. I can put you on somec, Batta, right now. I can put you under for five years and when you woke up they'd have learned to take care of themselves and you could go see them and know that everything was all right."

"Do you have that kind of money?"

"When you get enough power in this lovely little empire," Abner Doon answered, "money becomes unnecessary."

"When I woke up they might be dead."

"Perhaps. And then they'd definitely not need you."

"I'd feel guilty, Ab. It would destroy me."

But Abner Doon was persuasive, and by small stages he got her to lie down on a wheeled table and he put a sleepcap on her head and taped her brain. All her memories, all her personality, all her hopes, all her terrors were recorded and filed in a tape that Abner Doon tossed up and down in his hand.

"When you wake up, I'll play it back into your head, and you won't even notice that you were asleep."

She laughed nervously. "But anything that happens now, the somec wipes out, right?"

"True," Doon answered. "I could ravish you and perform all kinds of obscene acts, and when you woke up you'd still think I was a gentleman."

"I never have thought such a thing," she said.

He smiled. "Now let's get you to sleep."

"What about you?" she asked.

"I told you. I'm a year away. I'll be a year older when I wake you up, and we begin our life together, with or without benefit of contract. Good enough?"

But she began to cry, and she kept crying until it was near hysteria. He held her, rocked her back and forth, tried to find out why she was crying, tried to understand what he had *done*, but she answered, "Nothing. Nothing."

Until finally he brought out the somec bottle (but no one has a private supply of somec! It's the law—) and a needle and reached for her to lay her on the table. She pulled away, retreated to the other side of the room.

"No."

"Why not!"

"I can't run away from my parents."

"You've got your own life to live!"

"Ab, I can't do it! Don't you see? Love isn't just a matter of liking somebody. I don't like my parents very much. But they trust me, they lean on me, I'm their whole damn foundation, and I can't just walk away and let them fall down."

"Sure you can! Anybody could! It's sick, what they've done to you, and you have a right to your own life."

"Anybody could do it except *me*. I, Batta Heddis, am a person who does *not* walk away. That's who I am! If you want the kind of person who would, then go look somewhere else!" And she ran from the apartment to the tube station, returned home, closed the door and lay on the sofa and wept until her father called impatiently from the other room and she walked in and lovingly stroked his forehead until he could go to sleep.

* * *

When the brothers and sisters were there, Batta could pretend there was variety. Now, there was no pretense. Now, she was the entire focus of their lives and she was being slowly worn down, at first by the constant work and constant pressure (but she grew stronger than ever and soon settled into the routine better than ever until she couldn't conceive of another way) and later simply by the utter loneliness even while she was utterly unable to be alone.

"Batta, I'm doing embroidery, they do it with real cotton in the rich houses but there's no way we could afford that, of course, on your father's pension, but see what a lovely flower I'm making—or is it a bee? Heaven knows, I've never seen either, but don't you see what a lovely flower it is? Thank you, dear, it's a lovely flower, isn't it? They do it with real cotton in the rich houses, you know, but we could never afford that on your father's pension, could we? So this is a synthetic. It's called embroidery, will you look at the lovely bee I'm making? Isn't it lovely? Thank you, Batta dear, you have such a wonderful way of making me feel just lovely. I'm doing embroidery, you know. Oh, dear, I think your father's calling. I must go to him—oh, will you? Thank you. I'll just sit here and embroider, if you don't mind."

And in the bedroom, stolid silence. A groan of pain. The legs starting normally at the hip and then suddenly, abruptly, ending (not two centimeters from the crotch) in a steep cliff of sheets and blankets that fell away and left the bed flat and smooth and unslept-in.

"Do you remember?" he grunts as she turns the pillow and brings him his pills. "Do you remember when Darff was three he came in and said, 'Daddy, you should have my bed and I should have yours, because you're as little as I am.' Damnfool kid, and I picked him up and gave him a hug and wanted to strangle the little bastard."

"I didn't remember."

"Science has done everything else, but they can't figure out how to heal a man when he's lost his hams, lost his legs, lost every damn nerve. But one, thank heaven, but one."

She loathed bathing him. The tube had caught him slantwise in the mouth of the tubeway. If he'd been turned around, it would have ripped out his abdomen and killed him on the spot. As it was, he had lost his buttocks to the bone, his intestines were a mess, he had no bowel control, and his legs were a fragment of bone. "But they left me enough," he so proudly pointed out, "to father children."

And so it went endlessly day after day and Batta refused to remember Abner Doon, refused to admit that she had once had a chance to get away from these people (if only) and live her own life (if only) and be *happy* for a while (if only I hadn't— no, no, can't think that way).

Then Mother decided to make a salad while Batta was away shopping and cut her wrist with the knife and apparently forgot that the emergency call button was only a few meters away because she had bled to death before Batta could get home, a look of surprise frozen on her face.

Batta was twenty-nine.

And after a while Father began making hints about how a man's sexual drive doesn't diminish with nonuse, but only increases. She ignored him with gritted teeth until he too died one night and the doctor said it had only been a matter of time, the accident had messed him up so badly, and in fact if he hadn't had such excellent care he wouldn't have lasted *this* long. You should be proud of yourself, girl.

Age thirty.

She sat in the living room of the apartment that she alone controlled. Her father's pension would continue—the government was kind to victims of chance in the transportation system. She kept staring at the door and wondering why in the world she had longed to get away. After all, what was there to do outside?

The walls closed in on her. The flat bed in her parents' room looked just as it had when Father lay there all day, at least from where his legs would be on down. But when she rolled up blankets to look like legs and stretched them under the sheets on the bed, putting legs where she had never seen legs before, it occurred to her that she had lost her mind.

She packed her few belongings (everything else belonged to them and they were dead) and left the apartment and went to the nearest colony office because she couldn't think of anything better to do with the rest of her disastrous life than to go off to a colony and work until she died.

"Name?" asked the man behind the counter.

"Batta Heddis."

"This is a wonderful step you've decided to take, Miss Heddis—single, yes?—because these colonies are the Empire's newest way of fighting and winning the war. Only peacefully, you understand. Heddis, did you say? Come this way, please."

Heddis, did you say? Why had he looked so surprised? And so excited (or was it alarmed)?

She followed him to a room a corridor away, a plush convenient room with only the one door. A guard stood outside it, and she thought with terror that something was wrong, that Mother's Little Boys were going to accuse her of something, and she was innocent but how can you ever prove innocence to people already convinced of their own infallibility?

The wait was interminable—two hours—and she was reduced to a wreck by the time the door opened. Reduced to a wreck, that is, by her own perception. To an impartial observer coming in the door she was utterly calm—she had learned to exude calm no matter what the stress years before.

But it was not an impartial observer who walked in the door. It was Abner Doon.

"Hello, Batta," he said.

"My God," she answered, "my dear sweet God, do I have to be punished like this?"

His face went tense somehow, and he looked at her carefully. "What have they done to you, lady?"

"Nothing. Let me out of here."

"I want to talk to you."

"We forgot it years ago! I forgot it! Now don't remind me!"

He stood by the door, and it was obvious that he was horrified and fascinated—horrified because as she spoke so passionately her voice remained flat and calm, her body remained erect, there was no hint that she was in any kind of turmoil; fascinated because the body was still Batta, still the woman he had loved and had been willing to share his dream with not that many years before, and yet she was a complete stranger to him now.

"I've been on somec for several years," he said. "This is my first waking. I had them all warned—a code was to be set off when your name came up for colonization."

"What made you think it would?"

"Your parents had to die sometime. And when they did, I knew you'd have nowhere to go. People with nowhere to go, go to the colonies. It's politer than suicide."

"Leave me alone, please. Can't you have a little forgiveness for my mistake?"

He looked eager. "Did you call it a mistake? Do you regret it?"

"Yes!" she said, and now her voice raised in pitch, and she actually looked agitated.

"Then, by heaven, let's undo it!"

She looked at him with contempt. "Undo it! It can't be undone! I'm a monster now, Mr. Doon, not a girl anymore, a robot that performs services for revolting people without complaint, not a woman who can respond to anything the way you wanted me to. Nothing can be undone."

And then he reached into his pocket and held out a tape.

"You can go under somec right now and let the drug wipe out all your memories. Then I'll play this back into your mind, and you'll wake up believing that you did not decide to go back to your parents. That you decided to stay with me in the first place. You will be unchanged. The last few years will be erased."

She sat, uncomprehending for a few moments. Then, hoarsely, huskily, she said, "Yes. Yes. Hurry." And he led her to a tape-and-tap where they taped her brain and put her under somec and her mind washed away in the drug.

"Batta," a voice said softly, and Batta awoke, naked and sweating on a table in a strange place. But the face and the voice were not strange.

"Ab," she said.

"It's been five years," he said. "Your parents both passed away. From natural causes. They weren't unhappy. You made the right choice."

She was conscious of being naked, and the eternal virgin in her made her flush with embarrassment. But he touched her (and the memory of the night they first almost made love was still fresh—it had been only a few hours ago—and she was already aroused, already ready) and she was no longer embarrassed.

They went to his apartment, and made love gloriously, and they were blissfully happy for days until she finally admitted what was gnawing at the back of her mind.

"Ab. Ab, I have dreams about them."

"Who?"

"Mother and Father. You've told me it's been years and I know that. But it still feels like yesterday to me, and I feel terrible for having left them alone."

"You'll get over it."

But she did not get over it. She began to think of them more and more, guilt gnawing at her, tearing at her dreams, stabbing like a knife when she made love with Abner Doon, destroying her as she did all the things that she had wished, since she was a child, she could do.

"Oh, Ab," she wept one night—only six nights since waking—"Ab, I'd do anything, anything to undo this!"

He stopped moving, just froze. "Do you mean that?"

"No, no, Abner, you know I love you. I've loved you ever since we met, all my life, even before I knew you existed I loved you, don't you know that? But I hate myself! I feel like a coward, like a traitor for having left my family. They needed me. I know it, and I know they were miserable when I left them."

"They were perfectly happy. They never noticed you were gone."

"That's a lie."

"Batta, please forget them."

"I can't. Why couldn't I have done the right thing?"

"And what was that?" He looked afraid. Why is he afraid?

"To stay with them. They only lived a few years. If I'd stayed with them, if I'd helped them through the last few years, then Ab, I could face myself. Even if they were miserable years, I'd feel like a decent person."

"Then feel like a decent person. Because you did stay with them."

And he explained it to her. Everything.

She lay silently on the bed, staring at the ceiling.

"Then this is a fraud, isn't it? Secretly, truly, I'm a miserable

bitch of an old maid who rotted away in her parents' house until
they had the courtesy to die, a woman without the guts to com-
mit suicide—"

"Absurd—"

"Who was only saved from her fate by a man who contrived
to play God."

"Batta, you have the best of both worlds. You *did* stay with
your parents. You *did* the right thing. But you can go on with
your life now without having the memories of what they did
to you, without having to become what you became."

"And was I so horrible?"

He thought of lying to her, but decided against it. "Batta,
when I saw you in that room in the colonization office, I nearly
cried. You looked dead."

She reached over and stroked his cheek, his shoulder. "You
saved me from the penalty of my own mistake."

"If you want to look at it that way."

"But there's a contradiction here. Let's be logical. Let's call
the woman who decided to stay with her parents Batta A. Batta
A actually stayed and went crazy, like you said, and *she* chose
to go off to the colonies and keep her madness to herself."

"But it didn't happen that way—"

"No, listen," Batta insisted, quietly, intensely, and he listened. "Batta B, however, decided not to go back to her parents.
She stayed with Abner Doon and tried to be happy, but her
conscience wore at her and drove her mad."

"But it didn't happen that way—"

"No, Ab, you don't. You don't understand. Understand at
all." Her voice cracked. "This woman lying on the bed beside
you—this is Batta B. This is the woman who turned away from
her parents and didn't fulfill her commitment—"

"Dammit, Batta, listen to reason—"

"I have no memory of helping them. They suddenly—end. I
walked out on them—"

"No you didn't!"

"In my own mind I did, Ab, and that's where I have to live!
You tell me I helped them but I can't remember it and so it isn't
true! That choice—that was the choice that the real Batta made,
staying with them. And so the real Batta was shaped by that

experience. The real Batta suffered through those years, even if they were awful.''

"Batta, they were worse than awful! They destroyed you!''

"But it was *me* they destroyed! *Me!* The Batta who chooses to do what she believes she ought to!''

"What is this, the old-time religion? You have a chance to be spared the consequences of your own suicidal sense of right and wrong! You have a chance to be *happy*, dammit! What difference does it make which Batta is which? I love you, and you love me, lady, and *that's* the truth, too!''

"But Ab, how can I be anything but what I am?''

"Listen. You agreed. Instantly. You agreed to let me erase those years, to wake you up and have you live with me as if that agony had never happened. It was voluntary!''

She didn't answer. Only asked, "Did they tape me when they put me under somec? Did they record the way I really am?''

"Yes,'' he said, knowing what was coming.

"Then put me under again and wake me up with that tape. Send me to a colony.''

He stared at her. He got up from the bed and stared at her incredulously and laughed. "Do you realize what you're saying? You're saying, please take me out of heaven, God, and send me to hell.''

"I know it,'' she said, and she began trembling.

"You're insane. This is insane, Batta. Do you know what I've risked, what I've gone through to bring you here? I've broken every law concerning the use of somec that there is—''

"You rule the world, don't you?''

Was she sneering?

"I pull all the strings, but if I make a mistake I could fall anytime. I've deliberately made mistakes for you—''

"And so I owe you something. But what about me? Don't I owe me?''

He was exasperated. He hit the wall with his hand. "Of course you do! You owe yourself a life with a man who loves you more than he loves his life's work! You owe yourself a chance to be pampered, to be coddled, to be cared for—''

"I owe me myself.'' And she trembled more and more. "Ab, I haven't. I haven't been happy.''

Silence.

"Ab, please believe me, because this is the hardest thing I've had to say. Since the moment I woke up, something was wrong. Something was terribly, terribly wrong. I had made the wrong choice. I hadn't gone back to my parents. I have felt *wrong*. Everything has been colored by that. It's wrong. *I wouldn't choose to live with you, and so everything about it is wrong!*" She spoke softly, but her voice was intense.

"I would not be here," she said.

"You are here."

"I can't live a lie. I can't live with the contradiction. I must live my own life, bitter or not. Every moment I stay here is pain. It couldn't be worse. Nothing I suffered in my real life could be worse than the agony of living falsely. I must have the memory of having done what I knew was right. Without that memory, I can't keep my sanity. I've been feeling it slip away. Ab—"

And he held her closely, felt her tremble in his arms. "Whatever you want," he whispered. "I didn't know. I thought the somec could—make things over."

"It can't stop me from being who I—"

"Who you are, I know that, I know it now. But Batta, don't you realize—if I use that other tape, you won't remember this, you won't remember these days we had together—"

And she began to sob. And he thought of something else.

"You'll—the last thing you'll remember is my having told you I could erase all the pain. And you saying yes, yes, do it, erase it—and then you'll wake up with those memories and you'll think that I lied."

She shook her head.

"No," he said. "That's what you'll believe. You'll hate me for having promised you happiness and then not giving it to you. You won't remember this."

"I can't help it," she said, and they held each other and wept together and comforted each other and made love one last time and then he took her to the tape-and-tap where the past was washed away and a crueler life would be restored to her.

"What, is she a criminal?" asked the attendant as Abner Doon substituted the tapes—for only criminals had their minds wiped and an old tape used to erase all memory of the crime.

"Yes," said Doon, to keep things simple. And so her body was enclosed in the coffin that would satisfy her few needs as her body slowed down to a crawl through the years until he awakened her.

She would awaken on a colony. But one of my choosing, Abner vowed. A kind one, where she might have a chance of making something of her life. And who knows? Maybe hating me will make it all easier for her to bear.

Easier for her. But what about me?

I will not, he decided, spend any more of myself on her. I will close her from my mind. I will—I will forget?

Nonsense.

I will merely devote my life to fulfilling other, older, colder dreams.

15
Lifeloop

Arran lay on her bed, weeping. The sound of the door slamming still rang through her flat. Finally she rolled over, looked at the ceiling, wiped tears away delicately with her fingers, and then said, "What the hell."

Dramatic pause. And then, at last (at long last) a loud buzzer sounded. "All clear, Arran," said the voice from the concealed speaker, and Arran groaned, swung around to sit on the bed, unstrapped the loop recorder from her naked leg, and threw it tiredly against the wall. It smashed.

"Do you have any idea how much that equipment *costs*?" Triuff asked, reproachfully.

"I pay you to know," Arran said, putting on a robe. Triuff found the tie and handed it to her. As Arran threaded it through the loops, Triuff exulted. "The best ever. A hundred billion Arran Handully fans are aching to pay their seven chops to get in to watch. And you gave it to them."

"Seventeen days," Arran said, glaring at the other woman.

312

"Seventeen stinking days. And three of them with that bastard Courtney."

"He's *paid* to be a bastard. It's his persona."

"He's pretty damned convincing. If you get me even three minutes with him, next time, I'll sack you."

Arran strode out of her flat, barefoot and clad only in the robe. Triuff followed, her high-heeled shoes making a clicking rhythm that, to Arran anyway, always seemed to be saying, "Money, money, money." Except when it was saying, "Screw your mother, screw your mother." Good manager. Billions in the bank.

"Arran," Triuff said. "I know you're very tired."

"Ha," Arran said.

"But while you were recording I had time to do a little business—"

"While I was recording you had time to manufacture a planet!" Arran snarled. "Seventeen days! I'm an actress, I'm not going for the guiness. I'm the highest paid actress in history, I think you said in your latest press releases. So why do I work my tail off for seventeen days when I'm only awake for twenty-one? Four lousy days of peace, and then the marathon."

"A little business," Triuff went on, unperturbed. "A little business that will let you retire."

"Retire?" And without thinking, Arran slowed down her pace.

"Retire. Imagine—awake for three weeks, and only guest appearances in other poor slobs' loops. Getting paid for having fun."

"Nights to myself?"

"We'll turn off the recorder."

Arran scowled. Triuff amended: "You can even take the thing off!"

"And what do I have to do to earn so much? Have an affair with a gorilla?"

"It's been done," Triuff said, "and it's beneath you. No, this time we give them total reality. Total!"

"What do we give them now? Sure, you want me to crap in a glass toilet!"

"I've made arrangements," Triuff said, "to have a loop recorder in the Sleeproom."

Arran Handully gasped and stared at her manager. "In the Sleeproom! Is nothing sacred!" And then Arran laughed. "You must have spent a fortune! An absolute fortune!"

"Actually, only one bribe was necessary."

"Who'd you bribe, Mother?"

"Very close. Better, in fact, since Mother hasn't got the power to pick her nose without the consent of the Cabinet. It's Farl Baak."

"Baak! And here I thought he was a decent man."

"It wasn't a bribe. At least, not for money."

Arran squinted at Triuff. "Triuff," she said, "I told you that I was willing to act out twenty-four-hour-a-day love affairs. But I choose my own lovers off-camera."

"You'll be able to retire."

"I'm not a whore!"

"And he said he wouldn't even sleep with you, if you didn't want. He just asked for twenty-four hours with you two wakings from now. To talk. To become friends."

Arran leaned against the wall of the corridor. "It'll really make that much money?"

"You forget, Arran. All your fans are in love with you. But no one has ever done what you're going to do. From a half hour before waking to a half hour after you've been put to sleep."

"Before waking and after the somec." Arran smiled. "There's nobody in the Empire who's seen that, except the Sleeproom attendants."

"And we can advertise utter reality. No illusion: you'll see *everything* that happens to Arran Handully for three weeks of waking!"

Arran thoughtfully considered for a moment. "It'll be hell," she said.

"You can retire afterward," Triuff reminded her.

"All right," Arran agreed. "I'll do it. But I warn you. No Courtneys. No bores. And no little boys!"

Triuff looked hurt. "Arran—the little boy was five loops ago!"

"I remember every moment of it," Arran said. "He came

without an instruction booklet. What the hell do I do with a seven-year-old-boy?''

''And it was your best acting up to then. Arran, I can't help it—I have to spring surprises on you. That's when you're at your best—dealing with difficulty. That's why you're an artist. That's why you're a legend.''

''That's why you're rich,'' Arran pointed out, and then she walked quickly away, heading for the Sleeproom. Her eligibility began in a half hour, and every waking moment beyond that was a moment less of life.

Triuff followed her as far as she could, giving last-minute instructions on what to do when she woke, what to expect in the Sleeproom, how the instructions would be given to her in a way that she couldn't miss, but that the audience watching the holos wouldn't notice, and finally Arran made it through the door into the tape-and-tap, and Triuff had to stay behind.

Gentle and deferent attendants led her to the plush chair where the sleep helmet waited. Arran sighed and sat down, let the helmet slip onto her head, and tried to think happy thoughts as the tapes took her brain pattern—all her memories, all her personality—and recorded it to restore her at waking. When it was done, she got up and lazily walked to the table, shedding her robe on the way. She lay down with a groan of relief, and leaned her head back, surprised that the table, which looked so hard, could be soft.

It occurred to her (it always had before too, but she didn't know it) that she must have done this same thing twenty-two times before, because she had used somec that many times. But since the somec wiped clean all the brain activities during the sleep, including memory, she could never remember anything that happened to her after the taping. Funny. They could have her make love to all the attendants in the Sleeproom and she'd never know it.

But no, she realized as the sweet and deferent men and women soothingly wheeled the table to a place where monitoring instruments waited for her, no, that could never happen. The Sleeproom is the one place where no jokes are played, where nothing surprising or outrageous is ever done. Something in the world must be secure.

Then she giggled. Until my next waking, that is. And then the Sleeproom will be open to all the billions of poor suckers in the Empire who never get a chance at the somec, who have to live out their measly hundred years all in a row, while sleepers skip through the centuries like stones on a lake, touching down only every few years.

And then the sweet young man with the darling cleft chin (pretty enough to be an actor, Arran noticed) pushed a needle gently into her arm, apologizing softly for the pain.

"That's all right," Arran started to say, but then she felt a sharp pain in her arm, that spread quick as a fire to every part of her body; a terrible agony of heat that made her sweat leap from her pores. She cried out in pain and surprise—what was happening? Were they killing her? Who could want her to die?

And then the somec penetrated to her brain and ended all consciousness and all memory, including the memory of the pain that she had just felt. And when she woke again she would remember nothing of the agony of the somec. It would always and forever be a surprise.

Triuff got the seven thousand eight hundred copies of the latest loop finished—most of them edited versions that cut out all sleeping hours and bodily functions other than eating and sex, the small minority full loops that truly dedicated (and rich) Arran Handully fans could view in small, private, seventeen-day-long showings. There were fans (crazy people, Triuff had long since decided, but thank Mother for them) who actually leased private copies of the unedited loops and watched them twice through on a single waking. That was one hell of a dedicated fan.

Once the loops were turned over to the distributors (and the advance money was paid into the Arran Handully Corporation credit accounts), Triuff went to the Sleeproom herself. It was the price of being a manager—up weeks before the star, back under somec weeks after. Triuff would die centuries before Arran. But Triuff was very philosophical about it. After all, she kept reminding herself, she might have been a schoolteacher and never had somec at all.

* * *

Arran woke sweating. Like every other sleeper, she believed that the perspiration was caused by the wake-up drugs, never suspecting that she was in that discomfort for the five years of sleep that had just passed. Her memories were intact, having been played back into her head only a few moments before. And she immediately realized that something was fastened to her right thigh—the loop recorder. She was already being taped, along with the room around her. For a brief moment she rebelled, regretting her decision to go along with the scheme. How could she bear to stay in character for the whole three weeks?

But the unbreakable rule among lifeloop actors was "The loop never stops." No matter what you do, it's being looped, and there was no way to edit a loop. If there was one thing—one tiny thing—that had to be edited out in mid-action, the loop could simply be thrown away. The dedicated fans wouldn't stand for a loop that jumped from one scene to another—they were always sure that something juicy was being left out.

And so, almost by reflex, she composed herself into the tragically beautiful, sweet-souled yet bitter-tongued Arran Handully that all the fans knew and loved and paid money to watch. She sighed, and the sigh was seductive. She shuddered from the cold air passing across her sweating body, and turned the shiver into an excuse to open her eyes, blinking them delicately (seductively) against the dazzling lights.

And then she got up slowly, looked around. One of the ubiquitous attendants was standing nearby with a robe; Arran let him help her put it on, moving her shoulder just *so* in a way that made her breast rise just *that* much (never let it jiggle, nothing uglier than jiggling flesh, she reminded herself); and then she stepped to the newsboards. A quick flash through interplanetary news, and then a close study of Capitol events for the last five years, updating herself on who had done what to whom. And then she glanced at the game reports. Usually she only flipped a few pages and read virtually nothing—the games bored her—but this time she looked at it carefully for several minutes, pursing her lips and making a point of seeming to be dismayed or excited about individual game outcomes.

Actually, of course, she was reading the schedule for the next twenty-one days. Some of the names were new to her, of course—actors and actresses who were just reaching a level where they could afford to pay to be in an Arran Handully loop. And there were other names that she was quite familiar with, characters her fans would be expecting. Doret, her close friend and roommate seven loops ago, who still came back now and then to catch up on the news; Twern, that seven-year-old boy, now nearly fifteen, one of the youngest people ever to go on somec; old lovers and old friends, and a few leftovers from feuds on ancient loops. Which ones would be catty, and which ones would want to make up? Ah, well, she told herself. Plenty of chances to find that out.

A name far down on the list leapt out at her. Hamilton Ferlock! Involuntarily she smiled—caught herself in the sincere reaction and then decided that it would do no harm—the Arran Handully character might smile in just that way over a particular victory in a game. Hamilton Ferlock. Probably the one male actor on Capitol who could be considered to be in her class. They had started out at the same time too, and he had been her lover in her first five loops, back when she only had a few months on somec between wakings. And now he was going to be in *this* loop!

She thought a silent blessing for her manager. Triuff had actually done something thoughtful.

And then it was time to dress and leave the Sleeproom and walk the long corridors to her flat. She noticed as she walked along that the corridor had been redecorated, to give the illusion that somehow even the halls she walked along had class. She touched one of the new panels. Plastic. She refrained from grimacing. Oh well, the audience will never know it isn't really wood, and it keeps the overhead down.

She opened the door of her flat, and Doret screamed in delight and ran to embrace her. Arran decided that this time she should act a little put out at Doret for some imagined slight. Doret looked a little surprised, backed away, and then, like the consummate actress that she was (Arran didn't mind admitting the talents of her co-workers), she took Arran's quite subtle cue and turned it into a beautiful scene, Doret weeping out a confession that she had stolen a lover away from Arran several wakings ago, and Arran at first seeming to punish her, then forgiving.

They ended the scene tearfully in each other's arms, and then paused a moment. Dammit, Arran thought, Triuff is at it again. Nobody entered to break the scene. They had to go on after the climax, which meant building it to an even bigger climax within the next three hours.

Arran was exhausted when Doret finally left. They had had a wrestling match, in which they had ripped each other's clothes to shreds, and finally Doret had pulled a knife on Arran. It was not until Arran managed to get the weapon away from her that Doret finally left, and Arran had a chance to relax for a moment.

Twenty-one days without a break, Arran reminded herself. And Triuff forcing me into exhaustion the first day. I'll fire tho bitch, she vowed.

It was the twentieth day, and Arran was sick of the whole thing. Five parties, and a couple of orgies, and sleeping with someone new every night can pall rather quickly, and she had run the gamut of emotion several times. Each time she wept, she tried to put a different edge on it—tried to improvise new things to say to lovers, to shout in an argument, to use to insult a condescending visitor.

Most of her guests this time had been talented, and Arran certainly hadn't had to pull the full weight all by herself. But it was grueling, all the same.

And the buzzer sounded, and Arran had to get up to answer the door.

Hamilton Ferlock stood there, looking a little unsure of himself. Five centuries of acting, Arran thought to herself, and he still hasn't lost that ingenuous, boyish manner. She cried out his name (seductively, in character) and threw her arms around him.

"Ham," she said, "oh, Ham, you wouldn't believe this waking! I'm so tired."

"Arran," he said softly, and Arran noticed with surprise that he was starting out sounding as if he loved her. Oh no, she thought. Didn't we part with a quarrel the last time? No, no, that was Ryden. Ham left because, because—oh, yes. Because he was feeling unfulfilled.

"Well, did you find what you were looking for?"

Ham raised an eyebrow. "Looking for?"

"You said you had to do something important with your life.

That living with me was turning you into a lovesick shadow."
Good phrase, Arran congratulated herself.

"Lovesick shadow. Well, you see, that was true enough,"
Ham answered. "But I've discovered that shadows only exist
where there is light. You're my light, Arran, and only when I'm
near you do I really exist."

No wonder he's so highly paid, Arran thought. The line was
a bit gooey, but it's men like him who keep the women watching.

"Am I a light?" Arran said. "To think you've come back to
me after so long."

"Like a moth to a flame."

And then, as was obligatory in all happy reunion scenes (have
I already done a happy reunion in this waking? No) they slowly
undressed each other and made love slowly, the kind of copu-
lation that was not so much arousing as emotional, the kind that
made both men and women cry and hold each other's hands in
the theatre. He was so gentle this time, and the lovemaking was
so right, that Arran felt hard-pressed to stay in character. I'm
tired, she told herself. How can he carry it off so perfectly? He's
a better actor than I remembered.

Afterward, he held her in his arms as they talked softly—he
was always willing to talk afterward, unlike most actors, who
thought they had to become surly after sex in order to maintain
their macho image with the fans.

"That was beautiful," Arran said, and she noticed with alarm
that she wasn't acting. Watch yourself, woman. Don't screw up
the loop after you've already invested twenty damned days.

"Was it?" Ham asked.

"Didn't you notice?"

He smiled. "After all these years, Arran, and I was right.
There's no woman in the world worth loving with you around."

She giggled softly and ducked her head away from him in
embarrassment. It was in character, and therefore seductive.

"Then why haven't you come back before?" Arran asked.

And Hamilton rolled over and lay on his back. Because he
was silent for a few moments, she rubbed her fingers up and
down his stomach. He smiled. "I stayed away, Arran, because
I loved you too much."

"Love is never a reason to stay away," she said. Ha. Let the fans quote *that* piece of crap for a couple of years.

"It is," Ham said, "when it's real."

"Even more reason to stay with me!" Arran put on a pout. "You left me, and now you pretend you loved me."

And suddenly Hamilton swung over and sat on the edge of the bed.

"What's wrong?" she asked.

"Damn!" he said. "Forget the stupid act, will you?"

"Act?" she asked.

"The damn Arran Handully character you're wearing for fun and profit! I know you, Arran, and I'm telling you—*I'm* telling you, not some actor, *me*—I'm telling you that I love you! Not for the audiences! Not for the loop! For you—I love *you*!"

And with a sickening feeling in the pit of her stomach Arran realized that, somehow, that stinking Triuff had gotten Ham to be a dirty trick after all. It was the one unspoken rule in the business—you never, never, never mention the fact that you're acting. For any reason. And now, the ultimate challenge—admitting to the audience that you're an actress and making them still believe you.

"Not for the loop!" she echoed back, struggling to think of some kind of answer.

"I said not for the loop!" He stood up and walked away from her, then turned back, pointed at her. "All these stupid affairs, all the phony relationships. Haven't you had enough?"

"Enough? This is life, and I'll never have enough of life."

But Ham was determined not to play fair.

"If this is life, Capitol's an asteroid." A clumsy line, not like him. "Do you know what life is, Arran? Life is centuries playing loop after loop, as I've done, screwing every actress who can raise a fee, all so I can make enough money to buy somec and the luxuries of life. And all of a sudden a few years ago, I realized that the luxuries didn't mean a damn thing, and what did I care if I lived forever? Life was so utterly meaningless, just a succession of high-paid tarts!"

Arran managed to squeeze out some tears of rage. The loop never stops. "Are you calling *me* a tart?"

"You?" Ham looked absolutely stricken. The man can act,

Arran reminded herself, even as she cursed him for throwing her such a rotten curve. "Not you, Arran, don't even think it!"

"What can I think, with you coming here and accusing me of being a phony!"

"No," he said, sitting beside her on the bed again, putting his arm around her bare shoulder. She nestled to him again, as she had a dozen times before, years ago. She looked up at his face, and saw that his eyes were filled with tears.

"Why are you—why are you crying?" she asked, hesitantly.

"I'm crying for us," he said.

"Why?" she asked. "What do we have to cry over?"

"All the years we've lost."

"I don't know about *you,* but my years have been pretty full," she said, laughing, hoping he would laugh, too.

He didn't. "We were right for each other. Not just as a team of actors, Arran, but as people. You weren't very good back then at the beginning—neither was I. I've looked at the loops. When we were with other people, we were as phony as two-bit beginners. But those loops still sold, made us rich, gave us a chance to learn the trade. Do you know why?"

"I don't agree with your assessment of the past," Arran said coldly, wondering what the hell he was trying to accomplish by continuing to refer to the loops instead of staying in character properly.

"We sold those tapes because of each other. Because we actually looked real when we told each other we loved, when we chattered for hours about nothing. We really enjoyed each other's company."

"I wish I were enjoying your company now. Telling me I'm a phony and then saying I have no talent."

"Talent! What a joke," Ham said. He touched her cheek, gently, turning her face so she would look at him. "Of course you have talent, and so have I. We have money too, and fame, and everything money can buy. Even friends. But tell me, Arran, how long has it been since you really loved anybody?"

Arran thought back through her most recent lovers. Any she wanted to make Ham's character jealous over? No. "I don't think I've ever really loved anybody."

"That's not true," Ham said. "It's not true, you loved me. Centuries ago, Arran, you truly loved me."

"Perhaps," she said. "But what does it have to do with now?"

"Don't you love me now?" Ham asked, and he looked so sincerely concerned that Arran was tempted to break character and laugh with delight, applaud his excellent performance. But the bastard was still making it hard for her, and so she decided to make it hard for him.

"Love you now?" she asked. "You're just another pair of eager gonads, my friend." That'd shock the fans. And, she hoped, completely mess up Ham's nasty little joke.

But Ham stayed right in character. He looked hurt, pulled away from her. "I'm sorry," he said. "I guess I was wrong." And to Arran's shock he began to dress.

"What are you doing?" she asked.

"Leaving," he said.

Leaving, Arran thought with panic. Leaving now? Without letting the scene have a climax? All this buildup, all the shattered traditions, and then leaving without a climax? The man was a monster!

"You can't go!"

"I was wrong. I'm sorry. I've embarrassed myself," he said.

"No, no, Ham, don't leave. I haven't seen you in so long!"

"You've never seen me," he answered. "Or you wouldn't have been capable of saying what you just did."

Making me pay for throwing a curve back at him, Arran thought. I'd like to kill him. What a fantastic actor, though. "I'm sorry I said it," Arran said, wearing contrition as if she had been dipped in it. "Forgive me. I didn't mean it."

"You just want me to stay so I won't ruin your damn scene."

Arran gave up in despair. Why am I doing this anyway? But the realization that breaking character now would wreck the whole loop kept her going. She went and threw herself on the bed. "That's right!" she said, weeping. "Leave me now, when I want you so much."

Silence. She just lay there. Let him react.

But he said nothing. Just let the pause hang. She couldn't even hear him move.

Finally he spoke. "Do you mean it?"

"Mmm-hmm," she said, managing to hiccough through her tears. A cliché, but it got 'em every time.

"Not as an actress, Arran, please. As yourself. Do you love me? Do you want me?"

She rolled partway onto her side, lifted herself on one elbow, and said, the tears forcing a little catch in her voice, "I need you like I need somec, Ham. Why have you stayed away so long?"

He looked relieved. He walked slowly back to her. And everything was peaceful again. They made love four more times, between each of the courses of dinner, and for variety they let the servants watch. I've done it once before, Arran remembered, but it was five loops ago, about, and these are different servants anyway. Of course the servants, underpaid beginning actors all, used it as an excuse to get some interesting onstage time, and turned it into an orgy among themselves, managing every conceivable sexual act in only an hour and a half. Arran barely noticed them, though. They were the kind of fools who thought the audience wanted quantity. If some sex is good, a lot is better, they think. Arran knew better. Tease them. Let them beg. Let them find beauty in it too, not just titillation, not just lust. That's why she was a star, and they were playing servants in somebody else's loop.

That night Ham and Arran slept in each other's arms.

And in the morning Arran woke to find Ham staring at her, his face an odd mixture of love and pain. "Ham," she said softly, stroking his cheek. "What do you want?"

The longing in his face only increased. "Marry me," he said softly.

"Do you really mean it?" she asked, in her little-girl voice.

"I mean it. Time our wakings together, always."

"Always is a long time," she said. It was a good all-purpose line.

"And I mean it," he said. "Marry me. Mother knows we've made enough money over the years. We don't ever have to let these other bastards into our lives again. We don't ever have to wear these damned loop recorders again." And as he said that, he patted the recorder strapped to her thigh.

Arran inwardly groaned. He wasn't through with the games yet. Of course the audience wouldn't know what he meant—the computer that created the loop from the loop recorder was programmed to delete the recorder itself from the holo. The audience never saw it. And now Ham was referring to it. What was he trying to do, give her a nervous breakdown? Some friend.

Well, I can play his game. "I won't marry you," she said.

"Please," he said. "Don't you see how I love you? Do you think any of these phonies who pay to make love to you will ever feel one shred of real emotion toward you? To them you're a chance to make money, to make a name for themselves, to strike it rich. But I don't need money. I have a name. All I want is you. And all I can give you is me."

"Sweet," she said coldly, and got up and went to the kitchen. The clock said eleven-thirty. They had slept late. She was relieved. At noon she had to leave to get to the Sleeproom. In a half hour this farce would be over. Now to build it to a climax.

"Arran," Ham said, following her. "Arran, I'm serious. I'm not in character!"

That much is obvious, Arran thought but did not say.

"You're a liar," she said rudely.

He looked puzzled. "Why should I lie? Haven't I made it plain to you that I'm telling the truth? That I'm not acting?"

"Not acting," she said, sneering (but seductively, seductively. Never out of character, she reminded herself), and she turned her back on him. "Not acting. Well, as long as we're being honest about things, and throwing away both pretense and art, I'll play it your way, too. Do you know what I think of you?"

"What?" he asked.

"I think this is the cheapest, dirtiest trick I've ever seen. Coming here like this, doing everything you could to lead me into thinking you loved me, when all the time you were just exploiting me. Worse than all the others! You're the worst!"

He looked stricken. "I'd never exploit you!" he said.

"Marry me!" Arran laughed, mocking him. "Marry me, says you, and then what? What if this poor little girl actually did marry you? What would you do? Force me to stay in the flat forever? Keep away all my other friends, all my other—yes, even my lovers, you'd make me give them all up! Hundreds of men love me, but you, Hamilton, you want to own me forever, exclusively! What a coup that would be, wouldn't it? No one would ever get to look at my body again," she said, moving her body in such a way that no one in the world could possibly want to look anywhere else, "except you. And you say you don't want to exploit me."

Hamilton came closer to her, tried to touch her, tried to plead with her, but she only grew angry, cursed him. "Stay away from me!" she screamed.

"Arran, you can't mean it," Ham said softly.

"I have never meant anything more thoroughly in my life," she said.

He looked in her eyes, looked deep. And finally he spoke again. "Either you're so much an actress that the real Arran Handully is lost, or you really do mean that. And either way, there's nothing for me to stay here for." And Arran watched admiringly as Hamilton gathered up his clothing, and, not even bothering to dress, he left, closing the door quietly behind him. A beautiful exit, Arran thought. A lesser actor couldn't have resisted the temptation to say one last line. But not Ham—and now, if Arran played it right, this grotesque scene could be, after all, a genuine climax to the loop.

And so she played the scene, at first muttering about what a terrible man Ham was, and then progressing quickly to wondering whether he'd ever come back. "I hope he does," she said, and soon was weeping, crying out that she couldn't live without him. "Please come back, Ham!" she said pitifully. I'm sorry I refused you! I *want* to marry you."

But then she looked at the clock. Nearly noon. Thank Mother. "But it's time," she said. "Time to got to the Sleeproom. The Sleeproom!" New hope came into her voice. "That's it! I'll go to the Sleeproom! I'll let the years pass by, and when I wake, there he'll be, waiting for me!" She rhapsodized for a few more minutes, then threw a robe around herself and ran lightly, eagerly down the corridors to the Sleeproom.

In the tape-and-tap she chattered gaily to the attendant. "He'll be there waiting for me," she said, smiling. "Everything will be all right." The sleep helmet went on, and Arran kept talking.

"You do think there's hope for me, don't you?" she asked, and the woman whose soft hands were now removing the helmet answered, "There's always hope, ma'am. Everybody has hope."

Arran smiled, then got up and walked briskly to the sleep table. She didn't remember ever doing this before, thought she knew she must have—and then it occurred to her that *this* time she could watch the actual loop, see what really happened to her when the somec entered her veins.

But because she didn't remember any other administration of somec, she didn't realize the difference when the attendant gently put a needle only a millimeter under the surface of the palm of her hand. "It's so sharp," Arran said, "but I'm glad it doesn't hurt." And instead of the hot pain of somec, a gentle drowsiness filled her, and she was whispering Ham's name as she drifted off to sleep. Whispering his name, but silently cursing him under her breath. He may be a great actor, she told herself, but I ought to kick his head through a garbage chute for giving me a rotten time like that. Oh well. It'll sell seats in the theatres. Yawn. And then she slept.

The loop continued for a few more minutes, as the attendants went through a mumbo jumbo of nonsensical, meaningless activities. And finally they stepped back as if they were through, Arran's nude body lying on the table. Pause for the loop recorder to take the ending, and then:

A buzzer, and the door opened and Triuff came in, laughing in glee. "What a loop," she said, as she unstrapped the recorder from Arran's leg.

When Triuff had gone, the attendants put the real needle in Arran's arm, and the heat poured through her veins. Asleep though she had already been, Arran cried out in agony, and the sweat drenched the table in only a few minutes. It was ugly, painful, frightening. It just wouldn't do to have the masses see what somec was *really* like. Let them think the sleep is gentle; let them think the dreams are sweet.

When Arran woke, her first thought was to find out if the loop had *worked*. She had certainly gone through enough effort—now to see if Triuff's predictions of retirement had been fulfilled.

They had been.

Triuff was waiting right outside the Sleeproom, and hugged

Arran tightly. "Arran, you wouldn't believe it!" she said, laughing uproariously. "Your last three loops had already set records—the highest-grossing loops of all time. But this one! This one!"

"Well?" Arran demanded.

"More than three times the total of those three loops put together!"

Arran smiled. "Then I can retire?"

"Only if you want to," Triuff said. "I have several pretty good deals worked out—"

"Forget it," Arran said.

"They wouldn't take much work, only a few days each—"

"I said forget it. From now on I never strap another recorder to my leg again. I'll guest. But I won't record."

"Fine, fine," Triuff said. "I told them, but they made me promise to ask you anyway."

"And probably paid you a pretty penny, too," Arran answered. Triuff shrugged and smiled.

"You're the greatest ever," Triuff said. "No one has ever done so well as you."

Arran shook her head. "Might be true," she said, "but I was really sweating it. That was a rotten trick you pulled on me, having Ham break character like that."

Triuff shook her head. "No, no, not at all, Arran. That must have been *his* idea. I told him to threaten to kill you—a real climax, you know. And then he went in and did what he did. Well, no harm done. It's an exquisite scene, and *because* he broke character, and you, too, there at the end—the audience believed that it *was* real. Beautiful. Of course, everybody and his duck is breaking character now, but it doesn't work anymore. Everyone knows it's just another device. But the first time, with you and Ham"—and Triuff made an expansive gesture—"it was magnificent."

Arran led the way down the corridor. "Well, I'm glad it worked. But I'm still looking forward to a chance to rake Ham over the coals for it."

"Oh, Arran, I'm sorry," Triuff said.

Arran stopped and faced her manager. "For what?"

Triuff actually looked sad. "Arran, it's Hamilton. Not even a week after you went under—it was the saddest thing. Everybody talked about it for days."

"What? Did something happen to him?"

"He hung himself. Turned off the lights in his flat so none of the Watchers could see him, and hung himself from a light fixture with a bathrobe tie. He died right away, no chance to revive him. It was terrible."

Arran was surprised to find a lump in her throat. A real one. "Ham's dead," she said softly. She remembered all the scenes they had played together, and a real fondness for him came over her. I'm not even acting, she realized. I truly cared for the man. Sweet, wonderful Ham.

"Does anyone know why he did it?" Arran asked.

Triuff shook her head. "No one has the slightest idea. And the thing I just can't believe there it was, a scene they've never had before in a loop, a real suicide. And he didn't even record it!"

16
Breaking the Game

Herman Nuber's feet were asleep, and every time he shifted his weight they tingled unbearably.

"My feet are asleep," he complained to the Sleeproom attendant.

"Happens all the time," answered the attendant, reassuringly.

"I was under for three years," Herman pointed out. "Was the circulation to my feet cut off all that time?"

"It's the somec, Mr. Nuber," said the attendant. "It makes your feet feel that way. But your circulation was never cut off."

Herman grunted and went back to reading the lists on the wall. His feet tingled a little less, and now he began to shift his weight back and forth. The newsheet was boring. Same list of victories for the Empire, victories that half the time left the enemy in possession of the star system with a few Empire ships able to limp home. The gossip sheets were almost as boring. All the big-name lifeloopers screwing their way to fame and fortune. One looper committed suicide—a novelty, since people who wanted to take themselves out of circulation usually just signed up for the colonies.

The list he studied was, of course, the game sheet. He skimmed down to the International Games list, and there was the notice.

"Europe 1914d, now in G1979. Biggest news this week is that Herman 'Italy' Nuber is up on Thursday, so all non-Italy players, watch out!"

Very flattering, of course, to be named by the waking lists. But it was to be expected. The International Games had been around for years, dating back to well before somec. But there had never been a player like Herman Nuber.

He left the Sleeproom, pausing, almost as an afterthought, to dress. This waking would be for only six months—last time he had won more money than usual on the sidebets, which were strictly illegal but a very safe, pleasant investment. No one gave long odds against him—when he placed bets on himself the rate of return was only seventeen percent. But that was better than a savings bank or government bonds.

"Herman," said a quiet man, even shorter than Herman Nuber.

"Hi, Grey," Nuber said.

"Good waking?"

"Of course." Grey Glamorgan was a good business manager. He always remembered that even though he was something of a financial genius, with many good connections, he was *not* in business for himself. Trustworthy. A born underling. Herman liked to surround himself with men who were shorter than himself.

"Well?" asked Grey.

Herman looked unconcerned. "Buy Italy, of course."

And Grey nodded. It was a kind of ritual, but the game laws specified that a place in the game only be purchased when the player was awake—there must always be a waking player at the computer.

Well, I'm awake, Herman said. And unless things had changed considerably, this was the waking when he'd make the grand play—to end the game by conquering the world.

The computer wall was already warmed up when he got to

his flat—another thoughtful gesture from Grey. Herman tortured himself as he always did, ignoring the screen, refusing to look at it; pretending the computer wasn't waiting for him as he toured the flat, made sure all the arrangements were correct. Herman wasn't really rich; only mildly well-to-do. He couldn't afford to keep an empty flat while he was under. His belongings were stored, instead, or sold each time. Someday, though, I'll be rich enough, he thought. Someday, I'll get to the really high somec levels, like five years under for three months up. And I'll own a flat, not just lease one for a waking.

It was everyone's dream, of course. Everyone's plan. And one out of every seven million people in the Empire made it. Horatio Alger is alive and well forever.

At last, orange juice drunk, bed bounced on, woman for the night paid and picked out, toilet used, he allowed himself to settle down comfortably in the chair before the computer module. But still he kept the screen dead. He punched out the code for Europe 1914d.

He had been twenty-two when he had first decided to invest some money in the expensive hobby of International Games. It had cost him two months' salary, and he had only been able to buy a third-ranked position in Italy in the start of a new game. He had chosen Europe 1914, even though it was the fourth game of that name, because he had specialized in twentieth-century strategies in his small-game playing. And now, with an interplanetarily broadcast game, he'd have a chance to see if he was really as good as he had thought.

I *am* that good, he reminded himself now, flashing on the holo. The globe appeared before him, and he studied it. First the weather patterns were shown; then the political map.

"How is it?" asked Grey, appearing quietly behind Herman.

"Lovely. No one has tried anything rash. Good caretakers."

Italy showed up as pink on the map. Herman remembered the beginning—an Italy newly united, weak, unsure whether to join Germany and Austria-Hungary. In the real twentieth century, no one of any force had emerged in Italy until after the 1914 war. No one until that nincompoop Mussolini. But in Europe 1914d, Italy had Herman Nuber, and even though he was a third-ranked player, he had bet quite a bit on himself—and on Italy.

It was three years before his daytime work earned Herman enough money to go on somec for the first time. In that time he had married, had a daughter, and divorced. No time for marriage. She didn't like it when he spent all night on the game. But it had been worth it, in the long run. A bit painful, some emotional scenes, but at the end of the three years, Herman's bets paid off. Forty to one. He had driven out other, less skillful players, and when he went under somec, he did it as dictator of Italy, and Italy had turned savagely on Austria-Hungary, brilliantly defeated the Prussian army (oh, no, actually *German*, he reminded himself. Have to keep the periods straight) near Munich, and a peace treaty had been signed. America never joined the war, much to the chagrin of the players who had paid heavily for that choice position, only to see it become useless in the real game.

Italy, then, had been the major power in eastern Europe. But now, Herman saw with a smile, Italy *was* Europe, the entire continent pink, and most of Asia as well. His last waking had been the consummation of the struggle with Russia. And now Italy stood poised on the Pacific, on the Indian Ocean through Persia, and on the Atlantic, ready to try for everything.

"Looks very good, doesn't it?" Herman asked Grey, who was still silent.

"For the Italy player, it does," said Grey, and Herman turned in surprise. "You mean you didn't buy it?"

Grey looked a little embarrassed. "Actually," he said, "I was afraid of this."

"Afraid of what?"

"Someone's apparently been speculating in Italy. My staff gave me the report when I came up three weeks ago. Someone's been buying and selling Italy in closed bids ever since you went under last."

"That's illegal!"

"Weep, then. We've done it ourselves, you know. Shall we call in an investigation? All the books open?"

"Why didn't you get a good proxy and keep it?"

"They pulled it off again, Herman. The bidding was last night at midnight. Not precisely prime time. But I placed my bid.

Frankly, it was ridiculously high. But no taker. The player who got it bid twice what I did.''

"Then you should have bid higher still!''

Grey shook his head. "Couldn't. I only have fifty percent power of attorney, remember?''

Herman gasped in spite of himself. "Fifty percent! Grey, fifty percent? It was more than fifty?''

Grey nodded. "More than fifty liquid, anyway. I couldn't match it. Not from your funds. And I just don't have enough loose money around to add any of my own.''

"Well, who's the player?''

"Believe it or not, Herman, it's an assistant minister of colonization, a real flunkie. It's his first time in the broadcast games. No record at all. And no way he could have the money to buy that place in the game himself.''

"Find out who the organization is, Grey, and buy that position.''

Grey shook his head. "I don't have enough money. Whoever's buying it is serious, and they've got more money than you.''

Herman felt weak and cold. This was not expected. Of course there were always speculators in the games. But Herman always paid well for his position, and because he had contributed most to the slot, when he was awake no one could buy Italy but him, as long as he offered at least fifteen percent over the last purchase price. But now the purchase price had been more than half his wealth.

"It doesn't matter,'' Herman told Grey. "Borrow. Liquidate. I'll give you ninety percent power of attorney. But buy Italy.''

"What if they won't sell?''

Herman leapt to his feet, so that he towered (delicious) over Grey. "They can't! They can only sell to me. They have to be speculating on stripping me. Well, let 'em. This time Italy takes over the world, Grey. And the bets won't be just seventeen percent. We'll be in for the long odds. Do you understand?''

"They don't have to sell to you, Herman,'' Grey said. "The player who has it isn't on somec.''

"I don't care. I'll outlast them. They have to quit sometime. Pay their price. They have a price.''

Grey nodded, unsure. Herman turned away, and heard Grey

shuffle softly through the carpet as he left. Herman switched on the screen as his stomach churned. Italy was valuable, but only because of Herman Nuber. Only a genius could have taken that second-rate country and made it a world power. Only Herman Nuber, the greatest International Game player in history, dammit. They're just trying to rob me, Herman concluded. Well, let 'em.

And then, though he knew it would torture him, he flashed the screen through to a close-up of current military operations by the Italian Empire. There was a border skirmish in Korea. India was becoming hostile. The Italian agents were doing well at subverting Japanese rule in Arabia.

Everything's perfect, Herman said softly. In three days I can have this game flying. In three days, if I can once get Italy.

Grey didn't come or call all day. By evening, Herman was a nervous wreck. He had already had to watch as three perfect opportunities for quick, decisive action had been passed by the idiot playing Italy. Of course, that kind of thing happened all the time when Herman was on somec—but he was asleep, he didn't have to watch. And still Grey didn't come.

The buzzer. Not Grey, since the door opened to his hand. Must be the woman. Herman stroked the release strip and the door opened. She was young and had a beautiful smile. Just what the doctor ordered.

At first, because she was beautiful and cheerful and good at her job, Herman forgot the game, or at least was able to concentrate on something else. But then, even as she tried to arouse him again, the pent-up worry flooded back, and he sat up on the bed.

"What's wrong?"

Herman shook his head.

"Too tired?"

Good a reason as any. No reason to pour out your heart to an edna.

"Yeah. I'm tired."

She sighed, leaned back again on the pillows. "Don't I know it, I get tired, too. They give me shots so I can keep going for hours, but it's so nice to get a breather."

A talker. Damn. "Want something to eat?"

"We aren't supposed to."

"Diet or something?"

"Naw. Sometimes they try to drug us."

"I won't drug you."

"Rules are rules," the woman insisted. The girl, rather.

"You're pretty young."

"Working my way through college. I'm older than I look. But they can rent me juvenile too, so we all get more money."

Money money money. Pay for sex and you get a treatise on the state of the economy. "Look, kid, why not go now?"

"You paid for all night," she said, surprised.

"Fine. You were wonderful. But I'm tired."

"They don't like giving a refund."

"I don't want a refund."

She looked doubtful, but when he started dressing, so did she. "That's an expensive habit," she said.

"What is?"

"Paying for love and then not using up what you pay for."

"Well, right," Herman said, then added wryly, "wouldn't want any extra love lying around, would we?"

"Everybody's a comic," she answered, but even at that the habits of the trade stayed. It was sexy, her smile and her tone of voice, and for a moment he wondered if he really wanted her to go. But then he thought of Italy and decided he'd rather be alone.

She kissed him good-bye—it was company policy—and then left him alone. He sat up all night, watching Italy. The imbecile was letting things go. He could have had Arabia around three in the morning. But instead, he made a ridiculous peace treaty that actually gave up land in Egypt. Stupid! By morning, Herman had fallen asleep, but he woke with a headache and called Grey.

"Dammit, what's happening?" Herman demanded.

"Herman, please," Grey said. "We're working hard here."

"Yeah, and I'm just sitting around here watching Italy turn to crap."

"Didn't you get an edna tonight?"

"What the hell business is that of yours?" Herman snapped. "Buy Italy, Grey!"

"This Abner Doon, the assistant minister of colonization, he's pretty adamant."

"Offer him the moon."

"It's already owned. But I offered him everything else. He just laughed. He just told you to watch the game and you'd see a real genius at work."

"Genius! The man's a moron! Already he—" And Herman launched into a description of the stupidities of the night before.

"Look, I'm not into International Games," Grey finally said. "You know that, that's why you hired me. Okay? So let's just have me do my job and *you* follow the scoreboard."

"So when are you going to do your job?"

Grey sighed. "Do we have to do this on the phone, with Mother's Little Boys listening in?"

"Let 'em listen."

"All right, I've tried to trace who's controlling this Doon. The man has connections, but they're all legitimate. I can't find a bankroll, all right? So how can I get the people who are paying him to sell out if I can't find who's paying him?"

"Can't he have an accident or something?"

Grey was silent for a moment. "This is the telephone, Mr. Nuber, and it's illegal to suggest criminal activities over the telephone."

"Sorry."

"It's also very stupid. Do you want me to lose my license?"

"They don't listen to every conversation."

"All right, keep praying. But we don't do anything criminal. Now sit and watch the holo or something."

Herman punched off the phone and sat at the computer terminal. Italy had just launched a pointless, half-assed war in Guiana. Guiana! As if anything that happened there mattered. And it was such a naked act of aggression that the alliances were starting to form against Italy. Stupid!

He had to do something to take his mind off the delay. He punched in a private game, offered it for free for any taker, normal specs, and pretty soon he had a good five-man game of Acquitaine going. He won it in seven hours. Pathetic. The great players were all on the broadcast games. What's keeping Grey?

"Nothing's keeping me," Grey insisted when he finally came to Herman's flat that night. "I'm performing heroic tasks for you, Herman."

"Swinging on vines isn't doing a damn bit of good."

Grey smiled, trying to like Herman's sense of humor. "Look, Herman, you're my biggest client. And you're famous. And you're important. I'd have to be an idiot not to be doing my best for you. I've got three agencies out researching everything about this Doon. And all we can find out is that he's nothing like what we first thought."

"Good. What do we think now"

"He's rich. Richer than you could imagine."

"I can imagine infinite wealth. Give me credit."

"He's got connections all over Capital. He knows everybody, or at least knows the people who know everybody. Right? And all his money is in trusts and investments in dummy corporations that own dummy banks that own dummy industries that own half this damn planet."

"In other words," Herman said, "he's self-employed."

"Self-employed but he ain't sellin', you see. He doesn't need the money. He could lose everything you own in pinochle and still like the guy who won it."

Herman grimaced. "Grey, you sure have a way of making me feel poor."

"I'm trying to tell you what you're up against. Because this guy's twenty-seven years old. I mean, he's *young*."

But something didn't fit. "I thought you told me he wasn't on somec."

"That's the craziest thing, Herman. He isn't. He's never gone under at all."

"What is he, a religious fanatic?"

"His only religion seems to be wrecking your life, Mr. Nuber, if I may be so bold. He won't sell. And he won't tell why. And as long as he doesn't go on somec, he doesn't have to sell. It's as simple as that."

"What have I ever done to him? Why should he want to do this to me?"

"He said he hoped you wouldn't take it personally."

Herman shook his head, furious and yet unable to find a reason adequate for his fury—or an adequate way to express it. The man had to be reachable.

"You know what I said over the phone?"

"You'd be the first suspect, if anything happened to him, Herman," Grey warned. "And it wouldn't help a bit. The game would end for the duration of the investigation. Besides, I'm not in that business."

"Everybody's in that business," Herman said. "At least scare him. At least rough him up."

Grey shrugged. "I'll try it." He stood up to go.

"Herman, I suggest you go back into business for a while. Make a little more money, get the feel of it again. Meet some people. Try to get the game out of your system. If you don't play Italy this time, you can play it on your next waking."

Herman didn't answer, and Grey let himself out.

At three o'clock in the morning, Herman, exhausted, finally slept.

At about four-thirty, he was wakened by the alarms going off in his flat. He groggily pulled himself out of bed and staggered to the door of his bedroom. Alarms were pro forma—no one of his class was ever burglarized, at least not while the residents were at home.

His worries about theft were soon dispelled. The three men who came in all carried small, tight leather bags, filled with something hard. How hard they were Herman wasn't eager to find out.

"Who are you?"

They said nothing, just approached him silently, slowly. He realized that he was cut off, both from the front door and the emergency exit. He backed into the bedroom.

One of the men reached out a hand, and Herman found himself crushed against the doorjamb.

"Don't hurt me," he said.

The first man, taller than the others, tapped Herman's shoulder with his bludgeon. Now Herman knew how hard it was. The tapping continued, getting harder and harder, but the rhythm was steady. Herman stood frozen, unable to move, as the pain gradually increased. And then, suddenly, the man shifted his weight, swung the bludgeon backhand, and Herman's ribs were smashed. The breath left him in a grunt, and pain like great hands tearing apart his insides swept up and down his body.

The agony was unbearable.

They were just beginning.

"No doctors, no hospital, nothing. No," Herman said, trying to summon a forceful tone of voice from his battered chest.

"Herman," Grey said, "your ribs may be broken."

"They aren't."

"You're not a doctor."

"I have the best medical kit in the city, and it said that nothing was broken. Whoever those bastards were last night, they know what they're doing."

Grey sighed. "I know who those bastards were, Herman."

Herman looked at Grey in surprise, almost rising from the bed, though the pain stopped him as abruptly as if he were strapped down.

"Those were the men I hired to rough up Abner Doon."

Herman moaned. "Grey, no, it can't be—how could he have talked them out of it?"

"They had an ironclad contract. They've worked for me before. I have no idea how Doon subverted them." Grey looked worried. "He has power where I didn't expect it. They've been offered money before—a lot of money—but they always kept their contracts. Except when I hired them to teach Doon a lesson."

"I wonder," Herman said, "if he learned anything."

"I wonder," Grey added, more to the point, "if you did."

Herman closed his eyes, hoping Grey would drop dead.

"Forget the game. Buy Italy next time. Doon's got to go under somec sometime."

Herman didn't open his eyes, and Grey went away.

The days passed, and soon Herman was able to hobble back into the room where the computer screen dominated one wall, where the holo of the world of Europe 1914d rotated slowly. Whatever Doon's motive was, Herman saw countless proofs of the fact that Doon knew nothing about playing International Games. He didn't even learn from his own mistakes. The forcible occupation of Guiana was followed by a pointless attack on Afghanistan, which had already been a client state, driving several other client states to the enemy alliance. But Herman's rage finally faded, and he glumly watched as the position of Italy worsened.

Italy's enemies weren't particularly brilliant. They could have been defeated—could still be defeated, if only Herman could get to play.

It was when a revolution flared in England that Herman began to rage again.

From the beginning of the game, Herman had established a carefully benign dictatorship as the government of the Italian Empire, with local autonomy on many matters. It was not oppressive. It was guaranteed to eliminate any chance of revolution. Any rebellions were ruthlessly suppressed, while territories that didn't rebel were lavishly rewarded. It had been years since Herman had had to worry about the internal politics of Italy.

But when the English revolution began, Herman began to scan Doon's activities in the internal affairs of the empire. Doon had pointlessly changed things, taxing the populace, emphasizing the difference between the rich and the poor, the powerful and the weak. He had also oppressed local nationalities, compelling them to learn Italian, and the computer had brought the inevitable result—resentment, rebellion, and at last revolution.

What was Doon doing? Surely he could see the result of his actions. Surely he could tell that he was doing everything—or at least something—wrong. Surely he would realize he was out of his class in this game, and sell Italy while he still could. Surely—

"Grey," Herman said over the phone, "this Doon. Is he stupid?"

"If he is, it's the best-kept secret on Capitol."

"His game is too stupid to believe. Totally stupid. He's doing everything wrong. Anything that could be done right, he's done the opposite. Does that sound like him to you?"

"Doon's built up a financial empire from nothing to the largest I've ever heard of on Capitol, and done it in only eleven years since his majority," Grey answered. "That doesn't sound like him."

"Which means that either he's not playing the game himself—"

"No, he's playing, that's the law and the computer says he's following it—"

"Or he's deliberately playing to lose."

Grey's shrug was almost audible. "Why would anybody do that?"

"I want to meet him."

"He'll never come."

"On some neutral ground, someplace that neither of us controls."

"Herman, you don't know this man. If you don't control the ground, he does—or will, by the time a meeting takes place. There is no neutral ground."

"I want to meet him, Grey. I want to find out what the hell he's doing with my empire."

And Herman went back to watching as the revolution in England was put down brutally. Brutally, but not thoroughly. The computer showed armed bands still roaming in Wales and the Scottish highlands, and urban guerillas still alive in London, Manchester, and Liverpool. Doon could see that information, too. But he chose to ignore it. And chose to ignore the revolutionary movement gaining force in Germany, the brigands harassing the farmers in Mesopotamia, the Chinese encroachments in Siberia.

Asinine.

And the fabric of a well-wrought empire began to come apart.

The telephone sent its gentle buzz into the flexible speaker in his pillow, and Herman awoke. Not even opening his eyes, he said into the pillow, "I'm asleep, drop dead."

"This is Grey."

"You're fired, Grey."

"Doon says he'll meet with you."

"Call my secretary for an appointment."

"But he says he'll only meet with you if you can come to the C24b tube station within thirty minutes."

"That isn't even in my sector," Herman complained.

"So he isn't trying to make it easy for you."

Herman groaned and got out of bed, dressed in a suit that looked far from natty as he sagged out of the flat and into the corridors. The tubes were running at half-schedule at that time of morning, and Herman stumbled into one and followed the route that led him to station C24b. It was even less crowded than

Herman's own area, and there on the platform waited an unprepossessing young man, only a little taller than Herman himself. He was alone.

"Doon?" Herman asked.

"Grandfather,' the young man answered. Herman looked at him blankly. Grandfather?

"Not possible."

"Abner Doon, colt, out of filly Sylvaii, daughter of Herman Nuber and Birniss Humbol. An admirable pedigree, don't you think?"

Herman was appalled. After all these solitary years, to discover that his young tormentor was a relative

"Dammit, boy, I have no family. What is this, vengeance for a divorce a hundred years ago? I paid your grandmother well. *If* you're telling the truth."

But Doon only smiled. "Actually, Grandfather, I don't give a damn about your liaison and lack of it with my grandmother. I don't like her anyway, and we haven't spoken in years. She says I'm too much like you. And so now when she comes out of somec, she doesn't even look me up. I visit her just to be annoying."

"A trait you seem to specialize in."

"You find a long-lost grandchild, and already you're trying to cause division in the family. What an ugly way of dealing with family crises."

And Doon turned on his heel. Since they hadn't yet discussed the game, Herman had no choice but to follow. "Listen, boy," Herman said as he trotted doggedly behind the younger man's brisk walk, "I don't know what your purpose is with my game, but you certainly don't need any money. And you're certainly not going to win any bets, not the way you're playing."

Doon smiled over his shoulder and went on walking down the corridors. "It rather depends, doesn't it, on what I'm betting on."

"You mean you're betting that you'll lose? The way you're playing, you'd never get any takers."

"No, Grandfather. As a matter of fact, I'm holding bets made months ago. Bets that Italy would be destroyed and utterly gone from Europe 1914d within two months of your waking."

"Utterly destroyed!" Herman laughed. "Not a chance of that boy, I built too well, even for a games moron like you."

Doon touched a door and it slid open.

"Come in, Grandfather."

"Not a chance, Doon. What kind of fool do you take me for?"

"A rather small one, actually," Doon said, and Herman followed the young man's gaze to the two men standing behind him.

"Where did they come from?" Herman asked stupidly.

"They're my friends. They're coming to this party with us. I like to keep myself surrounded by friends."

Herman followed Doon inside.

The setting was austere, functional, almost middle-class in its plainness. But the walls were lined with real wood—Herman recognized it at a glance—and the computer that overwhelmed the small front room was the most expensive, most self-contained model available.

"Grandfather," Doon said, "contrary to what you think, I brought you here tonight because, for all that you've been a remarkably bad parent and grandparent, I feel some residual desire for you not to hate me."

"You lose," Herman replied. The two thugs grinned moronically at him.

"You haven't had much connection with the real world lately," Doon commented.

"More than I wanted."

"Instead you've devoted your life and your fortune to building up an empire on a shadow world that exists only in the computer."

"My Lord, boy, you sound like a clergyman."

"Mother wanted me to be a minister," Doon said. "She was always pathetically hunting for her father—you, if you recall—but this time a father who'd not desert her. Sadly, sadly, Grandfather, she finally found that surrogate parent in God."

"At least I thought I'd bequeath a child of mine some good sense," Herman said in disgust.

"You've bequeathed more than you know."

The world of Europe 1914d appeared on the holo. Italy was pinkly dominant.

"It's beautiful," Doon said, and Herman was surprised by the honest admiration in his voice.

"Nice of you to notice," Herman replied.

"No one but you could have built it."

"I know."

"How long do you think it would take to destroy it?"

Herman laughed. "Don't you know your history, boy? Rome was falling from the end of the republic on, and it took fifteen hundred years for the last remnant to fall. England's power was fading from the seventeenth century on, but nobody noticed because it kept gathering real estate. It stayed independent for another four hundred years. Empires don't fall easily, boy."

"What would you say about an empire falling in a week?"

"That it wasn't a well-built empire, then."

"What about yours, Grandfather?"

"Stop calling me that."

"How well have you built?"

Herman glared at Doon. "No one has ever built better."

"Napoleon?"

"His empire didn't outlive him."

"And yours will outlive you?"

"Even a total incompetent could keep it intact."

Doon laughed. "But we're not talking about a total incompetent, Grandfather. We're talking about your own grandson, who has everything you ever had, only more of it."

Herman stood up. "This meeting is pointless. I have no family. I lost custody of my daughter because I didn't want her. I don't know, and I certainly don't want her offspring. I'll be under somec in a few months, and when I wake up I'll take Italy, whatever damage you've done to it, and build it back."

Doon laughed. "But Herman. Once a country has ceased to exist, it can't be brought back into the game. When I'm through with Italy, it'll be a computer-standard country, and you won't be able to buy it."

"Look, boy," Herman said coldly, "do you plan to keep me here against my will?"

"You're the one who asked for a meeting."

"I regret it."

"Seven days, Grandfather, and Italy will be gone."

"Inconceivable."

"I actually plan to do it in four days, but something might go wrong."

"Of all criminals, the worst are those who see beauty only as an opportunity for destruction."

"Good-bye, Grandfather."

But at the door, Herman turned to Doon and pleaded, "Why are you doing this? Why don't you stop?"

"Beauty is in the eye of the beholder."

"Can't you wait until next time? Can't you let me have Italy for this waking?"

Doon only smiled. "Grandfather, I know how you play. If you had Italy this waking, you'd take over the world, wouldn't you? And then the game would end."

"Of course."

"That's why I have to destroy Italy now—while I still can."

"Why Italy? Why not go ruin somebody else's empire?"

"Because, Grandfather, it's no challenge to destroy the weak."

Herman left, and the door slid shut behind him. He went back to the tube, and it took him to his home station. At home, the holo of the globe was still dominated by pink. Herman stopped and looked at it, and even as he watched, a large section of Siberia changed colors. He no longer raged at Doon's incompetence. The boy was obviously compensating for a miserably religious childhood, which he blamed on his grandfather. But no amount of talent the boy might have could possibly dismember Italy. The computer was too rigidly realistic. Once the computer-simulated populace of Italy realized what Doon's character, the dictator, was doing, the unchanging laws of interaction between government and governed would oust him. He would be compelled to sell, and Herman could buy. And rebuild all the damage.

England rebelled again, and Herman went to bed.

But he woke gasping, and remembered that in his dream he had been crying. Why? But even as he tried to remember, the dream slipped from his mind's grasp, and he could only remember that it had something to do with his former wife.

He went to the computer and cleared it of the game. Birniss Humbol. The computer summoned her picture to the screen, and Herman looked as she went through a sequence of facial expressions. She was beautiful then, and the computer awakened memories.

A courtship that had been oddly chaste—perhaps religion was already in Birniss's blood, only to surface fully in her daughter. Their wedding night had been their first intercourse, and Herman laughed at how it had been—Birniss, worldly and wise, so strangely timid as she confessed her unpreparedness to her husband. And Herman, tender and careful, leading her through the mysteries. And at the end, her asking him, "Is that all?"

"It'll be better later," he had said, more than a little hurt.

"It wasn't half as bad as I expected," she answered. "Do it again."

They had done everything together. Everything, that is, but the game. And it was a crucial time for Italy. He began going to bed later and later, talking to her less, and even then talking of nothing but Italy and the affairs of his small but beautiful world.

There was no other man when she divorced him, and to satisfy a whim of curiosity he looked up her name in the vital statistics bank. He wasn't surprised when the computer told him that she had never remarried, though she hadn't kept his name.

Had there been something remarkable about their marriage, so that she'd never marry again? Or was it simply that she had only trusted one man, and then found that marriage wasn't what she'd wanted—or sex, either, by extension. Her hurt had poisoned their daughter; her hurt had poisoned Doon. Poor boy, Herman thought. The sins of the fathers. But the divorce, however regrettable, had been inevitable. To save the marriage, Herman would have had to sacrifice the game. And never in history, real or feigned, had there been such a thing of beauty as his Italy. Dissertations had been written on it, and he knew that he was acclaimed by the students of alternate histories as the greatest genius ever to have played. "A match for Napoleon, Julius, or Augustus." He remembered that one, and likewise the statement of one professor who had pleaded for an interview until Herman's vanity no longer allowed him to resist: "Herman Nuber, not even America, not even England, not even Byzantium compared to your Italy for stability, for grace, for power." High praise, coming from a man who had specialized in real European history, with the chauvinism of the historian for the era he studied.

Doon. Abner Doon. And when the lad had proven himself no match for his grandfather's gifts as a builder, what would happen to him?

Herman found himself, as he dozed at the computer, daydreaming of a reconciliation of some kind. Abner Doon embracing him and saying, Grandfather, you built too well. You built for all time. Forgive my presumption.

Even Herman's dreams, he realized as he awoke, even my dreams require the surrender of everyone around me. Birniss's image was still on the screen. He erased her, and began to scan Italy.

The entire empire was being swept by revolution from one end to the other. Even in the homeland on the Italic Peninsula. Herman stared in disbelief. It had only been overnight, and suddenly all the revolutions had come at once.

It was unprecedented in history. How could the computer have been so mad? It had to be a malfunction. Many empires had faced rebellion, but never, never so general—never universal revolution. Even the army was in mutiny. And the enemies of Italy were madly plunging over the borders to take advantage of the situation.

"Grey!" Herman shouted over the phone. "Grey, do you know what he's doing?"

"How can I help it?" Grey asked nastily. "All the games-players on my staff have been chattering about it all morning."

"How did he do it?"

"Look, Herman, you're the games expert. I don't even play, all right? And I've got work to do. Did you meet with him?"

"Yes."

"And?"

"He's my grandson."

"I wondered if he'd tell you."

"You knew?"

"Of course," Grey answered, "And I had his psychological profile. Do you think I would have let you meet him alone if I hadn't been sure he had no intention of harming you?"

"Not harming me? What about those walking turds he had beat me to a pudding last week?"

"Retaliation, Herman, that's all. He's a good retaliator."

"You're fired!" Herman shouted, slamming the button on the console that disconnected the conversation. And he watched grimly, hour after hour, as the loyal fragments of Italy's army attempted to cope with the mutiny and revolution and invasion all at once. It was impossible, and by late afternoon, the only pink areas on the globe were in Gaul, Iberia, Italy itself, and a small pocket in Poland.

The computer reported that Doon's persona, the dictator of Italy, had vanished, and would-be assassins couldn't put him to death. And as Rome itself fell to an invading army from Nigeria and America, he knew that now defeat and destruction were inevitable. Impossible yesterday, inevitable today.

Still he fought his despair, and sent an urgent message to Grey, forgetting that he had fired him that morning. Grey responded as deferently as ever.

"Offer to buy Italy," Herman said.

"Now? The thing's in ruins."

"I might pull it out. I still might. Surely he's proved his point by now."

"I'll try," Grey said.

But by late evening, there was no pink on the board. The other players and the computer's ironclad adherence to the laws of public behavior had left the game no chance of Italy's rebirth. The information appeared on the status lists. "Iran: newly independent; Italy: discontinued; Japan: at war with China and India over the domination of Siberia. . . ." No special notice. Nothing. Italy: discontinued.

Grimly Herman played back all the information he could find in the computer. How had Doon done it? It was impossible. But for hours he pored over the information the computer gave him, Herman began to see the endless machinations that Doon had set in motion, always postponing revolution here, advancing it there, antagonizing here, soothing there, so that when the full revolution erupted it was universal; so that when Italy's defeat was obvious, there was no lingering desire to have some fragment of it remain. He had gauged the hatred better than the computer itself; he had destroyed more thoroughly than any man had ever built. And in his bitterness at the wrecking of his creation, Herman still had to recognize a kind of majesty in what Doon had done. But it was a satanic majesty, a regal power to destroy.

"A mighty hunter before the Lord," said Doon, and Herman whirled to see Doon standing in his living room.

"How did you get in here?" Herman stammered.

"I have connections," Doon said, smiling. "I knew you'd never let me in, and I had to see you."

"You've seen me," Herman said, and turned away.

"It went faster than I thought it would," Doon said.

"Glad to know something could surprise you."

Doon might have said more, but at that point Herman's self-control, overstrained that day, broke down. He didn't weep, but he did grip the console of the computer far too tightly, as if afraid that when he let go the centrifugal force of Capitol's rotation would throw him into space.

Grey and two doctors came at Doon's anonymous call, and the doctors pried Herman's fingers away from the console and led him to bed. A sedative and some instructions to Grey, and they left again. It was only mild—too much in one day, that's all. He'd feel much better when he woke up.

Herman felt much better when he woke up. He had slept dreamlessly—the sedatives did their work well. The false sunlight streamed through his expensive artificial window, which seemed to open on the countryside outside Florence, though of course in reality nothing but another flat much like his own was on the other side of that wall. Herman looked at the sunlight and wondered if the illusion was good. He had been born on Capitol—he had no idea whether sunlight really streamed into windows that way.

Under the dazzling light, Abner Doon sat on a chair, asleep. Seeing him brought a flood of feelings back to Herman—but he retained his control, and the vestiges of the drugs made him oddly calm about things, after all. He watched his grandson's sleeping face and wondered how so much hatred could be hidden there.

Doon awoke. He looked immediately at his grandfather, saw that he was awake, and smiled gently. But he said nothing. Just stood and carried his chair closer to Herman's bed. Herman watched him silently, and wondered what was going to happen. But the drug kept saying, "I don't care what happens," and Herman didn't care what was going to happen.

"Is it all discharged?" he asked softly, and Doon only smiled more broadly.

"You're so young," Doon said. And then, so quickly that Herman had no time (and the drug gave him no inclination) to resist, the younger man reached out and touched Herman's forehead lightly. The hand was dry, and it traced the faint lines that had begun to cleave the skin. "You're so young."

Am I? Herman thought, as he rarely did, of how old he was in real time. He had gone on somec—what, seventy years ago? At his average rate of one out of four, that meant it had been only seventeen years of subjective time since he had first been able to use the sleeping drug, the gift of eternal life. Seventeen years. And all of them devoted to building Italy. And yet.

And yet those seventeen years hadn't even been half the time he had lived. Subjectively, he wasn't forty yet. Subjectively, he could start again. Subjectively, there was more than enough time for him to make an empire that even Doon couldn't break down.

"But I can't, can I?" Herman asked, unaware that his question arose from private thoughts.

Yet Doon understood. "I've learned everything you know about building, Grandfather," he said. "But you'll never understand what I've learned about tearing down."

Herman smiled wanly, the only kind of smile available to him under the drug. "It's a field of study I largely ignored."

"And yet it's the only one with eternal results. Build well, and eventually your beautiful creation, Grandfather, with or without my help, eventually it *will* fall. But destroy thoroughly, destroy effectively, and what was wrecked will never be rebuilt. Never."

And the drug took Herman's fury and hatred and turned it into regret and gentle grief. Tears spun from his eyelashes as he blinked.

"Italy was beautiful," he said.

Doon only nodded.

And as the tears now began to flow smoothly onto the pillow, Herman whimpered, "Why'd you do it, boy?"

"It was practice."

"Practice for what?"

"Saving the human race."

The drug permitted Herman to smile a little at that. "Quite a warm-up, boy. What can you destroy now, after Italy?"

Doon said nothing. He just walked to the window and looked through it.

"Do you know what's going on outside your window?"

Herman mumbled, "No."

"Peasants are pressing olives. And bringing food to Florence. A lovely scene, Grandfather. Very pastoral."

"Does that mean it's spring? Or Autumn?"

"Who remembers?" Doon asked. "Who cares? The seasons are what we say they are on every world in the Empire, and on Capitol we care nothing for seasons at all. We've mastered everything, haven't we? The Empire is powerful, and even the attempts of the enemy to attack us are only the annoyance of mosquitoes."

The word *mosquito* meant nothing to Herman, but he was too weary to ask.

"Grandfather, the Empire is stable. Not as perfect as Italy, perhaps, but strong and stable and with somec keeping the elite alive for centuries, what force could possibly topple the Empire?"

Herman struggled to think. He had never thought of the Empire as being a nation, like those in the International Games. The Empire was—was reality. Nothing would ever hurt it. "Nothing can hurt the Empire," Herman said.

"I can," Doon said.

"You're insane," Herman answered.

"Probably," Doon said, and then the conversation lagged and the drug decided that Herman would sleep. He slept.

* * *

"I want to see Doon," Herman told Grey.

"I would have thought," Grey answered mildly, "that you'd seen enough of him last month."

"I want to see him."

"Herman, this is becoming an obsession. The doctors say I can't let you do anything to upset yourself. If you'll just behave reasonably for a few months, we can get you back on somec and I can give you back fifty percent of your power of attorney."

"I don't like being considered insane."

"It's just a technicality. It's keeping you alive, you know."

"Grey, all I've done is try to warn—"

"Don't start that. The doctors are monitoring this call. Herman, this Empire isn't interested in your pathetic theories about Doon—"

"He said it himself!"

"Abner Doon destroyed Italy. It was ugly, it was cruel, it was pointless, but it was legal. Now to fantasize that he's also out to destroy the Empire—"

"It's not a fantasy!" Herman roared.

"Herman, the doctors said I have to call it a fantasy. To help you see reality."

"He's going to wreck the Empire! He can do it!"

"That kind of talk is treason, Herman. Stop talking like that and we can get you declared legally sane again. But if you say things like that when you're responsible for yourself, you can be executed very quickly by Mother's Little Boys."

"Grey, whether I'm sane or not, I want to talk to Doon!"

"Herman, drop it. Forget it. It was just a game. The man's your grandson. He was hurt, he tried to hurt you back. But don't let it damage you like this."

"Grey, tell the doctors I want to talk to Doon!"

Grey sighed. "I'll tell them on one condition."

"What's that?"

"That if they give you one meeting with Doon, you'll never ask for another."

"I promise. I only want one meeting."

"Then I'll do my best."

Grey switched off the phone, and Herman disconnected his

end. The telephone now would only connect him to Grey's office. He could make no other calls. He couldn't open the door. And his computer would no longer let him watch the broadcast games.

It was only an hour before Grey was back on the phone.

"Well?" Herman asked eagerly.

"They said yes."

"Connect me then!" Herman demanded.

"I already tried. Impossible."

"How can it be impossible? He'll talk to me! I know he will!"

"He's under somec, Herman. He went under only a few days after he wrecked—after the game. He won't be awake for three years."

And with a whimper Herman disconnected the phone again.

It took five years of therapy—five years without somec—for Herman at last to admit that his fear of Doon was abnormal, and that actually Doon had never hinted that he meant to wreck the Empire. Of course Herman had said that from the beginning, as soon as he realized that was what the doctors wanted to hear. But the machines enforced truth, and it was not until the machines told the doctors that Herman was not lying when he said those things that the doctors at last pronounced him cured and Grey's staff (Grey was under somec at the time) released fifty percent of Herman's power of attorney to him. Herman promptly signed it all back and went under somec, trying to snatch back the years of somec sleep that had been taken from him while the doctors cured him of his ridiculous delusions.

For nearly a century, Doon's and Herman's wakings failed to coincide. At first Herman hadn't tried to look Doon up—the cure had taken from him, for a while at least, any curiosity about his grandson. Then he had learned to look back on the strange episode that had so changed his life without fear or anger; and he had pored over the records of the famous game. Many books had been written on it—*The Rise and Fall of Nuber's Italy* was over two thousand views long. And as he philosophically studied the structure he had built and the way it had fallen, the desire grew in him to meet his opponent and grandson. Not *again*,

because the doctors had convinced Herman utterly of the truth
that he hadn't seen Doon at all after the battle.

But when Herman tried to look up Abner Doon's waking
schedule at the Sleeproom, he was informed that Doon's wakings were a matter of state security. That meant only one thing—
Doon was sleeping longer than the absolute maximum of ten
years and waking less than the absolute minimum of two months.
It meant he was in a power group inaccessible even to most
government officials. And it increased Herman's desire to see
him.

It was not until Herman had reached the subjective age of
seventy that he finally succeeded. Centuries of Empire history
had passed, and Herman followed them carefully. He read everything he could get into his computer on history—Empire and
otherwise. He wasn't sure what he was looking for; but he was
sure that he had never found it. And then one day his inquiry at
the Sleeproom brought him the information that Abner Doon
was awake. They wouldn't tell him how long Doon had been
awake or how soon he would sleep again, but it was enough.
Herman sent the message, and to his surprise, a message returned that Doon would see him. That Doon would even come
to him.

Herman fretted for hours, wondering now what it was he had
wanted to see Doon for. There was no filial feeling, Herman
decided. Family was nothing to him. It was the wish of a great
player to meet the man who had defeated him, that's all. Napoleon's wish, just before his death, to talk to Wellington. Hitler's
mad craving to speak to Roosevelt. Julius's dying passion to
converse, for just a moment as the blood poured from him, with
Brutus.

What's in the mind of the man who destroyed you? That was
the question that had nagged at Herman's mind for years, and
he wondered, now, if he would find the answer. And yet this
would be his only chance. Herman's five years of therapy had
cost him dearly, and he could see—as so few others could—his
mortality waiting around the corner. Somec only postponed, it
did not end.

"Grandfather," said a gentle voice, and Herman woke
abruptly. When had he fallen asleep? No matter. Before him

355

stood the short, now rather portly man that he recognized as his grandson. It was shocking to see how young Doon was, though. Hardly older than when they had locked horns so many, many years ago.

"My legendary opponent," said Herman, extending his hand.

Doon took the offered fingers, but instead of gripping them, he spread the old man's hand on his. "Even somec takes its toll, doesn't it?" he asked, and the sadness in his eyes told Herman that, after all, someone else understood the death that somec so cleverly carried within it's life-preserving promise.

"Why did you want to see me?" Doon asked.

And heavy, slow, inexplicable tears rolled out of Herman's aging eyes. "I don't know," he said. "I just wanted to know how you were doing."

"I'm doing well," Doon said. "My department has colonized dozens of worlds in the last few centuries. The enemy's on the run—we're going to outpopulate him if he doesn't do the same. The Empire's growing."

"I'm so glad. Glad the Empire's growing. Building an empire's such a lovely thing." Pointlessly he added, "I built an empire once."

"I know," Doon said. "I destroyed it."

"Oh yes, yes," Herman said. "That's why I wanted to see you."

Doon nodded and waited for the question.

"I wondered. I wanted to know—why you chose me. Why you decided to do it. I can't remember why, you know. My memory isn't all it was."

Doon smiled and held the old man's hand. "No one's memory is, Grandfather. I chose you because you were the greatest. I chose you because you were the highest mountain I could climb."

"But why did you—why did you tear? Why didn't you build another empire, and rival me?" That was the question. Ah, yes, that's the question, Herman decided. It was so much more satisfying—though he still felt a small doubt. Hadn't he once had a conversation with Doon in which Doon answered him? Never. No.

Doon looked distant. "You don't know the answer?"

"Oh," Herman said, laughing, "I was once quite mad, you know, and thought you were out to wreck the Empire. They cured me."

Doon nodded, looking sad.

"But I'm quite better now, and I want to know. Just want to know."

"I tore—I attacked your empire, Grandfather, because it was too beautiful to finish. If you had finished it, won the game, the game would have ended, and then what would have happened? It wouldn't have been remembered for very long. But now—it's remembered forever."

"Funny, isn't it," Herman said, losing the thread of the conversation before Doon finished speaking, "that the greatest builder and the greatest wrecker should both come from the same—should be grandfather and grandson. Funny, isn't it?"

"It's all in the family, isn't it?" Doon said with a smile.

"I'm proud of you, Doon," Herman said, and meant it for the time being. "I'm glad that if someone was strong enough to beat me, it was blood of my blood. Flesh of my—"

"Flesh," Doon interrupted. "So you're religious after all."

"I don't remember," Herman said. "Something happened to my memory, Abner Doon, and I'm not sure of everything. Was I religious? Or was it someone else?"

Doon's eyes filled with sorrow and he reached out to the old man sitting on a soft chair. Doon knelt and embraced him. "I'm so sorry," he said. "I didn't know what it would cost you. I truly didn't."

Herman only laughed. "Oh, I didn't have any bets out that waking. It didn't cost me a dime."

Doon only held him tighter and said, again, "I'm sorry, Grandfather."

"Oh, well, I don't mind losing," Herman answered. "In the long run, it was only a game, wasn't it?"

17
Killing Children

He heard the door click open but did not turn away from the tall pile of soft plastic blocks he was building. Instead he sought among the blocks scattered on the warm floor an orange block. Orange was definitely required since it helped make no pattern whatsoever.

"Link?" said an overfamiliar voice behind him, a strange familiar voice that, alone of all voices, could make him turn, startled. I killed her, he thought softly. She is *dead*.

But he turned around slowly and there, indeed, was his mother, flesh as well as voice, the slender, oh-so-delicious looking body (not forty-five! couldn't be forty-five!) and the immaculate clothing and the terror in her eyes.

"Link?" she asked.

"Hello, Mother," he said stupidly, his voice deep and slow. I sound like a mental cripple, he realized. But he did not repeat the words. He merely smiled at her (the light making her hair seem like a halo, the fabric of her blouse clinging slightly to the undercurve of her breast, no, mustn't notice that, must think instead of motherhood and filial devotion. Why isn't she dead? Was that, please God, the dream, and this the reality? Or is this vision why I'm in this place?) and a tear or two dazzled in his eyes, making it hard for him to see, and in the dimness he supposed for a moment that she was not blond, but brown-haired; but she had always been blond—

Seeing the tear and ignoring the continued madness in his dancing gaze, his mother held out her arms for a second, only a second, and then put her hands on her hips (note the way the point of her hips and the curve of her abdomen leave two slender depressions pointing downward, Link said to himself) and got an angry look, a hurt look on her face, and said, "What, don't I even get a hug from my boy?"

The words were the incantation required to get Link from the floor to his full 190 centimeters of height. He walked to her, reaching out his long arms for her—

"No—" she gurgled, pushing him away. "Don't—just a little kiss. Just a kiss."

She puckered for a childish kiss, and so he too puckered his lips and leaned down. At the last moment, however, she turned her head and he kissed her clumsily on the ear and hair.

"Oh, how wet," she said in her disgusted voice. She reached into her hipbag and pulled out a tissue, wiped her ear, laughing softly. "Clumsy, clumsy boy, Link, you always have been. . . ."

Link stood in confusion. And, as so many times before, puzzled as to what to do next that would not earn a rebuke. He remained in that confusion, knowing that there was something that he ought to do, something that he must decide, but instead deciding nothing, only playing again and again the same loop of thought in the same childish mental voice in which he had always played it, "Mummy mad, mummy mad, mummy mad."

She watched him, her lips forming a sort of half-smile (note the natural gloss on the lips, she never painted, never had to, lips always just slightly moist, partly open, the tongue playing gentle love games with the teeth), unsure of what was happening.

"Link?" she said. "Link, don't you have a smile for Mother?"

And Link tried to remember how to smile. What did it feel

like? There were muscles that must be pulled, and his face should feel tight—

"No!" she screamed, stepping back from him and encountering the closed door. She apparently had expected it to be open—as if this were not a mental hospital and patients were free to roam the corridors at will. She whirled and hammered on the door with her fists, shouting frantically, "Let me out of here!"

They let her out, the tall men with the pleasant smiles who also took Link to the bathroom five times a day because somehow he had forgotten to notice when he needed to. And as the door closed behind her, Link still stood, unable to decide what he should do, and wondering why his hands were stretched out in front of him, the hands set to grip something circular, something vertical and cylindrical, something, perhaps, the shape of a human throat.

In Dr. Hort's office, Mrs. Danol sat, poised and beautiful, distractingly so, and Hort wondered whether this was indeed the same woman who had wept in the attendant's arms only a few minutes before.

"All I care about is my son," she said. "He was gone, vanished for seven terrible, terrible months, and all I know now is that I've found him again and I want him home. With me!"

Hort sighed. "Mrs. Danol, Linkeree is criminally insane. This is a *government* facility, remember? He murdered a girl."

"She probably deserved it."

"She had supported him and cared for him for seven months, Mrs. Danol."

"She probably seduced him."

"They had a very active sex life, in which both were eager participants."

Mrs. Danol looked horrified. "Did my son tell you that?"

"No, the tenants downstairs told the police that."

"Hearsay, then."

"The government has a very limited budget on this planet, Mrs. Danol. Most people live in apartments where privacy is strictly impossible."

And Mrs. Danol shuddered, apparently in disgust at the plight

of the poor wretches that huddled in the government compound
in this benighted capital of this benighted colony.

"I wish I could leave here," she said.

"It would have been nice at one time," Hort answered. "Your
son hates this world. Or, rather, more particularly, he hates what
he has seen of this world."

"Well, I can understand that. Those hideous wild people—
and the people in the city aren't much better."

Hort was amused at her reverse democracy—she esteemed all
persons her infinite inferiors, and therefore equal to each other.
"Nevertheless, now Linkeree must stay here and we must attempt a cure."

"Oh, that's all I want for my boy. For him to be the sweet,
loving child he used to be—I can't believe he really killed her!"

"There were seventeen witnesses to the strangling, two of
them hospitalized when he turned on them after they pried him
away from the corpse. He definitely killed her."

"But why," she said emotionally, her breasts heaving with
passion in a way that amused Hort—he had known many such
closet exhibitionists in his time. "Why would he kill her?"

"Because, Mrs. Danol, except for hair color and several years
of age, she looked almost exactly like you."

Mrs. Danol sat upright. "My God, Doctor, you're joking!"

"Almost the only thing that Link has been consistent about
since he arrived here is his firm belief that it was you that he
killed."

"This is hideous. This is repulsive."

"Sometimes he weeps and says he's sorry, that he'll never do
it again. Most of the time, however, he cackles rather gleefully
about it, as if it were a game that he had, after many losses,
finally won."

"Is this what passes for psychology on this godforsaken
planet?"

"This is what passes for psychology on Capitol itself, Mrs.
Danol. That is, you recall, where I got my degree. I assure you
I have invented nothing." And dammit, he thought, why am I
letting this woman put me on the defensive? "We thought that
the fact of seeing you alive might have some effect on your son."

"He did try to strangle me."

"So you said. You also said you wanted him to come home with you. Is that really consistent?"

"I want you to cure him and send him home! Since his father died, whom else have I had to love?"

Yourself, Hort refrained from saying. My, but I'm getting judgmental.

The buzzer sounded and, relieved at the interruption, Hort pressed the pad that freed the door. It was Gram, the head nurse. He looked upset.

"It was time for Linkeree's toilet," he said, beginning, as usual, in the middle, "and he wasn't there. We've looked everywhere. He's not in the building."

Mrs. Danol gasped. "Not in the building!"

Hort said, "She's his mother," and Gram went on. "He climbed through the ceiling tiles and out the air-conditioning system. We had no idea he was that strong."

"Oh, what a fine hospital!"

Hort was irritated. "Mrs. Danol, the quality of this hospital as a hospital is indisputably excellent. The quality of this hospital as a prison is woefully deficient. Take it up with the government." Defensive again, dammit. And the bitch is still throwing her chest at me. I'm beginning to understand Linkeree, I think. "Mrs. Danol, please wait here."

"No."

"Then go home. But I assure you you'll be entirely in the way while we search for your son."

She glared at him and stood her ground.

He merely nodded. "As you will," he said, and picked up the door control from the desk, carried it with him out of the room, and slid the door shut in Mrs. Danol's face as she tried to follow. He got an altogether unhealthy feeling of satisfaction at having done so.

"Wouldn't mind strangling her myself," he said to Gram, who missed the point and looked a bit worried. "A joke, Gram. I'm not getting homicidal. Where did the fellow go?"

Gram had no answer, and so they went outside to see.

Linkeree huddled against the fence of the government compound, the miles of heavy metal fencing that separated civilization from the rest of the world. The evening wind was already blowing in from the thick grass and rolling hills of the plain that gave the planet its name, Pampas. The sun was still two fingers off the horizon, however, and Linkeree knew that he was plainly visible from miles away. Visible both to the government people who would surely be looking for him; but also visible to the Vaqs, who he knew waited just over the hill, waiting for a child like him to wander out to be eaten.

No, he thought. I'm not a child.

He looked at his hands. They were large, strong—and yet unweathered, as sensitive and delicate as an artist's hands.

"You should be an artist," he heard Zad saying.

"Me?" Link answered, softly, a little amused at the suggestion.

"Yes, you," she said. "Look at this," and her hand swept around the room, and because he could not avoid following her hand, he also saw: tapestries on tapestries on one wall, waiting to be sold. Another wall devoted to thick rugs and the huge loom that Zad used for her work. And another wall windowed ceiling to floor (glass is cheap, someone told the government architect), showing the shabbily identical government housing project in which most of the capital's people lived, and beyond them the Government Office Building from which the lives of thousands of people were run. Millions, if you counted the Vaqs. But no one counted them.

"No," Zad said, smiling. "Sweet, darling Link, look there. That wall."

And he looked and saw the drawings in pencil, the drawings in crayon, the drawings in chalk.

"You can do that."

"I'm all thumbs." Oh, you're all thumbs, he remembered his mother saying.

Zad took his hands and put them around her waist. "Not *all* thumbs," she said, giggling.

And so he had reached out, held the charcoal, and with her hand guiding his at first, had sketched a tree.

"Wonderful," she said.

He looked at the ground and saw that he had drawn a tree in

the ground. He looked up and saw the fence. They're chasing me, he thought.

"I won't let them catch you," he remembered Zad saying. He was ashamed at having lied to her and told her he was a criminal. But how would she have treated him if she'd known he was only the reclusive son of Mrs. Danol, who owned most of Pampas that could be owned? Then she would have been shy of him. Instead, he was shy of her. She had taken him from the street where he was wandering that night, already having been mugged and beaten up—the mugging by one man, the beating by two others who had found his hipbag empty.

"What, are you crazy?"

He had shaken his head, but now he knew better. After all, hadn't he murdered his mother?

A siren went off in the mental hospital. With a wrenching sense of despair Linkeree curled up tighter in a ball, wishing he could turn into a bush. But that wouldn't help, would it? This is a defoliated area.

"What have you drawn?" he remembered Zad asking, and he wept.

A stinger stung him, and he flicked the insect from his hand. The pain brought him up short. What was he doing?

What am I doing? he thought. Then he remembered the escape from the mental hospital, the run through the maze of buildings to the perimeter—the perimeter, because it was safety, the only hope. He vaguely recalled his childhood fear of the open plain—his mother's horrified stories of how the Vaqs would get you if you weren't good and didn't eat your supper.

"Don't disobey me again, or I'll let the Vaqs at you. And you know what part of little boys they like to eat first."

What a sick lady, Linkeree thought for the millionth time. At least it isn't hereditary.

But it is, isn't it? Aren't I escaping from a mental hospital?

He was confused. But he knew that over the fence was safety, Vaqs or no Vaqs; he couldn't stay at the hospital. Hadn't he killed his mother? Hadn't he told them he was glad of it? And when they realized he wasn't insane at all, that he really, seriously, in cold blood strangled his mother on the public streets

of Pampas City, without benefit of madness—well, they'd kill
him.

I will not die at their hands.

The barbed wire scratched him unmercifully, and the electric
shock from the top wire would have stunned a cow, he thought.
But grimly he hung on, his body shuddering in the force of the
voltage; climbed over; dangled a moment on the barbs until his
shirt ripped apart and let him drop; then lay, stunned, on the
ground as another alarm went off, this time nearby.

I've told them where I am, he thought. What an ass.

So he stood, his body still trembling from the electricity, and
staggered stupidly off into the high grass that began crisply a
hundred meters from the fence.

The sun was touching the horizon.

The grass was harsh and sharp.

The wind was bitterly cold.

He had no shirt.

I will freeze to death out here tonight. I will die of exposure.
And the part of him that always gloated sneered, "You deserve
it, matricide. You deserve it, Oedipus."

No, you've got it all wrong, it's the father you're supposed to
kill, right?

"Why, it's a painting of me, isn't it?" asked Zad, seeing what
he had done with the watercolors. "It's excellent, except that
I'm not blond, you know."

And he looked at her and wondered, for a moment, why he
had thought she was.

He was snapped out of his memory by a sound. He could not
identify it, nor ever, for sure, the direction from which it had
come. He stopped, stood still, listening. Now, aware of where
he was, he realized that his arms and hands and stomach and
back were scratched and slightly bloody from the rasping grass.
The suckers were clinging to his bare body; he brushed them
away with a shudder of revulsion. Bloated, they dropped—one
of the curses of the planet, since they left no itch or other pain,
and a man could bleed to death without knowing he was even
being sucked.

Linkeree turned around and looked back. The lights of the

government compound winked behind him. The sun had set, and dusk was only dimly lighting the plain.

The sound came again. He still couldn't identify it, but now the direction was more distinct—he followed.

Not two meters off was a feebly crying infant, the mucus of birth still clinging to his body, the afterbirth unceremoniously dumped beside him. The placenta was covered with suckers. So was the baby.

Linkeree knelt, brushed away the suckers, looked at the child, whose stubby arms and legs proclaimed him to be a Vaq. Yet apart from that, Link could see no other sign that this was not a human infant—the dark skin must come after years of exposure to the hot noon sunshine. He remembered clearly that one of the long line of tutors he had studied with had told him about this Vaq custom. It was assumed to be the exact counterpart of the ancient Greek custom of exposing unwanted infants, to keep the population at acceptable levels. The baby cried. And Linkeree was struck bitterly with the unfairness that it was *this* infant that was chosen to die for the good of the—tribe? Did Vaqs travel in tribes? If seven percent of infants had to die for the good of the tribe, why couldn't there be a way for seven-hundredths of each child to be done away? Impossible, of course. Linkeree stroked the child's feeble arms. It was much more efficient to rid the world of unwelcome children.

He picked up the infant, gingerly (he had never done so before, only seen them in the incubators in the hospital his father had built and which, therefore, Linkeree was "responsible" for), and held it against his bare chest, wondering at the warmth it still had. For a moment at least the crying stopped, and Link periodically struck off the suckers that leapt from the placenta to the baby's or his bare skin.

We are kin, he told the child silently, we are kin, the unwanted children. "If only you'd never been born," he heard his mother saying; this time a saying she had said only once, but the memory was sharp and clear, the moment forever imprinted on his mind. It was no act. It was no sham, like her hugs and kisses and I'm-so-proud-of-*yous*. It was a moment, all too rare, of utter sincerity: "If only you'd never been born, I wouldn't be getting old like this on this hideous planet!"

Why, then, Mother, didn't you leave me on the plain to die? Much kinder, much, much kinder than to have kept me at home, killing me seven percent at a time.

The baby cried again, hunting for a breast that by now was surely many kilometers off, leaking pap for the child that would never suckle. Did the mother grieve, perhaps? Or was she only irritated at the sensitivity of her breasts, only anxious for the last remnants of the pregnancy to fade?

Squatting there, holding the infant, Linkeree wondered what he should do. Could he bring the child back into the compound? Unquestionably yes, but at a cost. First, Linkeree would then be caught, would then be reconfined to the hospital where the fact that he was not, was *not* insane would soon be discovered and they would cleanly and kindly push the needle into his buttocks and put him irrevocably to sleep. And then there was the child. What would they do with a Vaq child in the capital? In an orphanage it would be tortured by the other children, who in their poverty and usual bastardy would welcome the nonhuman as something lower that they could torment and so prove their power. In the schools, the child would be treated as an intellectual pariah, incapable of learning. It would be shunted from institution to institution—until someday on the street the torment became too much and he strangled somebody and then died for it. . . .

Linkeree laid the baby back down. If your own don't want you, the stranger doesn't want you either, he said silently. The baby cried desperately. Die, child, Linkeree thought, and be spared. "There's not one damn thing I can do," he said aloud.

"What do you mean, when you can paint like that?" Zad answered. But Link saw more clearly than she. He had meant to paint Zad, but had instead painted his mother. Now he saw what for seven months he had been blind to—Zad's resemblance to his mother. That's why he had followed her through the streets that first night, had kept watching her, until finally she had asked him what the hell—

"What the hell?" Zad asked, but Link didn't answer, only wrinkled up the painting clumsily (You're all thumbs, Linky!), pressed the wad against his crotch, and struck the paper and thus himself viciously once. Cried out in agony. Struck himself again.

"Hey! Hey, stop that! Don't—"

And then he saw, felt, smelled, heard his mother lean over him, her hair brushing his face (sweet-smelling hair), and Link was filled with the old helpless fury, a helplessness made worse by clear memories of lovemaking hour after hour with this woman in an apartment filled with paintings in a government flat in the low part of the city. Now I'm grown up, he thought, now I'm stronger than her, and still she controls me, still she attacks me, still she expects so damn *much* and I never know what I should do! And so he stopped striking himself and found a better target.

The baby was still crying. Link was disoriented for a moment, wondering why he was trembling. Then another gust of wind reminded him that tonight was the night he would die in feeble expiation for his sins, he like the baby sucked dry by tiny bites, gnawed to death by the chewers that padded through the night, frozen to death by the wind. The difference would be, of course, that the infant would not understand, would never have understood. Better to die unknowing. Better to have no memories. Better to have no pain.

And Link reached down and put his thumb and forefinger around the baby's throat, to kill it now and spare it the brief agony of death later in the night. But when it was time to squeeze tightly and shut off blood and breath, Link discovered that he could not.

"I am not a killer," Link said. "I can't help you."

And he got up and walked away, leaving behind the child's mewling to be buried in the noise of the wind pushing through the grass. The blades rasped against his naked chest, and he remembered his mother scrubbing him in the bath. "See? Only I can reach your back. You need me, just to stay clean."

I need you.

"That's Mother's good boy."

Yes. I am, I am.

"Don't touch me! I won't have any man touch me!"

But you said—

"I'm through with men. You're a bastard and a son of a bastard and you've made me old!"

But Mother—

"No, no, what am I doing? It isn't *your* fault that men are like that. You're different, you, my sweet little boy, give Mother a hug—not so *tight*, for God's sake, you little devil, what are you trying to do? Go to your room!"

He stumbled in the near darkness and fell, cutting his wrist in the grass.

"Why are you hitting me?" he heard the brown-haired woman who ought to be blond crying out. But he hit her again, and she fled the apartment, ran for the stairs, stumbled out into the street. It was the stumbling that let him catch her, and there in the middle of the road he stifled her scream by showing her precisely what a man was like, by throwing her at long, long last away.

A knife pricked into his chest.

He looked up from where he lay in the grass at a short, stocky man—no, not a man, a Vaq—and not just one, a half dozen, all armed, though some were just rising from the ground and still seemed half asleep. He had stumbled in his daze into a Vaq camping place.

This is better, he thought, than the suckers and chewers, and so with a pillar of blackness and chill in place of his spine, he weakly stood, waiting for the knife.

But the knife pressed no deeper toward his heart, and he grew impatient. Wasn't he the heir of the man who had done most to hurt the Vaqs, whose great tractors had swept away the livelihood of a dozen tribes, whose hunters had killed Vaqs who chanced to wander on land marked out as his? I am the owner of half this world that is worth owning; kill me and free yourselves.

One of the Vaqs hissed impatiently. Press the knife, Link thought he seemed to say. And so he too hissed. Impatiently. Act now. Hurry.

In surprise at his having echoed his own death sentence, the Vaq with the knife at his chest withdrew a step, though he still held out the knife, pointing at Linkeree. The Vaq babbled something, something ripe with rolled *r*'s and hissed *s*'s—not a human language, they taught the children in the government schools, even though as Link well knew there were dozens of anthropological reports pointing out that the Vaq language was merely corrupted Spanish, and the Vaqs were obviously the descendants of the colony ship *Argentine* that had been thought lost in the first decade of interstellar colonization thousands of years ago, when man had first reached out from the small planet that they had utterly spoiled. Human. Definitely human, however cruel Pampas had selected for ugliness and ignorance and viciousness and inhumanity.

Savages have no monopoly on that.

And Linkeree reached out, gently took the hand that held the blade, and guided it back until the point pressed against his belly. Then he hissed again, impatiently.

The Vaq's eyes widened, and he turned to look at his fellows, who were equally puzzled. They babbled; some backed away from Link, apparently in fear. Link couldn't understand. He guided the knife deeper into his flesh; blood crept back along the horizontal blade.

The Vaq withdrew his knife, abruptly, and his eyes filled with tears, and he knelt and took Linkeree by the hand.

Link tried to pull his hand away. The Vaq only followed, offering no resistance. The others, also, gathered around. He couldn't understand their language, but he could understand the gestures. They were, he realized, worshiping him.

Gentle hands led him to the center of the encampment. All around, little braziers of peat burned brightly, sizzling constantly as the heat-seeking suckers left the Vaqs and gathered to die in the fire.

They sang to him, plaintive melodies that were only deepened and enhanced by the sweep and howl of the wind. They stripped him and touched him all over, gently exploring, then dressed him again and fed him (and he thought bitterly of the child who, because of the lack of food, was even now dying in the grass) and surrounded him and lay down around him to protect him as he slept.

You're cheating me. I came here to die, and you're cheating me.

And he wept bitterly, and they admired his tears, and after a

half hour, long before the cold moon rose, he slept, feeling
cheated but somehow utterly at peace.

Mrs. Danol sat in a chair in Hort's office, her arms folded
tightly, her eyes savagely watching every move he made—or
didn't make.

"Mrs. Danol," he finally said, "it would help everyone, including you, if you went home."

"Not," she answered acidly, "until you find my boy."

"Mrs. Danol, we are not even looking!"

"And that's why I'm not leaving."

"The government doesn't send searchers out on the plains in
the nighttime. It's suicidal."

"And so Linkeree is going to die. I assure you, Mr. Hort,
that the hospital will regret not doing anything."

He sighed. He was sure that the hospital would—the annual
gifts from the Danol family were more than half of the operating
budget. Some salaries would go immediately—primarily his,
there was little doubt. And so, knowing that, and also because
he was extremely tired, he tossed aside his politic courtesy and
pointed out some blunt facts.

"Mrs. Danol, are you aware that in ninety percent of our
cases, treating the patient's parents is the most effective step
toward a cure?"

Her mouth grew tight and hard.

"And are you aware that your son is not genuinely psychotic
at all?"

At that she laughed. "Good. All the more reason to get him
away from here—if he lives through this night out there in that
hell that passes for a terraformed planet."

"Actually, your son is quite sane, half the time—a very intelligent, very creative young man. Very much like his father."
That last was intended as a very deep dig. It worked.

She rose from her chair. "I don't want any mention of that
son of a bitch."

"But the other half of the time, he is merely reenacting childhood. Children are insane, all of them—by adult standards. Their
defense strategies, their adaptations, are all such that an adult
using them is regarded as utterly mad. Paranoia, acting out,

denial, self-destruction. For some reason, Mrs. Danol, your son has been kept penned into the relationship structures of his childhood.''

"And you think the reason is me."

"Actually, it's not just a matter of opinion. The only times that Linkeree was sane were the times when he believed he had killed you. Believing you dead, he functions as an adult. Believing you alive, he functions as an infant.''

He had gone too far. She shouted in rage and struck out at him across his desk. Her fingers raked his face; her other hand sprawled along his desk, shoving papers and books off onto the floor. He managed to push the call button while he grappled with her with his other hand. But he had lost a handful of hair and gained bruises in his shins by the time the attendants came in and held her back, sedated her, took her to a room in the hospital to rest.

Morning. The hairy birds of the plains were awake, foraging briskly in the dawn, eating the now sluggish suckers that had bloated themselves on the night life of the grasslands. Linkeree woke, mildly surprised at how natural and good it felt to awaken in the open, lying on a mat of grass, with birds crying. Is there some racial memory of life in the open land that makes me feel so comfortable? he wondered. But he yawned, stood, stretched, feeling vigorously alive, feeling good.

The Vaqs watched him, even as they pursued their morning tasks—packing up for the day's journey, fixing a skimpy breakfast of cold meat and hot water. But after the eating, they came to him, touched him again, knelt again, making arcane signs with their hands. When they were through (and Linkeree thought bitterly that it was strange that murder and worship were the only intercourse men could have with the Vaqs) they led Linkeree out of the camp, back in the direction he had come last night.

Now, in daylight, he could see why it was that the Vaqs were such deadly adversaries when met in their native habitat. They were short, and not one of them stood taller than the thickest part of the grass, though Link, not a tall man by any human standard, could see clearly over the crest of the blades. And the

grass ate up their footprints, closed behind them, hid their movements from any possible observer or follower. An army of Vaqs
could pass by unnoticed a meter from the keenest observer, he
thought, with some exaggeration.

And then they arrived. They had brought him back to where
the baby had been abandoned. It shocked Linkeree profoundly,
that they would return to the scene of their crime. Was there no
shame to the murders? At least they could have the decency to
forget the existence of the child, instead of coming back to gloat.

But they formed a circle around the small corpse (how had
they found him again in the grass?) and Linkeree looked down
at the child's body.

A chewer had come in the night, and then several others. The
first had (shades of Mother's nighttime threats) chewed off the
infant's genitals, gnawed into the abdomen at the soft entrails,
ignoring the muscle tissue entirely. But the baby and the placenta
had attracted a huge concentration of suckers, and these had
eagerly transferred to the much warmer chewer, bleeding it to
death before its meal was finished. The later chewers were bled
to death even faster, as more and more suckers came, sucked,
laid eggs, and died.

And then the birds, which had danced skyward when Link
and the Vaqs had arrived, eating the dying suckers, but ignoring
the sucker eggs which were implanted on the blades of grass,
where tonight they would hatch, and the lucky ones would find
food before they starved to death, find food and reproduce in a
mad, one-night life.

Except for the gnawed-away crotch, the child's body was intact.

The Vaqs knelt, nodded toward Link, and began cutting up
the child's body. The incisions were neat, precise. Breastbone
to crotch, a U-shaped cut around the breasts, a long slice down
the arms, the head completely removed; all cuts were quick and
deft, and in a moment the body was entirely skinned.

And then they ate.

Link watched, appalled, as they each in turn lifted a strip of
raw meat toward him, as if it were a votive offering. He shook
his head each time, and each time the Vaq murmured (in thanks)
and ate.

And when the raw bones were left, and the skin, and the heart, the Vaqs opened the skin smoothside up and laid it before Link. They picked up the pile of bones, and held it out to him. He took them—he was afraid, in the face of such inhumanity, to refuse. Then they waited.

What do I do now? he wondered. They were beginning to look a bit disturbed as he knelt, motionless, with the bones in his hands. And so, vaguely remembering some of his classical history, he tossed down the bones onto the blanket of skin and then stood, wiping the blood off his hands onto his trousers.

The Vaqs all looked at the bones, pointing to this one and that one, though they had landed in no pattern discernible to Link. At last, however, they began to grin, to laugh, to jump up and down and jig in delight at whatever the bones had told them.

Linkeree was more than a little glad that the portents had turned out so well. What would they have done if the bones had somehow spelled disaster?

The Vaqs decided to reward him. They picked up the head and offered it to him.

He refused.

They looked puzzled. So did he. Was he supposed to eat the head? It was ghastly—the stump had not bled at all, looked like a laboratory specimen, reminded him of—

No, he would not.

But the Vaqs were not angry. They seemed to understand—they only took the bones, buried each in a separate but shallow hole scrabbled out of the rich deep soil under the grass, and then took the skin and draped it over Link's bare shoulders. It occurred to him that they were signifying that *he* was the child. The leader's gesture confirmed that they believed that—he kept gesturing from the skin and the head to Linkeree, and then pausing, waiting for an answer.

Linkeree didn't know how to respond. If he denied he was the child's spirit or successor or something, would they kill him? Or, if he admitted that he was, would they finish their sacrifice by killing him? Either choice might end his life, and he was not feeling suicidal this morning.

And then, as he stared into the child's dead face, remembering that last night the infant had been alive, had responded to his

touch, he realized that there was more truth than they realized
to their belief. Yes, he was the infant, chewed and cut and eaten
and cast away to be buried in a hundred tiny graves. Yes, he was
dead. And he nodded in acceptance, nodded in agreement.

The Vaqs all nodded too and one by one they came to him
and kissed him. He was unsure of whether the kiss was a prelude
to leaving or to killing; but then they each kissed the child's head
that he held in his hands in front of him, and as he saw their
lips tenderly rest on the infant forehead or cheeks or mouth he
was overcome by self-pity and grief; he wept.

And, seeing his tears, the Vaqs grew afraid, babbled quietly
among themselves, and then disappeared silently into the tall
grass, leaving Linkeree alone with the child's relics.

Dr. Hort went to see Mrs. Danol as soon as he woke up in
the morning. She was sitting in one of the empty private rooms,
her hands folded in her lap. He knocked. She looked up, saw
him through the window, nodded, and he came in.

"Good morning," he said to her.

"Is it?" she answered. "My son is dead by now, Dr. Hort."

"Perhaps not. He wouldn't be the first to survive a night in
the grass, Mrs. Danol."

She only shook her head.

"I'm sorry about last night's fracas," he said. "I was tired."

"You were also too damn right," she answered. "I woke up
at four this morning, sedative or no sedative. I thought and
thought about it. I'm poison. I've poisoned my son just by being
his mother. I wish I could be out there on the plain in his place,
dying for him."

"And what the hell good would that do?"

She only cried in answer. He waited. The sobbing let up only
a few moments later. "I'm sorry," she said, "I've been crying
off and on all morning." Then she looked at Hort, pleading in
her eyes, and said, "Help me."

He smiled—kindly, not triumphantly—and said, "I'll try. Why
don't you just tell me what you've been thinking about?"

She laughed bitterly. "That's a rat's nest we hardly need to
go into. I spent most of the time thinking about my husband."

"Whom you don't like."

"Whom I loathe. He married me because I wouldn't sleep with him otherwise. He slept with me until I got pregnant; then he moved on. When Linkeree turned out to be a boy, he was delighted, and changed his will to leave everything to the boy. Nothing to me. And then, after he had slept with every girl on this planet and half the boys, he was run over by a tractor and I gave a little cheer."

"He was well thought of on the planet."

"People always think well of money."

"They often think well of beauty, too."

And at that she cried again. Through her sobs, in a twisted, little-girl voice, she said, "All I ever wanted was to go to Capitol. To go to Capitol and meet all the famous people and be on somec so that I could live forever and be beautiful forever. It's all I had, being beautiful—I had no money, no education, and no talent for anything, not even motherhood. Do you know what it means to have only one thing that makes other people love you?"

No, Hort thought to himself, but I can see what a tragedy it is.

"You were your son's guardian. You could have taken him to Capitol."

"No, I couldn't. It's the law, Hort. Planet money must be invested on the planet until it achieves full provincial status. It protects us from *exploitation*." She spat on the word. "No somec allowed until we're a province. No chance to have *life*!"

"There are some of us who don't want to sleep for years on end, just to stay young a few years longer," Dr. Hort said.

"Then you're the insane ones," she retorted, and he almost agreed. Eternal life didn't appeal to him. Sleeping through life seemed like a disgusting waste of time. But he knew the draw, knew that most people who came to the colonies were desperate or stupid, that the gifted ones or the rich ones or the hopeful ones stayed where somec was within reach.

"Not only that," she said, "my damnable husband entailed the entire fortune, everything. Not a penny could be taken from Pampas."

"Oh."

"So I stayed, hoping that when my son grew up we could find some way, go anyway—"

"If your son hadn't been born, the money would all have been left to you, unentailed, and you could have sold it to an off-worlder and gone."

She nodded, and began to weep again.

"No wonder you hated your son."

"Chains. Chains, holding me here, stripping away my only asset as the years made hash of my face and my figure."

"You're still beautiful."

"I'm forty-five years old. It's too late. Even if I left for Capitol today, they won't let someone over forty-one go on somec at all. It's the law."

"I know. So—"

"So stay here and make the best of it? Thanks, Doctor, thanks. I might as well have a priest as you."

She turned away from him, and muttered, "And now the boy dies. *Now*, when it's too late. Why the bloody hell couldn't he have died a year ago?"

Linkeree patted the last of the earth over the grave he had dug for the head and skin of the child. The tears had long since dried; now the only liquid on him was sweat from the exertion in the hot sun of digging through the heavy roots of the grass. No wonder the Vaqs had dug shallowly to hide the bones. It was already afternoon, and he had only just finished.

But as he had worked, he had forced himself back, coldly reassembling his memories in his mind, burying them one by one in the child's grave. It was not Mother I killed in the street, it was Zad. Mother is still alive; she visited me yesterday. That was why I fled the hospital; that was why I wanted to die. Because if ever there was a person who deserved to live, it was Zad. And if ever one deserved to die, it was Mother.

Several times he felt himself longing to curl up and hide, to retreat into the cool shade under the standing grass, to deny that any of this had ever happened, to deny that he had ever turned five at all. But he fought off the feeling, insisted on the facts, the whole history of his life, and then hid it under the dirt.

You, child, he thought. I am you. I came out here last night to die in the grassland, to be eaten alive, to have my blood sucked out. And it happened; and the Vaqs ate my flesh and now I'm buried.

I who bury you, child, I am the you who might have been. I am without a past; I have only a future. I will start from here, without a mother, without blood on my hands, rejected by my own tribe and unacceptable to strangers. I will live among the strangers anyway, and live unencumbered. I will be you, and therefore I will be free.

He brushed the dirt off his hands, ignored the painful sunburn on his back, and stood. Around him the sucker eggs on the grassblades were already hatching, and the newborn suckers were devotedly eating each other so that only the few thousand strongest would survive, fed by the others. Link avoided obvious comparisons, merely turned and headed back toward the government compound.

He avoided the gate, instead climbing the fence and enduring the electricity that coursed through him when he gripped the top wire. And then, as the alarms went off, he walked back to the hospital.

Dr. Hort was alone in his office, eating a late lunch from a tray that Gram had brought him. Someone tapped at his door. He opened it, and Linkeree walked in.

Hort was surprised, but out of long professional habit, he didn't show it. Instead, he dispassionately watched as Linkeree walked to the chair, sat down comfortably, and leaned back with a sigh.

"Welcome back," Hort said.

"Hope I didn't cause any inconvenience," Linkeree answered.

"How was your night in the grass?"

Linkeree looked down at his scratches and scabs. "Painful. But therapeutic."

Silence for a moment. Hort took another bite of his sandwich.

"Dr. Hort, right now I'm in control. I know that my mother's alive. I know that I killed Zad. I also know that I was insane when I did it. But I understand and accept those things."

Hort nodded.

"I believe, Doctor, that I am sane right now. I believe that I am viewing the world as accurately as most people, and can function in a capable manner. Except."

"Except?"

"Except that I'm Linkeree Danol, and as soon as it is known that I am capable of running things, I will be forced to take control of a very large fortune and a huge business that employs, in the long run, most of the people on Pampas. I will have to live in a certain house in this city. And in that house will be my mother."

"Ah."

"I don't believe my sanity would last fifteen minutes, Doctor, if I had to live with her again."

"She's changed somewhat," Dr. Hort said. "I understand her a little now."

"I have understood her completely for years, and she'll never change, Dr. Hort. More important, though, is the fact that *I'll* never change when I'm around her."

Hort sucked in a deep breath, leaned back in his chair. "What happened to you out on the desert?"

Linkeree smiled wanly. "I died and buried myself. I can't return to that life. And if it means staying here in this institution all my life, pretending to be insane, I'll do that. But I'll never go back to Mother. If I did that, I'd have to live with all that I've hated all my life—and with the fact that I killed the only person I ever loved. It isn't a pleasant memory. My sanity is not a pleasant thing to hold onto."

Dr. Hort nodded.

There was a knock at the door. Link straightened up. "Who is it?" Hort asked.

"Me. Mrs. Danol."

Linkeree stood up abruptly, walked around the office to a point at the far wall from the door.

"I'm consulting, Mrs. Danol."

Her voice was strident, even through the muffling door. "They told me Linkeree had come back. I heard you talking to him in there."

"Go away, Mrs. Danol," Dr. Hort said. "You will see your son in due time."

"I will see him now. I have a writ that says I can see him. I got it from the court at noon. I want to see him."

Hort turned to Link. "She thinks ahead, doesn't she?"

Link was shaking. "If she comes in, I'll kill her."

"All right, Mrs. Danol. Just a moment."

"No!" Link shouted, making spastic motions as if he wanted to claw his way through the wall backward.

Hort whispered, "Relax, Link. I won't let her near you." Hort opened a closet—Link started to walk in it. "No, Link." And Hort took his spare suit off the hanger, and a clean shirt. The suit, in the standard one piece, was a little long for Linkeree, but the waist and shoulders were not far wrong, and Link didn't look out of place in it when he had finished dressing.

"I don't know what you hope to gain by stalling, Dr. Hort, but I will see my son," Mrs. Danol shouted. "In three minutes I'll call the police!"

Hort shouted back, "Patience, Mrs. Danol. It takes a moment to prepare your son to see you."

"Nonsense! My son wants to see me!"

Linkeree was trembling, hard. Hort put his arms around the young man, gripped him tight. "Keep control," he whispered.

"I'm trying," Link chattered back, his lower jaw out of control.

Hort reached into his hipbag, pulled out his id and his cred, and handed them to Link. "I won't report them missing until you are on a ship out of here."

"Ship?"

"Go to Capitol. You'll have little trouble there, finding a place. Even without money. There's always room for someone like you."

Link snorted. "That's a damn lie and you know it."

"Right. But even if they send you back here, your mother will be dead by then."

Linkeree nodded.

"Now here's the door control. When I say, open the door."

"No."

"Open the door and let her in. I'll keep her under control until you get out the door and close it from the outside. There's no way out of here, then, except Gram's masterkey, and this note should take care of that.'' Hort scribbled a quick note. "He'll cooperate because he hates your mother almost as much as I do. Which is a terrible thing for an impartial psychologist to say, but at this point, who the hell cares?''

Linkeree took the note and the door control and stood beside the door with his back to the wall. "Doctor," he asked, "what'll they do to you for this?''

"Raise holy hell, of course,'' he said. "But I can only be removed by a council of medical practitioners—and that's the same group that can have Mrs. Danol committed.''

"Committed?''

"She needs help, Link.''

Linkeree smiled—and was surprised to realize it was his first smile in months. Since. Since Zad died.

He touched the open button.

The door slid open and Mrs. Danol swept in. "I knew you'd see reason," she pronounced, then whirled to look as Link stepped out the door, closing it so quickly that he almost got caught in it. His mother was already screaming and pounding as Link handed the note to Gram, who read it, looked closely at the man, and then nodded. "But hurry your ass, boy," Gram said. "What we're doing here is called kidnapping in some courts.''

Linkeree set the door control on the desk and left, running.

He lay in the ship's passenger hold, recovering from the dizziness that they told him was normal with a person's first mind-taping. The brain patterns that held all his memories and all his personality were now in a cassette securely stored in the ship's cabin, and now he lay on a table waiting for them to drug him with somec. When he woke up and had his memory played back into his mind in Capitol, he would only remember up to the moment of taping. These moments now, between the tape and the tap, would be lost forever.

And that was why he thought back to the infant whose warm body he had held, and why he let himself wish that he could have saved him, could have protected him, could have let him live.

No, I'm living for him.

The hell I am. I'm living for me.

They came and put the needle into his buttocks, not for the cold sleep of death, but for the burning sleep of life. And as the hot agony of somec swept over him, he writhed into a ball on the table and cried out, "Mother! I love you!"

18
And What Will We Do Tomorrow?

Of all the people on Capitol, only Mother was allowed to awaken on her own bed, the bed where she had slept with Selvock Gray before his death eight hundred years ago. She did not know that the original bed had fallen apart centuries ago; it was always remade, right down to the nicks and scratches, so that she could awaken on it and lie there for a moment in solitude, remembering.

No attendants murmuring. No flush of fever. Of all the people in Capitol, only Mother was given the delicate combination of drugs that made waking a delight—that cost more for each of her wakings than the entire budget of a colony ship.

And so she luxuriated in the bed, cool and not feeling particularly old. How old am I? she wondered, and decided that she was probably forty. I am probably middle-aged, she said, and spread out her legs until they touched both sides of the bed.

She ran her hands over her naked stomach, finding it not as flat and firm as it had been when Selvock had come to visit Jerry Crove and had, as an afterthought, seduced his fifteen-year-old granddaughter. But who had seduced whom? Selvock never knew it, but Mother had chosen him as the man most likely to accomplish what her grandfather was too good and her father too weak to accomplish—the conquest and unification of the human race.

It was my dream, she said to herself. My dream, that I needed Selvock to fulfill. He bloodied himself in a dozen planetside wars, sent fleets here and there at his command, but it was I who made the plans, I who set the wheels in motion, I who fired the starships and sent them on their way. I found the money by bribing, blackmailing, and assassination.

And then, on the day Selvock was confident of victory, that bastard Russian had shot him with (of all things!) a pistol and Mother was alone.

She lay naked on the bed, remembering the feel of his hand on her flesh, the tense, gentle hand, and she missed him. She missed him, but hadn't needed him after all. For now she ruled the human universe, and there was nothing she wanted that she could not have.

Dent Harbock sat in the control room, watching the monitor. Mother was playing with herself on the bed. If the people could only see a holo of this show! he thought. There'd be a revolution within the hour. Or maybe not. Maybe they really did think of her as—what had Nab called her?—an earth mother, a figure of fertility. If she was so fertile, how come no children?

Nab walked into the control room. "How's the old bitch doing?"

"Dreaming of conquest. How come she never had any children?"

"If you believe in a god, thank it for that. As it is, things are comfortable. The only royalty in the universe is a middle-aged woman we only have to wake up one day in every five years. No family squabbles. No war of succession. And nobody trying to tell the government what to do."

Dent laughed.

"Better start the music. We have a busy schedule."

* * *

The music started and Mother was startled into alertness. Ah, yes. It was time. Being Empress wasn't all luxury and pleasant memories. It was also responsibility. There was work to be done.

I'm lazy, now that I'm at the pinnacle of power, she said to herself. But I must keep the wheels turning. I must know what is going on.

She got up and dressed in the simple tunic she had always worn.

"Is she really going to wear that?"

"It was the style when she ruled actively. A lot of heavy sleepers do that—it keeps a touch of familiarity around them."

"But, Nab, it makes her look like a relic of the Pleistocene."

"It keeps her happy. We want her to be happy."

The first item of business was the reports. The ministers had to make the reports personally, and the new ministers who had been appointed since her last waking were on trial as she talked to them. The minister of fleets, the minister of armies, and the minister of peace were first. From them she learned about the war.

"With whom," she said, "are we at war?"

"We aren't at war," said the minister of armies innocently.

"Your budget has doubled, sir, and the number of conscripts is also more than twice what it was yesterday. That's a lot of change for five years. And don't give me any merde about inflation. Whom, my dear friends, are we fighting?"

They glanced at each other, fury barely concealed. It was the minister of fleets who answered, affecting contempt for his fellows. "We didn't want to bother you with it. It's just a border conflict. The governor of Sedgway rebelled a while ago, and he's managed to attract some support. We'll have it under control in a few years."

She sneered. "Some minister of fleets you are. How do you get something under control in a few years when it takes twenty or thirty years to get from here to there even in our lightships?"

The minister of fleets had nothing to say. The minister of armies intervened. "We meant, of course, a few years after the fleets' arrival."

"Just a border conflict? Then why double the army?"

"It wasn't that large before."

"I conquered—my husband conquered the known galaxy with a tenth as many soldiers as you have, *sir*. We considered it a rather large force. I think you're lying to me, gentlemen. I think you're trying to hide the fact that this war is more serious than you thought."

They protested. But even their doctored-up figures couldn't hide the truth from her.

Nab laughed. "I told them not to lie. Everyone thinks he can outwit a middle-aged woman who sleeps most of the time, but the bitch is far too clever for them. Wager you five that she fires them."

"Can she do that?"

"She can. And does. It's the only power left to her, and these fools who think they can make their reports without following my advice always end up losing their jobs."

Dent looked puzzled. "But Nab, when she fires them, why don't they just stay on the job and send an assistant to her?"

"It was tried once, before you were born, my boy. She was able to discover in only three questions that the assistant wasn't used to giving orders like a minister; it took only three questions more to know that she had been defrauded. She ordered the poor sap who tried to fool her brought into her chamber, and she sentenced both him and his assistant to death for treason."

"You're joking."

"To tell you how much of a joke it was, it took two hours to convince her that she ought not to shoot them herself. She kept insisting that she was going to make sure it was done right."

"What happened to them?"

"They were dropped from high somec levels and sent out to administer sectors on nearby planets."

"Couldn't even stay on Capitol?"

"She insisted."

"But then—then she does rule!"

"Like hell she does."

The minister of colonization was next to last. He was new in his job, and frightened to death. He, at least, had believed in Nab's warnings.

"Good morning," he said.

"Who are you trying to impress? One thing I hate is cheerful morning greetings. Sit down. Give me your report."

His hand was trembling when he gave her the report. She read it, quickly but thoroughly, and turned to him with an eyebrow raised. "Who thought of this cockamamy scheme?"

"Well—" he began.

"Well? What's well?"

"It's a continuing program."

"Continuing?"

"I thought you knew about this from prior reports."

"I *do* know about it. A unique way of handling war. Outcolonize the bastards. Great plan. It hasn't shown up on any reports until now, fool! Now, who thought of it!"

"I really don't know," he said miserably'

She laughed. "What a prize you are. A cabinet full of ninnies, and you are the worst. Who told *you* about the program?"

He looked uncomfortable. "The assistant minister of colonization, Mother."

"Name?"

"Doon. Abner Doon."

"Get out of here and tell the chancellor I want to meet this Abner Doon."

The minister of colonization got up and left.

Mother stayed in her chair, looking gloomily at the walls. Things were slipping out of her control. She could feel it. Last waking there had been little hints. A touch of smugness. This time they had tried to lie to her several times.

They needed shaking up. I'll shake them up, she decided. And if it's necessary, I'll stay awake two days. Or even a week. The thought was exhilarating. To stay awake for days at a time— the prospect was exciting.

"Bring me a girl," she said. "A girl about sixteen. I need to talk to someone who will understand."

"Your cue, Hannah," Dent said. Hannah looked nervous. "Don't worry, kid. She's not a pervert or anything. She just wants to talk. Just remember, like Nab said, don't lie. Don't lie about anything."

"Hurry up. She's waiting," Nab interrupted.

The girl left the control room and passed through the hall to the door. She knocked softly.

"Come in," Mother said gently. "Come in."

The girl was lovely, her hair red and sweet and long, her manner confused and shy.

"Come here, girl. What's your name?"

"Hannah."

And they began to converse. A strange conversation, to Hannah, who knew only the gossip of the younger members of upper-crust Capitol society. The middle-aged woman kept insisting on reminiscing, and Hannah didn't know what to say. Soon, however, she realized that there was no need to say much at all. She had only to listen and occasionally express interest.

And after a while the interest did not have to be feigned. Mother was a relic of an earlier time, a strange time when there were trees on Capitol and the planet was named Crove.

"Are you a virgin?" asked Mother.

Don't lie, Hannah remembered. "No."

"Whom did you give it up to?"

What does it matter? She doesn't know him. "An artist. His name is Fritz."

"Is he good?"

"Everything he does is beautiful. His pieces sell for—"

"I meant in bed."

Hannah blushed. "It was just the once. I wasn't very good. He was kind."

"Kind!" Mother snorted. "Kind. Who asks a man to be kind?"

"I do," Hannah said defiantly.

"A man who is kind is in control of himself, my dear. You wasted a golden opportunity. I gave my virginity to Selvock. Ancient history to you, girl, but it wasn't all that long ago to me. I was a calculating little bitch even then. I knew that who-ever I gave it to would be in my debt. And when I saw Selvock

Gray I knew immediately that he was the man I wanted to have owe me.

"I took him out riding horses. You don't know horses, there aren't any on Capitol anymore, more's the pity. After a few kilometers I made him take off the saddles so we could ride bareback. And after a few kilometers more I made him take off his clothes and I took off mine. There's nothing like riding a horse bareback, in the nude. And then—I can't believe I did this—I forced my horse to trot. Men don't enjoy trotting even when they have stirrups, but without stirrups and without clothes, the trotting was agony for dear Selvock. Damn near castrated the poor man. But he was too proud to say anything. Just gripped the horse, turning white with every jolt. And finally I gave in and let the horse run full out.

"Like flying. And every movement of the horse's muscles under your crotch is like a lover. When we stopped we were covered with horsesweat but he was so aroused he couldn't stand it and he took me in the gravel on the edge of a cliff. There were cliffs on Crove then. I wasn't very good, being a novice, but I knew what I was doing. I'd got him so hot he didn't notice I wasn't helping him much. And I bled all over the place. Very impressive. He was incredibly gentle with me. Led the horses so I could ride sideways, and we found our clothes and made love again before we went home. He never left me. Found plenty of women, of course, but he always came back to me."

It was an incredible world, to Hannah, where one could mount an animal and ride for kilometers without *meeting* anyone, and have sex on a *cliff*.

"Didn't the gravel hurt? Isn't gravel little rocks?"

"Hurt like hell. I was picking stones out of my back for days." Mother laughed. "You gave yourself too easily. You could have held out for more."

Hannah looked wistful. "There aren't any conquerors available these days."

"Don't fool yourself, girl. Hannah, I mean. There are more conquerors than you know."

And they talked for another hour, and then Mother remembered there was work to do, and sent the girl away.

* * *

"Good job, Hannah. Like a trouper."

"It wasn't bad," the girl said. "I like her."

"She's a nice old lady." Dent laughed.

"She is," Hannah said defensively.

Nab looked her in the eye. "She's personally murdered more than a score of men. And arranged for the deaths of hundreds of others. Not counting wars."

Hannah looked angry. "Then they deserved to die!"

Nab smiled. "She still weaves the old webs, doesn't she? She caught you well. It doesn't matter. You're on somec now, three years early. Enjoy yourself. Only one woman in every five years gets to meet Mother. And you can't tell anyone about it."

"I know," she said. And then, inexplicably, she cried. Perhaps because she had come to love Mother in that hour of conversation. Or perhaps because there were no horses for her to ride, and her first time had been in her parents' bedroom when they were away for an evening. Stolen, not freely taken in sunlight on a cliff. She wondered what it was like to be at a cliff. She imagined standing on one, looking down. But it was so far below her. Meters and meters down. In her imagination she shied away. Cliffs were for ancient times.

"So you are Abner Doon."

He nodded. His hand did not tremble. He merely looked at her steadily. His eyes looked deep. She was a little disturbed. She was not used to being looked at so easily. She could almost imagine that his gaze was friendly.

"I understand you thought of the clever plan to colonize planets behind the enemy's holdings."

Abner smiled. "It seemed more productive than wiping out the human race."

"A war fought by outbuilding the enemy. I must say, the idea is novel." She leaned her head against her hand, wondering why she didn't want to go to the attack with this man. Perhaps because she liked him. But she knew herself better than that, knew that she hadn't attacked because she wasn't yet sure where his weakness was. "Tell me, Abner, how extensive the enemy's holdings are."

"About a third of the settled planets," Doon answered.

* * *

Dent was startled, then furious. "He told her! He just told her! The chancellor's going to have his head."

Nab only smiled. "No one's going to have his head. I don't know how he figured it out, but he and that girl, Hannah—they both understand the bitch. The rule is be accurate, even when you lie."

"He's undoing everything!"

"No, Dent. The other ministers undid themselves. Why should he shoot himself down along with them? The shrimp is smarter than I thought."

She kept Doon with her for fifteen minutes—unheard of, when full ministers rarely got an audience of longer than ten. And the chancellor was outside cooling his heels.

"Mr. Doon, how can you bear being so incredibly short?"

Doon was finally taken by surprise, and she felt a small sense of victory.

"Short?" he asked. "Yes, I suppose I am. Well, it isn't anything I have control over. So I don't think about it."

"What do you have control over?"

"The assignments section of the ministry of colonization," he answered.

She laughed. "That isn't a complete list, is it, Mr. Doon?"

He cocked his head. "Do you really want an answer to that?"

"Oh, yes, Mr. Doon, I do."

"But I won't give an answer, Mother. Not here."

"Why not?"

"Because there are two men in the control room listening to everything we say and recording everything we do. I'll talk freely to you when there isn't an audience."

"I'll command them to stop listening."

Doon smiled.

"Oh. I see. I may reign, but I don't always rule, is that what you're saying? Well, we'll see about that. Lead me to the control room."

Doon got up, and she followed him out of the room.

* * *

"Nab! Nab, he's bringing her here! What do we do?"

"Just act natural, Dent. Try not to throw up on the looper."

The door to the control room opened, and Doon ushered Mother into the room. "Good afternoon, gentlemen," she said.

"Good afternoon, Mother. I'm Nab, and this petrified mass of terror is my assistant, Dent."

"So you're the ones who listen in and answer my every request."

"As much as possible, of course." Nab was the image of confidence.

"Monitors. Television! How quaint!"

"It was decided hololoops wouldn't be appropriate."

"Bullshit, Nab," Mother said sweetly. "This is a looper right here."

"Just for the historical record. No one ever watches it."

"I'm glad to know how closely I'm observed. I'll be more careful how I arrange my body in the morning." She turned to Doon. "Is there anywhere that we can meet where the birds won't be watching from the trees?"

"Actually," Doon answered, "I have the only place on Crove where the birds do watch from the trees."

She looked shocked. "Real ones?"

"Complete with droppings. You have to watch where you step."

Her voice was husky with eagerness. "Lead me! Take me there!" And she whirled on Nab and Dent. "And you two. I want this looper out of here. You can listen and you can watch, but there is to be no permanent record. Do you understand?"

Nab agreed pleasantly. "It'll be done before you return."

She sneered at him. "You have no intention of doing it, Nab. Do you think I'm a fool?" And she went out the other door, which Doon was holding open.

When the door swung shut, Dent gagged and retched into a wastebasket. Nab watched unconcernedly. "You haven't learned anything, have you, Dent? She's nothing to be afraid of."

Dent only shook his head and wiped his lips. Stomach acid burned in his sinuses and throat.

"Go get the technicians. We have to hook the looper up somewhere else. And have some phony spots ripped out of the wall, so that workmen will be repairing when they get in. It has to look like the lasers have been removed. Hurry it up, boy!''

Dent stopped at the door. ''What are they going to do to this Doon?''

''Nothing. Mother likes him. We'll simply use him to keep her happy later on. The man's a nonentity.''

Mother could sense Doon's increasing pleasure as they went (under heavy guard) through corridors that had been cleared before them, until finally they were at a door where Doon told the Little Boys to go wait elsewhere.

''This had better be good, Doon,'' Mother said, knowing from the way he acted that it would be good.

''It'll be worth the walk. Though you used to walk much farther than this in your childhood,'' he said.

''Kilometers and kilometers,'' she said. ''What a wonderful word. It even sounds like going up hills and down them again. A traveling word. Kilometers. Show me this place where the birds sing from the trees.''

And Doon opened the door.

She walked in briskly, then slowed, then stopped. And after a moment she began walking briskly among the trees, pausing only to strip off her shoes and dig her bare toes into the grass and the dirt. A bird fluttered past her. A breeze spun her hair out like a fan. She laughed.

Laughing, she leaned against a tree, put her hands on the bark, slid down the tree, sat in the grass. The sun shone brightly above her.

''How did you do it? How did you hold this spot of earth? When I last touched ground like this, I was twenty, and it was one of the few parks left on Capitol!''

''It isn't real,'' Doon answered. ''The trees and birds and grass are real enough, of course, but the sky is a dome and the sun is artificial. It can tan you, though.''

''I always freckled. But I said, 'Damn the freckles, I worship the sun!' ''

''I know,'' Doon said. ''I tell everyone that this place is modeled after Garden, a planet where they restrict immigration and industry is kept to a minimum. But you know what this place really is.''

"Crove," she said. "My grandfather's world! What this planet used to be before it was sheathed in metal like a vast chastity belt, blocking life from this place forever; oh, Doon, whatever it is you want, you can have, only let me come and spend an afternoon here on every waking!''

"I'll be glad to have you come. Only you know what it means.''

"But you want something from me, anyway," she said.

He smiled. "Want to swim?"

"You have water?"

"A lake. Crystal clear water. A bit chilly, though."

"Where!"

He led her to the water, and she unhesitatingly took off her clothes and dove in. Doon met her in the middle of the lake, where she floated on her back, looking upward as a cloud passed before the sun.

"I must have died," she said. "This must be heaven."

"You're a believer?" Doon asked.

"Only in myself. We make our own heavens. And I see, Doon, that you have created a good one. Well, Doon, you're the first man I've talked to today who wasn't an utter ass.''

"I do not aspire to surpass my superiors."

She chuckled, fanning her hands to propel herself gently in the water. Doon too lay on his back in the water, and they heard each other's words through the rushing sound of water in their ears.

"Now the complete list, Mr. Doon," she said.

"As I told you," he said. "Part of the ministry of colonization.''

"And?"

"The rest of the ministry. And the rest of the ministries."

"All of them?" she asked.

"Through one means or another. No one knows it, however. I just own the people who own the people who run it. I don't bother much with the everyday affairs.''

"Good of you. Let them think they're independent. And?"

"And?"

"The rest of the list?"

"That's the list. All the ministries. And the ministries control everything else."

"Not everything. Not somec," she said.

"Oh, yes. The independent, untouchable agency. Only Mother can make the rules for the Sleeproom."

"But you control that, too, don't you?"

"Actually, I had to take it over first. That let me control who woke up when. Very useful. It lets me get rid of people I don't want. I just put them on a lower level of somec, if they're weak, and they die out very soon. Or I put them on a higher level of somec, if they're strong, and they aren't around often enough to bother me."

"You rule my empire, then?"

"I do," Doon answered.

"Have you brought me here to kill me?"

Doon swung over and treaded water, looking at her in alarm. "You don't believe that, do you?" he asked. "I'd never do that, Mother, never. I've admired you too much. I've modeled my life on yours. The way you controlled the empire from the start, and everyone thought it was your husband, Selvock, the poor stud."

"He wasn't much of a stud," Mother mused. "He never fathered a child on anyone."

"No, Mother. You're the only person in the world, though, who could stop me. And I knew that sooner or later you'd realize who I was and what I was doing. I've looked forward to this meeting."

"Really? I haven't."

"No?" Doon broke into a crawl stroke and made his way to shore. Not long afterward, Mother followed, to find him lying on the grass.

"You're right," she said. "I have looked forward to meeting you. The thief who would take it all away from me."

"Not at all," Doon said. "Not a thief. Just your heir."

"I plan to live forever," she said.

"And if I have my way, you shall."

"But you don't want just to own my empire, Doon. You don't want to just inherit."

"Consider this a springboard. If you hadn't built this empire, I should have had to. But since it's built, I shall tear it up and use the building blocks to make something better."

"Better than this?" she asked.

"Can't you smell the decay? Nothing is alive on this planet. Not the people. Not the atmosphere, not the rock, nothing, it's all dead, all going nowhere. The whole Empire's like that. I'm going to kick it into gear again."

"Kick it into gear!" she giggled. "That was archaic when I was a girl!"

"I study old things," Doon answered. "Old things are the only things that are new anymore. You were great. You built a beautiful thing."

She was happy. The sun was beating down on her for the first time in decades (centuries, actually, but since she hadn't lived the years, she didn't feel them); she had swum in fresh water; and she had met a man who just might be, just might perhaps be her equal.

"What do you want me to do? Make you chancellor? Marry you?"

Doon said no, none of those things. "Just let me go on. Don't challenge me. Don't force my hand. I need a few more centuries. And then it'll all break loose."

"I could still stop you," she said.

"I know it," he answered. "But I'm asking you not to. Nobody was in a position to stop you. I'm asking for my chance."

"You'll have your chance. In return for one favor."

"And that is?"

"When you make your move and everything, as you put it, breaks loose—take me with you."

"Do you mean it?"

"There'll be no use for Mother in the universe you're making, Abner."

"But there'll be room for Rachel Crove?"

The name struck her like a hammer. No one had called her by her given name since—since—

And she was a girl again, and a man who was her equal, or nearly so, lay naked beside her, and she reached over and put her arms around him, whispering, "Take me with you. Take me."

He did.

They lay in the grass as the sun set, and she felt more fulfilled than she had since a day on a cliff in Crove when she had begun her career of conquests. Only this time she had been conquered, and she knew it, and she was willing.

"On every waking," she said, "you must tell me your plans. You must show me what you're building, and let me watch."

"I will," he said. "But you can't make any suggestions."

"I wouldn't dream of it. That would be cheating, wouldn't it?"

"You aren't very good at sex," Doon said.

"Neither are you," she answered, laughing. "Who gives a damn?"

Mother did not come back until half an hour before her grand entrance at the Mother's Waking Party, the highest high society event in Capitol. Nab was distraught.

"Mother, Mother, what a worry you've caused us!"

She only looked at him slantwise, and frowned. "I was in good company. Were you?"

Nab glanced at Dent. "Only second-rate, I'm afraid."

Dent laughed nervously.

Mother growled at him. "Can't you even get a little angry, boy? It's so damned boring when everybody tries to be nice. Well, the party's already under way, right? So what am I wearing this time?"

They brought her the dress, and seven women wrapped her in it. She was startled that her nipples showed. "This is really the fashion?"

Nab shook his head. "It's a bit more modest than most. But I thought that perhaps the image you need to present—"

"Modest? Me?" She laughed and laughed. "Oh, this is the best waking in years. Best in years, Nab. You can stay on, but fire the boy. Find an assistant with more gumption. The boy's an ass. And send the chancellor to me."

The chancellor came in, bowing and uttering apologies about the poor status of the reports this waking.

"Everybody's trying to lie to me," she said. "Fire them all. Except, of course, for the minister of colonization. And his assistant. The two of them impressed me. Leave them in. And as for you, I don't want to have another lie in a report again. Understand? Or if you must lie, at least contrive to do it well. None of these could have fooled a five-year-old child."

"I'll never lie to you, Mother."

"I know perfectly well that I'm Empress in name only, boy, so don't patronize me. You'd just better make sure that I don't get reminded of it by the sloppy work the cabinet does. Understand?"

"I understand."

"And that assistant minister of colonization. He was refreshing. I want him awake and ready to meet with me again next waking. And leave him in his job. Doubtless a sinecure, but he's sweet."

The chancellor nodded.

"Now give me your arm. To hell with the schedule. We're going down to the party."

Nab watched her go.

"Am I really fired?" Dent asked.

"Yes, boy. I warned you. Act natural. Too bad. You showed some promise."

"But what'll I do?"

Nab shrugged. "They always have good jobs for the people Mother fires. You don't have to worry."

"I want to kill her."

"Why? She did you a favor. Now you won't have to watch her act important every waking. The bitch. Wish she'd sleep for ten years."

Dent was surprised. "You really hate her, don't you?"

"Hate her? I suppose so." And Nab turned away. "Get on out, Dent. If she sees you here again, she'll fire me, too."

Dent left, and Nab went to the files and chose the next poor fool who would make a stab at satisfying Mother. He had to have an assistant. The assistant's stupidity always made Nab look better.

Do I hate her, Nab wondered.

He couldn't decide. He only remembered watching her in the morning, as she lay nude on the bed. It wasn't hate he felt then.

The party was long and boring, as all the others had been, but Mother knew the importance of being visible. She had to be seen at every waking, on a set day, or someone could make her disappear and no one would notice. So she circulated, and graciously met the young girls who were just getting to somec, and the fops and fags who hung about the court, and the old men and women who had first met her a few centuries ago when they were young.

She was a reproach to them all. No matter how high a somec level they achieved, she was higher. No matter how many centuries passed before they got old, they would never live to see her get older. I will live forever, she reminded herself.

But as she watched the people who actually believed this party was important, the thought of living forever made her very tired.

"I'm tired," she said to the chancellor, and he immediately waved a signal to someone and the orchestra struck up some stirring music from aeons ago (this was old when I was a child, she thought) and the guests lined up and for an hour she bade good-bye to all of them and finally they were gone.

"It's over," she sighed. "Thank heaven." And then she went upstairs to the room where workmen had obviously been knocking up the walls. Pretending to take the hololoop equipment out, she decided, and was amused that they thought she could be so easily fooled. That fellow Nab—a sharp one. A total bastard, too. The best kind of person to deal with. He'd be around for quite a while.

She sat on the edge of her bed and brushed her hair, not because it needed it but because she was in the mood for it. It felt good. She watched herself in the large mirror, and noticed proudly that she didn't yet sag. That she was still, though not young, desirable. I'm a match for Doon, she said to herself. I'm still a match for any man, and more than a match for most. I've played their games and won them, and if I'm just a figurehead now, I'm a figurehead they have to be careful with. And Doon—an ally. He was with her. She could trust him.

Or could she?

She lay back on the bed, looking up at the ceiling, where a fresco had been painted, duplicating an ancient one that had long since fallen to pieces on Earth. A nude man was reaching up to touch the finger of God. She knew it was God, because he was the most terrible creature on the ceiling, and that had to be God. I was that, she thought. I was the builder, I was touching fingers and bringing things to life. And now Doon is doing that. Can there be room for two of us?

I'll make room, she decided. He'll never feel threatened by me. Because he might win, and that would be terrible, and it would be more terrible if I won, because I'm lazy and finished and he's just starting. Let us be allies, then, and I'll trust him and he'll trust me, and I can see something new in the universe. A creation that, perhaps, will be better than mine.

"Was that what *you* hoped for?" she asked the bearded man on the ceiling. "Someone to top you? Or did you snick them all down to size whenever they got too big?" She remembered a story about people who built a tower to get to the stars. God stopped it, as she recalled. Well, we finally got to the stars anyway, but you had moved out by then, making space for us.

I'll move out, making space for Doon. But he'd damn well better not forget me.

"The bitch is asleep, Crayn. Call the Sleeproom people."

The new assistant, a nervous girl who would never last, Nab knew, called the Sleeproom people and they moved quickly but silently into the room, taping Mother's brain and then putting her under somec. When Mother was under, Nab came out into the room.

"Give me the tape," he said, and they gave it to him because he always sealed it away in a special vault. And then they wheeled her out to put her in her coffin in a private Sleeproom in a different part of Capitol from most others. With the tightest security.

But Nab still held her mind in his hands. She had slept with Doon, he knew. What the shrimp had, he didn't know, but she had slept with him, had liked him a lot, had asked to see him next time. And he had her tape. There was nothing to stop him from accidentally destroying it, was there? And then she'd wake up not knowing anything about this waking. They'd have to use the old tape, the one they had used this time.

It shouldn't be hard to erase, he thought, and he took the tape into the control room. "Go home, Crayn," he said. "I'll close up."

"What a day," Crayn said as she left.

The door closed, and Nab found the loop eraser. It would work just as well on a braintape. He would have done it, too, if a needle hadn't fired just then and killed him.

Mother's Little Boys took the body out and disposed of it, and Mother's braintape was put into safekeeping by those who would never harm it. A close one. But how had Abner Doon known Nab would do that? The man was an octopus, a finger everywhere. But that was why Mother's Little Boys obeyed him. He was never wrong.

Mother had not been asleep when the braintapers came. But she lay there limply, accepting their ministrations.

Today I met my successor and the first man I let make love to me besides Selvock. Today I fired most of the cabinet because they were fools and cheats. Today I stepped back into Crove the way it used to be when it was still beautiful.

Today passed with more variety than yesterday, or three weeks ago, or eight months ago.

Eight months ago. It was only eight months, only a thousand years ago that she had decided to go on somec at this level and live forever. She had noticed her first age wrinkle that day, and realized that she could, after all, get old. So she had decided to skim through time, only touching often enough to see if there was something worth living to experience.

Today she had found it.

And what, she wondered, will we do tomorrow?

Tales
from the
Forest of Waters

To Peggy Card,
who believed in these stories
even before they were true

During Jason Worthing's centuries of sleep, his children lived—and transformed themselves—on an obscure farm deep in the Forest of Waters. Some of their stories are told in *The Worthing Chronicle*—but only briefly, as they were remembered by later generations. Here are the tales in full.

19
Worthing Farm

Elijah stood in the dust of Worthing Farm and wiped his hand across the sweat on his face. The dirt on his hand turned to wet clay, but in a moment it was dry again, dust again, and the sweat left on his face was the only moisture in the field. Elijah picked up the empty buckets and walked on to the river.

It was a dark world, and the West River flowed from the heart of it through its blackest soil and deepest forest. Once at the east end of the river, and once at the west, cities burst through the ceiling of trees, and here and there the forest was interrupted by a small clearing and a house and a stand of grain. In distant lands cities had stood for centuries, nations had endured and grown and learned to be civilized, but none of this had touched the Forest of Waters. From the Heaven Mountains south to the Stipock Sea the wood was master, and the people who lived there were constant and desperate rebels against its sovereignty.

In recent years as the two cities of Hux and Linkeree arose, it appeared that at last the forest's rule would be thrown off. But the dark heart of the world seemed to realize that this was its fight to the death, its last battle, and that to survive and to rule, the forest would have to free itself of men.

It had only one weapon with which to fight. No snow fell during the winter, and all through the spring no rain came to the Forest of Waters. The roots of the trees burrowed deep and found last year's water. Grain threw roots down fast and far, but not fast and far enough, and they clung to dust.

The river was lower than it had ever been before, and it ran slow and thick and brown, twenty feet out from the old shoreline. Elijah dipped in the buckets and carried them sloshing back to Worthing Farm. When he came to the field again he stopped. The stalks of grain were still short, and they had turned brown in the sun. Faint traces of green still streaked the leaves.

Elijah reached his hand into the bucket and let water dribble from his fingers to the roots of a few plants. The drops of water immediately were glazed with dust and skittered across the surface, then slowed, then stopped and vanished without a trace. Elijah had long since given up trying to water his crops from the river. A hundred men couldn't carry enough water to bring life back to this field. The water was for Alana and John and little Worin. And for Elijah. To boil over the fire for a few minutes, then to drink as soup or tea or stew when Alana found good roots in the forest and Elijah killed a hare. From the farm they had nothing.

But this was Worthing Farm, and Elijah belonged to it.

"This Worthing Farm," his old grannam had said over and over until the ritual inhabited his dreams, "is the most important place in the world. It was for this piece of land that Jason brought the Ice People to life. It is our glory and power that we are the keepers of Worthing Farm. If you leave it, the world will die to no purpose, and you will die the deep death that no one wakes from." Grannam said it and stared down at Elijah with her blue eyes, the pure bright blue that stared without breaking. Elijah stared back with eyes just as blue, and he didn't break, either.

He never broke. Not during the winter when the fields stayed frozen and brown with no snow, and Alana began to murmur that the corn would never sprout. Not in the springtime when the ground was plowed and black but the rains didn't come to wet the soil. They had tried for a while to bring water from the

river. Weeks of ten trips back and forth every day, gently drib-
bling the water down the rows: at last the young green shoots
struggled to the surface. But no one noticed for two days as
Elijah and the boys nursed Alana back to health. Elijah had
come out the morning that Alana's fever broke and looked at his
field with the thin layer of green over the soil and knew that he
would have to let it die. They couldn't carry a rainstorm on their
backs, not forever.

Elijah picked up the full buckets and walked on through the
field. The plants crunched loudly when he stepped on them.
Where he had walked the dust rose three feet into the air in a
thick cloud that didn't dissipate for half an hour—just slowly
settled on the windless air.

When he got the buckets home there was a slime of dust
floating on the top. He pulled it off with a spoon and poured the
water into a large pot. Then he set it on the fire to boil.

"Can I drink some?" Worin asked. The four-year-old had
wet his pants, and dust clung thickly where it had dried. "I'm
thirsty."

Elijah didn't answer, just began to cut up chunks of rabbit
into the pot.

"I'm really thirsty."

The water isn't clean, Elijah thought. Go away until it's boiled.
But he said nothing, and Worin heard nothing and went away
outside to play. Elijah sighed. The sigh was echoed from a few
steps away at the other end of the room. He looked up into
Alana's eyes.

She was old. The fever had wrinkled her and greyed some of
her hair, and she always looked pale and faded now. Her hair
was snarled and her eyes waited heavy-lidded for some kind of
expression to come. None came. She just looked at Elijah with
heavy eyes. He looked back, refusing to break the trance. At
last Alana looked away, defeated, and Elijah was free to answer
her. "Never while I'm alive," he said.

She nodded, breathed heavily again, and sat on a stool to cut
up the roots she had gathered the day before. Her back was bent.
Elijah saw in his mind the woman she had been only six months
before, sharp tongued and violent at times, to be sure, but now
Elijah wished she would raise her hand and slap him just to show

she was alive. But she wasn't alive. Her blood had gone out with her sweat to water a field whose thirst could never be satisfied. She was as shriveled as last year's fruit. Elijah did not know why he loved her so much more and so tenderly now that her beauty was gone. He reached out and gently ran his hand down her back.

She shuddered slightly.

He took back his hand and picked up another haunch to cut into the pot. Outside the boys were quarreling loudly.

Silently he discoursed with Alana, and Alana listened but did not hear. I can't leave Worthing Farm, he said to her silently, I am owned, there is a stone at the southwest corner that swears I can never leave. You knew when you married me, he said. But he could hear her answer, though she didn't even think it: If you love me, let me live.

Elijah got up and went outside to where his sons were fighting. Five-year-old John had Worin on the ground, viciously forcing the younger boy's mouth into the dust.

"Drink it!" John yelled. "Lick it up!"

Elijah was filled with rage. Silently he strode to the cloud of dust where the boys wriggled. He reached down and picked John up by the trousers and lifted him high in the air. The boy shrieked, and Worin, unhurt, immediately leapt to his feet and started to yell.

"Hit him, Father! Hit him!"

And because the younger boy cried for it Elijah couldn't hit John, and so set him down to snivel in the dust. He looked at the two of them, John still whimpering in fear, Worin, his face covered with dust, jumping up and down taunting his brother. Elijah reached down and cuffed them both.

"You'll shut up now, both of you, and keep your hands to yourself, or by damn you'll both eat dust till you drown in it."

John and Worin fell silent, and watched him as he went back to the door of the house.

Elijah stopped at the door, not wanting to go in, not caring to stay out. The door was unpainted, weathered grey, and splintering. One of the boards was much newer than the others. Grannam's husband had put them there, Grannam used to tell him, before Elijah was old enough to find his way to the latrine. Elijah didn't remember. But he stepped back and looked at the house. It was old. Only two rooms and a few sheds built on, the roof rethatched in cornhusks and shocks a hundred times, a thousand times. Probably not a board in the house that was there when it was first built, Grannam said.

"Who builded it?" Elijah had asked her when he was young.

"Who?" she repeated, laughing. "Who makes the stars shine? Who makes the sun spin round and round us every day? Jason, boy, Jason builded this house when the world was brand-new and the forest trees were still little things that you could see over, clear to Mount Waters without climbing on the roof."

It was Jason's hand that held Elijah to Worthing Farm. Elijah tried to picture Jason in his mind. Grannam had said that Jason had the eyes. Clear blue just like hers and Elijah's. Elijah pictured him as huge and strong, with white hair and brown skin and hands that could break a tree and rip it down the middle to make boards. And in childhood nightmares that still sometimes came back to him in the shadows, he pictured Jason's hands gripping his shoulders, gripping deep, piercing him, and shaking him as a great voice said, "This dirt is your heart. If you leave it you will die."

But the hands weren't Jason's hands, and the voice was Grannam's husky whisper the day that Elijah tried to run away. He had quarreled with his brother, Big Peter, and at the age of ten he felt he was old enough not to have to bow to his brother's tyranny. So he did what he never had done. When he had run to the edge of the field, he boldly stepped out into the brush, and soon was lost among the trees.

There were paths in the wood. Some were made by the deer, some by the travelers going afoot between the far cities of Hux and Linkeree. Some were not paths at all, just openings in the brush that led to tangles and briars and fast-running brooks. Finally, when at dusk the sun cast no shadows within the wood, he fell exhausted and slept.

He was wakened by fierce hands gripping his shoulders. Startled, he whirled, and looked into Grannam's face. Her skin was scratched from fighting through the brambles, and her blue eyes burnt fiercely.

He felt fear rise within him and he got up and went with her.

She hurried, far too fast for the darkness and the difficulty of the path, but she found her way easily and ignored the branches that tore at their faces. Finally the forest broke open and they stood at the edge of Worthing Farm.

They walked along the edge of the farm to the southwest corner, and there she pointed to a stone in the briars. It had been cut into, deeply, though neither Grannam nor Elijah understood the writing. But there Grannam dug her hands into Elijah's shoulders and forced him to his knees, and then said, "This is the living stone that Jason left! It speaks to us. It says, never leave Worthing Farm or you will die the deep death. This dirt is your heart. If you leave it you will die." She said it over and over until Elijah was sobbing violently, and repeated it more, until Elijah was quiet and looked steadily into her eyes and repeated it with her. Then finally she fell silent, and he was also silent, and with their blue eyes locked she said, "Your eyes, Elijah, make you Jason's heir. Not Big Peter, not your father, not your mother. You, just like me, Elijah, you have the gift."

"What gift?" Elijah had quietly asked.

"It's never the same."

Elijah had wondered after that what Grannam's gift had been, but she had taken sick and died soon after, and he never knew. He wondered if it had to do with the way she unerringly found her way through the forest that night. Or perhaps it was the way she could hear the stone speaking and Elijah never could. But she died, and ten years later both his parents. He had only left Worthing Farm once in all that time, when he walked to the nearest farm and took Alana in marriage. Since then he had never come to the boundary of Worthing Farm and thought to cross it.

He didn't know how much he hated Worthing Farm. He thought he loved it.

He remembered all of this as he stood staring at the door. His sons were still watching him, puzzled at his silence. He didn't stir until the door opened and Alana stepped out. Their eyes met, and slowly Elijah realized that she had packed a bundle to carry with her. Defiantly she stepped past him to the boys.

"Come on, boys. We're going."

Elijah caught her arm before she could take a step.

"Going?"

"Out of here. You've lost your mind."

"You're not going."

"We're going, Elijah, and you're not stopping us! We're going to Big Peter's inn where my children can live and I can live, and you can stay on Worthing Farm and rot with the plants—"

He realized as the blood crept down from her lip that he had hit her. She lay on the ground, and tears came from her eyes. I'm sorry, he said silently. She didn't hear him. She never did.

Alana got up slowly, picked up her bundle, and took Worin's hand. "Come, Worin, John, we're leaving."

They started to walk across the field. Elijah followed, took her by the arm. She pulled away. He seized her shoulders, and as she struggled he got a firm grip on her waist and half carried, half dragged her back to the house. Soundlessly she struggled, elbows and hands flailing, connecting more often than not. He got her to the door, his anger turned to fury by the pain of her blows, and he threw her against it. She struck so violently that the door snapped open, and she fell inside.

Elijah stepped over her as she lay whimpering with pain in the doorway. Holding her under the arms, he dragged her in. As soon as he let go, she stood up and headed for the door. He threw her to the ground. She got up and walked to the door. He hit her and she fell to the ground again. On her knees she crawled to the door, and he thrust her back with his foot. Silent except for her heavy breathing, she pulled herself wearily to her feet, and started to walk toward the door. Elijah screamed at her then, and beat her again and again until she lay bleeding on the floor and Elijah, exhausted, knelt over her, sobbing in shame and pain and love for her. Softly he spoke, out loud this time, but she didn't hear, though her breath still came in short, hard gasps, "We can't leave. Worthing Farm is us, and if it dies, we die," he said, and then hated the words and himself and the farm and the forest and the air that would never weep until all his tears had been shed. He turned from his wife and looked out the door.

In the doorway his two sons stood watching. Their eyes wide, and as he walked toward the door they shied away, and as he reached the door they ran. They stopped twenty paces off and watched him. Stop watching me, he thought, but they didn't hear him. He walked to the south shed and stood on a cask to clamber to the low roof. He crawled along the thatch until he reached the roof of the house. Finally he stood on the heavy wooden beam that ran above the thatch along the top of the house, and he looked out over his farm.

The corn was the same color as the dust, yellowish white, and the fields seemed to be water, with billows stopped for a moment in mid-motion. In the far-off southwest corner Elijah saw a large stone. He turned away and looked out over the forest.

The trees were not unscathed by the drought. Some of them were dead, others greyed and dying, but most were still green, and the heavy green of the foliage mocked the death of Worthing Farm. Elijah cursed the forest in his mind. The Forest of Waters, it was called. Not for the many streams and rivers that ran through it. Rather for Mount Waters, the highest mountain in the world, which rose alone out of the middle of the forest, far from any other mountain. Even though no snow had fallen that winter, Mount Waters was still capped with snow from the year before, and if no snow ever fell again, Mount Waters would still hold water locked in its ice.

Elijah glanced a little to the south of Mount Waters and there, a few miles away from Worthing Farm, something rising above the level of the forest caught his eye. It was a tower, made of bright new wood, and on its roof Elijah could make out figures moving, thatching it. It was his brother Big Peter's new inn; the drought wouldn't hurt his brother, Elijah thought; his brother who had left the farm was prospering while he, Elijah, who had stayed, was losing his crops and his family.

Elijah hated his brother Big Peter, who was not hurt by the drought, and the trees of the Forest of Waters, which were not hurt by the drought, and Mount Waters, whose snow didn't melt in the drought, and then he looked down at his farm and hated the dust that rose above the corpses of the corn plants, and hated the boundary of the farm that locked him and his family into this place of death, and hated most of all the stone in the southwest corner that had spoken to Grannam and that now spoke to him, though he heard nothing, saying that if he left he would die and the world would die and that all Jason's work would be undone. And he hated Jason and wished that all his work would be undone.

Then he looked again at Mount Waters and in the fury of his hatred he imagined a white cloud rising from the snow of the mountain, stealing the water hidden there in plain sight to taunt him. He imagined the cloud, and wished for the cloud, and demanded the cloud, and for the first time in all the silent speeches of his life Elijah was heard. For a moment he did not recognize the white streak that emerged from the snow on Mount Waters. But it was a cloud. It was his cloud.

Elijah imagined, wished for, demanded that the cloud grow. It grew. He demanded that it fill the horizon, that its belly turn black and heavy with rain. It did. Then he demanded that the cloud come to Worthing Farm, that the Forest of Waters be covered by the cloud.

Wind arose from the west, a hard wind that tore at Elijah's hair and clothes as he clung to his perch on the roof of the house. Dust was whipped up from the field into his eyes, so that he couldn't see. When at last he could see again the entire sky was covered with clouds in every direction. The clouds were black. It had taken five minutes.

Then, with hatred for the farm and the forest still raging in him, Elijah demanded that it rain. Thunder rolled from the sky, a great peal from horizon to horizon. A flash of lightning stabbed to the earth, then another. More thunder. Elijah called for lightning to strike the tower of his brother's inn. A blinding flash funneled from the cloud to the new tower, and it burst into flames. Then Elijah felt the first drops start to come.

The drops were huge and heavy, and at first they were instantly buried in the dust, so that though Elijah could see rain falling, the ground looked dry. But soon the drops began to spread on the surface, and the dust settled, and as Elijah watched John and Worin walk in the field with their mouths held open to the sky to catch raindrops, he noticed that no dust rose from their feet. The earth was settling, and soon it turned black.

He called to his sons, and told them to go in. Slowly they walked across the field to the house. As they did, the rain began to fall faster, the drops heavier, and water began to stand in the field in thin puddles. The falling drops splashed, large splashes that spread for five feet. The sound of the rain changed from pattering to a roar, and the forest seemed to recede fifty yards as it dimmed through the curtain of rain.

Elijah was soaked to the skin and his hair hung matted around his face, water dripping from every strand. His hands hurt as the great drops struck. He laughed.

It was hard but in spite of the wind and the wet thatch Elijah clambered off the roof, off the shed, and onto the ground. The dust had turned to thick mud, and it sucked at his feet as he walked. He stopped when he got well out into the field, and there he looked up into the clouds, the raindrops bruising his face as they fell hard and fast, and he cried out silently for the rain to come like knives to kill the Forest of Waters. The rain became a single thing, falling again and again hard as an axe on the wood. Leaves were ripped from the trees, and Elijah was knocked to the ground where he stood. The rain beat him, the mud sucked on him, and the heavy drops knocked him unconscious as he demanded that the rain go on.

The hands touched his face gently, but still quick stabs of pain followed every motion. He tried to open his eyes, and found they were already open and he was looking up into the eyes of his wife. Her hair was matted with sweat. She looked worried, and he remembered what had last passed between them. I'm sorry, he thought, but she didn't hear. So he opened his mouth and said, "Alana."

She answered with fingers on his lips. And she pursed her mouth and said, "Shh." He fell asleep.

He awoke again lying on his straw-stuffed bed in a corner of the house. Food was cooking in the kitchen. A stew, maybe the same one he had started. Sun was streaking the room as it came through cracks in the east wall. Morning. But yesterday—was it yesterday?—there had been no such cracks there.

His body was stiff and sore, but he was able to rise from the bed. He was naked when he cast off the blanket. He fumbled for his clothes. It hurt him to put them on. Still tying the front of his shirt, he walked stiffly into the kitchen.

His wife and sons sat in front of the fire, slurping stew out of wooden bowls. They watched him silently. Finally he nodded, and his wife dished some up for him. He stood and ate a little, then set down the half-full bowl and went outside. Eyes but no people followed him.

Worthing Farm was a sea of mud, with huge standing puddles everywhere. The trees at the edge were still dripping, and the thatched roof was sagging under the weight of the water it had absorbed. Not a single stalk of grain was standing. There was no sign that any of it had ever been there. Nothing but thick black mud.

There was nothing left to save on Worthing Farm. It was too late in the year to plow and plant again. He reached down and plunged his hand up to the forearm into the soft mud. Groping in it he found a stem or two, and pulled out his hand with a great sucking noise. He looked closely at the broken stalks in his fingers. Absentmindedly he broke the dead plants into pieces.

He got up. The house had been soaked, and the wood was shrinking quickly in the sun. The walls and the door would have to be replaced. Winter would kill them unless the house was tight. There was plenty of time to repair the house—if he didn't have to hunt for food. Plenty of time to hunt for food if he didn't have to repair the house. Not time enough to do both.

If they stayed, they would die. If they left, they would live but the curse would fall on Elijah. Somehow, looking at the ruin of his farm Elijah no longer feared anything the curse might bring. Death, perhaps. And he wondered why he should fear even that.

He walked back into the house, where his family was through eating. They looked up, their eyes following him as he emptied the cupboards in the kitchen into the large sacks that a few months ago had held grain. John and Worin got up and began to help. Alana put her face into her hands.

Elijah left the boys to load the sacks and went outside to the north shed, where a small wheeled cart was loaded with wood and bronze farm tools. He emptied the tools out of it, flinging them far across the field, and when the cart was empty he pulled it to the door. He went inside. When he came out his arms were full of two rolled-up straw beds. The next load was a stack of blankets. Then he brought out the sacks and the bundles of clothing and soon the cart was full. He took several ropes and tied the load on the cart.

Then he went in to Alana and took her by the hand. She looked at the ground as he led her out of the house. He still held her hand as he stepped into the cart harness and slowly began to pull the cart across the sea of mud.

In a few minutes the cart was bogged down. The boys got behind the wheels and pushed. They sank up to their hips in mud, but the cart moved. It became a game to the boys, sloshing through the slime and shoving the cart out of every mudhole it stuck in. They laughed as Elijah pulled silently. They laughed as they entered the forest and the ground firmed. They were still laughing as Worthing Farm dropped away out of sight behind them and they were surrounded by trees and thin pillars of sunlight streaming through the leaves.

They did not stop until the forest opened up again to a wide track with deep wheel ruts. Here the trees did not close above the top of the trail, and as they continued west and a little south the sun was directly in their eyes.

The sun was just setting in red light as they heard the sound of hammering and sawing up ahead. Human voices soon reached them, the great shouts of men working.

"Faster, dammit, you'll break your backs."

Elijah recognized the voice of his brother, Big Peter, and just then the forest cleared away for many acres and in the middle of the huge clearing stood the inn.

It was all made of new wood, and it rose three stories high off a heavy foundation of piles sunk into the earth. At the south end of the inn stood a tower rising another twenty feet or so off the top floor. It had windows all around it, and it stood higher than the highest of the trees. The roof of it had recently burned, and men standing in the tower were straining to pull up a load of wood from the ground. They held long ropes, and on the ground a giant of a man with flaming red hair bellowed up at them, "Pull it up! I've lifted heavier loads myself!" And to prove it he bent and lifted the stack of lumber alone. The men on the tower gave a great heave and the wood moved higher up, out of Big Peter's reach, and he shouted up, "That's the way, boys! Pull!"

Elijah, Alana, Worin, and John stood at the edge of the forest road. They had never seen such a building in their lives, and they didn't believe that it could stand. Yet the tall tower didn't even sway as the lumber slowly crept skyward at the end of the ropes. Suddenly a boy about eight years old with light blond hair pulled away from the crowd by the building and walked curiously toward the family at the edge of the clearing.

"Who are you!" he called out in a high, piping voice. Elijah and Alana didn't answer, but when the boy came close enough Worin spoke up. "I'm Worin. This is John."

The eight-year-old thrust out his hand and said, "I'm Little Peter. This is my father's inn."

Elijah only looked at him. The boy was attractive, looked like Elijah's brother. But his eyes were blue. Like Elijah's. Like Grannam's. He had the gift, and Elijah looked at the boy with hatred.

Then Big Peter took his eyes off his work and noticed them.

"Well come!" he cried, striding toward them on huge legs. "You're early but there's room for you at the inn, if you don't mind sleeping on the— Elijah!" He was already going fast, but when he recognized his brother he broke into a run. In a moment he arrived and embraced his passive brother and threw John and Worin into the air and caught them, laughing and saying, "Well come, I'm glad to see you, here's my inn, do you like it? Borrowed the money in Hux and the workmen in Linkeree and in a year I'll be a very rich man!"

Big Peter asked no questions and so Elijah said nothing as they walked to the inn, Big Peter pulling the cart with one arm and conversing as if it were no burden. "Trade goes downriver from Hux to Linkeree, and overland from Linkeree to Hux. Here we get them both. The road passes by here, and up that trail there I've builded a landing on the river where even the biggest riverboat can pull in and moor for the night. There are twenty and three rooms and a huge kitchen and a common room that cries out for ale and drinkers and loud songs, and more room to store food than you've ever seen. It's gone up so quick I swear that Jason and all the Ice People are pulling with us. By Jason, Elijah, it's good to have you here! This drought has wiped out many a farmer in the forest, and I promise you that both Hux and Linkeree are buying food from the Heaven Plain, there's not a kernel of corn or a bushel of wheat in the whole Forest of Waters. But we broke the drought yesterday, didn't we by damn, near flooded away everything that wasn't already nailed into the inn, but there we are, the rain put out the fire when the lightning struck and we didn't even lose a whole day's work!''

They arrived at the front of the inn where two men were nailing in place a large sign with the words *Worthing Inn* painted on it in black. Elijah stopped cold, looking at the sign.

''What does it say?'' he said, for the first part of the sign was the same as what was printed on the stone at the southwest corner of Worthing Farm.

''Worthing Inn,'' Big Peter answered proudly. ''Oh, I know, Elijah, you don't like that. The farm is Worthing, it always will be, I know that. But I thought to keep the memory alive. And if the farm is ruined now you can go back there, you can look at that stone, you can keep track of how the world runs from there, but this—this is where the name of Worthing will be kept alive. We'll have a town here, soon enough. How's that? Worthing Town, where before there was just a single farm, lost out in the middle of the Forest of Waters. Don't pout, Elijah. Come in and have supper with us. Have you met my son Peter?''

The boy, who was running around them with Worin and John, stopped and smiled, his blue eyes flashing. ''I said well come before you, Papa.''

''Good,'' his father answered, tousling his hair. ''And you'll say it to many a traveler before the season's through.''

They went inside to supper, Elijah hiding his grief and his fury behind a mask of indifference, while Alana's silence masked nothing at all. She did not eat though she sat at the table, and when all of them went to bed, Alana did not undress, but lay instead on the floor on the other side of the room from the bed where Elijah lay, and slept little until the sun was near to coming up.

Then she finally drifted off to sleep, and when she woke the men were already hard at work outside, and the cries were human and warm and Alana realized that she had been lonely for the last ten years, since she had left her home to live with quiet Elijah with the strange blue eyes. She had been lonely and now there were voices of other people but it was too late. The lone-liness was in her blood and she knew that the cure was beyond any amount of cheer these strangers might give her. She belonged to Elijah, who was not in his bed. She got up to find him elsewhere in the house. Big Peter was not inside, but Little Peter and her two sons were stuffing breakfast down themselves in the kitchen.

"Where's your mama?" Alana asked.

"Dead, mum," Little Peter answered calmly, stuffing more bread into his mouth.

"Do you know where Papa went?" Alana asked her sons. They shook their heads and ate more cheese. She went outside and found Big Peter lashing thatches on the roof of a stable near the inn.

"Have you seen my husband?" she asked the innkeeper.

"Not a sign. Is he up? Did you sleep well? You're the first guests of my inn, you know. Just for that, it's free!" His laugh was a great booming one, and Alana smiled before she went off to look for Elijah.

He was nowhere in the inn, nowhere in the clearing, and he had taken nothing with him. Big Peter refused to send anyone looking for him.

"And why? Goodwife Alana, you know how he loved Worthing Farm. He damn near killed me when I decided to leave, except that I'm twice his size, and even so I barely escaped with my life. He loves that farm, now how quick do you think he'll be set to settle down here? Let him be. He'll be back when the hurt's worked out of him a little."

So saying, he went back to building the stalls for the horses of thirty guests, wondering loudly whether the stable was too small.

Little Peter offered to go looking for Elijah, but Alana said no, he was too small. He grinned, and took off running outside.

As the sun came up Elijah awoke to find himself lying on soft ground under a tree. Only the sun in the east gave him an idea of direction, and he couldn't remember which way he had come from in the night. Only that Worthing Farm was east, and the sun was east, and groggily he got to his feet and started walking.

The forest made no paths for him, and as he pried his way through thorns and low branches he remembered his escape as a child, when Grannam had caught him. Only this time he was fleeing toward Worthing Farm, not away from it.

The sun was high when he stumbled out of the forest and into what had been the field of Worthing Farm. It was drier now than when he had left it the day before, and only a few places were still black with mud. Large cracks were opening in the sun-dried soil, and a thin film of dirt was forming on top of the solid floor. Nothing was green from one edge of the clearing to the other. A bird flew past Elijah's face.

Elijah walked along the edge of the clearing until he reached the northwest corner, then turned right and walked to the northeast, then right again to the southeast corner, and then right again until he stopped in front of the speaking stone.

The rain had washed it clean. Elijah recognized the word that Big Peter had put on the front of his inn. Worthing. He could not read the rest of the sign, and the words would have made little sense to anyone else in the world, for the language had changed since the time of the writer. The stone said,

Son of Jason, Keeper of Worthing,
If you open this stone you will summon the stars.
Unless you are ready to teach the stars,
Keep this stone closed in Worthing.

Elijah sat on the stone and looked out over the field. He remembered how the clouds had come when he called, how the rain had fallen when he ordered it, how it had killed when he demanded it. But it was impossible, for if that was true, then Elijah could command the sky, and if that was true, then Elijah had murdered Worthing Farm.

Three broken stalks near him caught his eye. He looked at the stalks and told them to be green. They didn't hear. He spoke out loud. "Live," he said, but they didn't hear him. Then he imagined them green and thriving, wished them green, demanded that they live and as he watched, green streaked up the stalks and they straightened and stood tall and lived. Elijah reached down and touched one of them. It was real. It bent gently under his pressure. His power was real. His gift, even as his Grannam had said, his gift was a great thing, his gift was a terrible thing.

Elijah stood and stepped on the three plants he had caused to live, grinding them into the soil. He twisted and twisted until they were crushed and split and broken. Then he stopped and surveyed the farm for the last time.

I killed you, he said silently, because you would have killed me. Curse me if you will, I accept it, damn me to any suffering you want but I'll never come back here again.

There was a sound behind him and he whirled. At the edge of the forest, peering around a bush, stood the little boy, Big Peter's son. His blue eyes flashed and he smiled.

"They're looking for you at the inn," the boy said.

Elijah remained silent, looking at the boy's eyes.

"Are you all right?"

In answer Elijah reached out his hand, and the boy took it. Elijah turned him so he could see the stone.

"There's writing on that stone," Little Peter said.

Can you read it? Elijah asked silently.

"No," said Little Peter. "Except that it says Worthing, like the inn."

Elijah gripped the boy's shoulder so tightly that it hurt and the pain made the boy wince. "This is the speaking stone," he told the boy. "This stone has power over anyone who has eyes like mine."

Little Peter looked up into Elijah's eyes and realized that their eyes were alike. Elijah's hand on his shoulder began to tremble.

"There's a curse on us, Little Peter, because we have left the farm. But there's a worse curse even than that, and we carry it with us."

"What kind of curse?" Little Peter whispered.

"You'll discover yours," Elijah said, "as I discovered mine. When you do, destroy it. Tear it out of you."

"Tear what?" Little Peter asked.

"Tear out your gift." Then the hands on Peter's shoulder relaxed, and Little Peter slowly turned to face the tall man standing by him. Elijah's face was hard and dark, and his blue eyes were half-closed. But a shudder passed over Elijah's body and a grimace passed across his face and even as Little Peter watched there was a great cracking sound and the speaking stone split in half. Both halves tipped over and the writing was hidden in the weeds. The speaking stone was down.

Elijah ran his hand through his hair and opened his eyes wide again.

"I've broken the stone," he said defiantly. "I've killed it." But as they walked back through the forest on the way to Worthing Inn, Elijah knew that the curse was still on him, that he was being punished for his hate and his disobedience, that breaking the stone had only worsened his crime. He closed his eyes and wept empty tears of despair all the way home as Little Peter led him by the hand.

As for Little Peter, he clearly heard Elijah's grief and all that he silently said to himself. Peter did not wonder how he could hear words that Elijah's lips didn't speak. It was enough to hear, and understand, and fear, and lead this old man home.

20
Wortling Inn

In the darkness, Little Peter lay in bed and stared at the ceiling, at the broad beams that held the heavy straw thatch. Outside it was raining, which made a soft rustling sound in the straw many layers above. A warm breeze blew in his open window. It was heavy and misty with the rain. He could imagine the dusty road outside reaching up with a million wide-open mouths to drink it. The thought made him laugh.

He kicked his legs high and his light blanket flew. He lay down flat, and felt it settle coolly on each part of his tingling naked body, and watched the air pockets slowly collapse. He kicked again, and then again, but this time left his legs high in the air, and supported them by gripping his hips with his hands. The blanket settled into a tent high above him. Around the bottom it was a foot off the bed—he could see faint light coming in through the window. Suddenly a gust of wind blew rain in the room. He felt the cold spray, and when he let his legs down onto the bed it was damp and deliciously cold. The rain was beating steadily in the window now, and he lifted his eleven-year-old body off the bed, and reached out the window for the shutters.

The rain beat hard on his thin shoulders. When he had the shutters closed, he walked to the center of his room and shook like a dog. He was cold now. He ran and jumped on his bed, pulled the blanket over him, and immediately tossed it off again. It was soaking wet. Pouting, he got up, tossed it on the chair, and stood with his hands on his hips, surveying the small room.

No more blankets, of course. He would have to wear one of the woolen nightshirts, he supposed. His mother made him put one on before going to bed, but every night as soon as she left he took it off and lay naked under the covers. Even in winter. But to be naked *without* the covers would be tempting fate. What if his mother came in on him before he woke up? She'd be furious. Although she and Father often slept without clothes, on "those nights." He laughed inside. If Mother knew that he had listened in on "those nights"—the first time he had stared at the ceiling, his shockingly blue eyes wide open, his fists clenched at his sides. Now he just listened calmly, taking turns hearing Mother and Father. If they knew that, he'd be thrashed. So they never would know. No one knew, except his friend Matthew, and he'd never tell, either. And, of course, the dark man in the cellar knew.

The dark man had been there the first time Little Peter listened. His father was talking softly to his mother in the kitchen. Peter was straining to hear, and suddenly something opened, and he could hear the great, burly man clearly. He could hear him even when his lips didn't move. Then he realized that he could hear his mother too and suddenly both were a hodgepodge in his mind. In a moment he had them sorted out, and realized that he wasn't hearing their words, he was hearing their thoughts. He plugged his ears and heard them just as well. He then listened to his cousin Guy, and his cousin John. They were very distinct, and their thoughts were so funny, he almost laughed aloud. He tried to listen to people who weren't in the room. That was harder, but he soon could hear every tenant in every room in his father's inn.

And then he had noticed the dark man, his uncle Elijah, sitting in a corner of the room, carving a small piece of wood.

Elijah's brow was heavy, and his white hair made his sun-blackened skin seem even darker. Elijah had looked up then, and their eyes met. Peter was frightened of the dark man's blue eyes, so blue and deep. It was unnatural. Father had said that his, Little Peter's, eyes looked just like that, but Peter didn't believe him.

The dark man looked back down to his carving, and Peter listened to his mind. He heard a great storm, saw flashes of lightning, and was frightened. At that moment the dark man's mind clamped shut, Peter heard nothing, and looked up to see Elijah's blue eyes, now burning, look at each person in the room. And at last those terrible eyes fell on Little Peter, and rested there. Peter was frozen in that gaze, terrified. For a long time the dark man pinned him there, until Peter saw him savagely form the word *no* with his lips. And then he went back to his carving.

Since that time as Peter listened in the night, he had sometimes tentatively listened for the dark man who lived in a solitary room in the cellar. But always he heard nothing, could not find his strange uncle who could shut his mind. And when they met by chance in the house, the huge, dark man would stare down at him until Peter wasn't able to stop himself, and would run away. They never spoke, never acknowledged the other's existence in the house, but Peter watched every move the dark man made, and he knew the dark man watched him, too.

Once Peter had seen him in the yard, where the tombstones were: old Elijah had stood over the grave with the single word *Deb* marked on the stone. It was the grave where they had laid Elijah's wife within a month of their first coming to the inn. Little Peter couldn't understand why the dark man had a look of fury, instead of a look of grief. His uncle had stared heavenward, into the sky; and Little Peter felt a burning of hatred deep in his bowels, and he knew it came from Elijah. He had run away from him then, as always, but he never forgot that hot burning.

He hated his uncle Elijah. And tonight he had decided to kill him.

He felt a little warmer now that he was dry. He touched the blanket; it was still too wet to use. Never mind, he thought, I have a lot to do before I'll want to sleep.

Little Peter lay on the bed again, but this time without covers. He spread-eagled and gradually relaxed his body. He let his mind wander.

In the next room his father and mother were asleep. His father was having a dream in which he was flying through the air, and the ground was a brown ocean below him. Peter was tempted to follow his father's wanderings—but when he listened to dreams he often fell asleep. Mildly disappointed, he let his mind wander to the room where Guy and John slept. Guy, age twelve, was the only one home: John had been apprenticed to a carpenter in Switten a year ago and would come home only once a year. Guy himself would be going to Linkeree in the spring. But now Guy was busy forcing open the trunk where John was storing his belongings while he was gone. Peter almost laughed aloud. John had expected it, and had placed a large deer's head in the trunk, and nothing else. His real valuables were stored here, in Peter's room, because John trusted him.

Sure enough, he heard Guy's reaction of consternation and shame at having been so fooled. He listened to Guy plan a revenge when John returned. Peter knew that Guy would soon forget; he always did.

Peter started listening outside the inn. Next door, in the stable, he heard old Billy Lee, the aging horse-boy, viciously cursing the master's favorite mare, for having bitten the horse-boy's apprentice that evening. At the same time he was firmly brushing it down, and now and then caressing its nose and patting its shoulder. For all that his words were angry, the only emotion Peter could hear in the old man was love for the great beast. But Billy Lee was through now, and as he left the horse, Peter's mind listened on through the town, chasing the idle dreams and conversations of his neighbors.

He woke up suddenly, cold and afraid. He had dozed off in his wanderings. Quickly he listened through the house. No one was awake yet. The sky was still dark, though the rain had stopped. He could still do it. Calming himself, he lay out flat again, and now he prepared to kill the dark man in the cellar.

He had discovered the power today. He had been walking through the weeds near the stable watching the rainclouds come in the dusk. He stumbled, and suddenly a swarm of wasps rose buzzing at his feet. He ran, but was stung several times. His arms and legs were swelling, his face hurt excruciatingly, but dominating the pain was a fierce anger. He saw one of the wasps hovering a few feet away, and instinctively he seized the whole of the insect's structure in his mind and then he mentally squeezed it, broke the fine muscles and ripped open the tiny brain. The wasp fumbled in mid-flight and was lost in the weeds.

Still furious, Peter had turned back to the buzzing horde at the site of the ruined nest. One by one, faster and faster, he destroyed them, and then, panting with the exertion, he walked over and looked at the twisted bodies strewn around the nest. A strange feeling washed over him. He shuddered, and a chill ran from his limbs to his head. He had killed them with his mind. He started to laugh, delighted in the realization of his power. And he turned, and saw the huge dark man watching him from his dapple stallion. He hadn't heard him ride up.

For a full minute their eyes had locked. And this time, his power still strong in him, Little Peter refused to give way to those heavy brows and the rinsing gaze. He stood—afraid but *standing*—until Elijah, expressionless, dismounted in one quick movement, rung on the reins, and led his horse smoothly around the corner of the stable.

Peter was drained, felt like a wrung-out rag. He turned away, and stepped into the wasps with a crunch. The pain of the wasp-stings returned and he stumbled to the wall of the house. It was then he thought of using his power to heal himself. He imagined his own body, held it in his mind, and began to smooth out the pain, to carry away the poison. In fifteen minutes not a trace remained of the swelling. He had never been stung.

His mind could heal and his mind could kill. Tonight he would kill the dark man as he slept in his shadowy cellar room. Slowly and carefully Little Peter pictured Elijah's body in his mind. Every detail must be perfect. He pictured him lying on his back, breathing slowly, his eyes shut, his mouth frowning.

Inside the great barrel chest Peter found the heart, pumping rhythmically. In Peter's mind the heart began to slow, to writhe, to twist out of shape. He made the lungs begin to collapse. He moved down to the liver, made it release bile into the blood. And now in Peter's mind the heart had stopped. He had done it.

Suddenly Peter flew straight up into the air and slammed into the beam above him. Then he was slammed down to the floor. His mind spun. He didn't know what was happening. He couldn't breathe from the force of the blows. He was lifted up again and held in midair. His back arched, farther, painfully arched until his heels touched his head. He wanted to scream, but his voice wouldn't come. His body flew straight out, and he hit the wall, and fell crumpled to the floor.

He didn't dare move. A strange hot burning started in his stomach, a great nausea. He retched and heaved, but couldn't vomit. A great pain tore at his head. Then cold washed through his body. He shivered miserably. His skin itched terribly. Huge boils erupted on his skin; and then, suddenly, he was blind. Agonizing cramps seized his muscles. The floor was a thousand knives cutting his bare skin. He wept, beyond panic, crying for mercy in his mind.

Slowly he felt the pain ebb away, the itching stop. He was on the cold sheets of his bed. He sobbed hysterically, wheezing and shuddering, aching from his great exertions. His sight returned. The first light of dawn was coming through the window. And there in the doorway stood Elijah, the dark man, his face terrible. He had done this with his mind.

"Yes." The thought pulsed in his brain and his head throbbed. Peter stared with fear at Elijah as he walked to his bed.

"You will never use this power again, Little Peter."

Peter whimpered.

"This power is evil. It brings pain and suffering, Peter, as you suffered tonight. You will never use this power again. Never to kill, never to heal, never to wash the forehead of a dry world, however you may wish it. Do you understand, Little Peter?"

Peter nodded.

"Say it."

Peter struggled to form the words, then said, "I'll never use it again."

"Never, Peter." The blue eyes softened. "Now sleep, Little Peter." And cool hands stroked Peter's body, and took away the pain, cool fingers drew the terror from his mind. And he slept, and dreamed a long time of his uncle Elijah.

* * *

Peter's uncle Elijah was dead. They stood around the hole where they had placed his coffin, and sang a slow hymn. Peter's father, old now, and soon to join his brother, read words from the Holy Book.

Elijah had died with a great, wracking cough that seemed to split and rip him inside. Sitting by his deathbed, Little Peter had looked for a long time into his eyes, without speaking. And then he had said to him, "Heal yourself, Elijah, or let me." Elijah shook his head.

And now he was dead, covered with thick shovelfuls of wet soil that slopped on his coffin. He had died willingly: he had had the power to keep himself alive, and had refused to use it.

Peter tried to remember his fear of him, but that was long ago. After that one, terrifying night, Elijah's eyes had never frightened him again. That blue, still deep, was no longer hard: it was awash with softness.

At first Peter had stopped using the power out of fear of Elijah. But gradually his fear had ended. He passed through puberty, became a man in body, taller than Elijah, who was not so large as he had once thought. And he began to view Elijah as an equal, another man plagued with the same curse. He began to wonder what had happened to Elijah, how he had discovered the power. But he never dared to ask.

And now, standing alone at Elijah's grave, the ceremony over and the others gone, he was grateful for the lesson Elijah had taught that night. Oh, Peter now and then felt a pang of regret in remembering those nights of listening. But as he had abandoned his power out of fear before, so now he discarded it out of gratitude, out of respect for Elijah, out of love.

Peter knelt and scooped a handful of dirt off the new pile. He squeezed it into a ball in his hand. It became hard, like steel, this piece of earth. He walked off into the road of the town of Worthing, tossing the ball into the air and catching it, until it broke into dust in his hands. He felt very sad, looking at the grains of dirt. He brushed them off on his pants and walked on,

21
The Tinker

Night came to the forest as suddenly as an owl stooping, and John Tinker barely had time to pile leaves together under the bluemaple tree. He lay down and looked through the branches above him. Occasionally a star shone through the shifting pattern, and John Tinker wondered which of them might be the particular star he dreamed of.

And as he slept that night the dream came again, and again he woke sweating and trembling in the cold of predawn light. Rushing through the night the star had come toward him, with the terrible roaring in his ears, until it was larger than the sun, then larger still, and he felt it swallow him up. It was hot, so that he could barely breathe, so that he sweated until he was too dry to sweat and his body was sandpaper. Then he woke shivering and panting, with the finches perched on a high root, watching him.

He smiled at the finches and reached out his hand. Playfully they backed away, then came closer, toying with him as if he were part of their mating dance. Then at once they both leapt onto his hand, and he brought them close. Looking at the male, John Tinker cocked his head. The male finch cocked his head, too. John Tinker blinked. The finch blinked. Then with a soft laugh John Tinker threw his arm out straight and the finches were in flight, making tight, incredibly quick circles around the glade. And on their wings John Tinker rode their mad flight with them in the sickening drop of the organs of the birds diving, the exhilaration of rising quickly, looping, turning tighter and tighter until the wings are exhausted and straining. Then a few minutes of panting and rest, the finches on a branch, John Tinker on the ground, feeling the birds' weariness and slight shoulder pain as if it were his own. Hard flight, and then sweet pain. He smiled, and removed himself from the birds.

He got up and gathered his tinker's tools, the wooden mallets and shapers, the melting pot, and most important the thin patches and scraps of tin that he would shape into Goodwife Wimble's new spoon handle, Goodwife Smith's vegetable pan, or Sammy Barber's strophook. The scraps were tied to his clothing and his staff, and as he walked they jangled and clanked so loudly that whenever he came to town the wives would be on their porches waiting long before he was in sight. "Tinker's in town," he'd hear them calling, and he knew business would be good. Had to be good. Not another tinker between Hux and Linkeree, not in all the broad Forest of Waters, and John Tinker was smart enough not to come to the same town twice in a twelvemonth.

But it was near winter now, and John Tinker was coming home. To Worthing, the darkest, least-known little town in the forest, where no one came to him asking for tin. What they wanted in Worthing was a winter's worth of magic. What he would give them he would call a winter's worth of pain.

After only an hour John Tinker struck the road, knowing the spot to be about a quarter-mile out of town. He rarely used the roads, for in these days robbers murdered passersby to take their wealth. And though he knew many of them and had often tinkered for them and spent the night, he knew that if they saw him on the road he'd be dead before they had time to notice it was John Tinker, the forest man, or John Bird, the magician with the finches.

And there were places in the forest where his name wasn't

known at all, but where he had come once, covered with tin, to a cabin with no smoke from the chimney because the people inside were too sick to cut wood. He appeared in the doorway, and feebly a dying old woman lifted a knife, or a six-year-old boy struggled to lift an axe to protect his delirious parents. John Tinker whispered a soft word then, and smiled, and the finches would fly from his shoulders and alight on the bed of the sick. When he left the folk slept peacefully and there was wood in the hearth.

They awoke healthy and whole, and soon forgot John Tinker, whose name they never knew, except that every now and then as a mother covered her sleeping son in the night she remembered the hands of the healer, and as a man regarded his wife early in the morning while sleep still covered her eyes he thought of the large man with birds for friends who touched her and let her sleep.

Sammy Barber looked out the window of his shop on the main square, and saw the flashes of light from John Tinker's tin. He hurried back to the chair where Martin Keeper was covered with soap, waiting for a shave.

"Tinker's in town."

Martin Keeper sat bolt upright. "Dammit and the boy's the only one at the inn."

"Too late, anyway, he's already turned in." Sammy fingered his razor. "Might as well go home with a shave as go home with stubble, now, don't you think, Master Martin?"

Martin grunted and sat back in the chair. "Make it quick then, Sammy boy, or it'll cost you more than the tuppence you hope to gain."

Sammy set to work scraping at Martin's face. "I don't see why you don't like him, Martin. Sure, he's a cold man—"

"If he's a man—"

"He *is* your cousin, Master Martin."

"Which is a lie." Martin was turning red under the remnants of shaving soap. "His father and my father were cousins, but after that I swear no relationship except that he gets free lodging in my inn."

Sammy shook his head as he stropped his razor. "Then why, Master Martin, does your little boy Amos have his eyes?"

Martin Keeper jumped from the chair and turned on the little barber savagely. "My boy Amos has my eyes, Sammy boy, blue like mine, blue like his mother's. Give me the towel." He wiped his face quickly, missing a few places, including a spot of soap on the end of his nose which made his face look ludicrous. Sammy restrained his smile as the big innkeeper strode out of the shop. When the door slammed shut he went ahead and laughed, a giggle high in his head that shook his whole fat body.

"Blue like mine, he says. Blue like my wife." He sank into the chair still warm from Martin Keeper's body and giggled and sweated until he fell asleep.

Amos, Martin's son, sat on the tall stool in the common room, where he was to tend the desk—which meant an hour or two of looking through his father's counting book and wishing he could go outside. It was another thing to keep desk in winter, when the fire roared and everyone was inside drinking and singing and dancing to keep warm. Now it was the last few days of warm weather before the cold rains came, and then it would be winter and deep snow, and he wouldn't be able to swim until the thaw. His fingers itched to take off all his clothes and dive into West River. Instead he turned pages in the counting book.

A jangling noise distracted him and he looked up to see a tall man standing in the door, shutting out the light. It was John Tinker, the winter tenant of the south tower, the man that no one spoke of and everyone knew. Amos was afraid, of course, just as everyone else in Worthing was afraid. And he was even more afraid because for the first time in his life he had to see the Tinker all by himself, without his father's hand on his shoulder to calm him and make him safe.

John Tinker walked up to the wide-eyed boy at the counter. Amos only stared at him. John Tinker looked into his eyes and saw blue. Not common blue. Not the eyes of every blond forest dweller. Deep, uninterrupted, unfathomable blue, surrounded by a clear, veinless white. Eyes that could never twinkle or look merry or speak of friendship, but eyes that could see. The same blue eyes that John Tinker had, and it made him sad somehow

to know that this boy, his cousin Amos, had those same true
eyes. Amos had a gift. Not John Tinker's gifts, perhaps, but a
gift, and John Tinker shook his head and reached out his hand
and said, "Key."

The boy fumbled with the key on the rack and handed it to
the tinker, who said, "Get my things from the cupboard," and
walked away toward the stairs to the south tower. Amos got off
his stool slowly and made his way to the cupboard where the
tinker's bags were kept. They were covered with dust after a
summer's storage, but they were not heavy, and Amos carried
them easily to the tinker's room.

It was up a high flight of stairs, past two floors of tenants'
rooms, all full, and a floor of rooms that were not full this year,
and at last up a winding stair and then a short ladder through a
trap in the ceiling; and he was in the tinker's room.

The south tower was the tallest place in the town, with shut-
tered windows that had no glass on them so that when they were
opened the wind rushed through from all around and you could
look and see forest in every direction. Amos had never been up
here before with the windows opened—he had only snuck up a
few times to play here, had been caught once and thrashed. He
looked out west and saw Mount Waters rising high and clear and
snowcapped from the deepest part of the Forest of Waters. He
could see the West River flashing and shining away north and
west, and he could see, way to the north, the purple horizon of
the Heaven Mountains. From this tower you could see all the
world that Amos had ever heard of, except for Heaven City itself,
where the Heaven King lived, and that was not part of the world
anyway.

"You can see the whole land from here." Startled, Amos
turned away from the window to see the tinker sitting on a stool
in a far corner. The tinker went on. "From here you can pretend
the town is nowhere around." Then the tinker smiled, but Amos
was still afraid. He was alone in a high tower with the tinker,
with John Tinker the magic man. Too frightened to leave, yet
unwilling to stay, he stood silently by the window and watched
the tinker work.

John Tinker seemed to have forgotten the boy was even there
as he heated his melting pot over the fire in the hearth. In a few

minutes the tin was soft, and with wooden tongs he laid it over a hole in a flat pan. Working quickly before the metal was cool, he hammered and pounded with his wooden mallet until the patch was perfectly joined to the pan. Then he heated another patch and put it on the other side, and when it was done, he held it up for the boy to see. There was no sign that there had ever been a hole in the pan, except that the patch was shinier than the rest. But Amos still said nothing. And John Tinker said the same, continuing to rub and smooth the pan until the whole thing shone like new.

Then the tinker stood suddenly and took a step toward the boy. Amos shied away, and stood with his back to a farther window. But John Tinker only picked up the bags that Amos had carried up and took clothing from them to hang on the hooks on the window posts. Then he took a few bottles and tools and a brush and set them on the night table. All of this Amos watched in silence.

At last the tinker was through and sat on the edge of his bed, yawned, and lay back against the bolster. In a few moments he'll be asleep, Amos thought, and I can go. But the tinker didn't shut his eyes, and his young prisoner began to wonder if the magic man never slept. Of course he wouldn't sleep, and now he'd never get away.

Just then a bird flew in the window. It was bright red, and it flew in a streak of color three times around the room and landed on the tinker's chest.

"Do you know this bird?" the tinker asked quietly. Amos was silent. "Red Bird. Sweetest singer." And as if to prove it the bird fluttered to the sill and began to whistle and chirp, with such comic tiltings of its head that in spite of himself Amos smiled. Then John Tinker began to whistle with the bird, first the man and then the bird on quick little passages that went faster and faster until when they stopped Amos was laughing out loud.

The boy was won. John Tinker smiled and said, "You can go down now." Amos sobered immediately and bolted toward the trapdoor. "Oh, Amos," John Tinker called after him. The boy's head reappeared through the door. "Would you like to hold a jay in your hand?" The boy looked at him. "Next time," the tinker said, and the boy was gone.

* * *

"I don't like it! And by damn I don't have to have it."

"Hold still," Sammy Barber said softly, "or I'll cut your throat."

"You'll cut my throat whether I move or not," Martin Keeper bellowed. "Not a man in town would put up with it, but I have to." Sammy stropped the razor loudly. "Sammy Barber, do you have to strop so loud!"

Sammy leaned in close to his patron's face. "Have you ever been shaved with a dull razor, Master Martin?" The innkeeper grumbled and held still. Finally Sammy Barber reached for the wet towel and daubed it on Martin's face. Immediately the burly keeper leapt to his feet, tossed two coins at the barber, and said, "I don't like your attitude."

"Haven't got an attitude," the barber replied meekly, but Martin thought he heard a note of mockery.

"Haven't got an attitude, my father's *donkey*!" Martin roared, and reached for the barber's smock.

"Careful," said the barber.

"This whole town of lily-livered chicken-hearted dumpling eaters has an attitude and I won't stand for it!"

"The smock," said the barber.

"I don't care if the man's related to me or not! I won't have him at my house with my son another day!"

There was a sound of ripping cloth and a piece of the white smock came away in Martin's hands. Sammy Barber looked mildly chagrined. Martin plunged his hand into his coinpurse and came out with a penny. "Have it mended."

"Oh, thanks," the barber said.

Martin glared at him. "Why should I be the only one to keep the man around when the whole town benefits? Everybody wants a healer but nobody wants a magic man under their roof."

"He *is* your cousin—"

Suddenly the barber found himself gripped by the strongest arms in Worthing, staring into the angriest face in Worthing, being breathed on by a man who didn't brush his teeth any less often than Sammy but not any more often, either.

"If I hear," Martin hissed, "the word *cousin*—just one more time—I will make you swallow your stinking little strop and then I'll sharpen the razor on it inside your fat little belly!"

"Are you going crazy?" Sammy asked, politely trying to avoid inhaling near Martin's mouth.

"No!" replied the keeper, throwing him back. "I'm going home! And the tinker is going to pack up his tin and get out of my inn!" Martin found time to admire his own rhyme and then turned and barreled out of the barber's shop. He pretended not to hear Sammy giggling as he strode across the square to his building, the oldest in Worthing. The sign *Worthing Inn* badly needed painting.

"Pack up your tin and get out of my inn," he muttered as he walked. "Pack up your *damnable* tin," he muttered a little more loudly. A dog in the street got out of his way.

Amos was sitting on the counter when his father stormed in. He immediately jumped off and stood at attention. He tried not to whimper or duck as his father reached for him, picked him up, and stood him on the counter.

"You are not," said his father, "going to go . . ." Here the man paused to swallow. "Up in the south tower to see the tinker again." Now Amos swallowed "Do you understand me?" Amos swallowed harder. Martin shook the boy so fast his head was a blur. "Do you understand me!"

"Oh yes sir I do," replied the boy, his head still shaking.

"Every day is far too often to be going to see the magic man!" When Amos didn't answer immediately his father got set to shake him again. Amos nodded quickly.

"Definitely, Papa."

Then they both turned to look at John Tinker standing in the doorway.

There was an awkward pause as Martin tried to figure out how much John Tinker had heard. Then he decided he shouldn't take any chances.

"I hope you didn't misunderstand," he said in a voice not accustomed to being meek. "It's just that the boy's been neglecting his chores."

The tinker nodded, then walked to the door and turned to face the innkeeper. "Goodwife Cooper wants to see me. It's her boy. I need a helper."

Martin Keeper took a step backward. "Definitely too busy, John, sorry, maybe next time, you see how business is, I just haven't the time to spare right now—"

"But the boy can come," John Tinker said quietly and left the inn. Martin looked after him for a few moments and then, without looking at his son, said, "You heard the man. Go help him." Amos was out of the room before his father could change his mind.

At Goody Cooper's the house was dark, and four or five children were grouped in a corner of the main room when John Tinker and Amos came to the door. John knocked politely on the doorpost. The children didn't move. Finally there was a thundering noise as a huge woman in a work-stained apron came down the stairs. She stopped cold when she saw John, and then nodded for him to come in. She motioned toward the stair, and then allowed him plenty of room before she followed him up.

Her boy was lying naked on his side. The tumor had so distended his belly that the rest of his body seemed superfluous, an afterthought. The bed was stained from blood and urine, and the smell was terrible. The boy moaned.

John Tinker knelt by the bed and placed his hands on the boy's head. The boy shuddered and his eyes closed.

Without looking up from the boy's face John whispered, "Goody Cooper, go downstairs and fetch water, and give it to Amos to bring up to me. When I want you back up here, I'll send Amos for you."

The woman bit her lip and then bundled down the stairs again. She found her children clotted at the foot of the stairs and shooed them away with a slap that vaguely hit somebody. She returned with water and handed it to Amos—and then, because his eyes were as blue as the magic man's eyes, she backed away. But because he was small and she knew the boy, she asked him, "Will Calinn be all right?"

Amos didn't know. So he turned and went upstairs, leaving the woman to wring her apron and wait.

Calinn lay somewhere inside himself, vaguely aware that there were sounds around him, that someone touched a head somewhere in the distance, that someone spoke words that far-off ears could hear. He paid no attention, though. He was standing in a corridor with only one door, and beyond that door waited his body, and his body was a monster that tore at him. It had taken weeks to shut that door, for Calinn had found that to shut out the pain he had to shut out everything, sounds, smells, sights, and all the people who came to touch him, touch his terrible belly, and now should he open the door again because somebody new was whispering new words at him and touching his head? He lay still, and felt his distant mouth open and heard his far-off voice moan. He shuddered.

John Tinker closed his eyes and looked at the boy through his hands. Oddly, he could find no pain, almost no sensation at all. He began to whisper softly, "Where is the pain, Calinn, where are you hiding it?" Still he looked and found nothing.

Amos came in with the bucket of water. John dipped Calinn's hand into it. He looked for the sensation and couldn't find it.

"Pick up the bucket, Amos, and splash it on his head."

Where Calinn lay hiding he felt the rush of water on his head, and with that sensation he felt his monster body lunge at the door, nearly breaking through. Frightened, Calinn gasped, and pushed against the door with all his might.

John Tinker felt the little thread of feeling, seized it, followed it, careful that it didn't fade away, careful that it led where he wanted to go. At last he found himself inside a little room, and at the other side of the little room there was a door. He moved toward it. Suddenly he felt something clawing at him, pulling at him, pushing at him to keep him from the door. He pushed past the little guard and reached for the door handle.

(After he set down the bucket Amos watched. Strange shadows passed over the tinker's face as his hands still held the dying boy's head. Suddenly Calinn reached up limp hands and began to clutch at the tinker's face, feebly enough, for he was weak, but still with enough force to tear the skin and draw thin stripes of blood down the tinker's face. Amos was unsure whether he should help. Then the grotesque body contracted violently and the mouth opened, and from it came a long, high, helpless scream. It seemed to last forever, getting louder and louder until it was so loud it couldn't be heard anymore and it was gone, like silence, into the background as Amos watched the distended belly start to shrink.)

When John opened the door the monster leapt out, and it was terrible. He too heard the boy's scream, but not in the distance as Amos had. It was close and terrible as John grappled with the pain, held it, swallowed it, tore it, suffered it into submission, then followed it, every trace that was left, until he had the boy's whole cancer in his mind's grasp.

Then he began to kill the sickness. It was long and arduous, but he kept it up until he had killed it all. When he was sure, he began to heal the great gap, and Amos watched the skin gather tightly around Calinn's now slender waist, then smooth until it was tight and firm. He watched as the boy's body began to relax. The boy's mouth closed and he rolled onto his back, sleeping calmly for the first time in uncountable centuries. At last John took his hands from Calinn's head and looked up at Amos. There was pain on his face and his voice was a whisper as he told his assistant to gather up the sheets.

John stood and lifted the boy as Amos gingerly removed the foul bedding and piled it on the floor.

"Turn the mattress over," John whispered, and Amos complied. "Now go get clean sheets, and take the dirty ones with you."

Goodwife Cooper was chewing her fingers, which she had put in her mouth when Calinn screamed. She took them out again when she saw Amos come down the stairs with his arms full of sheets. He handed them to her and asked for clean ones. "And fill another bucket. He says you'll need to wash the floor now."

"Can I come up?"

"Soon, I think." Amos disappeared upstairs, and after a few minutes leaned his head down and nodded vigorously. Goodwife Cooper climbed the stairs, quickened by her hope and slowed by her fear. When she entered the boy's room the shutters were open, the curtain was thrown wide, and the sun was streaming in the window to show her Calinn sitting up on the bed, his stern little face smooth and untwisted by pain, his body normal, his stomach tight. She sat on the edge of the bed and put her arms around him and held him. He put his arms around her and whispered, "Mama, I'm hungry." Neither of them saw John Tinker and Amos leave.

But that night three children came to the door of the inn and gave Martin Keeper two fine buckets and a tight little cask. "For the magic man," they said.

Then the cold rain came, and in a week the Forest of Waters turned yellow, then brown, and then became spidery bare branches punctuated with a few evergreen trees. There was snow on Mount Waters.

Amos spent his days close around the inn now, cutting up the great logs of firewood into burnable faggots, cleaning rooms, running errands in the town, and then in his free moments rushing up the stairs to the south tower to be with John Tinker.

On the few days without rain the tower windows would be wide open, and sometimes a dozen birds would be gathered on the sills and in the room. Usually they were the small birds from the forest, particularly the two finches that seemed to be the tinker's most intimate friends, but occasionally one of the predators would come—owls at night or hawks in the afternoon—and once a great eagle from Mount Waters came. Its wings spread from the bed to the wall, with such power in them that Amos was afraid and stayed in the corner. But John Tinker stroked the bird's neck, and when the eagle flew away, its left leg, which had been slightly askew, was straight again.

And when rain pelted hard against the barred shutters, Amos would sit and talk to John Tinker. Not that John Tinker always listened—often enough Amos would ask him a question and the tinker would stir from a doze and ask him to repeat it. But when he did listen he replied to Amos's ideas respectfully. And one day Amos asked John to teach him to heal people.

After the healing of Calinn the Cooper's son, John had only rarely taken Amos with him on his calls, probably because he did not want the onus of being the magic man to attach to the boy. But Amos had watched carefully those few times, and he thought he was catching on.

"I've seen how you do it, sometimes."

John looked at him intently. "Have you?"

"Yes. You touch them, first. On the head or the neck or the back."

"Touching them doesn't heal them."

Amos nodded. "I know. And you say words, and people sometimes think they're magic words."

"Are they?"

"No," Amos answered. "You say things to calm them down. Make them relax a little."

John smiled, but there was no pleasure in it. "You watch pretty well."

Amos smiled back proudly. "And then you just find their hurt and fix it."

John Tinker reached out and took the boy by the arm. His grip was tight and Amos thought he was angry when he said, "How do you know that?"

"I just know. I watch you, and you close your eyes and think. And then every time they really hurt badly, you heal them. The hurt tells you where it is."

John leaned in closely and whispered, "Have you ever felt their pain?"

Amos shook his head. "I want you to teach me how."

John Tinker leaned back in relief and spread his arms along the sills of the windows. "I'm glad," he said.

"Then you'll teach me?" Amos asked.

"No."

And then John Tinker sent him downstairs.

Winter came early, hit hard, and stayed long. For three months not a day was warm enough for the ice to melt, and the wind never let up. Sometimes it came from the north, and sometimes for the northwest, and sometimes from the northeast, but every change of wind brought snow and hail, and every breeze found its way through chinks in the walls. After the first week the village was snowed in, and no one dared go into the forest, even on snowshoes, until the thaw.

After a month, people started dying. First it was the very old, the very young, and the very poor. Then it was the not-so-old, and the not-so-young, and it began to strike even in the solid houses of the well-to-do. They called on John Tinker.

Every day they would be waiting at the door to the inn, bun-

dled in a dozen layers of wool. Every day he went out early in
the morning and came back late at night. He couldn't keep up.
The cold worked more quickly than he could, and people died
before he could reach them. And every time a group of people
huddled through the street carrying a stiffening corpse, resentment began to grow toward the magic man who had let the loved
one die. Graves for the dead became shallower as the ground
became harder to work, and at last the dead were laid on top of
the ice and covered with snow that was packed down hard enough
that the wolves couldn't get through.

In a town of three hundred people, the death of fifteen touched
almost every home, and there was sorrow throughout Worthing
Town. And though John Tinker saved far more than died, still
people would trek out to the graveyard and look at the mounds
in the snow and then turn and look at the tall south tower of
Worthing Inn. Every day a little more snow fell, and none
melted, and sometimes much more than a little snow fell, until
it became impossible to keep the streets clear. Many families
were now entering and leaving their houses from the second
floor.

And then, from deep in the forest where there were no more
seeds and no more insects and from lands to the south where
this hard winter had brought snow for the first time in memory,
the birds came. At first only a few sparrows and finches, be-
draggled and cold, lighted on the roof of Worthing Inn. Then
many birds, large and small, and then hundreds, and then a
thousand or more perched on roofs and rails and windowsills
throughout Worthing. Their fear conquered by cold and disease,
the birds stood still when the children petted them, and didn't
fly away unless they were pushed.

At night people began to notice that behind the shutters of the
south tower the lights burned late into the night, and a window
would open from time to time, releasing birds and letting more
come in. At last they realized that at night John Tinker the magic
man was using his gift to heal the birds.

"There are those," said Sammy Barber to Martin Keeper,
"who don't think it's right for the tinker man to spend his time
healing birds when there's people who are dying."

"There are those," said Martin Keeper, "who stick their

noses into things that are none of their business. Don't shave me, the beard keeps me warmer at night. Just the hair here.''

The scissors clipped quickly. "There are those," Sammy Barber went on, "who think people are more important than birds."

"Then those who think so," Martin answered, "can bloody well go to the tinker and tell him their opinion."

Sammy stopped clipping. "We thought a man of his own blood could say it to him better than a stranger."

"Stranger! How is any man in Worthing a stranger to John Tinker! He's been in every house, he's lived here since a boy, and suddenly I'm his bosom friend and everyone else is a stranger! I have no quarrel with him and his birds. He keeps his nose clean. He helps people, and he leaves me alone. And I intend to leave him alone, too."

Sammy was unperturbed. "But there are those—"

Martin sat bolt upright. "There are those who're going to be eating scissors if they don't shut their mouths." He sat back down. The scissors started clipping again. But Sammy Barber did not giggle this time.

They started killing birds the next day. Matt Cooper found sparrows in his pantry, eating at the wheat he was storing for the winter. Because his wife was sick and he hadn't enough food to finish out the winter anyway and his good friend the old smith had died the day before when the tinker didn't come in time, Matt Cooper picked up the birds and set them on the ground and one at a time stomped them to death. As cold and slow and sick as they were, the birds made no effort to get away.

With blood on his boots Matt Cooper rushed outside and picked sparrows and finches and robins and redbirds off the sills and rails and threw them against the wall of his house. Most of them burst open and died.

By now he was cursing at the top of his voice, and his oldest sons were outside killing birds, and they were cursing too, and before long other men and women in other houses were picking up the slow, cautionless birds and breaking them, or strangling them, or stomping them to death.

Until suddenly they stopped, and silence spread down the streets, and all of them looked at John Tinker, who was standing on a mound of snow in the center of the square. He turned and looked in all directions, at the snow bloodied with the bodies of hundred of birds, and then at the people with bloodstained hands.

"If you want me," he cried out, "to heal your sick—then not one more bird will die in Worthing Town!"

His answer was silence. His answer was hatred for having made them feel ashamed.

"If another bird dies in Worthing, then all these people can die!"

After he went inside the silence was quickly broken.

"He acts like birds was more important as people."

"He's gone crazy."

"Magic man had *better* heal people."

But they all went into their houses and went about their business and no more birds died. Those slaughtered that day were quickly eaten by the eagles and the vultures, and even the predators ate birds that others had killed, until hardly a trace of the day's deaths remained.

By nightfall another two people had died, and the mourners looked with hatred at the south tower where a light was burning in the early dusk and the birds went in and out.

John Tinker woke at the sound of knocking on the trapdoor. It was not yet dawn, and when he cast the covers back a dozen birds that had been nestled against his body scuttered off into corners of the room. John lifted the trap and the head of Martin Keeper poked through.

"It's the boy, Amos, he's gone cold and so sick we don't know what to do." John pulled on his trousers and a blouse and a coat and followed the innkeeper down the stairs.

At the bottom of the last flight of steps Martin Keeper stopped suddenly and the tinker ran into him. Martin stood aside, staring at the floor, and John Tinker looked down to see the bodies of two sparrows. They had been strangled to death with string. Attached to one string was a paper with the name "Little John Farmer" scrawled on it. The other had the name "Goody Stover."

"Little John and Goody Stover died yesterday," Martin Keeper whispered.

John Tinker said nothing.

"When I find out who did this I'll wring their neck," Martin Keeper said.

John Tinker said nothing.

"Will you see my boy?"

John Tinker followed him to the north wing of the inn, into a little room with a hot fire burning in it. Kettles were boiling on the fire and steam filled the room, but Amos's forehead was cold and his hands were blue. He didn't answer when his father spoke to him. The boy's mother stood near the fire, quietly refilling kettles and putting leaves in the boiling water.

"See how it is?" Martin Keeper asked. "Will you heal him?"

John Tinker sat by the boy and put his hands on his head and began to whisper softly. After a moment he looked up with surprise on his face.

Martin Keeper asked, "Is something wrong?"

John just closed his eyes and touched the boy's head. Then he rolled the boy over and put his hands on his neck, and his spine, and then his head again, trying a dozen different places. There was nothing to be felt. Amos was as closed to him as a dead man, and yet the boy was breathing. No one had ever been closed to him before.

Amos's eyes opened, and he looked up at John Tinker. The tinker looked down at him.

"Have you found the hurt yet?" the boy asked.

John Tinker shook his head.

"Please hurry," the boy said, and his eyes closed again. The tinker took the boy's hand and bowed his head for a few moments. Then he stood up and walked to the door of the room. Martin Keeper clutched at his sleeve.

"Well? Will he be all right?"

John Tinker shook his head. "I don't know."

"Didn't you heal him?" Martin insisted.

"I can't," John answered, and left the room. Martin followed him.

"What do you mean you can't!"

"He's closed to me," John said, walking toward the south tower stairs. "I can't find it."

"You can't find what! Everybody else in this town you can

cure, but my son you can't do anything for—'' They passed the bodies of the birds, and Martin stopped and stared at them.

"It's the dead birds, isn't it! I heard your threat, another dead bird and everyone dies!" Martin bellowed up the stairs after the tinker. "Come back down here, magic man! I won't let you murder my boy!"

The tinker came back down the stairs. Martin rushed toward him. "My son didn't kill your damned birds. *I* didn't kill them! If you're going to punish somebody, punish whoever killed them!"

"I'm not punishing anybody," John whispered.

Martin shouted at him, "My boy is dying and you're going to save him!"

"I can't," John whispered. "It's his gift. He's closed to me."

Martin put his hand on John's coat. "What do you mean, his gift?"

"The eyes. A gift goes with the eyes. My gift is to feel things and fix them. His gift is to be the only person in the world who can shut me out."

"You mean your magic doesn't work on him?"

John nodded, and turned to go up the stairs. Martin grabbed him by the arm and whirled him around. "Don't give me any of that! You can cure anybody you *want* to cure! You've lived for thirty years free under my roof, you've taken my son and made him worship you and hate his own father, now get in there and heal that boy or I swear I'll kill you!"

John Tinker looked him in the eye. "I would cure him if I could. I can't." Then he removed Martin's hand from his coat, turned, and walked upstairs. When he had closed the trap he sat on the edge of the bed and leaned his elbows on his knees and put his head in his hands. Some of the birds moved closer to him and a finch lit on his shoulder.

He could hear a crowd forming downstairs, and the rumble of their voices was punctuated by a few loud calls. But the tinker didn't move until they started coming up the stairs. Then he slid his bed over the trap and piled everything he had with any weight to it on the bed. It was still not too heavy for a few men to lift, but a few men couldn't easily get on the ladder to the trap, and it would take them time to get the door up.

As they began to pound on the floor of his room John Tinker put on two more shirts, another pair of pants, and both of his coats. He stuffed a few tools and a few clothes and a little bit of food into his bag, and tied his snowshoes around his neck so they hung on his back. Then he opened the west window of the tower.

Sixteen feet below him the main roof of the inn sloped steeply away. John stood on the sill of the window, and with his bag tightly looped around his wrist he jumped.

He was barely clear of the window when he heard the part of the crowd that was outside the inn start to shout. Then he hit the deep snow on the roof and slid slowly to the edge.

The drop to the ground was even farther, but the snow was deep. For a moment when it closed over his head he wondered if he would be smothered, but he soon had his hands to the surface, and using the bag to pack down the snow, he clambered to the top and tied on his snowshoes. Then the crowd found him.

They came around the southwest corner of the inn and began to shout. Some of them struggled to follow him, but the snow was too deep and one of them nearly lost himself in a drift. The rocks they wanted to throw were buried so they could only make snowballs with broken-off bits of icicles in them. Though some of them hit the tinker as he moved slowly away, none of them hurt him, and in a few minutes he had disappeared into the trees.

As soon as he was out of sight the birds began to call. The mob looked up at the roof of Worthing Inn. All the birds were gathering there until the roof was no longer white but grey with small spots of red and blue. The birds stayed on the roof making a deafening noise for almost half an hour, and the people went to their homes, frightened that some type of vengeance would be taken on them for having expelled the tinker. Then the roof of Worthing Inn seemed to rise raggedly into the air, and in a few minutes the birds were gone. They flew like a low cloud all the way to Mount Waters, where the few people who watched couldn't see them anymore.

That night the wind stopped. The silence was so sudden and so complete that more than a few in Worthing Town awoke and walked to their windows to see what was happening. As they watched the snow started to fall again, slowly and softly and nearly straight down. The people went back to bed.

In the morning two feet of new snow covered the streets in Worthing, and a few of the men started the ritual of scraping paths. But since the snow was still falling thick and fast they gave it up and decided to wait until the snow stopped.

It didn't stop. Before nightfall the new snow was five feet deep, and some of the people in little houses far from the center of Worthing heard their roofs cracking under the weight of it. A few of the more timid souls packed some belongings into bags and shuffled off to Worthing Inn, where they sheepishly asked if they could spend the night. Martin Keeper laughed them out roundly, but he let them spread blankets near the fire in the common room and they slept well.

The snow fell even thicker that night, and still no wind came to sweep it off the roofs of the houses. Early in the night the roofs of the little homes collapsed under the weight of the snow, but so silently, with the cries of those trapped under beams so muffled by the snow, that even their next-door neighbors didn't know it.

And by early morning there were few roofs in Worthing Town that had held up completely under the strain. Dawn found many people struggling through a tumble of wood and snow to reach the surface, where still white flakes fell so thick that the tower of Worthing Inn could not be seen from the other side of the square. And in far more homes than not, there was no one struggling at the surface.

At noon the snow became a few flakes lazily drifting down. By two o'clock the sky was clear and the sun came out, shining wanly far to the south. By two-thirty the first of the survivors reached Worthing Inn.

They came to a second-story window, and Martin Keeper reached out to help them in. By three o'clock two dozen people had made it to the common room of the inn, where a few of the women were mourning the children they had been unable to find in the wreckage of their houses and the men were standing by the counter, too numbed to talk or even think.

Then the wind came up. It blew from the north, gently at

first, but at the first sound of its coming the men cocked their heads.

"Drifts," one of them said, and without even planning it they raced to the makeshift door on the second floor.

"By twos!" cried Martin Keeper as they sped on their snowshoes out to the houses of Worthing Town. They didn't need his warning. None of them wanted to be alone if he fell into a drift.

Soon the first of them came back, leading an old woman and a couple of little children. More came quickly, but these were the near ones, the easy ones to find, and the wind was blowing harder all the time. Fewer and fewer returned, and some searchers began to return without having found anyone. Then two of them came back carrying someone.

It was Matt Cooper and he was dead. He had been knocked unconscious when his roof caved in and froze to death during the day. The people in the common room, more than sixty of them now, stepped back and looked at the corpse. One of his arms had frozen straight up in the air, and now as it thawed it began to sink to the floor. Mothers hid their children's faces, but the children refused to not see. And then a terrible wail came from the stairs.

It was Goody Cooper and her children. They had just been brought back by a rescue team and were coming downstairs from the new door. Still keening loudly, Goody Cooper lumbered over to her husband's body and fell to the ground. Kissing the corpse and trying to warm its hands she wept and called out his name and finally, when she knew that Matt was dead, she fell silent, and then threw back her head and screamed. It seemed that the scream went on forever. It seemed to the people standing around her, watching, that the scream was their own, and when she at last fell silent there were many voices that were still faintly echoing her cry. Just then Martin Keeper's voice came clearly from upstairs.

"No more. It's dark. You'll only get lost yourself." There was an obscure response, and Martin's voice came again, louder. "You'll not go out any more tonight!"

Then there was silence again and the people drifted to the far reaches of the common room.

Martin soon came downstairs and assigned people to go to

various rooms in the inn. "There are too many to sleep in the common room, though heaven knows with this wind we'd be warmer all huddled together." The people gathered the few things that they had saved from the ruin of their homes and straggled off to sleep. When Martin saw where they had taken Matt Cooper's body he had two of the men carry it to the cold room. One of them laughed when he told them to take it there. "Cold room. Is there another?"

Next morning the sun shone, and the wind settled down to a gentle breeze. At ten o'clock it shifted around until it came from the south, and Sammy Barber turned to Martin and said, "This'll thaw us a little, Master Martin."

Martin agreed, and soon the survivors were tramping through the snow, two by two, trying to get into the houses that were beginning to show themselves as the sun and the breeze cleared a little snow away.

But this day's harvest was dismal. Only three people were found alive. In front of the inn, however, a pile of bodies began to grow. By nightfall there were more bodies on the pile outside the inn than there were living people inside it. They counted seventy-two alive and eighty dead, and nearly half the people of Worthing still not accounted for.

The day's work told on them. There was little weeping, though there was plenty to mourn for. Instead the survivors wandered from room to room to sit with each other, occasionally saying something or asking something, but always thinking of the pile of bodies in neat crisscrossed rows. The magnitude of their disaster left them beyond private grief. Of three hundred people in Worthing only seventy-two alive. Little hope of finding the others. Little hope of all seventy-two remaining alive, as children who had spent a night and a day in the snow violently coughed their lives out. Their parents looked on helplessly, or struggled with disease themselves.

Sammy Barber was helping Martin and Goodwife Keeper in the kitchen. He stirred the soup lazily, whistling softly as he did. When the soup boiled he swung it off the fire and set it aside to simmer.

"One thing," Sammy said to no one in particular, "We won't

run out of food. More than enough to feed everyone that's alive in Worthing this winter.''

Goody Keeper looked at him coldly and went back to cutting meat. Martin Keeper said gruffly as he filled a keg of ale from the great barrel, ''Come next spring there'll be too few hands to plant, and too few hands to harvest come fall. Some of us who've lived in town all our lives'll be back in the fields or starve.''

''Not you,'' Sammy Barber said. ''You've always got the inn.''

''And what good is that,'' Martin murmured, ''if there's no one to sleep here and no food to feed them if they come?''

When they carried supper into the common room a man was bearing out the body of a woman who had just died. They stood aside to let him pass.

''Nobody could help him carry her?'' Martin asked.

''He wouldn't,'' a woman said softly, and then they were in a crowd around the food as Sammy and Martin and Goody Keeper dished it out. There was more than enough, and as the women and children went back to the soup bowl for more, the men refilled their mugs at the ale barrel, saying that ale gave them more warmth to the blood than thin soup.

Martin was interrupted in ministering to the ale-drinkers by a tug on his sleeve.

''Take your turn, I've got two hands,'' he said, but the answer was not in a man's voice.

''Papa,'' Amos said.

''What are you doing out of bed!'' Martin turned away from the keg, and the men lost no time in keeping cups under the free-flowing spout. ''Get back to bed if you want to live,'' Martin said.

Amos shook his head weakly. ''I can't, Papa.''

Martin picked him up in his arms and said, ''Then I'll put you there. I'm glad to see you feel better, but you have to stay in bed.''

''But John Tinker's here, Papa.''

Martin stopped and set down his son. ''How do you know?'' he asked.

''Can't you see him?'' Amos answered, and glanced toward the stairs to the second floor. There John Tinker leaned against the wall, a few steps up and higher than the crowd. Already some had noticed him and were backing away, muttering.

"He's come back," Amos whispered, "to save us."

And then the whole crowd fell silent as all of them saw the tinker. They backed farther way, and he staggered down the stairs and fell to his knees on the floor. His chin was caked with ice where his four-day beard had gathered it, and his hands were stiff. He seemed unable to move normally, as if he had no feeling in his arms or legs. Without looking at anyone he struggled to his feet and lurched forward. The crowd made more space for him, until he was alone in the center of the room. He wavered as he stood there.

The murmuring in the crowd became louder, and then the man whose wife had died came down the stairs from the second floor.

He walked down the corridor that John Tinker had opened in the crowd until he faced the magic man. They stood that way, face to face, and the crowd fell silent.

"If you'd been here," he said softly, "Inna'd be healed now."

After a long pause, the tinker slowly nodded. And then the grieved man's face began to work, and his shoulders began to shake, and he began to cry for the crowd. And then for the crowd he raised his hand up and slapped the tinker across the face. The crowd was silent, except that Amos back in the corner gasped.

The man lifted his hand again, and struck harder. A few people in the crowd moved in. He struck again, and again, and again until the tinker slowly sank to his knees.

"Can't you stop him, Papa?" Amos whispered, urgently. Martin didn't take his eyes off the man standing in the middle of the floor. "Stop him, Papa, they'll hurt him!"

The man stepped back a pace from where John Tinker knelt facing him. He bent over a little, and then kicked the tinker powerfully in the face. The tinker flew backward and sprawled on the floor.

"Magic man!" cried his tormentor. "Magic man! Magic man!"

The crowd picked up the chant quickly, and drew together, making a tight circle where the tinker lay. *Magic man. Magic man. Magic m*⸱⸱⸱ ⸱⸱d as they watched, the tinker rolled over and struggled to his knees, his face bleeding, his nose broken, an eye puffed up and turning brown. But he opened the other eye and gazed unwaveringly at the man who had kicked him. The man backed away. John looked at another man, then slowly turned and with one blue eye gazed for a moment into the eyes in the front row of the crowd. The chant died away and there was silence as John Tinker struggled to stand.

He pulled one leg under him and tried to rise, but he lost his balance and caught himself with his arm. He tried again, and again his legs wouldn't hold him. Woodenly he tried the other leg. He failed again. And when again he tried he didn't catch himself at all, but lay on his side, his eyes open, his body shaking.

For a moment the crowd was still, like vultures unsure whether their prey is dead. Then a few of them stepped forward to where the tinker lay shivering. Silently they began to kick him. They kicked him viciously until they were exhausted and moved away, and their place was taken by others. The tinker never made a sound.

At last the crowd dispersed, many of them leaving the room, some staying near the fire, a few others going to where the keg still held a little ale. John Tinker's body lay in the middle of the room. His skull had broken, as had his skin in dozens of places, and a vast pool of blood lay around him. Footprints of blood led away from the body, following those who had stepped in it, until distance wore the blood off their feet. The tinker's face was not a face, his eyes were not eyes, his lips were not lips, and his split and splintered hands spread like roots over the floor.

After a while Martin Keeper looked away from his cousin's body and turned to face his son. Amos looked up at his father with no expression whatever on his face. But his eyes were as blue as the tinker's eyes had been, and they were cold and penetrating and Martin felt accused, condemned, ashamed. He couldn't hold his son's gaze. He looked at the floor until Goody Keeper came and quietly took Amos off to bed.

Then Martin carried his cousin's body up the stairs, and when he came back he spent the night washing the blood from the floor. Every print. In the morning there was no trace of it left.

All of Worthing Town lived in Worthing Inn until the spring thaw came. When the weather turned it turned sharply, and suddenly the days were hot and dry. As the snow melted, the people started to drift back to their houses, but soon found a more urgent task at hand. The bodies in the square were starting to rot.

They couldn't break the ground yet, and so they took lamp oil and poured it over the bodies and set them afire. The stench was horrible, and the fire burned for days, though they threw wood on it to make it burn hotter and faster. And as it burned they went into the houses and found the bodies of those who had been lost all winter and threw them on the fire too, until all the corpses in town were burned. They might have thrown John Tinker's body on the fire too, but the birds had come to him during the winter and picked his body clean, so that only bones were left, and those Amos silently gathered up and when the ground was soft he buried them but made no marker.

The town was not rebuilt at all. The houses that were still livable were few, but they were enough for the few left to live in them. Instead all the people went to the fields and plowed, and then to the fields and planted, and then they hoed. At night a few of them plied their trade, though Sammy Barber nicked a few faces by candlelight and Calinn Cooper's weary and little-trained hands made few casks that didn't leak.

Most of the people preferred to live as far as possible from the center of town, and when they did come to the square they always walked around the space where the pyre had been. The ashes stayed in the soil until the spring winds and rain washed them away.

And from time to time a family was seen with a loaded cart passing by the inn on the Linkeree road, or going the other way toward Hux. By summer Worthing claimed only forty citizens, and they were weary to the bone and grieved to the soul and bitter. There were no songs in the common room of Worthing Inn.

One day when Martin Keeper came home from the field he couldn't find his son Amos, who was still a boy, of course, but who like all the other boys left in Worthing had forgotten how to laugh loud and play in the streets in the evenings. He and his wife searched through all the rooms of their part of the inn, and out in the yard, until finally Martin Keeper climbed the south tower stairs. As he had at last guessed, the boards he had nailed over the trapdoor to the south tower room had been pried off.

He climbed the ladder and lifted the door. All the windows were open and the forest spread wide in all directions. Martin found his son standing by the west window watching the sun set near Mount Waters. He said nothing, but after a time his son turned to him and said, "I will sleep in this room from now on." Martin Keeper went away downstairs.

Afterword
by Michael R. Collings

The worlds of Worthing first appeared in October 1978, when *Analog* published Orson Scott Card's "Lifeloop." Within four months, four more Capitol-based stories appeared—"Killing Children," "A Thousand Deaths," "Second Chance," and "Breaking the Game" . . . the foundation of Card's first collection, *Capitol*.

The eleven stories in *Capitol* suggested the sweep of vision that would become Card's trademark, a suggestion amplified into fact by the appearance of *Hot Sleep*, a novel based on *Capitol* but exploring portions of its history in greater detail.

Capitol concentrated on the social consequences of an illusory immortality offered by the drug somec, and on the human community as it spread through multiple worlds. Somec allowed for space travel, but it also undercut moral, spiritual, and ethical values. From beginning to end, *Capitol* traced the threat somec represented as its artificial immortality destroyed the human community, isolating individuals until their lives rarely touched those of others; they became like stones skipping over the waters of time.

In *Hot Sleep*, Card focused on Abner Doon's plans to change all of that. Doon appeared in *Capitol*, but his full story was not told there. In *Hot Sleep*, Doon assumed center stage with his protégé, Jason Worthing. He coerced Worthing to captain a colony ship bearing three hundred of the best and most restless minds of the Empire light-years into the heart of the Galaxy. When an accident destroyed the colonists' mindtapes, Worthing accepted his role as pseudogod in awakening and educating adult-sized infants. The second half of *Hot Sleep* dispensed almost entirely with Capitol and emphasized the development of Jason Worthing's isolated community.

Even here, however, Card's vision extended beyond the confines of the novel. In the final chapters, Worthing sank his spacecraft into the ocean and instructed the computer to wake him when the ship is disturbed by other humans—the implication is that if his "children" develop sufficiently to carry out sophisticated exploration of the oceans, they would be able to handle the complexities of somec and Jason Worthing. The novel concluded optimistically, with Worthing's hope that the trials and pains his people suffer would lead to great good.

But Card was not yet finished. *The Worthing Chronicle* appeared in 1983, announcing that portions had "appeared previously as parts of the author's books *Capitol* and *Hot Sleep*." The comment served notice that *The Worthing Chronicle* was not simply a sequel; instead, it reexamined the worlds of Worthing, extending some fifteen thousand years further into the future and, through the rewakening of Jason Worthing, recounting the final resolution of his plan.

The Worthing Chronicle did not incorporate parts of *Capitol* and *Hot Sleep* by simply integrating chapters into new frameworks. Instead, Card compressed and condensed earlier histories until an entire chapter of *Capitol* became a single paragraph or less. What became critical was not so much the individual narrative as the meaning that narrative conveyed.

This characteristic reflects the most important backgrounds to understanding Card—his commitment to the Church of Jesus Christ of Latter-day Saints and the influence of *The Book of Mormon* on him as person and as writer. *The Book of Mormon* is one of four books of scripture accepted by Mormons, but is the only one that functions as a single, continuous narrative. It was particularly important to Card, since he read it many times during his childhood. It would be surprising if it did *not* turn up as a major influence on the style and form of his own writings. In an interview for *The Leading Edge*, a science fiction journal published by students at Brigham Young University, Card said that in spite of his interest in such fantasists as Ray Bradbury,

Stephen R. Donaldson, J.R.R. Tolkien, and C. S. Lewis, the writer who had most influenced him was Joseph Smith; the language of *The Book of Mormon*, he said, coupled with that of two other books of scripture, the *Doctrine and Covenants* and *The Pearl of Great Price*, "had such impact, as well as the stories that are told there, that it colors everything I do and everything I am."

The last chronicler in *The Book of Mormon*, Moroni, speaks of that book as a distillation of previous chronicles. From beginning to end, there is a sense that the history in *The Book of Mormon* is carefully formed, streamlined, and compressed to explore the shifting moral and spiritual values of its people. As a result, the book reads like a verbal rollercoaster: nations live righteously and prosper, become complacent, then fall into unrighteousness and destruction, to prosper again only when they rediscover the blessings of righteousness. Episodes are tightly focused, often less concerned about individuals than about the stories they lived. Even important characters are as much abstractions as individuals, their lives functioning as motifs in a grand tapestry of meaning.

As fiction, *The Worthing Chronicle* does precisely the same thing. Earlier stories are compressed until, in the case of the tales in *In the Forest of Waters*, they virtually disappear. "Worthing Farm" and "Worthing Inn," the first two written, are alluded to in the chapter called "Worthing Farm" (pp. 200–218), blended and combined, but without the intense personal sense of the stories. There is more emphasis on the drought in the novel version, less on the transmission of the Worthing curse and the Worthing eyes. Only "Tinker" retains much of its flavor as it appears in *The Worthing Chronicle*. Originally published in *Eternity SF* in 1980, this draft of "Tinker" was written later and, consequently, is more developed than either "Worthing Farm" or "Worthing Inn." It is, in miniature, the sort of narrative Card has explored since "Ender's Game" appeared in 1977—a single individual, possessed of a peculiar talent, must assume responsibility for the welfare of a community unable to understand the nature of its own savior. Card's characters recreate this pattern with ingenious variations: Lanik Mueller from *Treason*; Ansset from *Songmaster*; Patience, in *Wyrms*; the

Shepherd in "Kingsmeat." And, in its fullest manifestations to date, Ender Wiggin in *Ender's Game* and *Speaker for the Dead*, and Alvin Miller, Jr., in the Tales of Alvin Maker. Unlike these other versions, however, "Tinker" verges on the tragic. The savior-figure is sacrificed, bringing further death and suffering that only later transmutes into great hope. John Tinker is one with Card's Christic characters, although not the greatest among them. His function is more localized, narrower, but critical nonetheless. Perhaps for that reason, *The Worthing Chronicle* incorporates more of his history than it retains of "Worthing Farm" and "Worthing Inn."

In a chapter appropriately titled "Winter Tales," Card reproduces the essence of John Tinker's tale. The child Sala speaks the tale from the memories of Justice, a descendant of Jason Worthing and, in the context of the novel, a god-figure. The story is stripped of much of its descriptive and narrative power, becoming appropriate to the vocabulary and sentence structures of a child herself unsure of the true import of her tale.

At the same time, Sala incorporates specific instructions as to how to interpret the story. John Tinker is killed because, she says, the people of Worthing "had no use for a god who couldn't save them from everything" (p. 135). To this extent, Card's purposes in writing "Tinker" become even clearer through the process of distillation. Condensing the original story into a few paragraphs highlights the Christic pattern of mediation, suffering, and death—just as Moroni's distillation of the earlier histories highlights the spiritual movement in *The Book of Mormon*. As "Tinker," the story is highly emotional, charged with altruism and humanity; as an element in a larger narrative framework, it becomes paradoxically narrower and broader. It loses some of the impact of the minutiae of narrative while gaining the strength of moral vignette.

The publication of "Worthing Farm," "Worthing Inn," and "Tinker" in this present collection does more than merely restore several tales to full narrative completeness, however. Even more importantly, it suggests the extent to which Card's stories function on multiple levels. In this instance, the transformation of tale into episode heightens Card's ultimate purposes, effectively concentrating his interests as they focus in *The Worthing Chronicle*. To return once again to the image of *The Book of Mormon*, we now have, in essence, the original documents which Card distilled into his summary of the worlds of Worthing. The altered focus, the intensified sense of mission and purpose, the streamlining of character to create increased depths of empathy and understanding, and most specifically, the infusion of a sense of moral weight as the stories appear in *The Worthing Chronicle* all suggest how closely Card's vision parallels that of the writers of *The Book of Mormon*. In each instance, the narrative is fascinating on its own terms, yet finally communicates far more than the basic outline of history, whether real or imagined. In Card's hands, stories become modes of power, characters become icons for meaning, and the storyteller approaches the level of poet-priest, speaking Truth through the illusion of fiction.

Thousand Oaks, California
January 1989

THE BEST IN SCIENCE FICTION

THE BEST IN FANTASY

☐ 53954-0 SPIRAL OF FIRE by Deborah Turner Harris $3.95
   53955-9   Canada $4.95

☐ 53401-8 NEMESIS by Louise Cooper (U.S. only) $3.95

☐ 53382-8 SHADOW GAMES by Glen Cook $3.95
   53381-X   Canada $4.95

☐ 53815-5 CASTING FORTUNE by John M. Ford $3.95
   53826-1   Canada $4.95

☐ 53351-8 HART'S HOPE by Orson Scott Card $3.95
   53352-6   Canada $4.95

☐ 53397-6 MIRAGE by Louise Cooper (U.S. only) $3.95

☐ 53671-1 THE DOOR INTO FIRE by Diane Duane $2.95
   53672-X   Canada $3.50

☐ 54902-3 A GATHERING OF GARGOYLES by Meredith Ann Pierce $2.95
   54903-1   Canada $3.50

☐ 55614-3 JINIAN STAR-EYE by Sheri S. Tepper $2.95
   55615-1   Canada $3.75

Buy them at your local bookstore or use this handy coupon:
Clip and mail this page with your order.

Publishers Book and Audio Mailing Service
P.O. Box 120159, Staten Island, NY 10312-0004

Please send me the book(s) I have checked above. I am enclosing $_____
(please add $1.25 for the first book, and $.25 for each additional book to
cover postage and handling. Send check or money order only — no C.O.D.s.)

Name _____

Address _____

City _____ State/Zip _____

Please allow six weeks for delivery. Prices subject to change without notice.

BESTSELLING BOOKS FROM TOR